P9-DUE-881

ACKNOWLEDGMENTS

Michael Baram, Seth Nadel, Michael Najjar,
Andrew C. Tillman, John L. Tillman

HAROLD COYLE'S STRATEGIC SOLUTIONS, INC.

VULCAN'S FIRE

HAROLD COYLE
AND
BARRETT TILLMAN

FORGE®

A Tom Doherty Associates Book
New York

This is a work of fiction. All of the characters, organizations, and events portrayed in this novel are either products of the author's imagination or are used fictitiously.

VULCAN'S FIRE: HAROLD COYLE'S STRATEGIC SOLUTIONS, INC.

Copyright © 2008 by Harold Coyle

A Forge Book
Published by Tom Doherty Associates, LLC
175 Fifth Avenue
New York, NY 10010

www.tor-forge.com

Forge® is a registered trademark of Tom Doherty Associates, LLC.

ISBN 978-0-7653-5237-8

First Edition: November 2008
First Mass Market Edition: November 2009

Printed in the United States of America

0 9 8 7 6 5 4 3 2 1

PART

I

VIRGINIA

1

SOUTH GOVERNATE, LEBANON

The stalkers awaited the signal.

It came in the dappled gray light of 5:00 A.M. because delay was as much an enemy as the dedicated men inside the remote building.

Outside the five-room house, the assault leader gave a quick *click-click* of his tactical headset. The eleven members of his team recognized it as the preparatory signal. Receiving no response, he proceeded with his countdown.

"Ready . . . ready . . ."

A long three-second wait allowed anyone to delay the inevitable. No one did. The four men on perimeter guard saw nothing to interfere with the operation. Meanwhile, the two assault teams and the command element were tensed, leg muscles coiled to propel them from the shadows.

The team leader licked his lips. He had extensive experience but it was always like this: an eager dread. He glanced around. Only his radio operator returned his gaze; everyone else was focused on the objective. It looked good: they had probably achieved surprise, but surprise without violence was useless.

"Ready . . . go!"

Two explosions shattered the Mediterranean air, two seconds apart. The first was a Chinese-made RPG whose high-explosive warhead blew a hole in the brick-and-mortar wall facing the sunrise. The second was another RPG near the opposite corner that smashed through a window and detonated on the interior wall.

Assaulting together, each section was preceded by Rheinmetall flash-bang grenades to compensate for any defenders who escaped the RPG blasts.

A quick two-count, and both teams entered through the holes. It was doctrine: avoid the usual entrances, which could be mined.

The attackers' mission was simple: kill or capture everyone present. Take no unnecessary chances.

There were no novices on either side of the door.

The raiders held the advantage, exploiting the stunning effects of the grenades and flash-bangs. Moving with fluid rapidity, they "ran the walls," closing the distance on the defenders, firing short, disciplined bursts. The Egoz reconnaissance unit allowed its members a great deal of latitude: most chose 7.62 Galils but a few carried AK-47s. Both were lethally effective.

Three defenders were shot down in the front room; only one got off a round and it went high. A fragmentation grenade arced through the entrance to the next room. Before it exploded, the men inside opened fire with their AKs. The 150-grain rounds shredded the blanket separating the two rooms, and some were deliberately aimed low. One raider dropped with a Kalashnikov's bullet through the left thigh.

The grenade fizzled. Too long in storage—the result of clandestine acquisition policies—it exploded in a low-order detonation that inflicted minor wounds. Inside the small room, a close-range firefight erupted. It was fought at near muzzle contact.

One raider was killed, taking a round above the ballistic plate of his tactical vest. Another was clipped in the right bicep.

The defenders were shot down in an ephemeral moment of loud noise, bright muzzle flashes, and icy terror. Each body received one or two rounds to the head before the last brass clattered on the wood floor.

One man escaped the house, fleeing through the back door. The designated marksman with a scoped Galil shot him from sixty meters.

Order, if not quiet, returned to the shattered structure.

"Clear!"

"Clear!"

Without awaiting instructions, the raiders moved through the house according to their individual priorities. Two guarded the bodies on the floor while two others secured the victims' hands with flex cuffs. The fact that they were dead was irrelevant; some of the raiders had seen dead men kill the living.

The number two man turned to his superior. "No useful prisoners, Chief. Sorry."

The team leader shrugged philosophically. "I know. It couldn't be helped." As papers were gathered, the radioman began taking photos with his digital camera.

Hearing the all-clear, the team medic entered through the door—the only one to do so. He had one immediate case and two lesser. He was experienced and calm; combat triage was nothing new to him.

"Arterial bleeding here," said one man, leaning over the first casualty. The medic went to work, knowing that his friends would treat other casualties for the moment. He glanced at a green-clad form, not moving. One of the raiders merely shook his head. The decedent's family would be told that he died in a training accident, body unrecoverable. Knowing it was a lie, the parents would accept the fabrication.

The other killers began tearing the place apart. They searched thoroughly, quickly, indelicately. They opened every cabinet and drawer, spilling the contents, and pulled mattresses off beds. They searched for loose boards and pried at the ceiling. Finally one of them returned to the living room.

"Nothing here, Avri."

"It has to be here. Look again. Everywhere."

Abraham pulled the kaffiyeh off his head and allowed it to drape over his tactical vest. "We've already looked everywhere. Twice. I'm telling you, it's not here."

Avri looked around the house. "God damn it!" For the grandson of a rabbi, he was famously profane.

He grabbed the radioman. "Get me Capri Six. Priority."

The RTO handed over the instrument. "Scramble mode selected."

"Capri, this is Purchase. Pass." The commander released the transmit button, allowing the scrambler to do its work. In an instant the carrier wave was back.

"Purchase, I read you. Pass."

"The well is dry. Repeat, the well is dry. End."

The response was decidedly nonregulation, but the transmission from the south drew no comment. After all, this time the offending voice belonged to an agnostic.

SSI OFFICES, ARLINGTON, VIRGINIA

"Ladies and gentlemen, we're in trouble."

Rear Admiral Michael Derringer had been retired for longer than he cared to remember but he had lost little of his command presence. As founder and CEO of Strategic Solutions, Incorporated, he had conned the company through its early years, building success upon success as the military contractor market expanded. Working around the world, performing often clandestine tasks for the U.S. Government, SSI had become the go-to firm when DoD or State needed something done without official recognition.

But that was then; this was now.

"Still no new contracts?" George Ferraro, SSI vice president and chief financial officer, had no problem guessing the admiral's intent.

"Correct." Derringer's balding head bobbed in assent. "SecDef canceled our electronic warfare project in Arabia and State vetoed us for another African job. Oh, we're still getting business but it's paper-clip money: security work, training assignments, small-scale jobs. About the only advantage is that they keep some of our regulars on the payroll. But they don't reduce the red ink, and we can't operate on our stock portfolio indefinitely."

Among the nine people sitting around the polished table was Lieutenant General Thomas Varlowe, U.S. Army (Retired), the gray presence who never quite shed the three stars he once wore. As chairman of SSI's advisory board, he had little financial stake in the firm but remained interested in the fascinating projects that came down the Beltway. Though he seldom spoke up in board meetings, the situation called for an exception.

"Ahem." Heads turned toward the former West Point track star. "I wanted to talk to Admiral Derringer before the meeting but I didn't get the chance. In case there's any doubt about the company's lack of work, I can elaborate."

Derringer barely managed to suppress a tight smile. The two retirees were "Admiral" and "General" to one another in SSI meetings but friendly rivals named Mike and Tom the rest of the time—especially in November for the Army-Navy game.

"Go ahead, General." The Navy man knew what was coming.

Varlowe shoved back from the table. "It's that job with the Israelis. Damned poor situation to get into . . ." He came within an inch of adding, *As I tried to tell all of you.* Instead, he pushed ahead. "I've snooped around and found that new business dried up almost before that ship sank . . . what was it? Three or four months ago? Sure, our people prevented the uranium ore from reaching Iran, but that hardly matters."

"I've been traveling in Europe, General. What *does* matter?" Beverly Ann Shumard, with a PhD in international relations, was one of two women on the board of directors, and among the most outspoken of all.

Derringer interjected. "Dr. Shumard, the mission summary is still being prepared owing to, ah, security concerns. But the short version is, our training team in Chad got involved in a double play set up by the Israelis, presumably against the Iranians. Colonel Leopole can provide some operational details, but basically our tasking changed from instruction to interdiction, preventing a load of yellow cake from being shipped to Iran."

Shumard shook her head. "I'm sorry, Admiral. As I said, I've been away and didn't know the particulars. But why would Iran want ore from Chad? I mean, Iran has its own mines."

Derringer nodded to the chief of operations.

Lieutenant Colonel Frank Leopole looked, talked, and acted as Central Casting would expect of a Marine Corps officer. He was tall, lean, and hard with a high and tight haircut that screamed "jarhead" to the Army and Navy men in the office. His tenure with SSI had been marked by some notable successes and few failures.

"Deniability, ma'am. At least that's what our intel said. Presumably Tehran wanted foreign yellow cake to use in a weapon and avoid the nuclear fingerprints of its own ore. So our team went chasing off across Chad and Libya, then through the Med and down the west coast of Africa to overhaul the shipment. All the time we were working with the Israelis, who provided most of the information and logistics. We caught the ship, which was scuttled with its cargo, so presumably everybody was happy."

"But I take it nobody really is happy."

"Nobody but the Israelis," Varlowe added. It was an uncharacteristic interjection from the normally taciturn soldier. "As I was going to say, our team—this firm—was stiffed by Mossad. The Israelis concocted the plot in the first place to distract us—the U.S.—from their genuine concern. They had their own operation going against Iran's nuclear program but were afraid we would learn about it and bring pressure to bear. Apparently their real plan failed but what matters is, they tossed us a straw man: something credible that we could pursue and leave them alone." He gave an eloquent shrug. "It worked."

George Ferraro spoke up. "See, that's what I don't understand. We did what the government and the administration wanted done. So why are we the heavies now?"

"There are several major players," Derringer replied. "Not least of which is the CIA. The agency accepted the Israelis' ploy, apparently almost at face value. Our own sources—mainly David Dare—sniffed out the facts but too late to affect the operation."

Shumard accepted that explanation without reservation. Though not involved in intelligence or operations, she and everyone connected with the firm knew the eye-watering reputation of the former NSA spook. It was said that if you wanted to know what Japanese porn film Kim Jong Il watched last night, ask Dave Dare.

"So Langley's embarrassed that SSI figured out what was going on, and wants to cover its hindquarters."

Derringer spoke again. "It's bigger than that, Doctor. We've taken hits before from various agencies, and I admit that a few were justified. But usually when some agency tries to stiff us, it's as you say: embarrassment or jealousy or some sort of perceived rivalry. In this case, we're criticized by State and Langley and to an extent by DoD." He grimaced, then adjusted his glasses. "In a way I can understand it. Considering the high stakes involved in any Israeli-Iranian conflict, nobody this side of the pond wants to be blamed if something goes wrong."

Marshall Wilmont spoke up for the first time. As SSI president and chief operating officer, he had a finger in most of the company pies. "So much for the reason for our drought. What I want to know is, what can we do about it?"

The question hung suspended above the polished table, lurking in brooding silence.

SOUTH GOVERNATE, LEBANON

The dream returned again.

"Afrad mosallah!"

At the command, the executioners assumed their positions: squatting or kneeling with their rifles aimed at the condemned men's chests.

The sequence usually resembled a grainy black and white newsreel, for the sleeper was one of those who seldom dreamed in color. When awake, in the rare moments when he had nothing else in mind, Ahmad Esmaili sometimes pondered the odd situation. As a participant in the event that stalked his nights, he expected to relive the glorious, dreadful moments from behind the sights of a Heckler & Koch rifle. But more often his perspective was that of an observer, seeing himself and his colleagues from several meters away.

In 1979, at eighteen, Esmaili's first full-time job had been on a revolutionary firing squad. The first day had been dreadful, and if anything the second day was worse. But by the end of the week it was tolerable. After a while, to display his revolutionary fervor, he notched the wood stock of his G3 for each of the Shah's vermin he shot. However, as the imams noted, hell was reserved for infidels—those who rejected Islam. Presumably even Muslims who oppressed others of The Faith had a chance to achieve Paradise.

Apart from former government officials and Savak policemen, Esmaili also had dispatched evildoers such as drug addicts, perverts, and Kurds.

Esmaili had to admit that most of the dictator's men had died reasonably well, some with the Koran in hand. Resigned to their fate, they had stood their ground, eyes bound but hands free, and accepted the ayatollah's justice delivered almost from powder-burn distance. But the former revolutionary guard seldom alluded to that aspect of the process. A few early attempts from twenty meters or more had resulted in some messy episodes, and eventually the range was diminished almost to muzzle contact.

"Atesh!"

Esmaili felt the heavy trigger pull, then somebody was shaking him awake. It was two hours before dawn.

Forcing his consciousness to swim upward through the haze of REM sleep, he surfaced to think: *No good news arrives in darkness.*

He was right.

Esmaili sat upright on his cot, rubbing his eyes and stifling a yawn. He merely said, "Tell me."

"It is Malik's team." The tone of the messenger's voice told Ahmad Esmaili as much as the words. "They are all with God."

The Iranian was fully awake now. He focused on the face of his colleague, a young man from Tyre who called himself Hazim: Resolute. He was more enthusiastic than capable but occasionally he showed promise. Esmaili had decided to cultivate him.

"All of them?"

Hazim nodded gravely.

Esmaili swung his bare feet onto the floor of the small

house. His toes found his sandals and slid into them, rising in the process. Otherwise he was already dressed. "When?"

"Early this morning. We only got word a little while ago."

The senior man shook his head. "They could not have been more than forty kilometers from here. Why the delay?"

Hazim defaulted to his passive setting. "I do not know, Teacher. I only pass the message from the courier."

"Then I need to speak with him, not an errand boy." The words were selected to cut, to hurt. To teach. He stalked from the house, making for the larger building that served as headquarters for a few days.

Hazim trailed in his master's wake, biting down the pain. Belatedly he realized that he should have informed himself of more details before awaking the Iranian. *Or I could have brought the messenger with me.*

He was learning.

In the main building Esmaili found the courier drinking thick tea and devouring some biscuits. Showing deference to the Iranian, the Lebanese fighter stood and inclined his head. "Teacher . . ."

Esmaili waved a placating hand. "Please sit, brother. You are a guest here."

The two men were within three years of one another's age, both in their mid-forties, both dedicated and competent. But few Hezbollah operatives possessed Ahmad Esmaili's depth of experience. From the revolution onward, through the nightmare of the Iraq war of the 1980s and what the Zionist lackeys called the present "terror" war, the Iranian liaison officer had been constantly engaged. His masters in Tehran knew his worth—and so did his acolytes in The Lebanon.

The messenger was called Fida, and while he surely had sacrificed much of his earthly life to the service of

God, it had been a willing sacrifice. This night, he knew what the Teacher wanted to know without being asked.

"We were to meet Malik and his team this morning for a joint reconnaissance. When they did not appear, we searched for them." Fida sipped more tea but did not taste it. "We probably arrived two or three hours after . . . after the Jews."

Esmaili's obsidian eyes locked on to the courier's face. "You are certain it was Israelis?"

Fida reached into his vest pocket and produced a metal object. From across the table, Esmaili recognized an IDF identification disk. Neither man read Hebrew but both recognized the characters.

The Iranian's mind churned through various options. "This might be a ruse to mislead us. The killers could be local militia trying to drive us from the area." He thought for an additional moment. "Was there expended brass?"

"Yes. It was unmarked—no head stamps."

So it was the Jews.

"In any case, Malik and his men are dead," Fida continued. "We buried them properly and came here. I thought it best to avoid the radio. We are almost certain that the Jews have learned our frequencies again. We will have to change . . ."

"You did well, my friend. Now rest here. I have much to do this night."

SSI OFFICES

The intercom buzzed on Derringer's desk. "Admiral, there's a message for you at the front desk."

Derringer turned from his copy of *Naval History*. There wasn't much else to occupy him that morning, and besides, as an admiral himself, he often sympathized with Takeo Kurita's dilemma at Leyte Gulf. "What is it?"

Mrs. Singer's contralto voice crackled over the line. "Cheryl said it's just a calling card in an envelope addressed to you. She can bring it up."

"No, I should stretch my legs. Tell her I'll be right down."

In the lobby fronting on Courthouse Road, Derringer greeted the receptionist. "Hello, Miss Dungan. I understand there's a message for me."

"Here it is, Admiral." With her Peach Street drawl, Cheryl Dungan pronounced it "hee-yer." She handed over the envelope and beamed a heartbreaking smile. Office gossip said that she had been engaged twice but was having too much fun to change her marital status after just twenty-six years.

Suppressing his sixty-something male hormones, Derringer forced himself to concentrate on the message. It was a plain white envelope with the recipient's name and "PERSONAL" typed on the front. The CEO opened the envelope to find a business card.

Mordecai Baram, Minister for Agriculture and Scientific Affairs, Embassy of Israel, 3514 International Drive Northwest.

There was also a handwritten note that Derringer read in a glance. He turned to the receptionist again. "Who delivered this?"

"Oh, a man who spoke with an accent. Maybe thirty, thirty-two. Kinda cute." She said "kee-yute."

Minutes later Derringer walked into Wilmont's office and closed the door. "Marsh, take a look at this."

Wilmont looked up with a furrowed brow. "Agriculture and science? That's got to be some kind of cover."

"Concur. If I'm not interested, I'm to leave a phone message. Otherwise the note says to meet him at Natural History, 1100 tomorrow. At the evolution exhibit."

The SSI president slid the card across his desk. "What do you plan to do?"

"I see no reason to pass this up. I admit that I'm curious."

Wilmont's paunch bulged beneath his vest as he leaned back. "Obviously that's what Mr. Baram intended. But I wonder why he didn't just call or send an e-mail." He thought for a moment. "Have you ever met him? I've never heard the name."

Derringer shook his head. "Me neither. But that's probably the way he wants things."

"So you're going to keep the appointment?"

"Affirm. But I'm not going alone."

2

MUSEUM OF NATURAL HISTORY
WASHINGTON, D.C.

The Hall of Human Origins was a well-attended exhibit, partly because it generated such fervent debate on both sides of the Darwinian fault line. As Michael Derringer paced down the millennia of human evolution, he found himself more interested than he had expected. From arboreal hominids to fire starters and *Homo erectus* tool crafters; from hunter-gatherers to the incredible spurt of the last 150,000 years.

"It makes you wonder about intelligent design, doesn't it?"

Derringer was caught off guard by the voice. It seldom happened to the SSI founder, who prided himself on his situational awareness. But the man had seemingly materialized beside the former naval officer.

"Mr. Baram?"

The Israeli extended a hand. "Mordecai."

They shook, openly regarding one another. Derringer saw a slender man in his mid to late fifties, slightly taller than himself with a close-cropped beard showing traces of gray.

"Mike." They released their mutual grip. "How'd you recognize me?"

Baram smiled tightly. "I did a Google image search. Do you know that your name produces 447 hits? Of course, not all are actually photos of you, and you share a name with a well-regarded artist. But there were enough likenesses that I could pick you out."

It was Derringer's turn to smile. "That's odd. I couldn't find any images of you."

The diplomat spread his hands in a deceptively helpless gesture. "Alas, the result of an obscure career in an obscure field."

For the first time Derringer wondered if the man's name actually was Mordecai Baram.

"Mordecai, why do I doubt that you're approaching me about agriculture? If that actually is your area of expertise."

Baram seemingly reacted to the American's skepticism by rocking back on his heels. "Oh, my, yes. It truly is. I was a *kibbutznik*, you know. I grew up with dirt beneath my nails—hands and feet—so I come by my earthy trade quite honestly." The ironic grin was back. "But I deal in other areas as well."

Turning away from Australopithicus, Derringer asked, "Should we talk here or go somewhere else?"

"I suggest the cafeteria. It's on the lower level and we can find a quiet corner there."

The American nodded. "Very well." He glanced at his Rolex. "Ah, how long do you want to talk?"

The Israeli shrugged. "As long as it takes, Adm . . . er,

Mike. If you have another appointment . . . or need to meet somebody else . . ."

"Oh, no. I'm alone."

Baram, who knew about a good many things besides agriculture, had already made Derringer's close escort. The athletic young man known as Breezy was fairly discreet, but spent too much time watching his principal. However, the hefty black woman was the more accomplished at trade-craft. Martha Whitney had logged time with the agency in some interesting venues, having long since mastered the ability to fade into a crowd.

"I too am alone," Baram responded. "So we're both foot-loose and free." He stepped back, allowing the American to precede him toward the lower level. Baram's chauffeur maintained visual contact but mingled with a group of schoolchildren. Breezy missed the mark; Whitney did not.

Braced with coffee and tea, the two professionals se-lected the farthest two-seat table from the serving line. Derringer noted that the Israeli sat facing the entrance, back to the wall.

"Mike, I am here to make you an offer. More exactly, I can make SSI an offer."

Derringer sipped his coffee. "I guess it doesn't involve farming."

"No, it does not involve agriculture."

Derringer nodded. "Go on. Please."

The diplomat allowed some girls from a Catholic school to pass, herded by two nuns. When the giggling crowd had moved on, he resumed his pitch.

"You follow the news, Admir . . . ah, Mike. You know that Israel's 2006 incursion into Lebanon stirred up a hor-net's nest. In fact, the heavy resistance we met from Hezbollah was described as a defeat in some quarters."

"Including inside Israel, I hear."

Baram closed his eyes briefly, nodded, and seemed to choke down something in his mouth, and refocused his concentration on the American. "We cannot afford to allow Hezbollah and its Iranian sponsors to gain more strength and influence in southern Lebanon. The outcome could only bring greater conflict, possibly disaster. But neither can we provide open support to the Druze communities that oppose those factions. It's just not a political possibility, no matter the prospects on the ground."

"So how does this involve SSI?"

Baram leaned closer. "We want to hire you both as an operational asset and as a cutout—a cover, if you will."

The American sat back, trying to formulate a response. "SSI in Lebanon? Why us?"

"Well, Mike, at risk of seeming flippant, I'll say that apparently SSI has no other business at present." He allowed that intelligence to sink in. Then he smiled. "I believe the timing is fortunate for you. Isn't it?"

Derringer was careful to keep a level gaze with his new colleague. "Well, as somebody once said, the devil is in the details. Tell me more."

Mordecai Baram told him.

SOUTH GOVERNATE, LEBANON

"It's your call, Avri."

The pudgy, balding man in his late fifties wore regulation green fatigues devoid of rank or emblems. His relationship with the thirtyish officer in working clothes and Israeli military boots was part professional, part personal. The younger man was the son of the elder man's sister.

Captain Avrim Edrim slumped against a cedar and mussed his hair. Ordinarily thick and curly, it was matted with sweat and dust. "We're short three men now. One dead, two wounded."

Colonel Yakov Livni studied his nephew. The senior officer wanted to reach out and touch the youngster's arm, but people were watching from a respectful distance. "That's why it's your decision, boy. We can't get any replacements for two or three days. They'll be good men, well qualified, but of course they won't be fully integrated into your team."

Edrim raised his chin and locked eyes with Livni. "The briefing stressed that we need to keep up the pressure here. We don't have enough teams to cover the area adequately, even with our Druze contacts. At least not yet."

"My information is that nothing has changed."

Edrim could not keep the irony from his voice. "No, nothing's changed. The information was wrong, Yakov. There was no sign of 'the package' that we were sent to find. I'm not convinced it even exists."

Livni ignored the gibe. "You know that any such 'package' is too important to ignore. I cannot reveal sources, of course, but there have been persistent reports that Hezbollah is working to deploy tactical weapons."

"Well then . . ." Edrim's mind was set. "If Mossad believes it's worth the risk to keep understrength teams in the field, I have to accept that assessment."

The older man felt a twinge of guilt. "Avri, you know I asked Mossad's special operations division for some help. Twice, in fact."

"Yes, I know. They're more involved in assassination and kidnapping and sabotage than . . ."

"Well, yes. But with the current political climate in Tel Aviv, our friends in the *Metsada* are, well, gun-shy, as the Americans would say." Livni thought for a moment, resting an elbow on his paunch. "Of course, we could try some bureaucratic tricks. We used to call it 'shuffling the deck.' You know, transfers from one agency to another on a 'temporary' or 'liaison' basis. The trouble is, when we try that, anybody who looks closely sees through it right away."

Edrim squinted at his uncle in a parody of the colonel's nearsightedness. Yakov Livni was too vain to wear glasses for anything but reading. "So you're telling me that head-quarters has tried shuffling the deck before?"

A blink and a smirk. "Youngster, I am not telling you anything."

"Aah . . . I see." The familiar grin was back on the captain's tanned face.

"Look here, enough bantering. Hezbollah is trying hard to establish a larger operating area here and in Nabatiyeh Governate. We don't think they expect to control both regions simultaneously—at least not yet. But they keep probing, keep pushing to gain a secure base of operations. The indications are for a bigger effort than before. What form it might take, we can only guess." Livni wriggled his eyebrows suggestively. "In any case, we cannot let them consolidate more than they already have."

Edrim leaned forward, away from the tree. Standing upright, he replied, "Well, Uncle, that's clear. You said it's my choice, and I choose to continue. I have some really good boys; we'll be all right."

Mentally, Livni berated himself. *Damn it! I was speaking of the large picture, not Avri's team.*

But there was no turning back: Edrim would not permit it of himself. "All right, then. Where do we go next?"

Livni pulled a topographical map from his satchel and spread it so they both could see the area. A pudgy finger stabbed the grid north of Bint Jubayl. "Right here."

SSI OFFICES

Frank Leopole lost his patented leatherneck cool. "Work with the Israelis again? Admiral, you gotta be shitting me!"

Milliseconds later the erstwhile O-5 realized his gaffe. His face reddened beneath his tan and he murmured, "Ah, I'm sorry, sir. That kinda slipped out. But . . ."

The three grades between the two retired officers had long since melted in the warmth of their professional relationship. Derringer continued, his aplomb largely intact.

"Gentlemen—and ladies—you should understand something. We're not here to debate the issue. The board has already approved it, and much as I'd rather work for somebody else, we really have no choice. I hate to sound like a bean counter, but with our accounts receivable problems, and accounts payable only accumulating, we have to take this contract."

Sandra Carmichael, an Army lieutenant colonel in a previous existence, approached the situation from an operational perspective. Foreign ops were, after all, within her realm. "Sir, I have two questions. One: I agree with Frank. How do we know we can trust the Israelis? And two: what happens when DoD and the rest of the administration hears about this?"

Though Marshall Wilmont was present, the firm's chief operating officer deferred to the CEO and founder. Having fought the battle for approval with the board of directors, he nodded to Derringer, who accepted the conn for the current meeting.

"After the previous mission, it's certainly understandable that many of us are wary of the Israelis. Yes, they stiffed us before and they're capable of doing it again. But to what end? They're in a bind, which is exactly why they offered us this contract. In fact, they're not even trying to lowball us. So if Tel Aviv hangs us out to dry, the government will be exposed not only to its political opposition, but to the world at large." He shook his head. "So no, I don't think we're taking any unwarranted risks. But I agree that we should proceed with caution. We'll get to that later.

"Now, as to your second question, that's problematic. Believe it or not, we still have friends in the Pentagon and on the hill. There's also the matter of practicality to consider. Some of the suits around town may not care to be seen in our company, but they know what's at stake in South Lebanon. If Hezbollah gains a permanent foothold, it'll certainly lead to a bigger, wider conflict. That's in nobody's interest, except Iran's. So like us or not, we're probably going to get a pass from the administration."

Carmichael sat back, drumming her manicured fingers on the table. "I see your point, Admiral. But I'd like to start planning right now for a way to extract our people on short notice. In fact, I want to develop a primary plan and an alternate."

Leopole took up the sentiment. "Concur with Sandy. Once we know how many operators we'll need, and how they'll be deployed, we should have our own assets in place. This looks like another potential job for Terry Keegan. After all, he's the resident expert in dustoffs on hot LZs." The former Marine grinned self-consciously. In recent years the dedicated leatherneck had bought a few rounds for Mr. Keegan, erstwhile squid and dedicated rotorhead.

"Very well," Derringer interjected. "However, I'll arrange for Frank and Sandy to meet with our Israeli liaison. He's the one who contacted me, and in fact he expects to coordinate with our operations officers in drafting a presentation for the people we'll use. It will probably be a few days."

"Sir, who is the contact?" Leopold asked.

"Mordecai Baram. Officially he's their embassy rep for science and agriculture but obviously he does other things as well."

Sandy Carmichael leaned her elbows on the table. "Frankly, sir, that makes me nervous. We relied on one major contact with the yellow cake mission and we got hammered as a result. I'd feel better if we had broader support, from their embassy and maybe some military folks. Later we'll need more . . ."

"Yes, that's been arranged," Derringer replied. He looked around the room. "Remember, everyone, this is a fairly large operation, requiring detailed coordination as well as secrecy. If you're thinking that's a tall order, you're right. There are multiple layers with multiple players, including third-party nationals. But we are not—I repeat not—going into this project with our eyes half open. I've had a couple of frank discussions with Mr. Baram, who seems to understand our concerns. He'll be here in person in a few days and I think you'll find him open and knowledgeable." He paused, sensing the mood in the room. It came to him as a mixture of anticipation leavened with skepticism.

"All right, then. Sandy, Frank, you're authorized to start compiling a preliminary list of operators. Matt Finch already has a heads-up, combing the data bank for those with instructor backgrounds, Mideast experience, and Arabic language. As usual, we'll go with Omar on a training program."

As the meeting broke up, Leopole and Carmichael retreated to a far corner. "Whatchutink?" he asked.

"I think, better the devil you know than the one you don't."

"Well, we know this one," Leopole replied, "and that's the devil we're dancing with."

SOUTH GOVERNATE, LEBANON

"There they are."

The Hezbollah scout was twenty-two years old and had nearly seven years of experience. He knew the area intimately, from the days he played hide-and-seek with his two brothers and five cousins.

Of those seven playmates, two cousins were still living; one remained addled after a miraculous survival from an Israeli shelling several years ago.

The scout had noticed the Israeli-Druze team taking a night defensive position just below the crest of a hummock. It was well chosen, for though the position was only about eight meters above the surrounding terrain, it afforded an excellent view of most approaches. If not for a metallic glint in the slanting light, the Zionists might have gone undetected.

Ahmad Esmaili squatted beside his Lebanese colleague and squinted into the sunset. He detected nothing—no reflection, no movement. "You are certain?"

Tawfiq merely nodded, keeping his eyes on the rock pile that was his reference point.

"What is on the reverse slope?"

"More rocks, a little steeper. They will have one or two men watching that side."

Esmaili thought for a moment. This was a rare opportunity and he wanted to optimize it. "Do you think these are the ones who have been hunting us?"

Another nod. Tawfiq was a man of deeds, not words.

Esmaili patted the scout on the shoulder. "Keep looking." Then the Iranian slid sideways, rejoining the rest of his patrol in the brush. Gathering his fighters around him, he sketched the situation in the dirt. "The Jews are on this small hill about seventy meters ahead. They are positioned to watch all approaches so we will wait."

"How long, Teacher?" Sarif was new; devout beyond all question and eager to learn but also too eager to act.

An orange-yellow wolf's grin shone on the evening's face. "Until they come to us."

"Why will they do that?"

"Because they must."

3

SOUTH GOVERNATE, LEBANON

Dawn's gray hues stretched themselves across the land-scape, revealing the eastern slopes of Al Janub's hummocks and hills. Well concealed within the shadows, the Hezbollah fighters had been deployed for nearly an hour before they saw movement on the hill.

Ahmed Esmaili had considerable knowledge of ambushes, and he was well enough educated to share the Christian sentiment that 'tis more blessed to give than receive. He was confident that the Zionists descending the higher terrain were unaware of the ballistic gifts he intended to dispense.

A WHISPER SLID THROUGH the dawn. "Avri, I've got something." Golem lowered the Galil with a Litton generation III thermal sight and compared the green image he had just seen with his unaided vision.

"What is it?"

The designated marksman leaned forward from his sitting position beside a Joshua tree. "About 120 to 150 meters or so, on the far side of that gully. It's not moving but there's some kind of heat source."

Avrim Edrim knelt beside the shooter. "Could it be an animal?"

The rifle was back on Golem's shoulder, his master eye scrutinizing the object. "Maybe. It's an irregular shape. Probably behind a shrub or something."

"Take your time. See if there's anything else out there." Then Edrim emitted a low whistle, catching the attention of the other eight men. The nearest pair saw him gesture palm down and passed the word. In seconds the team disappeared behind rocks and foliage.

Two minutes passed in the gathering light. At length, Golem lowered his Galil. "There's another source maybe one hundred meters northeast. The first target still has not moved."

The captain leaned close. "Go back to the top and scan the other side. If there's no sign, we'll leave that way. Use your radio."

Golem cradled his Galil and, taking care to guard the expensive optic, crawled toward the crest.

The radio operator snaked his way to the team leader. "Avri, how long can we stay here? If we don't get going we'll . . ."

"I know that!" The words snapped out, harsher than intended. But the youngster was right. If the team did not get off the hummock before long, the Israelis risked being trapped by the stalkers who might be waiting in the brush. Still, that was far better than getting caught in the open.

The carrier wave crackled in Edrim's headset. "Avri, there's nothing in the scope. But that doesn't mean nothing's there."

Edrim turned to his Druze guide. "Hamzah, you know this area."

The militiaman nodded gravely. "Surely. My family has—"

"What's the terrain west of here for three hundred meters?"

The Lebanese glanced over his shoulder, toward the dawn. "Just like that. Maybe more foliage, some trees . . ."

"Lots of places for an ambush."

Hamzah permitted himself an ironic grin. "Captain, this is Lebanon."

The officer rolled onto his stomach and pulled out his map. Using a red-lensed flashlight, he studied the geometry of the situation. His objective was a cluster of buildings four kilometers away. Intelligence—for whatever that was worth—thought that a Hezbollah cell led by a competent Iranian would be there sometime this morning. Deciding to enter the area on foot, Edrim had shunned helo and ground transport in an effort to surprise his quarry. Now he had to consider that his men were the target, afoot deep in hostile territory.

The shadows slowly receded on the hummock, forcing the Israeli into a decision. *We're running out of time*. Rising to a crouch, he signaled his men. With a motion of his left hand he indicated an exit over the crest, into the darkness to the west.

LESS THAN 150 METERS away, another radio carried a terse message. "They are moving. As you expected."

Esmaili almost smiled to himself.

The Iranian pressed his transmit button. "Wait my command."

AVRIM EDRIM GLANCED AROUND him. His team was deployed properly—a small wedge-shaped formation that provided both frontal and flank protection, though it was difficult keeping alignment in the broken ground. He wished yet again for his missing three men: they would have provided another maneuver element besides additional firepower. But as he had told Uncle Yakov, one had to accept risks, and the need was deemed urgent. If only . . .

Automatic fire. Both sides, under twenty meters. Muzzle flashes sparkling in the growing dawn. Men down. No time to stop. Choke down the bile rising in the throat, ride the adrenaline spike, focus it. Use it. Assault out of the kill zone.

Booted feet pounding over the rocks and scrub brush. Hosing short, ill-aimed bursts at the enemy muzzles. Nearly there, almost to the thicket.

Hammer blows to thigh and pelvis. Something awful happening down there. Legs not responding. Sudden realization of one's face in the brambles. Arms still work but fingers have lost fine motor function. Pull the rifle forward from belt level. Bolt locked back: reload. Hands fumble for a spare magazine.

It's so quiet!

That means it's over. They've killed us.

"Three men: I should have waited for three men." Coppery taste in the mouth, energy draining away . . . so . . . so tired.

"WHAT DID HE SAY?" Esmaili spoke little Hebrew.

Tawfiq had some difficulty understanding the Jew's words, choked as they were. "Something about more men. Three men."

Two gunshots snapped out behind the Iranian. He did not bother to look back; his men were experienced and did what needed doing.

"This one was the leader," Tawfiq added. He leaned down and picked up the officer by the hair. "He will not last." He retrieved the officer's map case and handed it over.

Esmaili accepted the documents but wasted no time. He could examine them at leisure in more secure surroundings. Finally he took in the scene: it was much as the aftermath of most ambushes. He had been on the receiving end himself on two occasions. "None left to question?"

Hazim trotted up. "No, Teacher. Most were already dead. The others . . ."

The youngster had picked up a Galil with an impressive optic. Other Hezbollah fighters were slinging additional Israeli rifles and satchels over their shoulders.

Hazim saw a chance to ingratiate himself with his mentor. "An excellent plan, Teacher. Leaving two men to be seen by the night-vision device sent the Jews off the hummock, into the trap." He smiled in the fresh daylight. "They came to us, as you said."

The Iranian ignored the sycophancy but noticed that the boy had done reasonably well during the brief episode. He had even remembered to reload when it was over.

"Teacher, I wonder . . ."

"Yes?"

Hazim hefted the scoped Galil. "How did you know they would have night vision?"

Esmaili shrugged dismissively. "The Americans provide the Jews with everything they want. This time was no different."

"Ah, I see." Obviously he did not, but it mattered little. "But if they did not have the device?"

"Then I would have followed the alternate plan, of course." The Iranian found the youth's manner consistently irritating. Without elaboration, the leader formed up his team. "This position soon will be untenable so we are rejoining the others. But you all did well, brothers. We are one step closer to our goal in this area."

With that, Esmaili turned and began walking southeasterly. He could not admit to his men that he had not been told the nature of that goal.

SSI OFFICES

Marshall Wilmont opened the meeting. "So, who do we need for this job? And who's available?" He addressed the question to the room but intended it for Jack Peters.

As a former Army officer with experience in two other private military contractors, Peters was valued as SSI's human resources chief. However, he cordially detested the title, which Wilmont insisted upon for Beltway reasons. "I was a freaking S-1 in the Army," Peters insisted, "and I'm a freaking S-1 now, whatever the letterhead says."

Everyone present knew that Peters enjoyed minimizing his military record. He had been hired partly on the strength of his Special Forces background, and had been lured away from another successful PMC where he demonstrated a knack for scouting fresh talent.

Peters responded to Wilmont's rhetorical question with some specifics. "Well, sir, it's much as we expected. The contract calls for training experience, preferably with Arabic speakers. We're always short of those, but I'm reaching out to Dave Main again." He smiled to himself. "After he raided the gene pool at Fort Bragg for the last job, he probably has to grow a mustache and carry a broom to get near anybody down there anymore."

Even Wilmont appreciated the humor. As the firm's DoD liaison, Colonel Main was not above dipping his PMC ladle into sensitive waters when SecDef wanted something done quickly and quietly. "Well, he certainly delivered the goods for the Chad operation," Wilmont conceded. "I just wonder how many more Arabic linguists we can pilfer . . . er, recruit . . . who can also perform as weapons and tactics instructors."

Peters shuffled his briefing papers. "Well, sir, we have commitments from most of the Chad team except Gunny Foyte." He glanced at Frank Leopole. "I understand that Gunny has a redheaded priority these days."

Leopole did not try to suppress a grin. "That's affirm. Besides, he didn't relate real well to the Africans. Kept lapsing into his redneck mind-set and calling them 'boys.' He didn't mean it as 'house boys' or anything—he just meant 'guys' but you can imagine how that went over."

"In that case, it's just as well we won't have him calling Lebanese militiamen 'ragheads' or worse," Peters replied. He returned to his roster. "We can count on Bosco and Breezy, of course—they're always willing to add to their IRAs—plus Chris Nissen and Josh Wallender. Chris is golden: small-arms instructor and Arabic speaker. Josh is a good man, mostly a commo guy, who speaks French." Peters looked up. "Some of our clients are likely to be French speakers so that can help."

"What about Johnson?" Leopole asked.

"I have a call in to him. Some of you know that J. J. has, well, issues about going into the field again. I can't blame him after the way al Qaeda tortured him in Afghanistan. Frankly, I was surprised he went to Chad, but of course that also was a training mission."

"I'd like to have him if we could," Leopole replied. The former Foreign Legion veteran was not only fluent in French, but an excellent instructor who spoke a smattering of Arabic.

"Hey," Leopole exclaimed. "What about Vic Pope? He outdid himself in the Chadian maritime op."

Peters shook his head. "I already asked. He's not interested in most jobs above the high tide mark these days."

The former Marine was clearly disappointed. "I'd feel better if he were with our people. I never knew a better man in a tight spot." He grimaced as much to himself as anyone. "But I guess SEALs like to keep their feet wet."

"Who else, Jack?" Wilmont wanted to keep things on track.

"Several other operators we've used before, but none with language skills. Ashcroft, Barrkman, Furr, Green, Jacobs, Olson, a couple of new guys. Then there's . . ." He flipped through his papers again.

"Pitney. Robert Pitney. Former cop, been to Lebanon and speaks good Arabic."

Leopole leaned forward on his elbows. "But what's his military background?"

Peters shook his head. "None. Main heard about him through shooting circles. He's a nationally ranked action pistol shooter, won the Bianchi Cup two years ago."

"How's a guy like that speak Arabic?"

"He married a Jordanian gal and learned the language to please her family. Ah . . . he also converted to Islam."

Wilmont rubbed his chin. "He converted to marry this lady?"

"Affirmative. They have two children."

Leopole drummed his fingers on the table. The cadence was a tattoo accompanying the silent strains of John Philip Sousa. For the Eighth and I parade ground Marine at HQ in D.C., "The Thunderer" beats "Stars and Stripes Forever" every time. "Sounds like a great catch, especially knowing the culture and the language. But . . ."

"Yeah," Wilmont interjected. "How's he going to fit in with the others?"

"Well, I figure he'll fit in because that's his job, if nothing else."

Wilmont asked, "You mean he's officially on board?"

"No, sir. He's officially interested. So far we haven't formally signed anyone to this job."

Wilmont, who knew that elemental fact, cleared his throat. He recovered his poise by changing the subject. "Dr. Mohammed, I think we should hear your thoughts on the training angle. After all, that's what the contract is about."

The director of training was, as always, prepared for questions. "Based on Mr. Baram's information, this is a straightforward assignment. We are to help improve the standard of readiness and training for selected Druze militia units and villages in southern Lebanon. We will receive covert logistic support from the Israelis, and our team will be broken into smaller units depending on where our services are needed.

"As of now, it looks like a bread and butter operation, the kind we have done so often before: small-arms use and maintenance, basic infantry tactics, and undoubtedly defensive measures. Hezbollah is active and often aggressive in the area, trying to expand its influence and seeking fresh advantages. It is especially interested in gaining more high ground, either for launching rockets into northern Israel or for spotting purposes."

Sandra Carmichael interjected, being one of the senior operations officers. "Doctor, one thing troubles me. Given the tactical and political situation on the ground, how can we reasonably expect our people to remain uninvolved? I mean, any of them could come under attack almost anytime."

"Quite so. That is the nature of the work, especially in Lebanon. Obviously, it is also why we have been offered so lucrative a contract." He thought for a moment. "In their own way, the Israelis are being generous to us. After all, they could have—as you might say—low-balled us, knowing our financial situation."

Wilmont expressed the dominant sentiment in the room. "Let's be thankful for small favors."

NORTHERN ISRAEL

"It's better you don't look, Yakov." The words were nearly lost in the dust and noise of the departing UH-60 Owl helicopter.

Colonel Livni stared at the shrouded bodies laid in a row. It did not occur to him that perhaps only in the Israeli Army would a first sergeant address a field-grade officer by his given name.

But *Rav samál rishón* Maier Boim was more than a fellow soldier, let alone merely a subordinate. They had first served together when Livni was a *ségen*, the executive officer of an infantry company. They had shared much over the years, including loss. But seldom like this.

Livni knelt beside the longest shroud, knowing intuitively that it contained the body of his nephew. *His mother will never forgive me,* he told himself. *Even if it wasn't my fault, she would never forgive me. But it is my fault. I gave him the latitude to continue, knowing he would take it.*

In his mind's eye, Yakov Livni saw the face of his sister. Even in her youth, Esther had been no beauty, and neither was her brother. But her son and his nephew *was* beautiful. *In so many ways.*

Captain Avrim Edrim had lived by IDF law codified in the Purity of Arms. With a quiet, fierce pride, Livni recalled the time when Avri had risked censure or worse to abide by the code, protecting an obviously guilty Palestinian gunman from an outraged crowd of armed Israelis demanding street justice.

Livni braced a hand on his knee and levered himself upright. Maier Boim moved to help his friend, then stopped in midreach. The colonel looked at the sergeant and merely nodded. "You are right, Maier." He even allowed himself a public gesture by patting his comrade on the shoulder. "I do not need to see him like this. I should remember him as . . . he was."

"We'll take good care of him, Yakov. The battalion's rabbi is on the way."

The pudgy old soldier straightened up, squared his shoulders, and looked around. He knew that Avri and the others would be laid in Israeli soil within the prescribed time. Taking in the ancient, disputed hills to the north, he forced his mind back to the present and the recent past. *Anything to get Esther off my mind.*

"Tell me, Maier. How did it happen?"

The first sergeant recalled the scene. It was terrible, ugly. Years had passed since he had seen nine dead Israeli soldiers.

"It was an ambush. The boys had left a night defensive position on a small hill, apparently intending to complete their mission. We had intelligence that the Iranian . . ."

"Yes, yes. I remember."

"Well, they got about 150 meters before they entered the trap. Apparently two died immediately. The others assaulted through the kill zone but didn't get very far. Avri . . . got the farthest."

Livni nodded silently, slowly, knowingly, still facing south. "Was he . . ." The officer's voice trailed off.

"Tortured? No. Multiple hits. He didn't last long."

The colonel was in control of his voice now. "What of the other boys?" He reminded himself that eight other families were about to be aggrieved.

"Two were finished off. Head shots."

Yakov Livni turned in the midday sun to face the veteran NCO. "All right, Maier. You have told me what happened. Now I need to know *why* it happened. How did Hezbollah track Avri's team and force it into a trap? He was too old a soldier, too smart an officer, to fall for a simple trick."

Boim spread his hands in a futile gesture. "Colonel, that is above my pay grade. I think you should ask the special operations branch."

"I intend to, First Sergeant. I intend to."

4

SSI OFFICES

Robert Pitney was on trial, and he knew it.

While driving the 120 miles from Reading, Pennsylvania, to Arlington, Virginia, the prospective Lebanon team member had time to contemplate his interview with Frank Leopole and Jack Peters. Making his way to SSI's office took some doing in the D.C. area traffic, but he parked his

Nissan Xterra in the employees' lot as directed and entered the lobby eighteen minutes beyond his ETA.

Pitney introduced himself at the front desk and waited for his hosts to appear. It was immediately apparent who was whom: the former Marine O-5 with the high and tight haircut and the ex-Navy officer who looked completely at home in a three-piece suit.

"Colonel Leopole, I'm Robert Pitney." The erstwhile cop extended his hand and exchanged grips with the operations officer, hard and fast. Peters's handshake was equally firm without the same testosterone dose. "I apologize for being late," Pitney hastened to add. "I hope you got my cell phone message."

"Not a problem," Leopole replied. "The receptionist passed your call while we were meeting with Admiral Derringer."

Peters was aware that the two shooters were sizing up one another. He sought to ease the atmosphere, which was neither tense nor warm. "You did well to get here when you did . . . Robert?"

Pitney nodded. "Yes, sir. My father was Bob and I didn't like 'Bobby' so I've always been Robert." He grinned self-consciously. "Some people think it sounds pretentious but it's better than 'Hey kid.' "

Leopole showed the way past the desk into the office spaces. "How long did it take, Robert?"

"I allowed three hours. I took Thirty to East York, then Eighty-three to Baltimore and Ninety-five on down, but there's more construction and delays than I expected between here and 495."

"Always is," Leopole replied. "But I don't suppose it would've been much of a saving if you'd flown."

"No, sir. Besides, I don't fly anymore unless I have to. The security bothers me, and it can be tedious traveling with a gun."

"Ah, do you have one on you?" Peters asked.

"In the car. I figured I shouldn't wear one in here without permission."

Leopole felt himself warming a bit. "Well, don't sweat it, Robert. We're a gun-friendly outfit. Besides, you still carry a badge, don't you?"

"Actually, Colonel, I do not. I left my department in Massachusetts after a couple of disagreements with the chief." He paused, testing whether the SSI men were interested in the details. He took their silence as curiosity and ventured a brief explanation. "I'm a gun guy, but most law enforcement officers, LEOs, aren't. When I became our training sergeant I requested a bigger budget, more than just qualification. The chief wanted to put the money into surveillance gear and radios. Well, we had a couple of, ah, marginal shootings, and I told the investigators what I thought." He shrugged. "It cost the city some money and my services were no longer required. So I moved my family to Pennsylvania."

"What do you carry?" Leopole asked.

"I have two Springfield XDs in the car. A .40 and a .45."

Peters was puzzled. "Why two?"

"Well, sir, if I have to use one I still have the other to get me home."

Frank Leopole appreciated the practical aspects of Robert Pitney's philosophy. "I'm a 1911 man myself, but it's not about gear. It's about training, which is what we'd like to discuss with you." He motioned toward a chair in the conference room and the three men settled down to business.

Peters took the lead, as he expected. "Robert, as you know we're forming a training team to work in Lebanon. Frankly, we're quite enthused about your background, especially since you're well qualified on weapons and you speak Arabic."

"Well, thank you, Mr. Peters. But I should say up front that I'm a pistol shooter and rifleman, mainly from IPSC three-gun competition. I don't know much about belt-fed weapons and nothing about explosives. But I do have a lot of experience as an instructor, and you have the references from my police and military clients. As for the language, well, it's mainly conversational. I'd have to study some to get up to speed in terminology for weapons and tactics."

Peters said, "We'll introduce you to Omar Mohammed, our head training officer. He speaks all the major Muslim languages and can brief you on some of the technical aspects we're addressing."

Leopole threw out a toss-up question. "Have you been to Lebanon?"

Pitney's green eyes narrowed slightly. *He's testing me to see how I think on my feet.* "Twice. My wife's family used to have business there and I've seen Beirut, Tyre, and Sidon."

"May I ask what kind of business?" Peters interjected.

"Import-export. Last time was in 2002, but I'm not involved in that."

Leopole decided to cut to the religious chase. "Robert, I understand that you converted to Islam. Is that correct?"

Pitney gave the SSI man a three-count before answering. "Colonel, Shareefa's family is Sunni, like ninety percent of Jordanians. So that's my affiliation, and our children's. But if you're wondering about me because I'm officially a Muslim, well, you already mentioned your Mr. Mohammed . . ." He allowed the sentiment to dangle in midair.

Leopole shifted in his seat. "No, no, nothing like that, Robert. You're right about Dr. Mohammed. He's invaluable here. But he was born a Muslim, and I just want to clarify things. You understand that some of the operators you'd be working with might wonder why an American would convert to Islam in . . . times like these."

Pitney leaned forward, elbows braced on the table. "Colonel Leopole, I married Shari nine years ago. Some of my fellow policemen wondered the same thing, before

9-11. Most of them saw I was the same guy, doing the same job to the same standards as before. I was still Sergeant Pitney, not Sergeant Abdullah. The ones who let it interfere with their work got transferred to other divisions.

"Now, my daughters inherited a tough situation. They're growing up with kids who've never known anything about Islam but the war on terror. Their knowledge of Muslims is limited to suicide bombers and religious zealots. But my little girls were born in this country and they're going to be raised as loyal Americans." He leaned back, fingers drumming on the table. "Next question."

Leopole looked at Peters, who looked back at Leopole. Finally Peters asked, "Mr. Pitney, when can you start?"

NORTHERN ISRAEL

Colonel Yakov Livni brushed a topographical map with the fingers of one hand. "Solly, we need to reassess our operations in Lebanon. We're already overextended, and it's . . . costing us good men."

Brigadier General Solomon Nadel knew exactly what Livni meant. The brigade commander had attended the burial, then put it behind him. Though two years younger than his subordinate, he had more than a year in seniority, and was connected besides. Not that it mattered: they were both professionals who respected one another's opinions, however infrequently they meshed.

Nadel scratched his head, habitually sunburned beneath his thinning hair. He often wore his beret stuffed in an epaulette rather than wearing the ridiculous cap. Away from the troops he preferred an American boonie hat, which at least afforded some protection to the face and neck, but a *Tat alúf* had to set an example.

"Yakov, I do not disagree with you. My God, you know the situation in Northern Command as well as I. The whole brigade is overextended, guarding its assigned area and supporting your Egoz boys across the border. For that matter, so is most of the Ninety-sixth Division." He spread his hands in frustration. "I have made two requests through channels for more assets or fewer operations. The division commander supports me but Mossad and the cabinet want to keep the pressure on Hezbollah, and supporting the Lebanese is the best way to do that."

Livni turned away from the chart table and slumped into a camp chair. He almost upset the Galil rifle leaning against a file cabinet. The general's personal weapon reminded him that Solomon Nadel had not always been a map reader or logistics pervader. Not so long ago he was an enthusiastic shooter, and he still kept dust on his boots most of the time.

"All right, Solly. All right. We'll continue doing what we can, but hear this: I refuse to commit any more understrength teams to an operation. You hear me? I absolutely refuse! If we cannot accomplish a mission with the men on hand, then I'll pull in others to get the job done and let the other mission wait. But Ari was . . ."

Livni choked off a sob. He swallowed hard, looking around for a glass. Nadel read the signs and handed his colleague a plastic bottle. The colonel thanked the general with a quiet nod, drank deeply, and handed back the water. When he looked up at his superior, he could not think of anything else to say.

Nadel pulled another chair across the wood floor and sat beside the veteran commando. "Yakov, listen. The word *is* getting through at cabinet level. There is more support for covert operations with friendly Lebanese, especially the Druze. In fact, there's a growing Druze presence outside the traditional areas around Beirut. I know of a couple of areas along the Syrian border. As far as I'm concerned, you're already eligible for distribution of that intelligence, so come back tomorrow and we'll talk again."

Livni stared at the floor, nodding again. At length he looked at Nadel and trusted himself to speak. "You know, Solly, I was just thinking what old Colonel Baharof used to say in command and staff school."

"Yes? What's that?"

"We operate on incomplete information, and things are seldom as good or as bad as they seem."

SOUTH GOVERNATE, LEBANON

Ahmad Esmaili believed in thoroughness. It was one of the many reasons he was still walking the earth, praise be to Allah. Secretly, he admitted to himself that he had been fortunate on several occasions, but far be it for a holy warrior to doubt that Fortune often represented the Will of God.

At least that is what he told his superiors, let alone the occasional imam who crossed his path. The revolution had taught him nothing if not the utility of carrying a Koran and quoting it at opportune moments.

Unlike many Hezbollah leaders, Esmaili believed in marksmanship and weapon maintenance. The former had just been put to good use, though admittedly the element of superior firepower at close range had been a major factor in slaying the Zionists. But now, after the excitement his men felt in the wake of the successful ambush, the Iranian insisted that they disassemble and clean their weapons. Properly.

Essam Tawfiq was reassembling his RPK faster than the others manipulated their AK-47s. But then Tawfiq was Esmaili's most experienced man, one of the few who seemed genuinely enthusiastic about small arms. That was why the Iranian had designated him the machine gunner.

Leaning against the wall of the command building, Esmaili inserted a loaded magazine in his own rifle. Then he began refilling the one magazine he had used in the ambush. Loose rounds rolled on the tarp serving the five men nearest him. He noted that young Hazim was the next fastest in pounding his receiver cover into place, cycling the bolt twice, and tripping the trigger. True, the newcomer's muzzle was pointed at Abdullah's foot, but if the latter was unaware of the indignity, Esmaili was not inclined to make an issue of it. He thought, *One accidental discharge now and then serves to focus the men's attention.*

As Hazim laid his weapon on the tarp—muzzle pointed away from the group—the boy looked around, obviously pleased with himself. He accepted his leader's tacit praise, expressed by a nod of the head and the faintest of smiles. It had been a very good day for the neophyte fighter. He had claimed two of the Israelis, being certain of at least one, proven his worth to his fellow jihadists, and won the quiet approval of the man he most respected.

And something more. Hazim reached behind him and produced his prize, the Galil with side-mounted dovetail base to accept the weight of the American night scope. Nobody else had tried to usurp the treasure, but neither had Esmaili nor Tawfiq pronounced that he might keep it. Rather than delay the resolution, he ventured a question.

"Teacher, what shall we do with this?"

The Iranian extended a hand, and noticed the boy's ephemeral delay in passing it over. When the weapon was relinquished, Esmaili made a point of grunting at the nine-kilogram weight. Some of the other men laughed in appreciation, exchanging knowing glances. One whispered to a friend, "Perhaps now Hazim knows why none of us wanted it!"

Esmaili removed the magazine and locked the bolt open. The muzzle incident moments before had happened to someone else. This latest breach had occurred to the leader. "Did I fail to teach you proper manners, boy? I believe that

I did when you joined us. But that was weeks ago, and my dimming memory serves me poorly these days."

Hazim blushed beneath his tan. His eyes lowered to the tarp as he muttered a muted apology.

Tawfiq shot a mirthful glance at his friend and colleague. *He always enjoys times like this. Now he will regain the young fool's devotion.*

The leader made a point of visibly checking the chamber, then pretended to look through the Litton optic. With a dissatisfied grunt he handed the Galil back, followed by the magazine. "For your lapse in weapon handling, your punishment shall be to carry this burden for as long as it remains workable."

Hazim's carpenter hands wrapped around the scarred stock, then cradled the captured rifle in a gesture more befitting a parent with a child. "Thank you, Teacher! I promise my best efforts to learn this rifle's proper use."

The Iranian waved a cautionary finger. "That means you will have to find a source of American ammunition for it and suitable batteries for the scope."

Hazim's smile faded at the realization of the challenge he now faced. He did not even know the designation of the 7.62×51 NATO cartridges remaining in the magazine. As for batteries . . . where did they fit in the scope?

Esmaili and Tawfiq smiled broadly at one another. Each knew that the Iranian possessed both ammunition and batteries, but would reveal neither until the boy had worked himself into a quandary trying to solve the problem he had just brought upon himself.

5

The Lebanon team was taking shape.

Frank Leopole and Omar Mohammed presided over the first assemblage, Leopole as operations officer and Mohammed in charge of training.

"Now," Leopole began. "Since I have no other pressing commitments, I'll take the lead with our in-country team, at least in the beginning."

Some knowing glances were exchanged in the audience. The message was tacitly clear: since SSI lacked meaningful employment with the U.S. Government, the firm's operations officer had nothing to keep him home. Besides, he had not smelled gunpowder since the Afghanistan contract and was between significant others. In short, the timing and circumstances were favorable.

Sitting near the back of the room, Lieutenant Colonel Sandra Carmichael folded her arms and feigned indifference. Alternating with Leopole as the company's director of international operations, by rights the option to take a foreign-deployed team should be hers. But not even a West Point ring and "U.S. Army (Ret)" behind her name could overcome most cultural barriers. Not for the first time she regretted that so many SSI contracts involved Islamic nations, where a white American female would not be well received. She let her notepad slide to the seat beside her, musing that while Leopole got the potential for some trigger time, she was obliged to produce some additional overseas business.

The dozen men occupying the chairs in the briefing

room were mostly known to one another but Leopole wanted everyone familiar with their teammates. He began by introducing most of the regulars.

"I think all of you know Jason Boscombe and Breezy Brezyinski. But Bob Ashcroft, Phil Green, Jack Jacobs, and Jeff Malten also are among our old hands. More recently we've acquired the services of two of Fort Bragg's finest, Chris Nissen and Josh Wallender, who have deployed with us to Africa. They're well qualified in small-arms and small-unit tactics and are cross-trained as medics or communicators.

"Our snipers are Rick Barrkman and Robbie Furr. They sort of lurk in the background and don't talk very much, except to themselves." Since the pair had in fact sat in the rear row, the observation drew the chuckles he expected. "They deployed with us to Afghanistan a while back, and they'll introduce our clients to precision rifles in Lebanon."

Leopole glanced around, taking stock of the audience. His gaze came to rest on the newest acquisition. "Also, I want to recognize Robert Pitney, who's probably known to you who follow the shooting sports. Robert, would you introduce yourself?"

Pitney briefly stood and faced the audience. "I'm Robert Pitney, Reading, Pennsylvania. Former police training officer, full-time firearms instructor and competition shooter." With that brief statement, he sat down.

Leopole interjected. "Robert's being modest. In case any of you don't know, he's one of the best pistol shooters in the country. He's won the Bianchi Cup and he's also a top-ranked competitor in three-gun matches. He's married to a Jordanian lady and speaks pretty good Arabic." For the moment Leopole decided to omit Pitney's religious preference.

Chris Nissen raised a hand. "Excuse me, sir. What's the Bianchi Cup?"

Leopole nodded to Pitney, who obviously did not want to be seen blowing his own horn. "It's the national action pistol championship. There's categories for iron sights or red dots." He grinned. "I finally put it all together and won the open category."

Two rows away, Breezy leaned over to Bosco. "Man. If that guy can shoot with Leatham and Koenig, he's gotta be some talent."

Bosco was unconvinced. "Dude, shooting falling plates ain't the same as whacking bad guys who want to whack you." He looked at Pitney from behind, noting the former cop's well-developed shoulders. "I wonder if he ever capped anybody."

Marc Brezyinski regarded his partner and saw an opportunity for mischief. "Why don't you, like, ask him?"

Jason Boscombe shrugged off the suggestion. Both operators knew The Code: you never asked another shooter if he had ever scored. It was just plain rude, like asking someone his bank balance. Besides, eventually the word got out, either by professional reputation or in the course of relating war stories.

Privately, Bosco considered himself a superior trigger man. He prided himself on his marksmanship, but it had nothing to do with his expert rifleman badge. He knew that he was better than Breezy, who was generally unconcerned with interpersonal rivalries. Among those present, only Barrkman and Furr were acknowledged better riflemen but they plied the sniper's arcane art, which was distinct from the stand-up kind of combat that Bosco practiced.

Leopole was speaking again. "As usual, we're short of language specialists. Pitney and Nissen speak passable Arabic while Wallender is qualified in French, but Mr. Baram assures me that there'll be English speakers on the other end."

"Hey, speaking of French, any word from J. J.?"

Boscombe seldom was reluctant to interrupt anyone. His partner Breezy said, "You know Bosco: never an unspoken thought."

"No, it looks like Johnson's sitting this one out." Leopole decided that he did not need to elaborate. The former Foreign Legionnaire had endured a brutally brief time in al Qaeda captivity in Pakistan, accepted a subsequent training job in Chad, then returned to Idaho. "But he's still available for domestic work."

The former Marine officer resumed his personnel rundown. "Malten and Brezyinski have combat medic ratings, and we'll have them update everybody before we leave."

Chris Nissen's baritone rose out of the second row. Sandy Carmichael would never admit it, but she always enjoyed the Special Forces sergeant's Barry White voice. "Colonel, I realize this is a preliminary briefing, but I'm wondering how much we can expect to get shot at."

"Well, I'd put the odds at better than fifty percent. That's why you're getting the hazardous duty bonus in addition to the overseas base pay."

SOUTH GOVERNATE, LEBANON

"Teacher, you have a visitor."

At the sound of Hazim's voice, Ahmad Esmaili was immediately alert. The Iranian had hoped for an afternoon nap, an ambition that was as rare as his ability to accomplish it. Ordinarily he kept going, remaining focused on each task as it arose. He had not lived through the previous thirty years by taking anything for granted. Multitasking was fine for those who could do it, but inevitably most of them overlooked something. Therefore, Esmaili had taken to making lists. At least he did not yet require spectacles to read them.

The Hezbollah leader slid his feet into his sandals and arose from the cot. "Who is it?" He tasted the morning taste and wanted something to rinse out his mouth—neither tea nor water. *Banish such thoughts,* he told himself.

"He calls himself Mohammad. He said to give you this."

Esmaili accepted the business card. The Farsi inscription was as simple as an ice pick through the eye. "Dr. Gholamhossein Momen, Tehran." Below the printed name was a handwritten line: *My son, Please come with Mohammad Azizi. Dr. Momen.*

Hazim saw the expression on his master's face and felt a tiny shiver somewhere inside. In all the time the youngster had worked with Esmaili, never had the Iranian betrayed any emotion other than mild satisfaction or icy anger. The fact that Esmaili was obviously impressed with the obscure name on the card was in itself—impressive.

"Bring him in," Esmaili said. His voice was quiet, respectful.

Hazim and one of Esmaili's bodyguards returned with the visitor, who regarded the Hezbollah operative with a calm demeanor and steady eyes. He introduced himself as Mohammad Azizi, also of Tehran. Esmaili made a quick assessment and determined that it might even be the man's true name.

"Assalamu Alikum we Rahmatulah wa Barakatu." Esmaili spoke Arabic for the benefit of his Lebanese colleagues.

"And peace and the mercy, and blessings of Allah be upon *you,*" the guest returned, shaking hands. He accepted a seat at the table in the small kitchen while Hazim poured tea and produced a plate of thin wafers. After the perfunctory formalities were concluded, Esmaili dismissed his acolytes with a flick of his head.

He faced Azizi, mindful that whatever the courier knew about Dr. Momen, it could be a ruse. Therefore, Esmaili kept the table between them, his right hand on his belt with the holstered Sig. He noted that the visitor kept both hands flat on the tabletop, apparently as a sign of good faith.

Azizi spoke first. "I believe that you are familiar with Dr. Momen."

Esmaili nodded slowly, gravely. "Yes. I worked for him several years ago. As part of his security detail."

"At the research institute." It was a statement, not a question.

"Correct."

The courier drummed his fingers briefly. "He remembers you, brother. And your devotion to the cause of Islam."

There was only one response. "I am honored. May the blessings of Allah be upon him."

Azizi felt more confident, or at least more comfortable. He crossed his arms and leaned toward his host. "The doctor would speak with you again, in person. If you are willing . . ."

Ahmad Esmaili knew an order even when couched as an invitation. "Certainly I am willing. But obviously it will not be here."

"No, no. In Tehran." Azizi glanced around, as if ensuring there were no eavesdroppers. Esmaili suspected that the gesture was more for effect than for real. "You will understand the need for caution. Even our most secure radio links can be compromised, so I was sent to, ah, invite you to return home for a visit." He smiled knowingly. "It must be some time since you saw your family."

"When would I leave, and for how long?"

Azizi leaned back, fully at ease now. "If you can arrange matters here, in perhaps two days. We would be in Tehran for three or four days, then return." He ran the numbers in his head. "Say, ten days in all."

"Then we can leave day after tomorrow."

"That is excellent," the messenger replied. "But you

will not be coming back here. The plan calls for your group to move to an area closer to the Syrian border, so make arrangements before you leave."

Esmaili did not enjoy receiving orders from a stranger, but if Azizi spoke for Dr. Momen, there was no arguing. The Hezbollah chief heard his voice say, "It will be done."

6

SSI OFFICES

"In your American phrase, I'm not going to blow smoke at you," Mordecai Baram began. "This will be hard, dangerous work. You can expect to take casualties."

Baram's words had the desired effect. His audience—mainly composed of SSI operators—was focused, quiet, attentive. The Israeli had their full attention in the first of a series of Lebanon briefings.

"What's the opposition really like, sir?" Chris Nissen spoke the question on each American's mind.

"You have all heard about Hezbollah, the main Islamic force in Lebanon. Well, that's what you're up against. It's a Shiite organization with strong ties to Iran, which is almost ninety percent Shiite itself. There's also significant logistic support from Syria, which is mainly Sunni."

Breezy squirmed in his seat. "Sir, I gotta admit I don't understand the whole Sunni and Shiite thing. What's the story?"

Baram knew the answer, chapter and verse. But he did not want to be distracted from his main topic. "I will be glad to explain that after the briefing, Mr. . . . ."

"Brezyinski. But just call me Breezy."

Baram grinned in appreciation. "Thank you, Mr. Breezy. For the moment I will just say that to you gentlemen, the difference is largely irrelevant. It has to do with the leadership of Islam, whether by bloodline from Mohammad or by popular acclaim. Not unlike the difference between Protestant and Catholic, with the role of the pope. But in some cases, it assumes so much relevance that people kill each other over relatively minor differences."

"Oh. Gotcha." Mark Brezyinski was very much a lapsed Catholic, to the lasting consternation of his Polish family. By his grandmother's reckoning, young Mark Casimir had broken at least five Commandments (depending upon one's distinction between killing and murder), as he was blatantly guilty on Honoring Thy Parents, Keeping the Sabbath, Blasphemy, and what he called the "Coveting Thing." Though he did not care to discuss Adultery, he felt safe on the matters of Other Gods, Graven Images, Stealing, and False Witness.

Baram resumed his briefing, focusing on SSI's major concerns. "Hezbollah is wholly of Lebanese origin, formed in response to the Israeli invasion in '82. The name means 'Party of God' and that can be taken literally. Besides its terrorist and paramilitary activities, it's increasingly involved in the Lebanese government as a political party. In 2005 Hezbollah won fourteen seats in parliament, and there are some cabinet ministers, too.

"Now, Hezbollah has gained battlefield credibility as well. In the 2006 fight it surprised a lot of people in the region and impressed others around the world." The diplomat gave an eloquent shrug. "Some were ready to be impressed, I admit, but still it pays to be objective. My advice is, don't take anything for granted."

Baram thought for a moment, barely referencing his notes. "Another thing to consider. Though it's heavily Lebanese and Iranian, Hezbollah recruits internationally.

There have been reports as far afield as Singapore, and of course Indonesia is the world's largest Muslim nation." He looked at Frank Leopole in the front row. "Your linguists will, of course, have to speak Arabic but you might plan on Farsi as well."

Leopole shot a sideways glance at Omar Mohammed. SSI's training officer caught the motion and chose to ignore it. Having been operationally involved in Pakistan and Afghanistan, the Iranian-born Mohammed had seen quite enough of fieldwork, thank you very much.

Sandy Carmichael generally was a low-key presence but as one of two senior operations officers she had an iron in the fire. "Mr. Baram, could you maybe bring in somebody who's operated in Lebanon recently?"

The Israeli had anticipated the question. "Officially, no. Besides, none of our attachés have been on the ground there. However . . ."

"Unofficially?"

The shrug again. "Maybe I know somebody who knows somebody."

"Well, for the present, how about a general perspective?"

Baram thought carefully, wondering how much to reveal. Finally he decided to open up. "Frankly, we've lost a lot of good men in South Lebanon in recent weeks. Not so much in actual numbers, which have to be kept pretty small, but in terms of percentages. One team was wiped out and a couple of others were badly hurt. I shouldn't be too specific, you understand, but I think it's only fair that you know something of what you're up against."

Baram acknowledged to himself that he was gilding the Lebanese lily. One team had two survivors, only one of whom would ever return to duty. He had seen some of the classified debriefings and recognized a few names.

"It's not just our own people who are taking hits. We work with some Druze militias because we just don't have the strength to conduct such operations ourselves. Actually, the whole situation turns on the Druze. It's their territory, and many of them are fighting for their homes, their own land. They've been badly mauled in several actions but they keep fighting." A frown. "They have no choice, really. Fight or leave."

APPROACHING TEHRAN

The flight from Damascus to Tehran covered fifteen hundred kilometers and a little over two hours. Finally Esmaili decided to risk a question of his escort.

"You have not said why Dr. Momen wants to see me."

Azizi kept his face turned toward the window of the Airbus A320. The Syrianair flight was on schedule, descending toward Mehrabad International, and Esmaili's curiosity finally had overcome his usual caution. He did not want to learn the reason for his trek at the last moment, when it might be difficult or impossible to decline whatever honor was headed his way.

Mohammad Azizi spoke in a subdued voice, even though he had requested two seats well removed from other passengers. "That is correct. I have not said." He finally turned from the window, a wry smile on his face.

Before Esmaili could respond, Azizi interjected. "It speaks well of you that you have not pressed for more information until now. The doctor will be pleased at your patience." The smile vanished. "But in truth, it would speak better for you had you not asked at all."

The Hezbollah leader had not survived decades in the field without developing mental agility. Without blinking he replied, "The doctor knows my record, brother. Otherwise he would not have requested me. And he knew that I would not refuse him. Therefore, I believe that my time over the past few days could have been well spent in considering whatever he has in mind."

Azizi regarded his new companion through objective eyes. *He is much as the doctor said.* After a moment he said, "When you meet the doctor day after tomorrow, much will be revealed. For now, I can say that patience remains a virtue, brother." The grim smile was back. "As it always has been."

While Azizi dealt with customs—there was precious little baggage—Esmaili looked around the terminal. He had not been in Tehran for almost three years, but the sights and smells came rushing back at him. A city of more than seven million residents, home of half of the nation's industry including military, textiles, chemical, construction, and electronics.

But the expansion brought problems. Esmaili had seen the most evident example during the landing approach—a heavy layer of dirty air. The pollution was inescapable—it was said that two dozen people died there every day from respiratory diseases.

On the other hand, Tehran had a large cultural community with mosques, museums, art galleries—and even synagogues. *There's an irony for you,* Esmaili thought.

Taking a taxi from the airport, Esmaili saw the Azadi Tower's formidable bulk. There was no ignoring it. Built in 1971 to honor the 2,500th anniversary of the Persian empire, its fifty meters of gleaming white marble had originally been dubbed the king's tower, but the Islamic revolution led to renaming it Azadi—freedom.

Pondering the drastic changes in Iranian life since 1979, Esmaili reflected on yet another irony: how much freedom ensued from toppling the despot who called himself Shah?

He kept such thoughts strictly to himself.

The cab turned onto the Ashrafi Esfahani Highway, then north to Iran Pars Highway. There the driver made a right turn, heading east. It was apparent that he knew the address Azizi had given, as he asked no questions en route.

At length the cab stopped at an undistinguished building in the Evin district in the north of town. Azizi paid the driver and led Esmaili into the entrance. It proved to be an apartment complex with a dining area, evidently at one time for upscale patrons. Now, based on Azizi's easy mastery of the layout, it seemed to be owned or at least controlled by Dr. Momen's organization.

Esmaili was quickly shown to a small, well-appointed room with a bath and was instructed to make himself comfortable. Azizi said, "I will call for you tomorrow after lunch. We will see the doctor then. Meanwhile, talk to no one about your work. No one. But other than that, enjoy the area." He indicated the view from the window.

The Evin district was composed of the older section featuring orchards and gardens and the newer section with modern skyscrapers. Esmaili already knew that it lay near Shahid Beheshti University and Evin Prison with its notorious political prisoner's wing. SAVAK used it before 1979 and the Ayatollah's minions ever since.

After his guide left, Esmaili took a walk to familiarize himself with the building and the area. It was an acquired habit of long standing: he was unable to relax until he felt comfortable with his surroundings.

Strolling in the afternoon sunlight filtered through the perpetual smog, Ahmad Esmaili allowed himself to wonder what one of his nation's most prominent scientists wanted with him.

7

SSI OFFICES

Frank Leopole had no idea how many briefings he had delivered in his time at Strategic Solutions, but he was comfortable with his audience, and increasingly with his subject. Like any good O-5, he had done his homework.

"Gentlemen, as you know, our mission involves working with Druze militias in central and southern Lebanon. There's increasing Hezbollah pressure in the area, trying to expand the territory where Iranian-backed groups can train and equip for operations against Israel. As you probably know, the Beirut government is largely unable to defend its own interests in some provinces. So we've been asked to step in, providing training and actual defense of specific villages and tribal areas.

"The primary Druze area is southeast of Beirut, fifty or sixty miles from the Israeli border. But the region has excellent defensive terrain, and the Druze control some of the best artillery positions in the country, including hills east of Beirut. The Hezzies would like to grab some of it for artillery positions and observation.

"The fly in the ointment is the Israeli concern with appearances in the international arena. Tel Aviv does not want to be seen backing the Druze in any overt manner, even though it's an open secret that the IDF works inside Lebanon, especially since there are Druze in the Israeli Army.

"Basically this is another training mission. But to maintain the charade we'll be working with Israeli Druze who will provide liaison and translator services. However, I'm hoping to assign at least a couple of our Arabic speakers to this operation."

Jason Boscombe raised a hand in the second row. "Sir, if we're going to work with the Druze, shouldn't we know more about them?"

"Odd you asked," Leopole replied. He turned and said, "Dr. Mohammed?"

Omar Mohammed was SSI's resident Middle East expert. The Iranian native had been hired for his reputation as a training officer but with a PhD in international relations, fluent in most Muslim languages plus French and Russian, he was as Frank Leopole said, "A one-stop shopping center."

Typically elegant, Mohammed smoothed his Brooks Brothers suit coat as he stepped to the lectern.

"Most of you are familiar with Lebanon's recent history, which briefly stated is one of internal conflict, frequent foreign occupation, and government disintegration. As an aside, I can say that in my youth, Beirut was called the Paris of the Mediterranean. A beautiful, cosmopolitan city that has since been destroyed in repeated fighting among the Syrians, Israelis, and Lebanese themselves."

Mohammed opened his PowerPoint presentation with a map of Lebanon on the screen.

"Lebanon is smaller than Connecticut with about 3.8 million people. More than ninety percent are of Arabic ancestry though roughly forty percent are Christians who do not identify with the Muslim culture.

"The nation is divided into six *mohafazah*, or governates, including Beirut. Those are in turn composed of districts or what we would know as counties . . ."

"Excuse me, Doctor," Leopole interjected. "I was looking at the CIA World Book, and it says there's eight provinces."

Mohammed gave an eloquent shrug. He stroked his salt and pepper beard, then ventured, "Well, that's the agency for you." He waited for the laughter to abate, then proceeded.

"The country is geographically divided along religious lines. The Shia are concentrated in the south, Sunnis in the north and east, and Christians in the center. The Druze are mostly between the Shia and Christians in the south-central region around Beirut.

"For a moment I want to address the two southern governates bordering with Israel. They are the main source of conflict at present."

Using a laser pointer, Mohammed sketched the boundaries of both areas. "South Governate, or Al Janub on some maps, lies here along the coast and Nabatiyeh farther inland. These are the areas of most military activity. Hezbollah, with strong Iranian backing, has established enclaves in several districts in both provinces, and obviously intends to stay. In fact, it is making overt efforts to expand its control in the region with the obvious intent of increasing attacks on northern Israel.

"Now, the United Nations maintains a so-called peacekeeping mission called UNIFIL, for U.N. Interim Force in Lebanon. 'Interim' calls for some perspective, since UNIFIL has been there since 1978. It varies but has run as high as twelve thousand troops from several member nations. I would imagine that you will have some dealings with U.N. officials, but they are far more observers than enforcers. You will have liaison officers to meet with UNIFIL and other agencies, so don't be overly concerned."

"Don't worry, Doc. I'm not." Breezy's off-the-cuff response prompted chuckles in the audience and a smack on the head from Bosco.

Mohammed, who nursed a quiet fondness for the brash paratrooper, ignored the lad's flippancy.

"As far as the Druze themselves, they are an Islamic reformist sect, mainly in Lebanon but with adherents in Jordan, Syria, and Israel. I can explain the religious aspects, but few Druze consider themselves Muslims. They're actually monotheists."

Breezy turned to Bosco. "Monotheists?"

The erstwhile Ranger nodded. "Like, they believe in one God."

Mark Brezyinski wrinkled his forehead. "Well, so do we, dude. So what's the diff?"

"About that much." Bosco rubbed a thumb and forefinger together as if dispensing salt.

Mohammed was speaking again. "They have been in the region for about a thousand years but since they're neither Muslims nor Christians they're mistrusted by both. Most Americans never heard of them until their militia became a factor in the Lebanese Civil War of 1975–90 when they defeated the Christian Phalangist militia. Later an accord was reached, and the two parties became nominal allies.

"In Lebanon the Druze are seen as a separate religious community with its own courts. In Israel the Druze are loyal to the government. Many serve in the armed forces and even in the Knesset. Others along the Golan identify with Syria."

Bosco raised a hand. "I've heard of them but not much in a long time. If they're involved in all these different countries, why don't we know more about them? I mean, like Hezbollah or Hamas?"

"Well, remember," Mohammed replied. "They're not Muslims and they have nothing in common with Hezbollah or Hamas. But mainly we don't hear much about them because secrecy is a large part of their culture. The Druze seldom accept converts, owing to a long history of persecution."

"So can we trust them?"

Mohammed shrugged. "That depends upon the individuals. It's like Christianity: everybody quotes the Golden Rule but how many Christians actually practice it?" He permitted himself an ironic smile.

"If you deal with serious Druze, you are likely in good hands. The tenets of the faith include belief in one God, honesty, protecting the family and homeland, helping those in need, and respect for the aged. They disapprove of alcohol or tobacco, usually don't eat pork, and reject polygamy. They do not marry outside the faith. As a rule, they reject materialism though some are successful businessmen."

The Iranian-American felt himself warming to his subject. Though he realized that most of the door-kickers in the audience were only marginally interested in such things, he felt that he owed the operators the benefit of his knowledge.

"There are two main groups: *al-Juhhal* or The Ignorant are denied secret holy literature. They form the political-military leadership, about ninety percent of all Druze. Those are the ones you'll be working with."

"What about the others, Doctor?" Leopole asked.

"Well, the inner group is *al-Uqqal* or The Knowledgeable Initiates. They are entirely unlike Muslims since women are considered spiritually preferable to men. Female *al-Uqqal* often wear a loose white veil to cover their hair and long skirts to the ankles. Men usually grow mustaches, shave their heads, and wear dark clothes and white turbans."

Breezy enjoyed playing the hey-dude surf bum to the Oxford educated lecturer. "So, Doc. Does that mean, like, we can ID most of the Druze by their clothes?"

The lecturer squinted his brown eyes in concentration. "It means you can tell the Druze by their clothes if they want you to identify them." He paused for effect. "Or it means they are someone else who wishes to appear as a Druze.

"Now," Mohammed concluded. "The Druze have fought just about everybody at one point or another. In the 1860s they massacred a lot of Christians, leading to French intervention about the time that Maximilian was engaged in Mexico. Since then the Druze have been allied with Christians and Jews and various Islamic groups." He looked up. "In short, gentlemen, you should remember one thing. The Druze are expert survivors."

NORTHERN ISRAEL

Brigadier Solomon Nadel dismounted from a Merkava Mark III and tugged a shop cloth from his cargo pocket. Wiping some errant diesel fuel from his hands, he greeted his guest with a smile. "Yakov, I'm sorry if I kept you waiting." He nodded over his shoulder. "Sometimes even a brigade commander needs to get his hands dirty."

Colonel Yakov Livni recognized the flippant tone for what it was. "General, you don't fool anybody. You can't stay away from your Chariots."

Nadel grimaced dramatically. "You found me out. Once a charioteer, always a charioteer."

"Well, let's just hope that we don't need these Chariots north of the border." Livni gave his superior a penetrating look. "You know, Sol, the days of battle tanks may be coming to an end."

Pausing in midstride, Nadel turned to look at the Merkava. It was a tanker's tank: designed for survivability with severely angled armor to protect the four-man crew; a twelve-hundred-horsepower engine for speed and acceleration; and a 120mm smoothbore as main armament. There was even a 60mm mortar carried internally. Finally the veteran tanker replied, "Well, it's no secret anymore. We lost six Chariots in Lebanon in 2006 but one hundred crewmen were killed or wounded. That's four times what we would expect just based on tanks destroyed." He shrugged philosophically. "ATGMs are becoming more effective."

Nadel quickened the pace. "But come on. You don't

want to talk about tanks when there's covert operations to support in Lebanon."

The two officers adjourned to Nadel's office and closed the door. The general tossed his shop rag and his beret onto a file cabinet, showing no concern when the headgear missed the basket and fell to the floor. "All right, Yakov. What do you have for me?"

Livni eased his left buttock onto the edge of the desk and unfolded a map. "Solly, this is confidential for now, but you can tell your chief of staff. Formal notice will arrive in a few days, and there will be a planning conference with brigade and division commanders as well as my people and . . . others."

The brigadier allowed himself a sly grin. "You mean Mossad."

An eloquent roll of the shoulders was all the response needed. "Anyway, consider this a warning order. Your brigade and other elements of the division will be tasked with supporting our cross-border teams, especially those working with Druze militia."

Nadel leaned back in his chair. "Druze. Well, they're no friends of the Iranians, but my God, Yakov. Their areas are up around Beirut. How are we going to . . ."

Livni raised a pudgy hand toward the wall map. "Yes, most of their traditional areas extend south and east from Beirut. But there are also some Druze enclaves closer to our border." He used a blunt index finger to circle an area in southern Lebanon.

Nadel looked at the map and recognized the name. "Hasbaya."

"Yes, that's a promising area. It's about fifteen kilometers south of Mount Hermon and a similar amount from the Syrian border. We want to insert training teams into the area before Hezbollah gets a better foothold."

"Well, that's going to be a tall order. I mean, that close to the Syrians, there must already be some well-established Hezbollah supply routes and even some bases."

Livni nodded decisively. "There are. Which is why we cannot allow the situation to remain uncontested. My boys are already making contact with civic and militia leaders, building goodwill with the local population. But we're stretched too thinly, as . . . as . . . " He cleared his throat and looked away. When he turned back, he was composed again. "As we learned too often of late."

Scanning the map more closely, Nadel emitted a soft whistle. "That's almost twenty kilometers inside Lebanon. What sort of support are we expected to provide?"

"As we noted before, mainly logistics. Supplies, route security, and a powerful presence round the clock. Your reaction force should be fully briefed on the terrain and tactical situation. I am informed that intelligence will be updated frequently, but that's a matter for the full briefing in a few days."

Nadel arched his eyebrows. "Well, all right. But if Hezbollah wants to oppose the operation—and undoubtedly it will—things could get messy. I mean, it wouldn't take much to escalate into another 2006 situation."

"Yes, I'm afraid you're right. But the decision has been made. The mood in the government seems to be that we'll have another fight sooner or later, and we want our Druze friends to be as prepared as possible. While keeping a low profile."

"Yakov, you mentioned supplies. That means either trucks or helicopters, and both can easily be intercepted. We're bound to have casualties, and . . ."

"Well, maybe not so many this time."

Nadel shook his head. "What do you mean?"

Livni lowered his voice. "Yes, there will be IDF personnel, including Israeli Druze. But there will also be, ah, third-party nationals doing much of the actual work."

"Who would that be?"

The colonel leaned toward the general. "Americans."

TEHRAN

Of the capital's twenty-two municipal districts, Esmaili considered one as good as another. But Dr. Gholamhossein Momen favored the Amirabad area, west of Azizi's hostel, and that is where the meeting occurred. The fact that the district contained a nuclear research facility might have caused concern, but Esmaili reckoned that the doctor subscribed to what Americans called the "forest for the trees" method of hiding oneself.

Azizi escorted Esmaili to the scientist's office and left for a moment. During the short interval, the Hezbollah operative took in the ambience. It reflected his memory of Dr. Momen from their association several years before. Austere, functional, businesslike, without adornment.

From his awful days on the revolutionary firing squad, through the eight-year agony of the Iraq war to the more satisfying, less constrained campaign in Lebanon, Ahmad Esmaili had become an adept judge of men. That is, of character. Very few had earned his full respect and fewer caused him genuine fear. Gholamhossein Momen was the only one who filled both descriptions.

Esmaili forced himself upright in the straight-backed metal chair. With his hands folded, he tried to exude an air of confidence, or at least calm indifference, for whomever might be watching. He knew that Momen's acolytes never tired in their surveillance even of allies. Perhaps especially of allies. The doctor was too valuable to the national interest to take anyone for granted. And for that reason, few of the security operatives remained indefinitely. Esmaili recalled that they were transferred out, like himself, or otherwise disposed of, often for the smallest of reasons.

Or for no reasons but a doctrinal concern about any individual gaining too much knowledge or influence.

The door to the inner office opened and Azizi beckoned.

With an effort of will, Esmaili forced himself from the chair and strode through the portal into his future.

The office, if it was such, contained a desk and a few chairs. Besides Azizi, Esmaili saw three robed men, speaking quietly while facing away from the door. At length the shortest figure turned, his hands within the large sleeves of his robe.

Esmaili felt a shudder in his shoulders and worms in his belly. Belatedly, he realized that his tremor was visible.

Dr. Gholamhossein Momen extended his hands from his white robe. They were long, bony, manicured hands. "Peace and mercy and the blessings of Allah be upon you, my son."

Esmaili returned the greeting, bowing his head deferentially. To himself, he conceded ephemeral gratitude for a chance to escape the doctor's eyes.

Momen was cursed with dreadful vision. Most of his life he had worn thick glasses that gave an eerie magnification to his brown eyes. They were his dominant feature, seemingly widened unnaturally behind the lenses as if seeking to observe everything around him in minute detail. Which was exactly the case.

The years had not been kind to the scientist. Always short and stout, even his traditional robes failed to conceal his growing obesity. His face behind those spectacles was fleshy and wan, in contrast to his short, dark beard.

Momen stepped around the desk, moving to greet Esmaili in a gliding motion that almost seemed serpentine. It took an effort of willpower for Esmaili to hold his ground, not merely for fear of insulting his host, but for the sign of weakness that retreat would impart. He devoutly did not wish to appear weak in the presence of Dr. Momen.

They grasped hands, and Esmaili felt the clammy sensation of the doctor's skin. Then, with a start, he realized that the perspiration might as easily be his own. He forced himself to look into the magnified eyes and mutter a dignified response. "I am honored that you have called upon me, Doctor."

Momen released the grip and waved to a chair. "And I thank you for coming so quickly, brother." He glanced at Azizi, who seemed approximately relaxed in the doctor's presence. "Our friend assures me of the quality of your work in Lebanon." A tight, grim smile. "Not that I ever doubted it."

Momen returned to the swivel chair on the other side of the desk, motioning one of the other men to leave. It was tacit indication of the trust placed in Esmaili. Otherwise, Dr. Momen was seldom out of sight of at least two armed guards.

Ordinarily there would be coffee or tea, perhaps with wafers, and some preliminary small talk. But Momen had neither time nor use for polite conversation. He fixed his myopic gaze upon the visitor and said, "I have need of your services again. Arrangements have already been made with your superiors. Once you return to Lebanon, you will operate under Mohammad Azizi, who reports directly to me."

Esmaili had forgotten the doctor's penchant for speaking of people as if they were not present. Evidently Azizi was accustomed to the habit; at least he made no objection.

It occurred to the Hezbollah operative that he had not been asked to volunteer for anything. He was receiving an assignment that permitted no refusal. Harking back several years, Esmaili recalled what befell the only two men who had ever tried to decline the honor of an assignment from Dr. Momen.

"Certainly, Doctor." Esmaili managed to keep an even tone.

Momen leaned back in his swivel chair, hands inside his sleeves again. He reclined enough to look at the light in the ceiling, apparently entranced with it. Speaking in an oily, sibilating voice, he seemed lost in free association.

"I have brought you a long distance for this short meeting because you need to understand the gravity of my . . . our . . . plans. The operation has many layers, each independent of the others. No one but I and a few others know the entire plan, for obvious reasons. A degree of technical expertise is required, and specialists will be assigned to each cell as the schedule moves forward."

Momen finally turned his attention back to Esmaili. "My son, your cell will be responsible for delivering one of the technical teams to its destination. You have not been told, but your recent activities were planned months ago in order to gain a position of advantage for that purpose." The ghosting smile returned for a few heartbeats. "Again, secrecy is maintained for obvious reasons."

Another deferential nod. Then Momen was on his feet again. "You have done well. I am confident that you will continue doing so." He turned dismissively but then, as if an afterthought, he added, "I will dispatch a beloved colleague to assist you before long."

Esmaili expressed gratitude for the sentiment, then followed Azizi out of the room. In the exterior hallway, Azizi looked at his new partner. "Well? What do you think?"

Esmaili thought: *I think I am glad to be away from that man*. He said, "About what?"

"About the operation, of course."

A noncommittal shrug. "I do not know enough to form a judgment, brother." Then he remembered to add, "It is in God's hands."

Azizi seemed satisfied with the platitude. He said, "I have more meetings this afternoon. You return to Damascus tomorrow and on to Lebanon. I shall rejoin you in a few days." He raised a cautionary finger. "You must never speak to anyone about this meeting unless I clear it." He gave an ironic grin. "For obvious reasons."

"Certainly, my brother."

Esmaili shunned a taxi for the return to his room. It was only a ninety-minute walk, and he wanted to clear his head. Well before he arrived, he had the basics of the plan in his mind. *Momen is a physicist. That means I am part of a compartmentalized operation to deliver multiple nuclear or biological weapons against Israel.*

He also knew that the odds of surviving the mission were less than those of an infidel entering Paradise.

8

SSI OFFICES

Omar Mohammed convened the meeting of the Lebanon training team that would develop a training program for the Druze militiamen. He began, "Mr. Baram has obtained some information on the state of training of our clients, but since there are several locales we do not know exactly the needs of each. Therefore, we should have two contingencies: a very basic syllabus and a more advanced one for those militia who possess some basic knowledge."

Mohammed rose from his chair and flipped the cover off an easel. As an experienced briefer he knew that revealing subject headings always invited the audience to read ahead of the presentation, which interfered with comprehension. The first page had a list of topics: Organization, Communications, Weapons, Tactics, Combat Trauma.

"These are the areas that Mr. Baram told us to look at.

As you can see, the groups we'll be training are willing to learn many of the basics from us, even though many of them undoubtedly have combat experience. I consider that an encouraging sign. It means that most of them seem to have an open mind." He shrugged. "Considering what they are facing, perhaps that is as important as anything else. Actually, I suspect that in the end we may learn as much as they do."

Chris Nissen, the former NCO who would lead one of the teams, raised a point. "Doctor, it seems to me that a lot of the Druze will have some combat experience. They're likely to think they don't need any weapons instruction."

The suave Iranian native shrugged eloquently. "In that case they would not have hired us. True, we're actually working for the Israelis who need a cutout for political deniability, but the IDF is sending us where we seem to be needed the most. I believe, therefore, that most of the Lebanese will be receptive."

Mohammed took a marker and underlined each topic. "I have tentatively assigned each of you two areas of expertise: a primary and a secondary. For instance, Mr. Malten and Mr. Brezyinski are rated medics so they will mostly teach combat trauma with weapons as a secondary subject. Similarly, Mr. Wallender specializes in communications and doubles as a tactics instructor. Your briefing packets contain your specific assignments."

Frank Leopole walked to the easel and stood beside Mohammed. "Actually, weapons and tactics will be our bread and butter, pretty much like it is on most of our training contracts. That's why most of you were selected for this job. We'll break into five-man teams and discuss some of the specifics before we meet again this afternoon and hash out any questions about doctrine. The main things to keep in mind: keep it simple and keep it consistent."

While Leopole circulated among the team discussions, Mohammed sat in on the weapons group for starters.

Consulting his notes, he began, "Many experienced fighters in the Middle East have expended thousands of rounds without hitting anybody. At least not that they can tell. Mainly it's cultural. The more radical Islamists do not even bother to zero their rifles. They just point toward the enemy and pull the trigger, trusting God to guide their bullets. *Inshallah.* I am told that such attitudes are rare among the Druze who, after all, are not Muslims."

Pitney wriggled in his chair, apparently concerned about something. Mohammed noted the movement. "Yes, Robert."

"Well, sir, I think we should emphasize the fundamentals: grip, cheek weld, breathing, sight picture, trigger control, and follow-through. Especially trigger control."

Mohammed regarded the champion shooter. Obviously he was speaking as a national-class authority on the subject. "You seem to be saying that the trigger is more important than the others."

"Well, Doctor, they're all important. I mean, I wouldn't gloss over any of them. But the trigger's the man-machine interface, you know? When I was in high school we would've said it's where the rubber meets the road. In my experience, if you get a shooter to concentrate on a good surprise break every time, he'll learn a lot faster than otherwise. And he'll be more accurate as well."

Bosco fancied himself as a marksman and had some theories of his own. "You know, I've always wondered about follow-through. I mean, how can the shooter affect the shot when the bullet goes three thousand feet per second?" He spread his hands. "That's different from an early flinch, of course."

Mohammed looked to Pitney for a response.

"Sir, once I computed the dwell time in the barrel for a 5.56 round. I forget exactly but it's a few ten-thousandths of a second. So Bosco's right, once the primer goes, the shooter can't influence the course of the bullet. But if the shooter follows through on every round, pretty soon he begins to notice where the sights were, and that means he can begin calling his shots. After that, he can start correcting himself."

Mohammed appreciated Pitney's throwing a bone to Bosco. The ex-Ranger was a good shooter and a better rappel instructor, but Pitney could have turned the exchange to his own advantage. Instead, he remained professionally neutral. *He's trying to fit in,* Mohammed noted. *Good for him.*

"Now, I might add something. There's a saying: 'One round, two sight pictures.' What does that mean?" Since he knew that Pitney could write an encyclopedia on the subject, he looked elsewhere. "Anybody?"

Phil Green beat out Bosco. "It means you immediately get a second sight picture after the round goes."

"Correct. Whether you need it or not."

Chris Nissen asked, "What about full auto? I mean with rifles, not belt-fed guns."

Mohammed looked at Pitney who had his own thoughts on the subject but thought better of addressing a purely military subject. The snipers, Barrkman and Furr, gave each other disapproving looks while mouthing the words: *Waste of ammo.* Finally Green spoke up again. Though primarily a SWAT cop, he had done a tour as an artilleryman. "Doesn't that depend on how much time and ammo is available? From what we've heard about this job, it sounds as if we're not going to have much chance to teach more than the basics."

"That is probably the case," Mohammed replied. "But Sergeant Nissen's question is well taken. Undoubtedly most of our clients are accustomed to firing their AKs on full automatic. We can either show them the folly of that technique or try to teach them how to do it right."

Nissen said, "Sounds like a distinction between the beginners and the more experienced people. In other words, a syllabus decision. Now if it was just up to me, I'd say semiauto only at anything outside room distance."

Mohammed nodded in agreement. "Unless anyone has other thoughts on the subject, we will make that a doctrinal item. Full auto only at close quarters."

Pitney had a thought. "Doctor, are we likely to have people with sub guns?"

"You mean submachine guns?"

"Yes, sir."

"Well, I don't know. It hasn't come up."

The speed shooter bit his lip. "Sometimes it's better to have a pistol than a buzz gun, especially in tight spaces. I'm just wondering if we should decide if we want to try teaching SMGs or handguns. I mean, there probably won't be time for both."

Now Bosco's curiosity got the better of him. "You saying that a pistol's better than an MP-5 up close and personal?"

Pitney blinked his green eyes. After two heartbeats he replied, "I know it's better for *me*. And probably for most guys. Look, you don't have as much risk of leading with your muzzle around corners, and retention is easier with a handgun. There's no real advantage in the ammo, and in fact the pistols I'd carry are all bigger than nine-millimeter."

Bosco squirmed in his seat. "Yeah, but with one trigger pull of an MP you can dump ten, twenty rounds into somebody."

"What if there's two or three of them? I'm not trying to pump myself up here, but I can show you on the range that a pistol is better than a buzz gun against multiple opponents up close."

The erstwhile Ranger recognized an opportunity. Robert Pitney seemed to be challenging Jason Boscombe to a man against man contest. Bosco's Heckler & Koch against Pitney's Springfield XD.

"What sort of test would it be, dude?"

Pitney smiled. "Say, five targets at ten yards."

"What kinda targets?"

"Oh, eight-inch steel plates. Starting with both guns at low ready."

Bosco thought for a moment, then leaned back and laughed. "Hey, dude, I only *look* stupid. That's the kind of games you play all the time. I'd end up buying you a case of beer or something."

"No, no," Pitney insisted. "I'm not trying to sandbag anybody. I'm just saying that I've run that test several times, and the pistol usually wins. It's because the distance is too short for the sub gun's sight radius to be a real advantage, and that HK trigger can't be tweaked like most pistols. When we switch guns, after a few runs the guy shooting my pistol does better."

"Better than you?"

Pitney tried suppressing a grin and failed. "Well, better than he did with the buzz gun."

"That's what I thought." Bosco laughed.

PART

II

ISRAEL

9

SOUTHERN LEBANON

Ahmad Esmaili returned to the secure orchard area that sheltered his unit from overhead observation. He found Fida conducting weapon familiarization drills for the new men, some of whom appeared not quite through puberty.

"Do they really get so much younger, or are we so much older?"

The Lebanese fighter was both experienced and cynical. "Both, of course. As long as the world keeps turning, it supplies us with a new crop of volunteers every year. I accepted two of these boys because they had no place to go. Their families are dead or displaced, so I believe we are engaging in charitable work as well as military recruiting."

Esmaili emitted a noncommittal grunt. He looked at the youngsters who were learning to field strip an AK-47. Eventually they would be able to disassemble and reassemble a Kalashnikov blindfolded. Whether they could shoot one straight and fast was another matter.

Fida scratched his beard and examined his superior's face. Nothing registered, which was entirely normal. "Was your trip worthwhile?"

Leaving Tawfiq to supervise the newcomers, Esmaili took Fida several meters to one side. "I will tell you as much as I can. My trip was made for the purpose of spending about two minutes with a highly placed man in Tehran. We are to be honored with a significant assignment, but that will be determined later. Meanwhile, I will receive information and directions from Mohammad Azizi and we will conform to his directions until further notice." He paused.

"Yes?"

"There is something more. The . . . source . . . said he is dispatching 'a beloved colleague' to oversee our part of the operation. I do not know if the new colleague will replace Azizi or work beside him, but I want you to know that we are going to be under greater scrutiny than ever before."

Tawfiq scratched his beard again. It was showing faint traces of impending gray. "Well, that could mean anything, could it not? That is, a sign of trust and confidence or . . ."

"Or a lack of trust and confidence."

"What do you think, brother?"

Esmaili dropped into a crouching position, idly rearranging pebbles between his feet. Tawfiq joined him, back to the shade tree class under way. "No. I have thought of little else since leaving Tehran. Based on what the . . . source . . . told me, it seems to be considered an honor. Besides, I do not believe that we would be given a crucial mission if we were mistrusted."

Tawfiq grimaced. "There is a possible explanation, you know. We might be considered expendable and your . . . source . . . wants to ensure our compliance."

The Iranian made no comment. None was necessary. At length his subordinate whispered, "You think so, too."

Esmaili leaned back and sat on the ground, hands grasped between his knees. "I only know that the mission will involve a high degree of technical expertise, something beyond our capabilities. Therefore, we will almost certainly be assigned security for the operation."

Tawfiq knew better than to speculate on when or where, let alone to ask his commander for more details. He rolled his slender shoulders. *"Inshallah."*

A curt nod. "God's will."

NORTHERN COMMAND HEADQUARTERS
SAFED, ISRAEL

Frank Leopole had experience of women in a dozen nations. As he said, "There are two kinds: mothers and others." He was decidedly an Other kind of guy. Never married and presently minus a commitment, he was comfortable in doing without for an indefinite period. However, the *sabra* who escorted him into the office prompted him to reconsider his impending celibacy. Raven hair, huge brown eyes, and a face of chiseled marble atop a slender carriage caused the former Marine a momentary distraction.

It was obvious that the commanding officer had first choice of the base secretarial staff.

Major General Moshek Brafman greeted his guest by rising from his desk. He was a stout third-generation Israeli who looked more Middle Eastern than Polish. However, he caught the American's glance at the mobile decor and smiled approvingly. "Isn't she a beauty?" Brafman emitted a sigh. "My wife was a head turner in her day, but Gabriella . . ." He shook his head. "Hoof!" Despite his accent, the sentiment was clear.

"She must be a distraction, General."

"Yes, she is. She certainly is." A male bonding smile and a gesture toward a sofa. "Would you like some refreshment?"

"Ah, no, sir. Thank you." He took a seat, remaining erect and attentive.

Brafman plunked down beside Leopole and frankly

studied the SSI operator. "Colonel, from what I am told, you are a direct individual and a man of action. Therefore, I shall do you the honor of being blunt. Though this is an international operation, and ordinarily it would involve certain . . . diplomatic niceties. While I hope that our relations will remain cordial, all of us need to keep certain realities in mind."

The general paused a moment, ordering his thoughts. "As a professional, you must know that few plans remain unchanged. That especially applies to your upcoming work, for a variety of reasons that must be clear by now."

Leopole nodded. "Yes, sir. Mr. Baram and a few others gave several briefings before we left."

Brafman smiled slightly. "Well, he is not one to gild the lily, so to speak. Sometimes it's a wonder that he advanced so well in government work."

"You know him, then?"

The general squirmed slightly and gave a sideways glance. "We are acquainted, Colonel." His tone changed from jovial to matter-of-fact. "As I was saying, although you will be training our Druze friends to defend their villages, it's still an Israeli operation—which we of course will deny to one and all."

Leopole did not know how to respond to such candor from a foreign general so he merely nodded.

"Your people, Colonel, absolutely must keep as low a profile as possible. Naturally, if you are attacked, you may defend yourselves." Brafman set his thick hands on his knees and launched himself off the couch. He began pacing. "Frankly, it was foolish of our politicians to expect that third-party people could remain uninvolved. The area you will be working is of particular interest to Hezbollah, and once your presence is known, the pressure may increase rather than decrease. You understand?"

Leopole stood. "Certainly, sir. Mr. Baram said in his briefings that we might take casualties."

A decisive nod. "Good!"

After three or four heartbeats, Brafman held up a hand. "I did not mean that the way it came out, Colonel. Naturally . . ."

"Yes, sir. You approve Mordecai's honesty."

"Well, let us say that I know of *Mr. Baram's* honesty." The ironic grin was back.

"Certainly, General."

Brafman was pacing again. "Now, as I was going to say . . . although your team will operate directly with the militias, it will always be under IDF supervision. You will meet some of our own Druze officers before you proceed to Beirut. Some of them have worked with their Lebanese cousins before, some have not. But I want to emphasize this, Colonel: whatever you may think of a given situation, your actions will be guided by Israeli interests, not American."

Leopole shrugged. "General Brafman, I never expected anything else."

"So. How many training teams will you deploy?"

"Two or three, depending on local requirements. We can double up where needed."

Brafman absorbed that information, nodding solemnly. At length he said, "You must realize that some of the areas are remote, quite remote. Your men will be beyond our ability to help in anything less than several hours. More likely a day or more. Even helicopter reinforcements are no guarantee. Therefore, it is advisable to establish relations with other villages and other militias in each area. That is where our own Druze officers can help the most."

Leopole accepted the information stoically. "Yes, sir. It's pretty much what we were told in Arlington." He stepped to a wall map covering Israel, Lebanon, and much of Syria and Jordan. Tapping the paper he said, "General, besides reinforcements and supplies, I see our big concern as communications. We have cellular capability and may even be able to talk to headquarters in Arlington. But as I understand it, we're relying on your people for contact with you."

The Israeli nodded. "That is correct. Our liaison officers are well equipped. The militias . . . not so much."

Leopole turned away from the map to face his host. "You know, if I were a Hezbollah planner, I'd start working on a way to interrupt your comm. Then I'd drop the hammer before anybody here realized something was going down."

A taut smile. "Colonel Leopole, I admire men who think as I do. That is why our liaison and training teams have communications specialists with frequency-agile radios, encryption, and burst transmission capability." He raised an eyebrow. "And not all of it is made in the U.S.A."

"As long as it works, General. As long as it works."

Brafman then turned to the map. He ran a finger along the northeastern border. "Here we are fifteen kilometers from the border, well within range of Katyushas." He turned to his guest. "In 2006, some of us spent time in the bomb shelters, I can tell you. But you will be working opposite the area of the division in this area. Solomon Nadel, one of the brigade commanders, is tasked with supporting your mission, and he works with the special operations branch, which conducts our efforts in Lebanon." He looked at Leopole. "I can read your mind. Do not worry about too many layers of command authority. This is a streamlined operation, and as I just noted, your IDF liaisons will have direct contact with brigade, special ops, and with me."

"Very well, sir."

"Then we understand one another." He sat down at his desk and pressed the intercom. "Gabriella, would you bring us some refreshments?"

NABATIYEH GOVERNATE, LEBANON

Mohammad Azizi brought the word.

"Dr. Momen's colleague will arrive in two or three days. I am to escort him across the Syrian border."

Ahmad Esmaili set down his topographic map. "Who is he?"

Azizi slid into a chair. He felt more at ease with his fellow Iranian since returning from Tehran. "Imam Sadegh Elham. He is an old friend of Dr. Momen. They have much in common, especially The Faith . . . and science."

"Science. There are priests and scholars who insist that Islam should not become dependent upon science or technology. Such men cite the corruption of the West."

The liaison officer waved dismissively. "Well, Imam Elham is not among them."

"What do you know of him?"

"A devout servant of God. More a leader than a scholar, I believe."

"No, no. I mean his background. His influence." *His political connections.*

"Well, I know that he has ministered to various Hezbollah units in recent years, often with prestigious assignments. His name has been connected with our rocket forces."

Esmaili perked up. "Rocket forces? What is the need of an imam there?"

Azizi permitted himself an ironic smile. "My brother, God's minions are needed everywhere the faithful are found."

The commander squinted in concentration, staring at the floor. "Rockets. That could explain what Dr. Momen meant when he referred to 'technical experts.'" He raised his gaze. "Since the blessed doctor is involved in nuclear research . . ."

Azizi shook his head. "No, no. I do not think so." His voice was harsh, insistent. Clearly he did not like the sum of two and two. "Besides, there would have to be testing to match a nuclear warhead to any rocket."

"We do not know all that occurs in Iran . . . or Korea. Or elsewhere. Who is to say what has been tested and what has not?"

Esmaili referred to his map again. Spreading it on the table, he laid out the geography. "From this area there are not many worthwhile targets within range. Haifa is well beyond the 122mm Katyusha rockets but barely within range of Fajr 3s based just inside of the border, not to mention Fajr 5s. But from this area, Haifa is too far."

"What about the Zelzal rocket? One hears much of it."

Esmaili fidgeted, feeling mildly angry that he had little current knowledge of rockets and missiles, though he knew Zelzal was the latter. Many jihadists tended to use the terms interchangeably. Moreover, most of what he did know dated from his brief tenure with Dr. Momen.

But there was something else, more unsettling. It occurred to him: *Azizi does not know the plan.*

"Depending upon the model, Zelzal has a range of one hundred fifty to perhaps four hundred kilometers. I believe it carries a six-hundred-kilogram warhead." He thought for a moment, trying to dredge up the figures from his memory. "The Shahab 3 and 4 possess much greater range—from twelve hundred to two thousand kilometers. They are based on the North Korean No-dong, and probably carry a thousand-kilogram warhead."

"Then they would be better used here than closer to the border." Azizi flicked the map. "They can easily reach any point in Israel."

Esmaili rubbed his chin, then brushed his mustache. "Yes, but it makes no military sense. As soon as the Jews discover long-range missiles in this area they would destroy them."

"But how would they know? Surely the Shahab batteries would set up quickly, fire their rockets, and be gone."

The cell leader regarded his colleague. "The Americans must have satellites overhead almost constantly. They give any such information to the Zionists." He paused to allow that sentiment to set in. "No, the longest range weapons would only be fired from Iran itself, where retaliation would be most difficult."

"Very well, then," Azizi replied. "The Fajr series is too short-ranged and Shahab too sophisticated for use here. Therefore, let us assume a Zelzal with two-hundred-kilometer range. From here, that could strike Haifa, Netanya, and Nablus. But if we were to move thirty kilometers southwest, to Qiryat Shemona, a Zelzal could reach Tel Aviv."

Esmaili saw the logic: Zelzals could be deployed on trucks and dedicated launch vehicles—a definite advantage given Israeli air superiority. Still, something did not track quite right. "Brother, even assuming you are correct, consider the outcome. We would have to fire many missiles to achieve worthwhile damage, and even with mobile launchers they could be found and destroyed. That indicates a few missiles carrying massive warheads. Therefore . . ."

"Therefore," Azizi interjected, "either Imam Elham and Dr. Momen are planning nuclear rockets or something else entirely."

10

The SSI team was assembled at a secure compound that afforded a few days of preparation before proceeding to Lebanon. Frank Leopole allowed the men to settle in, get better acquainted, and enjoy the pool or exercise room. Then it was down to business.

At the initial briefing Leopole related the administrative details. "I met with General Brafman of Israeli Northern Command, and he laid out the situation. You already know we're working with Druze militia in southern Lebanon, and we'll have IDF Druze members as liaison officers and translators. Largely we'll be semi-independent, sometimes in fairly remote areas, but I am assured that we'll have secure, reliable comm via the IDF people." He stopped for a moment, then added, "If it works, that's great. If not, I have some backup that should permit us to talk directly to HQ in Arlington. It'll be on an as-needed basis, but Admiral Derringer said the board sprung for the extra gear just to cover the bases."

The operations officer mentally ticked off the topics he intended to cover. "Now then, as for our Druze contacts, you should know a couple of things. They're Israeli military personnel but obviously they have an interest in the welfare of their cousins in Lebanon. I have no reason to think that any of them are other than what they seem, but I'm not taking anything for granted. I want our relationship to be polite and professional, but there's no need to tell them everything we know. General Brafman was pretty plainspoken with me: we're under Israeli command and we'll act in accordance with their best interests, not ours. While I appreciate his candor, I think we could become expendable if things go south. But don't worry too much: as usual, SSI has a Plan Alpha and a Bravo to extract us."

Chris Nissen, though relatively new to the firm, was not timid. "Care to share that with us, sir?"

Phil Green added, "Yeah, I might sleep a little better."

Leopole did not want to reveal that neither plan was finalized: too many political and bureaucratic hoops still remained. So he said, "One is by land, the other by air. That's all I can say for now."

Seated in the back, Robert Pitney congratulated himself for his foresight. While he had no reason to doubt his new employer's concern for his welfare, he had a list of names, addresses, and phone numbers based on his in-laws' business contacts. None were located in the likely operating area, but he knew that if he made enough calls, somebody would come for him—either from devotion, greed, or both.

Breezy always asked the obvious questions. "Colonel, how do we get to our AO? I take it that we're supposed to keep a low profile."

"Lower than a snake's navel, son." Leopole allowed the laughter to abate, then added, "We'll address that when we meet with our IDF folks in a day or so.

"Now," Leopole continued. "Before you left, you had the standard in-country brief about local culture and customs. I'm going to add something else." He placed his hands on his hips and inclined his torso slightly forward, as if imparting physical emphasis to his words. "I am reliably informed that Lebanon produces some of the finest-looking women in the Middle East. Maybe *the* finest."

He lanced Jason Boscombe with a D.I. stare, and was rewarded when that worthy slid lower in his chair. Both personally and professionally Leopole believed the mantra "Time spent on reconnaissance is seldom wasted." His efforts had shown that celebrities of Lebanese descent included entertainers Yasmine Bleeth, Salma Hayek, Shakira, and supermodel Yamila Diaz. Bosco, however, being a leg man, was disappointed to find divided opinion on Paula Abdul's heritage but otherwise he was suitably impressed.

Leopole knew that Bosco and Breezy had enjoyed themselves immensely during some downtime in Haifa before the previous operation, which climaxed in a sea chase across the Mediterranean. While none of the local or visiting fillies had complained—in fact, a few were downright complimentary—the duo's antics had brought unwelcome attention.

"Now hear this," Leopole intoned. "What you do on your own time with consenting females is *not,* repeat *not,* your own business. In these circumstances it reflects on this firm and upon our contracting parties, so I expect you to bear that in mind at all times." He paused for effect. "If you meet some hottie who invites you to go skinny-dipping with her boobacious friends, I want to know about it."

Breezy turned to Bosco. "Boobacious? Did Lieutenant Colonel Leopole just say 'boobacious'?"

"Fershure, dude. I heard him five by five."

NABATIYEH GOVERNATE

Omar Razlavi stalked the dreamscape of Ahmad Esmaili. Ferretlike in his speed and agility, the Iranian teenager had become noted for his ability to snake in and out of barbed wire, finding and marking Iraqi mines. Nobody seemed to know exactly where Omar came from or the circumstances that placed him in the front lines in 1981. But the boy's innate ability to find mines buried beneath dirt or sand, in the dark, grew to near legendary status. As a *Sarjukhe* in the Twenty-third Special Forces Brigade, he refused every promotion above corporal. He insisted that God had made him for mine clearing, and that was what he would do.

Armed with his faith, a green headband, and a sack full of white flags, Razlavi probed the enemy ground with a hard plastic knife. Thousands of Saddam's mines—many of foreign manufacture—were avoided by the Ayatollah's soldiers during the long war. In an endeavor where survival often was measured in hours, Omar Razlavi thrived for seven years. And then some.

The next morning, Esmaili awoke with the beginning of a plan. He went in search of Fida and found him after breakfast. "I want to talk with you."

Fida recognized the statement as more a command than a desire. They walked a safe distance from the aspiring jihadists and sat on a stone wall.

"I had a dream last night. Usually I do not remember my dreams, but this was different. It dealt with reality."

Fida squirmed on the uncomfortable rocks. "Yes?"

"During the Iraq war, I knew a young mine hunter. Omar Razlavi."

"Yes, yes. I remember the name."

"I became acquainted with him late in the war, and served with him during operations with Hamas in Palestine. I learned then that Omar was an orphan. Thousands like him were taken into the army and fed into the war. We had no choice: we were fighting for our survival and full mobilization was required. But those boys, those young boys . . ." His voice trailed off.

Finally Esmaili spoke again. "Most of them went willingly. They were filled with revolutionary spirit and the excitement of serving the nation. And God," he hastened to add. "They had never known anything else.

"Sometime late in the war, when it was clear that there could be no winner, I began to wonder. How did a teenaged boy like Omar find his calling? He was by far the best at what he did; I never heard of anyone who came close to matching him. It was as if he was born to hunt mines. But what else might he have accomplished? Was mine clearing the only thing he was meant to do? What if . . ."

The what-if remained moot. But Fida grew wary; his well-honed sense of survival began twitching at the back of his cranium. He would not betray any doubt to his superiors, who were notably unsentimental about living heroes, but neither would he bare his professional neck, let alone the personal variety.

"What if? Do you mean, what if he had another calling?"

Esmaili nodded quietly. Then he turned to his colleague. "Something other than war."

Fida shifted his AK; he was seldom without it. "He was born into a time of war, brother. As you say, he served the revolution and he served God in the best way he could." When that comment drew no response, Fida prompted, "What became of him?"

"A few years after the truce, some of our commandos began passing their knowledge to Palestinian fighters. That was his end."

Fida grasped the essential facts. The traditional religious rivalry was set aside as Iranian Shiites worked with Hamas Sunnis against the common Zionist enemy. He could guess the rest.

One dark night, along the Gaza Strip, Ahmed Esmaili had seen the fatal explosion from well behind the mine hunter's position. It was not difficult to interpret the events: an Israeli sentry glimpsed movement through his thermal imager and flipped a switch. The command-detonated mine erupted six meters from the Iranian instructor, sending him directly to the right hand of God.

"You saw Razlavi in your dream?"

Esmaili nodded. "It gave me an idea." He licked his lips. "Obviously we have an important operation coming fairly soon. I think there is a way to create a diversion that will not deprive us of many men."

Fida was interested. "Brother, in God's holy ledger the loss of one man may benefit hundreds of others."

"So you approve of a sacrifice?"

"Certainly, if it yields a profitable return."

Esmaili accepted the assessment. No doubt their scientific sponsor would approve it as well.

"By the way," Fida added, "when do you expect Dr. Momen's colleague to join us?"

"I have not been told exactly, due to security concerns. But Azizi said he should return with the man in a few days."

"If God wills it."

Esmaili continued playing the righteous game. "Surely He does, brother. Surely He does."

SAFED, ISRAEL

Two-star generals seldom brief former lieutenant colonels, but Moshek Brafman wanted his American colleague to enter Lebanon as well prepared as possible. He had arranged for Leopole to meet Yakov Livni, who knew the lay of the land, both geographical and political.

"Tell me about Rafix Kara," Leopole said.

Livni shook his head as if recalling a favorite uncle. He stared at the floor, then raised his gaze to the American. "He is probably all that you have heard and more. Flamboyant, charismatic, and maddening to work with. At one time or another he's fought almost everybody in Lebanon, but when he's on your side there's no better ally. The fact that he is still among the living I can only attribute to divine intervention." He shrugged. "God has use for such people."

The SSI operative nodded slightly. "Yeah. I heard that he has a talent for walking away from ambushes and assassinations."

Livni raised his eyes and his hands in a dramatic gesture toward the ceiling. "Oh, the stories I could tell . . ."

"So you've worked with him?"

The Israeli turned serious. "Yes. Yes, I have worked with him." He decided not to relate that he had also worked against the Druze warlord when Israeli interests diverged from Kara's.

Leopole stretched his muscular arms behind his head. "Well, the main thing I need to know is if I can trust the guy. That's job one."

Livni nodded gravely. "As I said, Colonel, Rafix has been at odds with most of the major factions in the country at one time or another. The one thing I can count on is that he's totally opposed to the Syrians and Iranians. And the other thing I can count on is his courage. Many people may question his loyalty at a given moment, but never his courage."

"Okay, so he's a brave sumbitch who might shove a blade between my ribs. How does that make him worth working with?"

The Israeli operative waved a placating hand. "No, no. Do not misunderstand me. Rafix has a sense of honor to go with his courage. I have never known him to betray anyone. But as conditions change, so does his allegiance." He paused for emphasis. "Colonel Leopole, the key to understanding Rafix Kara is very simple. He is Druze to the core. As long as your mission benefits his people, he will be a loyal ally. But remember this." Livni wagged a pudgy finger. "If he ever has reason to doubt *your* commitment to his cause, he probably *will* shove that blade between your ribs."

11

Rick Barrkman and Robbie Furr seemed an unlikely pair. The former was athletically built and fond of working out; the latter was not. In fact, Furr claimed that he had been eating at his favorite Mexican restaurant since before he was born, and he could pack away a large platter of tacos and enchiladas with little effort. Nevertheless, after working together for years, each knew the other's strengths and vices. They had long since passed the point where they were professionally wedded: frequently they could communicate by something approaching mental telepathy. They even shot the same zero to eight hundred yards.

Now they needed to see how their rifles had fared the rigors of international air travel.

Barrkman uncased the Robar SR90, a customized Remington 700 with orthopedic stock and Leupold ten-power scope. Owing to their different physiques, the cheek piece and length of pull were optimized for Barrkman, though Furr could crawl the stock well enough to compensate. His own rifle was an SR60, a near duplicate of Barrkman's minus the orthopedic furniture.

Furr laid down on his mat, set up the spotting scope, and focused on the hundred-yard target taped to a riddled piece of plywood. He glanced around. "I guess I've seen worse ranges but I don't remember just where."

Prone behind the rifle, Barrkman thumbed three rounds into the Remington's magazine. Keeping his right index finger along the stock, he checked the Leupold's elevation knob and was satisfied with the setting. "Frank says we should be grateful for this place. Nothing else is available."

"Well, okay. Consider me grateful." Seated beside his partner, Furr focused the Kowa scope and said, "Spotter on."

Barrkman snuggled up to the twelve-pound SR90 and adjusted the butt's elevation with his left hand. Then he looked through the scope. "Sniper on. Upper left."

The spotter's attention went to the top row of four black aiming dots. He heard the shooter inhale, then exhale. Three seconds later the 2.5-pound trigger broke cleanly and the shot went. Barrkman cycled the bolt, lifting the knob with the heel of his right hand, rotating the palm, then pushing the bolt back into battery. It appeared one fluid motion. "Center."

"Six o'clock, low," Furr replied.

Barrkman ignored the call and fired again. "Center."

"On top of the other."

At the third shot, the marksman said, "Center."

Furr looked over at him. "Center. The cold bore shots are still a quarter to a half minute low."

"Well, it's consistent." He grinned. "Besides, the guy downrange never knows the difference."

The pair changed positions to verify each shooter's zero. When Furr was finished, his friend shook his head. "Dude! Three rounds, two holes. What happened?"

Furr pointed downrange. "Right to left mirage. I caught it just as I broke the last shot. Didn't you see it?"

"Nah, it must've been a pretty good gust of wind." He wriggled his eyebrows suggestively. "Or . . ."

"No way, man. Dead nuts center call."

Obligatory bantering concluded, the sniper team repeated the zeroing process with the SR60. Six more rounds of Black Hills .308 snapped downrange at 2,650 feet per second. The result was two ragged groups with one called flyer.

Barrkman asked, "How many rounds through your barrel now?"

Furr entered the latest data in his log. "That's 2,489."

"Getting a little high. You gonna rebarrel anytime soon?"

"Not as long as it prints like today," Furr replied. "Unless you want to spring for a new Schneider tube."

"In your dreams, amigo."

"Hey, where's the snout?"

Barrkman turned around and tapped the third gun case. He withdrew a Robar QR-2, actually a Ruger 77 adapted to accept ten-round M14 magazines with a detachable six-power scope and flip-up iron sights. The combination of sniper and scout rifle yielded the unlikely nickname "snout."

Furr accepted the precision carbine, handed to him with the bolt open. Nevertheless, he inserted a pinkie finger to be certain. Then he assumed a sitting position, cradling the Ruger's comfortable weight. He dry-fired three times, running the bolt rapidly each time. "It's beyond me why the military keeps buying honking big rifles that weigh sixteen or eighteen pounds when this does about eighty percent of the work at ten pounds."

Barrkman beamed a knowing smile. "Because that's what the gun club wants, man. That's the trouble with police and the military: they buy what they think they want instead of what the shooters need. Like the M40A3 the Marines got a couple years ago. The damn thing weighs about nineteen pounds: how'd you like to hump *that* piece of iron in Afghanistan where it's uphill in both directions?"

"Yeah, I know. I trained some recon dudes a while back. They said the Quantico benchrest shooters injected themselves into the process. They like heavy rifles because they only carry them from the jeep to the firing line."

"So why'd the sniper school go along with it?"

Furr shrugged. "Go along to get along, I guess."

"Well, let's shoot snout before we draw a crowd. If there's time left over I want to do some position shooting."

"Six-pack of beer on the best offhand group?"

Barrkman responded, "Sure. Are you buying Maccabee or Goldstar?"

"No way. You're buying *me* Heineken. They import it here, you know."

"Now how'n hell did you know that?"

Rob Furr enjoyed the gotcha. "Somebody once said, 'Time spent on Google is seldom wasted.' "

Barrkman tossed his partner a box of Black Hills. "You gonna talk or shoot?"

Inserting a magazine, Furr quipped, "I'm gonna shoot, then I'm gonna drink your beer."

"Well, all I can say is you'd better enjoy it while you can. Where we're going there's probably not much liquor."

"Hey, Lebanon's national beer is Almaza. It's considered an excellent pilsener. Most people drink it with salt."

"Google?"

"Pitney," Furr replied.

"Say what?"

"Robert Pitney, the new guy. His wife's family used to do business in Lebanon so I asked him about the culture and food and stuff."

Barrkman nodded quietly. "He doesn't seem the drinking kind."

"Well, neither do you. But he's not. In fact, he's Muslim."

"Muslim? You gotta be . . ."

"Hey, you gonna talk or shoot?"

NABATIYEH GOVERNATE

Hazim was a dutiful student in most aspects of his Hezbollah training, but none more so than his desire to become a sniper. He heeded Tawfiq's advice about not removing the scope too often, but he lavished considerable care on the action and the optics.

Esmaili nurtured the youngster's ambition, providing encouragement with some practical assistance. Returning from a supply run, the Iranian diverted to the practice range before delivering his goods to the warehouse. As expected, he found Hazim playing with his daytime scope. Esmaili dropped a canister beside the young Lebanese.

Hazim looked up, surprised. "Teacher! I did not see you." He leapt to his feet, almost stepping on the metal can.

"Stealthiness is a virtue for most warriors, but especially snipers." Esmaili almost smiled. "I admire your diligence, boy. Accept this gift."

Hazim forgot himself and bowed reverentially, as if to an imam. Then he knelt to examine the container. It was dark green with yellow stencils in the Jewish alphabet. Opening the tin, he withdrew a rectangular cardboard container. Though ignorant of Hebrew, he was adept at numbers. "7.62 NATO" held significance for him.

"Ammunition for the rifle!"

"Two hundred fifty rounds. Use it sparingly. I do not know when I may have more."

As Hazim all but genuflected, Esmaili returned to his vehicle. Tawfiq was waiting with a knowing smile. "You are spoiling that boy, you know."

The commander returned the grin. "Yes, I know." He glanced over his shoulder, observing the Lebanese fighter declaring God's bounty to his friends. "He will be useful one day. Or night—depending on how long the batteries last."

Esmaili stopped to ponder whether his manipulation of the youngster was much removed from the late ayatollah's exploitation of children in the Iraq war. Without reaching a conclusion, he asked, "How is he progressing?"

Tawfiq almost chuckled. That was significant, as he

was a man who seldom laughed—or had reason to. "Actually he shows some promise. He has read the sniping manual repeatedly and I believe he could recite long passages. I have worked with him on the mil scale, and since it is based on meters there is not much room for confusion."

"How is his marksmanship?"

"Well, not remarkable but he shows ability inside three hundred meters. He can hit a half silhouette about half the time, depending on wind. Beyond that, he might be useful for harassing fire . . ."

Tawfiq cocked his head at his colleague's sudden silence. "Yes?"

"I was just thinking. Do you remember our second trip to Iraq, supporting the resistance fighters?"

"Yes, yes. Two years ago, more or less."

"There were reports of an Iraqi sniper called Juba. He was said to use a Tabuk, the Iraqi version of the Yugoslavian rifle."

"I thought he was a fiction. A ghost to scare the crusaders."

Esmaili shook his head. "I believe he was genuine—for a while. If he was killed or went away, it mattered little. Other successful snipers could continue shooting in his name, and spread the fear." He gave a grim, tight smile. "We may have our own Juba growing right here."

Tawfiq was unaccustomed to guile beyond the tactical variety. The psychological aspect was new to him but he recognized the potential benefit. And the risk. "He may not last long."

"True." He paused for an ephemeral moment of self-examination. Then he asked, "What word is there about the next supply shipment?"

SAFED, ISRAEL

Colonel Yakov Livni was a man with many irons in the same fire. The fire was the impending clash in southern Lebanon, and few but his immediate colleagues knew how badly he had been burned. The loss of his nephew was seldom far behind his brown eyes, and alternately he rebuked himself for previous errors while striving to avoid making others.

Fahed Ayash was part of that plan.

Livni made the introductions, a quick turnaround since he himself had only met Leopole at their original briefing with Brafman. By way of explanation, Livni said, "Mr. Leopole, Major Ayash will be your primary liaison with the Druze militias. He has worked with some of them before, and he has as much experience as anyone I know in that area." Livni nodded to Ayash as if to say, "You're on."

Ayash spoke passable English, telling Leopole, "In Beirut you will meet a man named Rafix Kara. He is very important to our . . . ah, the mission." The Druze officer grinned self-consciously. "His influence alone could be enough to produce success, let alone his contacts and his support."

"Yes, Mr. Baram mentioned him during the planning sessions in Arlington. I trust that Mr. Kara knows we're coming."

Ayash nodded vigorously. "Oh, yes. In fact, we have arranged for you to meet him, as you say, one to one. That is how he prefers to operate, on an individual basis. He believes it is the best way to measure a man, especially someone he does not . . ."

"Trust?"

"Oh, no, Colonel. I was going to say, 'someone he does not know.'" The IDF man smiled, as much in satisfaction at his quick recovery as at the American's justified skepticism.

Leopole stood up and stretched. His lower back was cramped again; he wondered if it were occupational tension or the aging process. *Maybe both,* he told himself. "Major Ayash, I'll level with you. I've now dealt with six or seven people and I still haven't even set foot in Lebanon. Just how are we supposed to maintain security with all the people who've been involved in our meetings?"

The Druze seemed taken aback. He blinked twice, moved his lips, and then found the words. "We are all working together in the IDF: Jews, Druze, Army, special operations. I do not know your, ah, grasp of my people's culture but we Druze are all of the same blood. Family, you know? Nobody would do anything to risk hurt to others."

The SSI operator noted Ayash's heightened color, which could only be embarrassment or anger. It was obvious which was the more likely. Waving a placating hand, Leopole replied, "Oh, no, Major. Please do not think that I question anybody's loyalty. But I've been involved in ops that . . . er, operations . . . that were compromised because of a careless comment made without harmful intent. That's all I meant."

Ayash squinted at Leopole, as if assessing the American's honesty. Evidently satisfied, he concluded, "Mr. Leopole, we are all of the same boat, as you say. If anything goes wrong, I will be sinking with you."

"Fair enough, Major. Fair enough."

12

NABATIYEH GOVERNATE

Mohammad Azizi delivered Dr. Momen's colleague, on schedule.

Imam Sadegh Elham appeared to be in his mid-forties. In contrast to the corpulent Momen, Elham's was a thin, spare frame with few of the scientist's unctuous mannerisms.

However, Esmaili noticed that the cleric's eyes had the same look. While Imam Elham did not wear spectacles, his gaze—penetrating and perceptive—reminded the Hezbollah operative of Momen's. Ahmad Esmaili felt a tiny chill. *Both of them are probably mad.*

"Peace be upon you," Esmaili greeted the cleric. Elham replied in kind, apparently with genuine sentiment. Then he presented papers identifying him as spiritual advisor to the Hezbollah cell. That his bona fides were genuine there could be no doubt. His warrant was handwritten by Dr. Momen and countersigned by his deputy.

After the ritual greetings, Ahmad Esmaili showed the imam to his quarters, allowed him to settle in, and departed. Esmaili realized that he was glad to be out of the man's presence.

Azizi saw Esmaili standing alone and joined him. "Our guest is satisfied with the present situation. You have prepared well, and Dr. Momen should be pleased."

The Hezbollah leader managed a straight face. "Praise be to God that we have performed our mission . . . so far." He regarded Momen's acolyte. "You will be in frequent contact with the doctor?"

"Yes, yes." Azizi nodded eagerly. "My duty requires me to return to Tehran at various intervals. But do not worry, brother. You will be well mentioned in my reports for your work . . . so far."

Esmaili waved a hand. "Oh, please do not trouble yourself. Doing the work is reward enough." This time the sentiment did require some facial control. He wondered if Azizi were gullible enough to believe the statement or merely indifferent, knowing something of what was to come.

If Azizi were skeptical, he concealed it beneath an earnest demeanor. "Soon there will be plenty of work for your men to prove their devotion to the jihad." He actually smiled. "That should please them, should it not?"

"Most assuredly. I only pray that we are up to the task—whatever it may involve." *How long are we going to continue exchanging banalities?*

Azizi recognized that Esmaili was fishing for more details. But that did not bother him. Were it otherwise, he might have had reason for suspicion. "My friend, you know almost as much as I do at present. For now it is enough that Dr. Momen has entrusted an important mission to our hands, and favored us with his most valued advisor. We will learn more details when we need to know them."

"Then my fighters can be satisfied. I should check their progress this afternoon. Please excuse me."

Azizi nodded deferentially. "Of course, brother, of course. I shall see you at the evening prayer. The imam will conduct it himself."

"I shall be honored to pray behind him."

As he walked away, Ahmad Esmaili was careful to keep his head up and his shoulders back. He did not wish Mohammad Azizi to realize how the Hezbollah chieftain really felt: like the loneliest man in Lebanon.

HAIFA, ISRAEL

Chris Nissen convened the planning session with the entire SSI team. "Colonel Leopole is meeting with our main Druze contact in Beirut but he left a list of topics for us to cover." He set down his notes and jumped on one of his favorite subjects.

"What's the best way to take down a roomful of bad guys?"

"A Mark 82 through the roof," Breezy quipped. When his wisecrack drew no laughter, he went on the defensive. "Well, a five-hundred-pounder takes down a bunch of bee-gees."

"It's not a theoretical question," Nissen insisted. "If we're going to work with the Druze in securing their villages, we have to be ready to show them some interior tactics."

Bosco sought to cover his partner's gaffe. "We have the canned routine from the company's training manual. Use flash-bangs if possible, frags if necessary, and put at least a short stack of operators through the door or another entry. Then run the walls and hose anybody with a weapon."

Nissen nodded in agreement. "But what if there's known or possible noncombatants?"

"That's why we start with flash-bangs. Then secure everybody there and let the intel guys sort them out." He shrugged. "It's worked for us before."

Nissen returned to the main subject. "Well, let's realize that our clients will not have the latest gear that some of us brought. We need to stay focused on teaching them to use their own weapons as efficiently as possible."

Josh Wallender broke his usual silence. "Chris, what do we know about the Druze and their gear?"

"Not a lot right now. Mostly AKs. I don't think they have many sidearms. That means when we get to interior tactics we'll show them how to use what they've got. The more specialized weapons, like precision rifles, we'll address as they arise."

Phil Green, the ex-SWAT cop, had a lot of experience putting cuffs on uncooperative suspects. "I don't think we can be too dogmatic about this, Sergeant. I mean, there's too many variables, and good-guy bad-guy recognition is a biggie, especially when everybody looks alike. Besides, what if there's more suspects than operators? There's going to be a lot of noise and confusion, especially with women and kids screaming and crying. We'll have some guys slinging their own weapons while putting flex cuffs on everybody, and that reduces the number of shooters for emergencies." He shook his head. "I'd avoid an inside fight if at all possible."

Privately, Nissen agreed, but Leopole had wanted various scenarios discussed before meeting the militiamen in Lebanon. "Okay, you're right. It's likely to be dark and noisy and confusing. Lots of chances for distraction and surprises. But I'm talking a last-ditch situation. No way to solve the problem without entering the room.

"Just for consideration: a bud of mine did an exchange tour with the SAS. He said at Prince's Gate in 1980 one of the terrorists at the Iranian embassy was hiding among the civilians. They pointed him out so two SAS dudes scooped him up and pinned his arms against the wall. One of the other guys double-tapped him with his MP-5 and that was that. All twenty-six hostages were released and five of six terrorists were KIA. A real slick op."

"Not quite in line with our usual ROE, is it?" Bosco asked with wink.

"No, Mr. Boscombe. It is not."

Bob Ashcroft, who had trained as a police crisis negotiator, had another angle. "The only situation I can think of for entering a room would be a hostage situation. I mean, if the BGs have shot a couple of hostages and tossed the bodies out the door, then all bets are off. Otherwise, I'd maintain a perimeter and wait 'em out."

Nissen realized that the subject was far more varied than the training teams would have time to address with their clients, so he sought to simplify matters. "All right, then. Let's consider this: you have two or three men ready to enter a room full of hostiles. What's their best choice of weapons and tactics?"

Breezy turned serious for a moment. "I really like my suppressed MP-5 with a light. And I'd wear goggles and ear protection."

"Why ear protection if you've got a suppressed weapon?"

The operator unzipped a gotcha grin. "Because, Sergeant Nissen, the bad guys prob'ly don't have suppressed weapons."

"Okay, point well taken." He looked around. "Anybody else?"

Robert Pitney squirmed on his seat. After a moment, he spoke up. "It might sound odd, but I'd take a big-caliber race gun with a laser sight. And a light."

As a former Green Beret NCO, Chris Nissen had little experience with the civilian shooting world. But he was intrigued. "Okay, it does sound odd. But suppose I'm willing to be convinced."

Pitney was aware that everyone in the room was looking at him. He stood up. "I like a pistol for interior tactics for all the obvious reasons. And a double-column .40 or .45 gives me twelve to fifteen rounds, which should be plenty. If not, I carry my first reload at the front of my tactical belt. I can swap magazines in less than two seconds.

"I brought a compensated Springfield XD with me. It's loud, but like Mr. Brezyinski just said, we'll have ear protection. The integral compensator keeps the muzzle steady, and at typical distances you can do 'hammers' with both rounds inside two inches.

"The red dot or laser sight is a big advantage in dim light and against multiple opponents. At room-clearing distances—inside twenty-five feet—you can engage several targets very quickly."

Nissen was impressed. "Okay, that makes sense to me. But you're not going to carry a specialized weapon like that for everyday use."

"No, sir, I'm not. It's a special tool for special circumstances."

"What if the BGs have body armor that your ammo won't handle?"

Pitney shrugged. "Inside a room with a bunch of hostiles, I wouldn't rely on torso shots anyway. I'd shoot for the eyes."

The retired noncom frowned. "That's a *very* high standard of marksmanship, Mr. Pitney. Especially when people are shooting at you."

"Yes it is, Sergeant Nissen. It certainly is."

SSI OFFICES

Marshall Wilmont was overweight to the point of being fat. His goal was to remain shy of obese, and recently he would not have claimed victory in that campaign, for it was more than a battle. Privately, he envied the hell out of Michael Derringer, who in his mid-sixties tipped the scales barely twenty pounds more than his Annapolis weight.

On the other hand, Wilmont retained most of his hair and needed glasses only for newsprint.

Wilmont stopped at the top of the stairs, regaining his breath. At that moment Matt Finch dashed past, taking the steps two at a time. "Hey, Marsh," the personnel officer chirped. "Still avoiding the elevator? Good for you. Keep it up, man!" On that cheerful note, the slender forty-something was gone.

SSI's chief operating officer watched him disappear. *Damn marathoners. They're fanatics.*

At length Wilmont reached the second-floor landing and opened the door. Aside from his physical bulk, he felt as if he carried an equally onerous burden—a load to be shared with Mike Derringer.

Wilmont nodded to Peggy Singer, who broadcast a contralto "Good morning," ending on an upscale that bespoke cheerfulness. It also alerted her boss in the inner office that a visitor was inbound.

Derringer swiveled his high-backed chair, turning away from his computer console. "Good morning, Marsh." He stopped to scrutinize his partner more closely. "You look like yesterday's chow, if I may say so."

Wilmont plopped his bulk into the visitor's chair. "You may, and you did." He emitted a short wheeze and realized that he had left his handkerchief at home again. His marriage remained on the downhill slope, and tending hubby's laundry had never been a priority for Jocelyn Brashears Wilmont. He contented himself with extracting a partial tissue from his coat pocket and dabbed his mouth.

Derringer wondered if Sandy Carmichael or Frank Ferraro in the operations division maintained their emergency responder certification.

Finally Wilmont regained his breath and his voice. "Mike, I saw Brian Cottle last Friday night. He was at the club with some of his Foggy Bottom friends."

"Is he still running scared over State's embarrassment after our African outing?"

Wilmont nodded. "But he's only frightened, not terrified like he was a couple of months ago. I arrived late for happy hour and Brian was working on his third drink. So I eased him over to an empty table and bought him another round."

Derringer approved. "You sly dog, you."

"Actually, I don't know how much slipped out and how

much he actually wanted me to know. But he pretty much laid it out. State and CIA are still red-faced over the way the Israelis snookered them, and sending us chasing all over Africa and the Med and the Atlantic after that yellow cake. So I laid it on a little thick, you know? I said, 'Jeez, Brian, we did exactly what you guys wanted us to do and now we're the bastard cousin at the wedding.'"

"I hope he absorbed a boatload of guilt."

Wilmont shrugged his burly shoulders. "Well, he didn't argue. He just sort of acknowledged that maybe we'd got a raw deal, being denied other contracts because our team did the work that we'd been hired to do." Wilmont paused, trying to recall the conversation. "The fact that the yellow cake sank with that ship our guys took was all to the good. I mean, State understands that the cake never reached Iran. But once they realized that Mossad had been calling the shots through third parties and cutouts, there was some, ah, unwelcome scrutiny on the hill."

Derringer leaned back in his chair, arms behind his head. "Yes, I know. So what's the point of Mr. Cottle's unhappy hour?"

"Well, since I had him alone I pushed the man-to-man thing, you know? I said, 'Look, Brian. We're forced to do business with the damned Israelis, the same people who used us and got a couple of our guys killed. So when the hell are you,' and I emphasized *you*, 'going to let us out of detention?'"

"Good lad. So what'd he say?"

"Well, then he did get defensive. His voice went up a couple of octaves and basically he said, 'Shit, Marsh. I'm the one who approved SSI for the current Israeli job. If it'd gone to somebody else, the foreign contracts desk probably would've turned you down. Then you'd really be stuck.'"

"Is that true?"

Wilmont coughed again. While regaining his composure, he nodded. "Yeah, I think so. I mean, he's the deputy undersecretary for international security so he can direct traffic pretty much where he wants. I think that his boss rubber-stamps most of Brian's recommendations unless it's high visibility."

Derringer laughed. "Like Radar on *MASH*. 'Here, Colonel. Sign this.'"

"Well, maybe not quite like that. But I felt better after pumping Brian. He's a decent guy down deep—just has trouble showing it sometimes."

"So, does that mean that we might be considered for some U.S. Government contracts anytime soon?"

Wilmont squirmed his weight against the seat. "I'll know more on Wednesday. But I think things are easing up because when I left, Brian promised to stand me to a three-martooni lunch."

Derringer chuckled aloud. "Well, he might welch on a business deal, but a promise made when drunk is sacred."

"You got it, Mike."

13

NABATIYEH GOVERNATE

In a rare moment to himself, Ahmad Esmaili sat with his back against a tree and allowed his mind to wander. He could not remember the last time he had indulged in non-professional musings.

As the leader of a notably successful Hezbollah unit, Esmaili had grown accustomed to a degree of latitude in accomplishing his missions. But now, apparently entrusted with a more important operation than ever before, he was tacitly reduced to second in command to a zealous cleric possessing little military experience.

"Commissar" was the word that Esmaili attached to Imam Elham. Essentially a political appointee, the priest nonetheless wielded full authority over the fighters—and their commander. It would not be wise to question his orders, which meant that operational worries would have to be couched in diplomatic terms.

Esmaili was astute enough to know that he lacked diplomacy. He achieved results by force of personality and the threat of draconian enforcement for the few jihadists who resisted him. In recent years he had only been forced to execute two men: proof of the French concept *Pour encourager les autres*.

The Hezbollah chief reflected that almost immediately Imam Sadegh Elham began assuming de facto leadership of the unit. After barely asking permission, the priest convened a meeting and announced his intention of establishing a more devout routine. He began by uttering a smooth assurance of his belief that the Hezbollah fighters represented the fruit of Islam's warriors. Then he said that at dawn tomorrow he would begin the *Fad salat,* the five daily prayers conducted by a group praying behind an imam.

Esmaili had accepted the news in stony silence, trading the briefest of glances with Tawfiq and Fida. Azizi, the liaison between Momen and the men who would execute his mysterious plan, seemed satisfied with the situation. A trifle uncharitably, Esmaili thought, *He can afford to be satisfied. He probably does not have to perform our mission.* Esmaili weighed the situation and cataloged the operative factors. Because Hezbollah was dominated by Iranians such as himself, the movement was largely Shia. Therefore, Imam Elham possessed unquestioned power as a Shiite cleric.

Azizi had said, "Brother, you know that an imam must be obeyed because he speaks for God."

"Yes, of course," Esmaili had replied. "That is why Dr. Momen sent him. Aside from his position in the scientific organization, Imam Elham's religious authority cannot be questioned." Esmaili conceded that the double dose of power was bulletproof. And that knowledge chilled him to the marrow. Esmaili held not the ghost of a doubt that Momen and Elham were perfectly content sending their jihadists to destruction if there seemed some advantage.

"That is the wonder of it," Azizi insisted. "We achieve Paradise merely for the worthiness of the effort, not for the results."

Esmaili had concluded the discussion in the only way possible. Inclining his head, he had intoned, "Allah be praised."

Watching the westering sunlight slanting onto Southern Lebanon's cedared hills, Ahmad Esmaili contemplated his likely future and indulged in a silent heresy.

BEIRUT

Major Fahed Ayash deposited Frank Leopole at Rafix Kara's office building in the fashionable Verdun area of West Beirut. "I was going to introduce you in person," the Druze officer explained, "but I must meet with a, ah, supplier, before he leaves. I return in an hour, no more."

Leopole had no option but to make the best of his circumstances. He looked around, feeling ballistically naked in one of the region's riskiest cities, and longed for his Sig. *Better inside than an obvious Gringo on the street*, he concluded. He went upstairs, admitted by the lone secretary.

The office defined the man.

Leopole took in the ambience, which an interior decorator might call Post-Modern Ballistic. The place was strewn with weapons: rifles, pistols, a few shotguns, and two machine guns. Leopole recognized one as a Soviet

RPD, which he considered the finest LMG ever made. It rested on its bipod with hundred-round drum in place. The other was partly obscured behind some ammo boxes but Leopole thought the stock resembled an even older antique: a Lewis Gun.

Kara's desktop was clean, with two exceptions. One was the .455 Webley revolver of the same vintage as the Lewis. The other was a two-tiered organizer with roasted peanuts in the In basket and figs in the Out basket. A wastebasket and well-used chair completed the administrative suite.

Leopole was drawn to a Steyr SSG in the corner, complete with Kahles ten-power scope and ten-round magazine. He had owned one of the Austrian sniper rifles long ago but sold it when his logbook of rounds fired revealed that he had not shot it in four years. He seldom kept a gun that he did not fire at least semiannually. On the other hand, his partner, retired Master Gunnery Sergeant Daniel Foyte, had more firearms than he knew and simply bought a new safe now and then.

Leaning over, hands behind him in deference to gun culture etiquette, Leopole was interested to note four hash marks painted on the stock. Then the door opened behind him.

"Ah, Colonel Leopole."

The SSI operator turned to see a short, compact man with a Lebanese nose, thinning gray hair, and a brisk, cheerful manner that belied his well-cut business suit. Rafix Kara strode across the carpet, extending an arm. Leopole stood erect and grasped the proffered hand. The men shook briskly, both squeezing hard before releasing as if on mutual consent.

Kara nodded toward the Steyr. "I see you admire fine rifles," he said in French-accented English. "But one should expect that of a United States Marine!"

Every Marine a rifleman, Leopole thought. It was a catchy sentiment, if no longer true.

"Well, sir, I wish I'd kept the one I used to own. It was the most accurate production rifle I ever had. My hand loads would hold under three inches at five hundred yards."

The Druze leader wrinkled his brow. "Then why part with such a fine weapon?"

Leopole shrugged. "I didn't shoot it very often and was short of space in my safe."

Kara's eyes registered surprise. "A safe? Surely one such as yourself needn't hide fine weapons in a safe. That is for bankers and merchants!" He swept a hand around the room. "This is my gun safe, Colonel!" He laughed in appreciation of his own joke.

Leopole looked around again. Two walls and much of the floor did in fact resemble a walk-in gun vault. It occurred to Frank Leopole that Rafix Kara had acquired a veritable alphabet of weapons: AKs, FALs, a couple of AUGs, the RPD and SSG, even a couple of RPG launchers. He returned the Lebanese leader's broad smile. "How do you stay proficient with so many weapons, sir?"

"Oh, I do not. I merely have this . . . collection . . . to ensure a ready supply. I have guns in various calibers, you see? The Soviet round for AKs and RPDs; 7.62 NATO for FALs, sniper rifles, and MAGs; 5.56 for Galils, AUGs, and some M16s though they do not function well." He cocked a mirthful eye at his guest. "As you no doubt already know!"

"Uh, yessir. But what about these?" He pointed to the RPG launchers.

"Oh, those are no problem. Rocket projectiles are easy to get, Colonel. Last I heard, less than two hundred dollars here in Beirut." He unzipped a knowing grin. "Unless you want a volume discount. But the launchers will cost you three hundred each."

Despite his cautionary instincts, Leopole found himself

liking the merchant. "You're what we call a one-stop shopping center, Mr. Kara."

The Druze laughed loudly, more for emphasis than empathy. "One-stop shopping center! That is good, Colonel. Quite good." He shook his head in appreciation. "Some of my associates will enjoy that description." Gaining enthusiasm, he swept his hand around the room again. "This is just my personal stock, as you might say. Now, if you really want to bargain with me, we can discuss body armor, night vision, even light armored vehicles."

"Well, sir, I'll keep that in mind."

Kara returned to his desk and opened the nearby closet. He extracted soft body armor and a Browning Hipower. Donning both, he said, "Let us go out, Colonel. We can talk business while having some lunch."

On the street with his bodyguard, Kara indicated his preference for an open-air stall selling *pastirma*. He stepped to the counter and ordered two servings of the air-dried beef, insisting, "Please permit me. This is my favorite, Colonel."

Gunfire chattered two blocks away, stray rounds slapping the concrete wall above their heads. Leopole dived for cover, reaching for the pistol that was not there.

Kara knelt beside him, dripping aplomb. "Not to worry, Colonel Leopole. This sort of thing happens often in my city." He shrugged philosophically. "Probably a celebration of some sort. Many Lebanese have an unfortunate tendency to fire into the air when happy or excited."

Glancing left and right, the former Marine levered himself off the sidewalk. "Damn! I *knew* I should've ignored the State Department order about personal weapons."

The Druze leader turned to his bodyguard and passed a brief exchange. The burly security man raised his left leg and produced a .22 Beretta from an ankle holster. Kara handed over the backup piece, butt first. "This is Kamal's personal weapon but you may keep it until you remedy your, ah, unfortunate state of undress."

NABATIYEH GOVERNATE

Imam Elham professed to know little of military affairs but a great deal about religious doctrine. As near as Ahmad Esmaili could tell, the cleric did not exaggerate on either point.

However, Esmaili drew the line when theology interfered with operations.

After the dawn prayer, *Salat-ul-Fajr,* the Hezbollah leader reckoned that the rest of the morning belonged to him. But Elham had not dismissed the assembly. Instead, he launched into a philosophical discourse—the closest oration to a sermon that Esmaili had heard in several months.

Today's lesson centered upon the distinction between defensive and offensive jihad.

Elham began, "Defensive jihad is always justified since by its nature it preserves Islam from the aggressions of the unbelievers. Theoretically, offensive jihad is justified by bringing infidels into The Faith, as The Prophet Himself did. However, since the last caliphate in Turkey in 1924, there is no supreme leader of The Faith to sponsor offensive jihad." The discourse continued along those lines for several minutes.

Esmaili was unaccustomed to philosophical debate, being far more familiar with violent confrontation. But his tactician's mind defaulted to the analytical mode that had kept him alive in the region's worst conflicts. "Imam, please excuse me if I fail to understand something. It appears that we believers are placed in a dilemma. If The Faith is to expand to all the corners of the earth, it must be done by offensive jihad. But lacking a caliphate authority, that jihad cannot be implemented. So how is The Faith to achieve its rightful place in the world?"

Elham squirmed on his cushion, looking as if a needle had found its way into his posterior. He peered at the questioner with an ill-concealed mixture of curiosity and resentment. At length he found his tongue.

"We must find the middle path, neither violating The Word nor giving the unbelievers too much latitude. For instance, the Koran prohibits torture, mutilation, and burning prisoners alive. Muslims must not pillage homes or the property of noncombatants. Enemy crops, trees, and livestock are immune except as food for the army of Believers. Neither kill a woman, child, or aged man. But those who would strangle Islam must be scourged and destroyed. That is the way to convert the world to The Faith."

Esmaili nodded as if absorbing the priest's wisdom. *Not by conviction but by coercion,* he thought. Well, if that was the method, so be it. Ahmad Esmaili would play his role, just as he had since the Iraq war. But he fully intended to witness the end of the current mission just as he had the miserable conclusion to that sorry affair in 1988.

Afterward, while Tawfiq oversaw the morning's training, Elham drew Esmaili aside. For once the imam seemed almost relaxed. He even laid a hand on the leader's arm. "We are going to survey certain areas in preparation for the mission. I will have qualified men here within a few days."

"Yes, Imam." Esmaili hoped that he could elicit additional details. "How may we assist you?"

"We shall require security for the surveyors, who will operate in some fairly remote areas in this region. I estimate that only one or two days will be required for each site. There will, however, be several locations."

"Very well. I will assign qualified men as soon as we know how many teams are needed."

"Brother, your commitment is noted. And gratefully received." Elham almost smiled: a ghosting, ephemeral curvature at the ends of the mouth.

When Elham departed—he seemed to glide across the ground, barely raising his sandaled feet beneath his robe—Esmaili went in search of Fida. Since meeting him, the man had proven competent within certain limits, and was reliable thus far. Esmaili decided to feel him out.

"I have just spoken with Imam Elham. He instructs me—us—to provide security for some surveying crews."

Fida perked up. "Surveying? Well, that might explain it."

"Explain what, brother?"

Fida looked around, ensuring privacy. "My cell has received information, or rumors, that the rocket force may use this area."

"Yes, I have heard the same thing." Recalling his speculation with Azizi, Esmaili was pleased with their powers of deduction. He knew that Fida was unlikely to ask about sources.

"Well, then. It seems that possible launch sites are to be examined and surveyed. That would make perfect sense, because . . ."

"Exact firing positions and level ground would be necessary."

Fida nodded. "Just so."

Esmaili's risk assessment mode was activated in the left lobe of his brain. At first he had envisioned a suicide mission of some kind. Now it appeared that the upcoming operation was likely to draw Israeli air strikes. He had survived far worse. Among other things, Saddam's artillery had been purchased on a massive scale. And that did not include the poison gas.

For the first time in days, Ahmad Esmaili felt the onset of something like relaxation.

SAFED, ISRAEL

Colonel Yakov Livni entered Major General Moshek Brafman's office without knocking. He did not even indulge himself the pleasure of having Gabriella announce him.

The special operations commander stood inside the door and pointedly cleared his throat. Brafman looked up, saw what he saw, and politely dismissed his chief of staff. The colonel got the hint and closed the door as he left.

"What is it, Yakov?"

Livni plodded the few steps to the desk and sat down. "Real-time intelligence. It looks as if Hezbollah knows about the SSI mission."

Brafman took off his reading glasses and plopped them onto the desktop. "Tell me." When he got no immediate reply, the brigade commander leaned forward. "Signals intelligence, obviously. So tell me, Yakov!"

Livni leaned back, folding his hands over his bulging stomach. "I can neither confirm nor deny. But you grasp the essentials, as usual."

"Actually, I am patiently waiting for Colonel Livni to tell me—General Brafman—what they know. Details, Yakov! I have people at risk up there."

"As do we all." Livni rubbed his stubbly face and licked his lips. He wanted to ask for some wine but knew the general to be sadly deficient in appreciating such things.

"All right, General. Our sources"—he arched his eyebrows—"are more than halfway convinced. They have Hezbollah reports that Druze militia units in southeastern Lebanon are going on increased alert, and seem to know or at least suspect that third-party nationals will be involved. I don't know how else to interpret that information."

Brafman stood up and began to pace. "How many times

have we been down this road? I keep telling the army staff that sometimes we need unfiltered information, the raw data. At some point we have to be able to form our own opinions about intelligence from above." He looked at his colleague, as if inviting agreement. Receiving none, he asked, "Is Sol Nadel cut into the loop? I would think that the brigade commander supporting the operation should be told."

Livni spread his hands, as if to say they were tied. When Brafman glared at him, the spec-ops officer finally relented. "There may be a leak in Kara's organization. That's speculation. But right now it's as good an explanation as anything."

Brafman did some mental mastication. "Well then, are you going to tell Kara?"

Another set of arched eyebrows.

Brafman felt a shiver between his shoulder blades. "Are you trying to say that it might be Kara?" He was on his feet again. "I don't believe it!"

"Actually, neither do I. Apart from the fact that I've worked with him for years, he's far too dedicated to his cause. His people. In that regard, he's a lot like us."

Brafman spun on a booted heel. "The hell he is! He's as likely to fight us as help us." The general snorted. "You of all people should know that!"

"General, sit down. Take off some of the strain." Livni forced himself into an even more relaxed posture. "Look, I'm not taking anything for granted. After all, Major Ayash is in Beirut with the American Leopole right now. I'm certainly not going to put them in danger by withholding information. I'm just advising you of the situation." He pushed himself out of the chair. "I'll keep you advised. General."

Brafman smiled at last. "Good day, Colonel. And kiss Rachel for me."

A broad male-bonding wink. "I'd rather kiss Gabriella— for me!"

14

BEIRUT

It was a measure of Rafix Kara's charm that he could manipulate strong men who knew they were being manipulated. The day after their initial meeting he began the charm blitz by presenting Frank Leopole with two ultimately pragmatic gifts. "Accept these," the merchant began, "and wear them in good health."

Leopole opened the box, finding a Second Chance Kevlar vest and a Sig Sauer P229 with three loaded magazines plus a belt holster.

The American mercenary looked up, wide-eyed. "Mr. Kara, I certainly didn't expect any gifts. I mean, it's up to me to provide my own . . ."

Kara waved both hands vigorously. "No, no, my friend. Since that unfortunate demonstration by my people yesterday, it is up to *me* to provide for my guest." He smiled broadly, obviously pleased with his coup. "Besides, I confess a certain selfishness. How can we conclude our business if you need either of these items—let alone both of them—and do not have them?"

In his Marine Corps career, Leopole had served mostly with mission oriented professionals who tolerated the inescapable Charlie Sierra factor common to all militaries. Kara broached no trivialities, lest any of them divert him from the welfare of his cause. And his cause was far more than a corps: it was a people.

The Druze warlord—no other single word described him—would not have made a model Marine. He was stu-

diously flamboyant, though the Corps certainly had its
share of such types, including the mercurial Smedley
Butler with two Medals of Honor and the iconic Chesty
Puller with five Navy Crosses. But in their brief time together, Leopole recognized Kara as a natural leader, the
sort of commander who worked simultaneously behind
the lines and at the front of his organization. Beneath the
charming, almost boisterous exterior, the American dis-
cerned the steel core that Colonel Livni had described.

Considering Kara's charmed life and checkered affilia-
tions, it occurred to Leopole that the Druze matched the
Corps' self-proclaimed title: No better friend, no worse
enemy.

As Leopole tried on the vest, he wondered what he
would do with it. "I don't know if they'll let me on the
plane with these things, so maybe I should leave them with
you."

"Oh, I have plenty of both. After all, this is Lebanon."
He shrugged philosophically. "Why don't you keep them
until you leave? That way I can return Kamal's Beretta."

Leopole returned the grin. "Yes, sir. I appreciate the
loan." He laid the backup gun on the desk, slide locked
back and magazine removed.

Kara sat down and opened the folder marked "IDF-
SSI." He produced narrow-lensed reading glasses and
scanned his notes. Satisfied, he removed the spectacles
and regarded Leopole again. "You are doing well here,
Colonel. I appreciate it when a plan proceeds as drafted,
mainly because I know how rare that is. But after today
we should have a firm grip on things. Major Ayash seems
satisfied with our progress. He should be back shortly."

Leopole sat down opposite Kara. "Well, he and Colonel
Livni obviously have a lot of experience working together."

Kara laughed aloud, leaning back with his hands clasped
behind his head. "Yakov! What else did he tell you about

me?" Before Leopole could respond, Kara rebounded, hands on the desk. "Do not bother answering. It's only a rhetorical question, you know?" The smile was back—a semipermanent feature on the Druze's face. "Yakov and I have worked together for years, and we have fought as well. He probably did tell you that."

"Well, he . . ."

"Of course. That's the way of the world here. Shifting alliances, new priorities. Changing loyalties is one of the permanent factors in the Middle East. But Yakov and I . . . well, we serve different causes but whenever those causes overlap, we work together. Neither of us has ever betrayed the other." He jabbed the desktop with an emphatic finger.

"Yes, sir. That's what he told me."

"Now you and I, Frank. I will call you Frank from now on. You and I, Frank, we start fresh." He thumbed his chest. "I am Rafix now for you. No baggage, you might say. We take each other to face value, and because we both are honorable men, we work hand in hand." He grinned self-consciously. "Or better, hand in glove?"

"Affirmative, sir. Hand in glove." Leopole did not care to pursue a masculine hand-in-hand image.

"Now," Kara continued. "Our village and regional militias you already know about. You and Major Ayash will work with them in the way we all agreed. The Israeli government pays your employer, who pays you I trust." He did not wait for a perfunctory response. "But things are active down there, Frank, and they will get more active. I admit I do not know just what Hezbollah has in mind, but it wants more control of more land. Yakov and I are in contact about that but his masters will not want to admit that, you know?"

Leopole nodded. "Oh, yes. That's why the IDF Druze members are assigned to us: for liaison and for deniability."

"Yes, yes. Just so." Kara laughed aloud. "Deniability! It is big part of what you do, yes? You are there but you are not there even when everybody knows you are there. You are—what is your word?—indivisible?"

"Ah, that's 'invisible,' Rafix."

The warlord thoroughly masticated the etymological distinction. "In-visible. Ah, I see. Not visible!" He chortled again. "Hey, Frank, I see invisible! Makes me like Superman, yes?"

Leopole wondered about Kara's sudden giddiness. Maybe the arms merchant had imbibed something between breakfast and lunch. "Well, sir, ah, Rafix, that would mean you have X-ray vision."

"Then what is 'indivisible'?"

"It means undivided. That is, unable to divide. Remaining whole." Leopole decided not to recite the Pledge of Allegiance. Heaven only knew what an ebullient Rafix Kara would make of *that*.

Kara turned serious again. As if reading the American's mind, he declared, "Like your country, Frank." He shook his head side to side. "Not like mine. Poor-poor Lebanon. She is never united."

Leopole sought a chance to end the moribund discussion, or at least change its direction. "Well, Rafix, maybe when our mission is over, that part of your country will be more unified than before."

NABATIYEH GOVERNATE

For a man of action and violence, Ahmad Esmaili unexpectedly found himself gaining admiration for the philosophical, scholarly cleric who had taken control of the Hezbollah cell. Never mind that the imam's devout routine was unwavering: prayers every morning, noon, afternoon, evening, and night. The full ritual usually was observed, and Esmaili noted that even some of the most zealous fighters went along with the routine more for appearances than from conviction.

But Imam Elham—or, equally likely, Dr. Momen—had demonstrated exceptional foresight and attention to detail. Esmaili admitted to himself that the planning stages for the forthcoming operation were handled with military competence. For it was, ultimately, a military mission.

Following the afternoon *Salat-ul-Asr,* Elham beckoned to the Hezbollah leader. Esmaili resented the gesture, conducted more as an order than an invitation, but frequently he learned something new in such sessions.

Elham said, "Come, let us walk." It was, Esmaili realized, often a time for confiding an operational detail that had been withheld. Elham seemed to mete out such items as if they were cash to be spent sparingly. So it was today.

"In order to assure security for our mission, it will be necessary to secure some additional areas. The holy warriors under Dr. Momen's guidance will require some area for movement. You understand?"

"Certainly, Imam. But how much area? We have to know for planning purposes."

The cleric turned briefly away, profiling his hatchet face. At length he said, "Certain locations around Hasbaya."

"Hasbaya? That is a Druze area. I have operated there. Several villages are well defended with organized militias."

Elham's face remained expressionless, almost serene. "We know the strength of the Druze. In fact, I will confide to you that our operatives are watching those areas now, and conducting surveillance of their headquarters in Beirut and elsewhere."

Esmaili was astute enough to appreciate what such surveillance involved. "You mean Rafix Kara? The merchant who supplies so much money to the Druze and the warlord who keeps them armed?"

"We are well informed on all such men, my brother. But you need not concern yourself with those measures. Focus instead on the task at hand." He turned to begin walking, knowing that his colleague would follow. "You will have some assistance. We have been preparing for this mission for many months now, and reinforcements will be available."

Esmaili absorbed that information and the implications. "May I ask how many men? And their state of training or experience?" He did not enjoy having to cadge operational information from the imam, but had learned that if he did not ask, frequently he was not told until later.

"The details are still being finalized in Tehran and Damascus. We will have the information in ample time, though."

Damascus! So it is a larger operation than I thought.

As if reading Esmaili's thoughts, Elham continued. "I can tell you, my brother, that the technical material for our mission must come through Syria. That information is for your ears only."

"Certainly, Imam."

"I mention that detail because it may be necessary for you to dispatch some guards to conduct the shipment here. We cannot always rely upon our Syrian brothers for the public support that we might wish." He curled a lip, sneering at the niceties of diplomacy. "But they have often been most helpful in the past, and as long as our people are involved in the shipments, I am told that there should be little trouble."

Esmaili was enough of a strategist to grasp the essentials. "The goal, then, is deniability of direct Syrian support."

Elham almost smiled. "More precisely, the goal is *political* deniability. Our government, the Syrians, and the United Nations will conduct a masquerade. In such cases, each side knows that the others are being disingenuous but it is to the advantage of all to proceed with the charade. If no one objects, the result is the same as if nothing happened at all." A genuine smile unfolded itself. "Such people much prefer to avoid unpleasant facts than to deal with them."

"Then I suppose we should be grateful that there are such creatures."

"God is great, brother. God is great."

BEIRUT

Leopole had inherited Kamal Azzam, Kara's chief bodyguard, who was charged with getting the American and Major Ayash to the airport for their return to Israel. Before they joined Ayash, Leopole wanted another perspective on Rafix Kara. He had no option other than Kamal.

"Kamal, I am worried about Mr. Kara. Is he all right?"

Azzam was nothing if not loyal. "Yes, of course he is all right. What do you mean, Mr. Leopole?"

"Well, when I left him he was much more, uh, animated than before." Leopole recognized that Azzam's English had its limits. "I mean, he seemed free-spirited, almost playful."

The security man nodded in comprehension. "Oh, yes yes. That is medicine. Mr. Kara takes pills for pain." He touched his head with both hands. "Has been okay mostly but sometimes old wounds hurt him still."

The SSI operative filed that intelligence for reference. He wondered if Yakov Livni knew that the IDF's senior Druze contact might be subject to morphine highs now and then.

Leopole heard the ballistic crack; a high-pitched *snap* instantly followed by a supersonic object striking concrete. Several more followed.

Frank Leopole was too experienced a gunfighter to remain upright on a city street, looking for the source of the shooting. He dived behind a fruit cart outside a stylish shop, drawing his loaner Sig as he did so.

He peeked from behind the cart, trying to sort out the situation. More gunfire. People racing in every direction, some screaming, a few sobbing. Two or three had assumed awkward positions on the sidewalk. Typical confusion. He remembered to breathe, sucking in oxygen to fuel his system.

The cart provided decent concealment but precious little cover. A rifle round could easily penetrate it, and probably most pistol ammo from across the street. Call it twenty-five meters.

Then Leopole remembered: there had been no time to check the Sig's sights. He had no idea where it shot. Worse than that, he did not even know if it functioned. While it was extremely unlikely that Rafix Kara would own an inoperable weapon, one just didn't know until one tried.

Leopole saw a hanging sign across the street, advertising women's clothes. The Arabic script offered no decent aimpoint but the O in "Boutique" was a decent substitute for a zeroing bull's-eye. He raised the P229, gripping with both hands, and stroked the trigger. The 9mm round impacted the sign, moving it visibly, but at that distance it was impossible to tell where.

He felt fifty percent better.

Kamal.

Leopole looked behind him, seeking Kara's bodyguard. No sign of him. That was bad news indeed; the Druze was obviously a serious young man. Leopole was skilled at sizing up men, and Kamal had impressed him as dedicated to the point of obsession.

Where is *he?*

Twenty meters to his left front, Leopole glimpsed two men, one with an AK and the other with an FAL. They were walking briskly, diagonally across the street in his direction. He noted that they covered one another, the FAL man reloading while his partner scanned left and right. *They've done this before.*

The American looked again for his escort. The two shooters probably were hostile, but in West Beirut you never knew. They might be responding to an unseen threat. Leopole leaned back on his haunches and saw two forms on the sidewalk. One was a woman who was still moving; the other was Kamal Azzam, who was not.

That settled it. When the shooters got fifteen meters away, Leopole centered his borrowed Sig's sights on the right-hand man with the AK. The American's mind was rational; almost calm. His heart was not. He thought: *Squeeze between the beats.* Not enough time. He pressed the double-action trigger once, twice, three times.

Then he breathed and shifted targets.

The AK gunner had flinched visibly and turned partly away. In that interval Leopole had a new sight picture and was taking up the slack when more gunfire sounded to his left. *Somebody's shooting at the FAL guy.* The remaining hostile spun on a heel, fired two rounds semiauto, and collapsed. More shots followed him to the ground.

Leopole shifted his scan to the right again and saw the AK shooter backpedaling to the far curb, firing short, ill-directed bursts. *He must have a vest.* It was longish distance for a head shot, but Leopole tried. He fired once, saw no hit, and realized that he still did not know where to hold. People were running in the background. *Rule Four: be sure of your target and backstop.* He reached for the magazine pouch on his left side and managed a tactical reload. Then he thought: *Kamal.*

Staying low, Leopole dashed to the Druze. From ten meters away he realized the young man was dead. *Live people don't look like that.* Kamal had worn soft body armor that offered no protection against rifle ammunition.

A Lebanese in a uniform knelt beside the wounded woman, an AK-74 lying beside her. Leopole wondered if the gendarme—or whatever he was—had shot the second offender. Belatedly, the SSI man remembered to holster his pistol. It was not the time or place for a stranger to be seen packing.

A high-pitched European-style siren warbled up the block. Its two-tone, high-low bleat announced that Red Crescent had been summoned. With professional detachment, Leopole admired the response time. He knew of American emergency responders who refused to enter a crime area until the street was blue with police.

Abruptly, he remembered a National Guardsman who had responded to the Watts riots in '65. Leopole was not old enough to remember those days, when "African-Americans" were "Negroes." But he knew that black radicals had torched buildings, then shot at the fire trucks, killing a fireman and two cops. The firemen had withdrawn, quipping, "Burn, baby, burn."

Fahed Ayash was by his side. "Colonel, are you hurt?"

Leopole stirred himself from his reverie. He looked at the liaison officer. "Yeah, I'm okay. But . . ." He gestured at the body.

"Yes, I know." The Israeli Druze grasped the American by the arm and led him toward a cab. "We must get away from here."

Leopole resumed his scan of the threat sector. He was focused again. "What about Rafix? He's got to be told about Kamal."

A faint smile, condescending in execution if not intent.

"Colonel Leopole, he will know very soon, if not already. But we *must* go."

"What's the hurry, Fahed?"

Ayash shoved his charge into a Citroën taxi. "Colonel, they were after *us*."

15

SAFED, ISRAEL

Yakov Livni already had a report from Fahad Ayash but the IDF colonel wanted a personal account from the American operator. Livni got straight to the point. "Tell me about it."

Frank Leopole was brief. "I finished my meeting with Kara and was going to meet Ayash at a taxi stand with Kara's bodyguard." For reasons he did not fully understand, Leopole was reluctant to speak Kamal Azzam's name. "I heard gunshots, took cover, and returned fire at two shooters in the street. When I looked around, the bodyguard was dead with some other people." He shrugged it off. "Ayash showed up and got me to the airport. So here I am."

Before the Israeli could respond, Leopole interjected, "How'd they know about me, Colonel?"

Livni removed his glasses and rubbed his forehead. "I think that Major Ayash addressed that point."

Leopole leaned forward. "Yes, he *addressed* it. Hell, it's all we talked about on the plane. He had some theories but nothing solid. I think he knows more than he's telling me, Colonel Livni, and that makes me nervous. We have a saying, 'Nervous as a long-tailed cat in a rocking chair factory.' That's how nervous I am. Not just for me, but for my people. You understand?"

Despite the edge in Leopole's voice, Livni grinned in appreciation at the colorful humor. "Yes, Frank, of course I do. And you're right. Major Ayash does know a little more than he told you, but that's not his fault. He's under orders to reveal only what is operationally necessary. Do not blame him." He thumped his chest. "If you must, blame me."

"It's not about blame, Colonel. It's about trust."

Livni leaned back, more relaxed than before. "I can tell you that we recognized some Hezbollah operatives in Kara's area. It wasn't hard to add up two and two. They were undoubtedly watching his office, maybe even trailing him to see where he went, who he met. We knew that at the time but we judged the threat minimal." He grinned. "After all, you were armed."

"Well, I didn't even have time to test the pistol. I think I hit one of those guys but if the Lebanese soldiers hadn't shown up—"

Livni interrupted. "Tell me. Did he ply you with women, wine, or both?"

Leopole was startled. "None, Colonel. It was a straight-up business meeting. We confirmed the operating areas and the militias we'll be training."

Livni shook his head. "Well, if Rafix Kara didn't ply you with something, it's the first time I ever heard of. One of our previous consultants was two days late returning because he was so badly hungover in a bawdy house. When he could speak coherently, he said he only remembered the first night, and it was absolutely the best of his life."

The American gave an ironic smile. "Maybe I should've played hard to get."

"He never tried to bribe you or coerce you at all?"

"He just gave me the pistol and a Kevlar vest."

Livni's face split wide open in a beaming smile. "I

knew it! You see, I know how that pirate works. He's shrewd, Frank. He recognized that he didn't have to bribe you to get his way because you are one of those straight arrows. So, to cement the bonds, he gave you something you valued more than mere wine or women." The Israeli leaned close. "But I've seen some of his feminine stable, and a few of them would give Gabrielle a good run." He winked conspiratorially.

"That good, huh?"

The Israeli slowly shook his head. "Oooh, the women I've seen . . ." Abruptly he caught himself. "But to return to business. You are justifiably concerned about what Hezbollah knows or suspects about your upcoming operation. We do not know if they have identified you but we can assume they know you're American. Since you're not part of the diplomatic circle, they will deduce that you have a military connection. That's cause for concern, but it does not link you with your SSI team."

Leopole mulled over that thought. Finding no flaw in it, he agreed. "All right. Unless they have a lot more info than seems likely, there's not much chance they've connected me with the militia training plan." A thought belatedly pushed its way forward. "But maybe they do know about the plan."

Livni bit his lip. The American wondered if it were a giveaway or an unconscious habit. "We don't have any evidence that they are aware of the operation, Frank. But even if we did, there's not much we could do other than increase monitoring of, ah, some sensitive sources."

"Okay then. I'll brief my guys to proceed as planned, but maintain a heightened awareness."

"Yes, that's fine. Now, Major Ayash said you mentioned that Kara was in unusually high spirits when you left him. He's not usually erratic. You suspect he's medicated?"

"That's what . . . the bodyguard . . . said. Kara has occa-

sional pain from some wounds or injuries. I figured you'd
know about that."

Livni nodded. "Yes, he's probably been shot and blown
up more than anyone I know. And believe me, that's saying something. It stands to reason that he would require
pain medicine, but I've never seen it." He paused for a moment. "Do you think the morphine, or whatever it is, might
affect his judgment?"

"Damned if I know, Colonel. I hardly met the man."

"Well, if it's any comfort, he's acting normally since
you left."

"Oh? How's that?"

Livni decided to explain. "We learned that Kara dis-
covered a possible security breach in his organization. He
waited too long to correct it."

"So what happened?"

"He corrected it."

NABATIYEH GOVERNATE

Mohammad Azizi was back, and this time he brought
something besides encouragement and platitudes. He invited the imam and Esmaili to a private conference well
away from the other Hezbollah fighters.

"I have been in contact with our operatives in Beirut
and Damascus," Azizi began. Esmaili concluded that
since he did not allude to the all-powerful Dr. Momen, the
statement indicated either rare honesty or secrecy to protect sources. In either case, Esmaili acknowledged that he
could only accept the courier's assessments at face value.

"We have been watching several offices in Beirut, both
governmental and private ventures. The one that raised the
most interest was the doings of Rafix Kara, a patron of the
Druze cause throughout Lebanon. He has been meeting

with foreigners including a westerner who almost certainly is American, and a man believed to be an Israeli Druze officer."

Imam Elham absorbed that information. "Are the two working together?"

Azizi nodded. "It appears so. They were on the street outside one of Kara's buildings when two of our men saw an opportunity. Unfortunately, the westerner defended himself and some Lebanese police intervened. We learned that one of Kara's guard dogs was killed, as were some others. But that is of no concern."

"What of our men?" Elham's question surprised Esmaili. He did not expect the cleric to worry about lesser mortals.

"One was killed, the other wounded but escaped."

"Then that man is the source of your information?"

"Yes, Imam."

Elham was satisfied with the response. *I should have known,* Esmaili told himself.

"I have heard of this man Kara," Elham continued. "He would be a river to his people. Perhaps he seeks additional help from the Zionists and their bought dogs."

"Yes, perhaps. We had a man inside his office for a short time. He was well paid but produced little useful information. He has not reported lately."

Esmaili sought to maintain his standing in the group. "If Kara is supporting Druze causes, is it not logical to assume that he will be interested in whatever happens around Hasbaya?"

Azizi rubbed his close-cropped beard. "Yes, it is. But so far there has been no indication. Our agents report most of what happens in the Druze settlements in this area."

Elham stood, indicating that the meeting was over. "It does not matter. Events will take the course that God selects. We only serve Him and follow His path."

Azizi also rose. "His will, Imam."

"His will," intoned Ahmad Esmaili.

HAIFA, ISRAEL

"When we left Arlington, I told you that I would keep you informed at every step," Frank Leopole began. "Well, this will be your final briefing before we go to Lebanon." Leopole was the type of commanding officer who walked the walk. When it came to looking out for the troops, almost everyone in the room had served under men who merely talked the talk.

"Major Ayash and I met with Mr. Kara in Beirut and confirmed that our clients will be prepared for us. The Druze are eager to receive updated training, and I am confident that we'll find the militias receptive students. But as always, there are cultural concerns, and we're going to rely heavily upon our IDF liaison officers."

Leopole walked to an easel supporting a large-scale map of Lebanon with border areas of Israel and Syria. "We will fly into Beirut with our Israeli colleagues and spend a couple of days getting oriented. Then we'll proceed to the area around Hasbaya, about forty miles south-southeast. That's where the Israelis and the militias are concerned about growing Hezbollah activity. As you will recall from Mr. Baram's briefings, the Izzies . . . er, Israelis . . . took some heavy casualties operating against Hezbollah. So keep that in mind, gentlemen. If IDF spec-ops teams are having a tough time, we can expect the same."

In the second row, Leopole saw Breezy lean over to Bosco and mutter something behind a cupped hand. The hoarse whisper was faintly audible. "Ah, Mr. Brezyinski, would you care to give us the benefit of your wisdom?"

Breezy straightened up, looking much like a seventh-grader caught passing notes in class. "Oh, no sir. I mean, no thank you."

Leopole caught the titters in the audience. He was less miffed about whatever the ex-paratrooper may have said than interrupting the briefing. He placed his hands behind his back and paced forward, looking over the heads of those in the front row. "Oh, come now, Mr. Brezyinski. You're far too reticent. I'm sure that you would not interrupt the important facts I'm trying so poorly to communicate to everyone unless it were worthy of universal distribution." He gave a Clint Eastwood stare, complete with narrowed eyes and tic of facial muscles.

Bosco leaned back, hands comfortably clasped on his lap, trying hard not to smile.

Seeking succor and finding none, Breezy plunged ahead. "Well, if you put it like that, Colonel . . ." He almost said, *Sure thing, dude*. "I was just commenting to my esteemed Ranger colleague here that since the Israeli specops guys got hammered, we're going in because we're expendable."

Frank Leopole blinked once. Then twice. He thought: *That's* exactly *why we're going*.

Then he said, "Mr. B, you surprise me. *Of course* we're expendable. And we're very well paid for it. But since you're a bright, upstanding young man who already knew that when he signed up for this job, you merely state the obvious."

Breezy slumped in his chair. "Uh, yessir. I sort of thought the point could stand to be made again. Sir."

"And what does your esteemed Ranger colleague make of his own expendability?" Leopole switched his reptilian gaze to Jason Boscombe.

Bosco rose to the challenge. "Hoo-ah on the 'very well paid,' sir!"

Now the group's laughter was open and genuine. Even Frank Leopole, former lieutenant colonel of Marines, joined in. "Very well. As long as we have *that* settled, we shall return to the briefing."

The operations officer returned to the map. "As you can see, our op area lies about ten to fifteen miles north of the

Israeli border. We will receive covert logistic support from the IDF brigade in that region, but it's unrealistic to think we can get away with it indefinitely. There's just too much Hezbollah activity and supporters in the region. That means we'll stash a goodly supply of food and ammo on the initial runs in case air and ground transport is denied us. We could probably get by for a while on our own, but I do not want to impose upon our clients. Reportedly some outlying villages have had problems in the past."

Chris Nissen, who would lead one of the training teams, had a question. "Colonel, I understand the benefit of taking our own gear with us, especially radios. But if we get an Alamo situation in one of these villes, will there be enough Russian guns and ammo for us?"

"Good question, Sergeant. And the answer is yes. Mr. Kara is, ah, very well connected and well supplied. In fact, we may detail a couple of men to stay in Beirut and coordinate with him. That's one of the things Major Ayash and I discussed with him. So rest easy. If we use up our own stash, there will be AKs and LMGs and probably RPGs aplenty. Even mortars."

"Any chance of fighter or gunship support?"

"That's possible, more likely helos than fast movers. I'll know more before we leave."

Josh Wallender raised a hand. "Colonel, I'd like to know more about the covert nature of this mission. It seems that since we're doing weapons and tactics training, there's going to be a lot of shooting. That's gonna get the Hezzies' attention for sure."

Leopole nodded. "Undoubtedly it will. But remember, we're going to Lebanon. Things are different there. People shoot AKs in the air just to let off steam or to celebrate birthdays or weddings. So we'll blend in more than if we were operating elsewhere.

"Which reminds me. I know most of you brought your

favorite cammies or BDUs or whatever. When we get to Beirut, Mr. Kara will provide us with several sets of local clothes, which can be anything from blue jeans to burkas." He shot Breezy a quick grin. "And Brezyinski, I'd love to see you in a burka that's a lovely shade of blue.

"But a lot of shooters in Lebanon wear paramilitary clothes, sometimes a mixture of camo patterns. We'll try to blend in as much as possible, depending on what the locals are wearing." He looked around. "Anything else?"

Silence met the question so Leopole said, "Get your gear ready, gentlemen. We'll gear up in twenty-four hours."

PART

III

LEBANON

16

APPROACHING BEIRUT

"Hey, lookit!"

In his aisle seat, Bosco craned his head to look past Brezyinski. "What?"

Next to the window, Breezy pointed aft. "We're popping flares, man!" He turned back to his partner, eyes wide. Both men knew what flares meant.

A row behind them, Robert Pitney leaned forward. "Hey, what's going on?"

"We're in SAM country, dude." Bosco raised from his seat just enough to glimpse the last decoy burn itself to oblivion in thousands of degrees Fahrenheit. Then he sat down again and buckled his lap belt.

The Israeli pilot of the charter DC-8 made a belated announcement. "Ah, this is the captain. I apologize for not warning you gentlemen of our countermeasures. Please be assured that we drop chaff or flares only as a precautionary measure. The decoys are not, I repeat not, being used against a specific threat. We will be on the ground shortly."

Immediately the aged jetliner dropped its nose, inducing negative G. Breezy felt his butt try to leave his seat. "Whoa! Gnarly, dude!"

Bosco lanced his friend with a narrow-eyed stare.

"We're poppin' flares, making a kamikaze approach to Beirut International, and all you can say is 'gnarly'?"

Pitney managed a grin in Breezy's defense. "Well, it beats puking."

The McDonnell Douglas jetliner made a high sink-rate landing on Runway 03 that jarred items in the overhead luggage compartments. But nobody complained.

Chris Nissen was seated with Frank Leopole. "Hey, baby. I don't know much but I know that chaff and flare kits cost a bunch of shekels. The charter business must be makin' a ton of money."

Leopole shook his head. "I doubt it, Chris. This outfit does a lot of back-channel work and must go to some, ah, interesting places. More likely the Israeli government foots the bill."

Across the aisle, Phil Green expressed his opinion. "Colonel, I don't believe that for a hot minute. More likely the U.S. taxpayer foots the bill."

"Well, that same gentleman is footing *our* bill, so I'm not going to lodge a complaint, Mr. Green."

Green sat back. "Hoo-ah on footing the bill, sir."

From Beirut Rafic Hariri International Airport it was an eight-kilometer drive to the city center, paralleling the coast. Riding in two buses provided by Rafix Kara, the SSI operators noted the Lebanese ambience through windows screened to prevent grenades from being tossed inside.

"Kinda interferes with the view," Bosco observed. "Pretty country, though."

Robert Pitney had seen the sights before. "This is one of the best views of the Med that you'll get anywhere. Even with all the damage." He smiled self-consciously. "Great bikini watching, too."

Breezy turned around. "Now what would a married Muslim guy know about bikinis?"

Pitney flashed a self-conscious grin. "Hey, man, I'm married, not dead. Besides, some of these ladies are trolling for rich Americans. You guys could go back married men yourselves."

Bosco made a face. "Not me, dude. I ain't the marrying kind. But, uh, are there, like, any clothing optional beaches here?"

"Hey, how would I know? I'm the married Muslim guy."

Breezy perked up. "Hey, I saw a magazine in Haifa. It had a feature on these new bikinis, man. They're, like, minikinis so the gals are practically falling out of 'em."

"So this is Beirut." Phil Green's comment broke the salacious conversation in the rear of the bus. He looked around, absorbing the urban combat ambience of the battered, beautiful city.

"You know, a few years ago I trained with a guy who'd been a State Department rep here in the eighties. He said that some of the locals who worked in the embassy brought weapons and a change of clothes to work. During lunch they'd change into cammies or sweats, take their AK or FN and a satchel full of loaded mags and go shoot for an hour. Then they'd come back and return to work. Unless they got whacked, of course."

Bob Ashcroft eyed his partner, obviously unconvinced. "Well, you got to admire somebody who takes his work that seriously."

The buses arrived at a compound already prepared for the SSI men. Waiting to greet them was Rafix Kara himself.

Leopole stepped off the first bus and shook hands with the host. "Hello, sir. It's good of you to meet us in person."

In contrast to their previous meeting, Kara was serious, almost somber. "It is the least I can do, Colonel. Things have changed since we parted last week."

Leopole noted the formality, which he ascribed to Kara's wish to appear professional before the American team. Certainly he showed no sign of the giddy hospitality from the day Kamal was killed. *"I call you Frank from now on . . . I am Rafix now for you."*

Growing more expansive, Kara addressed the SSI men. "Gentlemen! Welcome to Beirut." He waved a hand at the walled enclosure. "This area is as secure as anyplace in the city. You will get to know the area while you are here. The U.S. embassy, American University, and American Hospital all are here in the northwest of the city. So you are among friends, yes?" He chuckled in an effort to provide a relaxed atmosphere.

Chris Nissen leaned over to Josh Wallender. "With the arty damage we saw and the small-arms holes in some of these buildings, it don't look like such a friendly neighborhood to me, bro."

Wallender cast a professional eye along the rooftops, looped with razor wire and patrolled by sentries. "Hoo-ah on the 'hood, my man."

Leopole assumed command of the situation. "We'll be quartered in two of the buildings to disperse our assets. Follow Mr. Kara's people, get settled in, and we'll meet in the dining hall in an hour."

Bosco and Breezy picked up their duffels and gun cases. Bosco asked, "Did you get what Frank said? 'Disperse our assets.'"

Breezy slung an MP-5 case over his shoulder. "Sure, man. Just good soldiering, you know? Put your eggs in different baskets so they don't all get smashed at once."

"Yeah, I know, Breeze. I'm one of the good eggs so I can figure that out by myself."

SSI OFFICES

Sandra Carmichael poked her blond head inside Derringer's door. "Admiral, did you copy Frank's e-mail?"

"No, I've been working on budget requests the past hour or so. What's the word?"

"They're in Beirut, arrived this afternoon local time. It's just a preliminary report but Rafix Kara has everybody installed at a compound in the city. Frank says it looks secure."

Derringer took in that information, anticipating the next move. "Very well. I suppose his IDF liaison people are with him?"

"I don't know, sir. But it stands to reason. That major went with him to confer with Kara last week. There are others who'll work with our team once they get to the militias around Hasbaya."

SSI's founder laid his reading glasses on the desk and leaned back in his overstuffed chair. "Come in, Sandy. Sit a spell." Then he added, "And close the door."

Sandy sensed that her boss wanted to talk about something more than the current operation. In her years with SSI she had learned of Michael Derringer's focus on his people more than a particular mission.

"You're worried about Frank and the guys?"

"Oh, well . . . yeah." He swiveled his chair ninety degrees. "You know me, Sandy. When there's an operation under way, sometimes I have trouble staying focused on other things, even though that's my job. After all, Marsh is supposed to keep an eye on our day-to-day business."

Sandy placed her manicured hands on the desk. "Sir, are you thinking about the shootout Frank was involved in last week?"

Derringer stared at a framed lithograph on the far wall. It showed USS *Constitution* engaged with HMS *Guerriere* in 1812. *Now* that *was a shootout. Twenty-four-pounders almost hull to hull.*

He turned to his operations officer. "Excuse me?"

She cocked her head, almost the same way she did when

she wanted to look extra cute. This time it was genuine curiosity. "Frank, Admiral. In Beirut last week."

Derringer forced his consciousness forward two centuries. "Oh, yeah. Excuse me, Sandy. But yes. I *was* thinking of Frank."

"What about him?"

"Well, it's just the nature of our business, you know? I mean, we live a pretty normal life here in the office. But once in a while, people we know—our colleagues—go in harm's way and sometimes they get harmed. For some reason, it just struck me that I'd never really envisioned Frank or most of our people actually doing what they do. Getting in gunfights, killing people to avoid being killed or maimed." He looked at her. "You know what I mean?"

Lieutenant Colonel Carmichael squirmed slightly. She sensed the potential for an interservice rivalry, but she was well paid to speak her mind on professional matters. "Well, Admiral, yes I do. I mean, that's pretty much what we do in the Army. I understand that the Navy has other roles and missions . . ."

Derringer flinched visibly. "Ouch. Or should I say *touché.*" He managed a grin. "But your point is well taken. I spent thirty years on active duty and never got shot at. Not once. For that matter, no submariners have been shot at in over sixty years and not many blackshoes. The only real combatants were aviators and SEALs."

Carmichael accepted victory gracefully. Besides, she harbored genuine affection for her boss. *He's such a dear man,* she told her daughters. But the Army-Navy thing was never far beneath her peaches and cream complexion.

"Well, I suppose that's just the luck of the draw, Admiral. I mean, the Air Force doesn't have much of a direct role in the war on terrorism, either. At least not the big-ticket items like air superiority fighters and stealth bombers and such."

He waved a hand. "Ah, you're just being magnani-mous, Sandy. But you don't have to coddle an old sea dog. We sailors grow pretty thick skins, you know, facing hurricane winds and staring into sun-bleached skies."

The SSI operations officer thought for a moment. "Ad-miral, it seems to me that we're doing a decent business because we *do* go to bad places. You must've seen that coming years ago when you started the firm."

Derringer swiveled slightly in his chair, obviously more receptive to the turn in the conversation. "It wasn't very hard to predict, Sandy. The way Bush Forty-one and Clinton and Congress rushed to downsize, the opportu-nity was there for anybody who could look downstream a few years. The military was bound to be caught short, and civilian contractors were well positioned to pick up the slack." He fought down a self-congratulatory grin. "Now DoD can't do without us."

She nodded. "So we're back to Square One. Our friends go to interesting places and get shot at."

Derringer squinted at the attractive Alabaman. He re-called that she had killed two of three Muslim assassins sent to destroy SSI's headquarters last year. "You'd go with them if you could, wouldn't you?"

"In a New York minute, Admiral."

"But what about your girls?"

"Well, Kippy's starting college, and Patty could stay with Nyle and Carol."

Derringer shook his head. "Nyle and Carol?"

"Oh, my brother's family. Actually, I've discussed it with them and it would be okay for a while." She smiled. "Besides, they'd love the chance to spoil her."

"Sandy, listen up." Derringer leaned forward on the desk, hands clasped before him. "There are some con-tracts I'd allow you to work in the field, but this job in Lebanon is not one of them. You receiving me, Colonel?"

She bit her lip. "Five by five, Admiral. Five by five."

NABATIYEH GOVERNATE

Mohammad Azizi found Esmaili working with the budding snipers. The man from Tehran crooked a finger at Esmaili, who left the shooters to continue under Essam Tawfiq.

Azizi led Esmaili off to a safe distance before speaking. "How are they progressing?"

"Three of the six are satisfactory, especially the boy, Hazim. But he is more motivated than the others."

"What of the other three?"

Esmaili shrugged. "One might progress, given more time. As for the others, I see more enthusiasm than dedication." He looked over his shoulder at the group. "I believe they volunteered for the prestige."

"Then we may consider them to be expendable?"

Ahmad Esmaili's professional antennae sensed the political atmosphere and sent a warning message to his personal receptors. *Be careful.* "Brother, we are all expendable in the jihad, are we not?"

Azizi regarded his colleague carefully, as if uncertain of the cell leader's intent. Finally he replied, "Surely, we all do Allah's will." He almost smiled. "But some can serve God sooner than others, if you understand my meaning."

Esmaili thought: *Larijani and Yazdi just volunteered to die.* "I understand, brother. When do you require them?"

"They must be in Beirut tomorrow night. There is a situation developing that will benefit us in the near future if certain measures can be taken soon."

"I do not understand the urgency. After all, there are much more experienced men in Beirut than any of these . . . boys."

Azizi glanced at the nascent snipers, then turned back to their leader. "The need is twofold, Esmaili. First is security. The target is already aware of the threat it faces, but that is localized. We can get your . . . boys . . . into the area without going through the usual channels. Secondly, the target area is well defended and capably manned. It is unlikely that the snipers will survive, but if they achieve even part of their mission, that is acceptable."

Esmaili wanted to ask *Acceptable to whom?* But he dared not. Instead, he nodded. "I see. That way, we preserve the more promising fighters for the future."

"Exactly so."

With no alternative, Esmaili yielded to the situation. "I will have them ready for you this evening."

Azizi raised a hand. "Oh, forgive me, brother, if I did not make myself plain. You see, I shall show the way, but they are going with you."

17

NABATIYEH GOVERNATE

The briefing was largely a lie but it had to be.

Azizi closed the door of the building that had served as headquarters for Esmaili's unit, and had been usurped by Imam Elham. The cleric was absent at the moment, but Azizi had dropped some hints that the forthcoming operation carried not only his knowledge, but consent.

Esmaili's sniper students sat on benches, appearing eager or pensive depending upon their state of training and motivation. All they knew was that a mission was pending, and that two would be accorded the honor of conducting it.

"Our unit has been selected for an operation in Beirut,"

Esmaili began. "Brother Azizi informs me that two men will be needed, and time is short. I think it best if you hear the details directly from him."

As he stepped aside, Esmaili glanced at Hazim. The boy seemed confident of himself, and not without reason. He was generally the best shooter in the class, always eager to earn approval. The others were interested in sniping; Hazim was devoted to it.

Azizi went straight to the point.

"There is an American mercenary team at a Druze compound in Northwest Beirut. Our operatives have been watching them since they arrived. We believe that the Zionist lackeys are about to move into this area to train the local militias, and we intend to prevent that from occurring." He paused for effect. "After consulting with brother Esmaili, I have selected two of you to undertake the dangerous task of destroying some of the Great Satan's minions."

Hazim squirmed in anticipation. He appeared positively radiant. *He is about to be disappointed,* Esmaili thought, *but he should be delighted.*

Azizi intoned, "Ebrahim Larijani and Moshen Yazdi, stand up."

The anointed pair immediately rose. Esmaili thought that Larijani appeared more enthused than Yazdi, but both presented an air of willing complicity.

"You will execute the plan that has been drafted. I will take you to your operating area, where Brother Esmaili will supervise the details."

Esmaili looked directly at Hazim. The boy's face was a mask. His superior realized that it reflected stunned disbelief. Esmaili thought: *He cannot believe that they have been chosen over him.*

Azizi was speaking again. "I am informing all of you about this plan for two reasons. First, so that you will realize the seriousness of your training. And secondly, so that those not selected for *this* mission can help the designated fighters prepare in the limited time." He nodded and the two shooters sat down.

"You have much to do. I want you to confirm the scope settings on your rifles, select the best quality ammunition, and pack whatever else you may need. If all goes well, you may be back here in three days.

"Meanwhile, Imam Elham will provide a benediction before you leave to take your place in the jihad." He glanced at Esmaili. "Be ready to leave by sunset, after *Salat-ul-Asr*."

Esmaili ignored Hazim's doelike eyes and followed Azizi from the building. While the others were congratulating Larijani and Yazdi on their great good fortune, the cell leader caught up with his superior.

"Azizi, I need a word with you."

The liaison man slowed and, reluctantly, turned. "We can talk on the drive north."

"Not without the others hearing us. Before I take those boys to this mission, I would know more of the intelligence behind it. Mainly, how is it known that the targets are Americans?"

With an obvious exertion of patience, Azizi replied, "There is no doubt, brother. It comes from direct observation. They are employed by a paramilitary contractor that works for the highest bidder. And in anticipation of your other questions, we believe their ultimate destination is a Druze area because their benefactor in Beirut is a well-known Druze operative. He seldom deals with other communities."

Esmaili absorbed that information and drew the logical conclusion. "And since we are operating in a Druze area, the Americans are likely to work against us here."

After a slow three-count, Azizi replied, "We are engaged in preventive measures, brother. Consider your mission in that light."

KARA COMPOUND, BEIRUT

Rafix Kara wanted to throw a welcome banquet for the SSI team, and while the Americans appreciated the sentiment, most were skeptical of Druze cuisine. Informed of the impending dinner, Frank Leopole laid down the law.

"We are dining in tomorrow night. You will not only eat what Mr. Kara feeds us, but you will *enjoy* it! These people have gone out of their way to welcome us, and by Chesty Puller's ghost, we are going to show our appreciation."

Breezy looked wide-eyed. "Chesty's ghost? You mean he's dead?" He searched the room with a say-it-ain't-so urgency. "My *God,* why didn't somebody tell me?" He turned to Bosco, laid his hands on his partner's shoulder, and cradled his head. Breezy's shoulders quivered in a fair impersonation of bone-deep grief, accompanied by soap-opera sobs. Bosco bought into the sudden drama fest by patting the former paratrooper's back in a there-there motion.

Leopole had to turn away to hide his smile. He decided to ignore the histrionics and proceeded with the briefing. Turning to face the audience again, he continued. "You got a briefing on Druze culture in Arlington but it didn't include food. However, I think we can expect lamb or chicken plus a vegetable dish, then some entertainment. If you can't choke that down, well, there's need for a couple of sentries on the roof tomorrow night. Somebody to back up one of our snipers."

Breezy raised his head from Bosco's shoulder. "Will Chesty's ghost be up there? I'd feel better if he was walking point."

Mark Brezyinski did not realize that he had just hung a high, slow one over the center of Frank Leopole's plate. The former Marine swung and connected.

"Well, I don't know, Mr. Brezyinski, but since you

demonstrate such concern, I could excuse you from the night's sampling of Lebanese cuisine."

Bosco was cautiously interested. "Colonel, if we stand guard duty, what would we eat?"

"Oh, I can get you some burgers and fries from a McDonald's in the neighborhood. Maybe some half-liter Cokes."

The trap was well and truly baited.

Breezy perked up. "Gosh, Colonel, that'd be great."

"All right, then. You go on duty at 1800. I'll send somebody for your burgers around 1930 and you'll be relieved at 2200. Of course, that means you'll miss the floor show."

"Floor show? You mean there's entertainment?"

Leopole fished a paper from his pocket and feigned difficulty reading it. Holding the note at arm's length, he said, "Jasmine and Bahiya. Apparently they're sisters."

Bosco asked, "What are they? Like, singers?"

The tight little smile was back on Leopole's face. "Actually, they're like belly dancers."

The room erupted in hoots and howls. Bosco and Breezy received hearty thanks for volunteering to miss the Druze cuisine and the evening's onerous conclusion.

18

BEIRUT

"There is the target area," Azizi said. "I leave it to you as to how you proceed."

Esmaili studied the compound, first from the north, then from the other sides. Keeping a block away with his binoculars, he drew sketches and set his men making notes about the guards' routine. As he expected, there was none. Unpredictability was a sure sign of professionalism.

The Iranian cast a look at the afternoon sky. The operation would be conducted after dark, affording his shooters a compromise between visibility and concealment. But the distances were fairly short—barely two hundred meters—and even Ebrahim Larijani and Moshen Yazdi should be able to get hits under those conditions. Esmaili wished for another night scope but the Dragunovs available to him had limited optics.

Esmaili was not overly concerned. The SVD rifle's standard four-power scope featured a battery-powered reticle and an infrared filter. He had ensured that everyone in his sniper class had some experience with night firing, at least under full moon conditions. Tonight was a waning moon but the city's ambient lighting would make up much of the difference.

As for the two shooters, Esmaili knew that they were not ready for combat, but perhaps they were ready for a couple of assassinations. He double-checked the figures on his crude range card and returned to the briefing point with Azizi.

"The tactical situation is favorable," Esmaili began. His two students were attentively wary. All they knew so far was that they would have a glorious opportunity to strike the Great Satan. "We will fire from the north and the east sides of the target building, coordinating by radio. Each of you will have two of brother Azizi's guards as your security element." He looked directly at each youngster, pinning their gaze with a practiced mixture of sympathy and intensity.

"We will synchronize our watches before deploying, because it is important to have precise timing. The main attack will fall within seconds of your shots, so any guards on the roof or the walls need to be eliminated before they can provide warnings."

Larijani spoke up. "What should we do after the main attack?"

Esmaili caught a sideways glance from Azizi. *He does not expect either of these boys to be alive at that time.* "Withdraw with your security element to this position and await orders."

"Where will you be, Teacher?" Yazdi was the more nervous of the pair, and that was saying something.

"I shall be on another rooftop, communicating by radio. Do not worry, brothers. I am never far from you."

KARA COMPOUND

Dinner was fair; the entertainment was memorable.

Leopole sat at the head table with Kara, his wife, and two sons. The boys were sixteen and nineteen, subdued for the offspring of a domestic warlord but astutely attentive. Leopole inferred that their education had been as practical as it was varied. They spoke excellent English—better than their father—and apparently were equally proficient at French.

As Leopole had predicted, the main courses were chicken and lamb. But Kara was insistent that everyone try a vegetarian dish. "This is *sulbeta*," he began. "It is a mixture of buckwheat with peas, zucchini, onions, and tomatoes, then it's spiced with salt, paprika, cinnamon, and pepper." He leaned affectionately toward his wife. "Nobody makes better *sulbeta* than Asala."

Mrs. Kara smiled appreciatively but said little. She sipped her wine, spoke occasionally to the boys, and otherwise held her own counsel.

Toward the end of dinner, Kara raised his glass. Leopole knew that Druze traditionally shunned alcohol, but apparently the Karas made exceptions for special events. Kara had drunk one glass of Chateau Kefraya throughout the meal, commenting that most wine comes from Baalbek in the Bekaa Valley. That esoterica was lost on the American, whose taste ran more toward single-malt scotch. He did not know that Druze families owned some of the vineyards, which tended to be located on tactically advantageous terrain.

"My friends," Kara intoned. The conversation dropped off as attention shifted to the head table. "My friends, though we have already met, I take this time to bid you welcome. Not only to my country, but to the cause of my people. In a few days you will be working with many of the militia leaders you have met here tonight. I wish all of us success, good health, and if it comes to pass, good hunting!"

The SSI men returned the sentiment with a hearty response, and the Karas made their farewells for the evening. Leopole suspected that Asala knew little of the planned entertainment, as her husband dutifully escorted her to the exit well before the dancers appeared.

Apart from two bodyguards, both sons carried weapons without concern for them being seen. Salim, the older boy, had a Romanian AK-47 while Walid favored an MP-5. *Whatever floats your boat,* Leopole thought.

After a short interval, one of Kara's men pressed the play button on a Sony Walkman. The music featured strings, percussion, and cymbals, bringing two barefoot dancers onto the floor. The audience erupted in a chorus of masculine shouts and enthusiastic applause. Even Robert Pitney sat up straight to get a better view.

Up on the roof, Bosco and Breezy heard the noise and recognized it for what it was. "How good could it be?" Bosco asked.

"Sounds pretty damn good," his friend replied. They

continued pacing in opposite directions, stepping around Rob Furr and his NVG-equipped rifle.

"How's it goin', dude?" Breezy envied Furr the cushy job of lying on a padded shooting mat, looking at a green-tinted world through his Litton scope.

"About going to sleep up here." He gave an exaggerated yawn, wondering how Rick Barrkman was enjoying the floor show. Then he nodded toward the Druze guards. "I wonder how they like walking their shoes off all night long, waiting for something to happen."

Brezyinski stifled a yawn himself. He wanted to sit down for a while but knew better. "Something always happens when you're not ready for it."

BEIRUT

Azizi appeared out of the urban darkness. "The operation is proceeding. You may tell your snipers to open fire in two and one-half minutes."

Esmaili had been tracking the sentries atop the target complex. Most were rovers, in keeping with the doctrine of unpredictability. But he had spotted two permanent stations through his second-generation-plus Russian device. They would be the most dangerous to his shooters, but because they lacked a good view down the chosen approach, they were low-priority targets.

Sacrifices must be made.

Since Azizi said that the main attack would come from the east, Esmaili had deployed his men to cover that approach as well as ninety degrees off axis to establish a cross fire. It was only necessary for Larijani and Yazdi to gain fire superiority long enough for the main blow to land, or merely to distract attention away from the street level.

Esmaili keyed his radio. "Two minutes. Acknowledge."

"North ready."

"East ready." Their voices sounded firm.

The Iranian leader watched his digital display tick down the remaining seconds.

"Activity at the main gate!" Larijani was excited about an unexpected development. "A limousine is leaving . . . no, two vehicles. Turning south."

Esmaili turned to Azizi. "This is the target? Not the building?"

The courier from Tehran shrugged eloquently. "Forgive me, brother. Secrecy was essential. But your men should proceed as planned."

Biting down his anger, Esmaili spoke into his handset again. "North and East, the plan remains. Repeat, the plan remains." He glanced at his watch. "Begin . . . now!"

KARA COMPOUND

One of the Druze sentries glanced down and recognized Kara's armored limousine. The Mercedes-Benz S600 had almost every option except self-contained oxygen against gas attacks. The trailing BMW was well equipped—it could run on flat tires a considerable distance—but boasted few amenities beyond minimal armor and a goodly supply of 7.62mm ammunition.

A gunshot split the night air, taking the Druze off his feet.

Across the intersection to the east, another round snapped out. It hit the brick facade of the building just below the concrete lip, forcing Bosco to take cover. Thirty meters away, Breezy turned toward his partner. Noting that Bosco was unharmed, Breezy reached his right hand to his left shoulder and pressed the transmit button on his tactical set. "Rounds fired, rounds fired! North and east corners."

"Look! Down the street!" Another Druze pointed down the boulevard, noting a speeding Citroën. The gray hatchback was followed by a black Peugeot sedan.

Bosco stuck his head up, took in the situation, and made another call. "Hostiles inbound, Colonel! Two cars. Looks like they're after the limo."

Frank Leopole heard the calls and forced his attention away from Jasmine and Bahiya's molded forms and lithe movements, visualizing the developing situation outside. He stood up, shouting over the music. "Gooks in the wire, people! Saddle up!"

ROB FURR HAD SPOTTED the second muzzle flash. He put his crosshairs on the spot, confident that it was inside the two-hundred-yard zero on his scope, and remembered to breathe. Prone behind the bipoded SR-60, he made a minute elevation adjustment by flexing his toes on the surface of the roof. As he sweetened up the sight picture, another shot flared in his night scope. He heard the round whip overhead, apparently aimed at one of Kara's men who ducked amid an exclamatory tirade in Arabic.

He began his squeeze. *Hold it, right . . . there.*

The .308 round left the custom barrel as the rifle recoiled straight back. Furr called the shot to himself. *Center.* He ran the bolt and recovered, finding his crosshairs steady.

Breathe.

He saw no sign of the shooter but another form was visible, leaning over something on the roof. Furr adjusted the sight picture, placed the crosshairs on the green humanoid form, and pressed the trigger.

Damn! A little left. He cycled the bolt again and saw a third form apparently dragging something out of sight.

Breathe.

Furr sucked in more of the night air, then shifted his scan left and right. Nothing else appeared in his scope.

He realized that his pulse was elevated, but his breathing was under control. So were his emotions.

BREEZY LOOKED DOWN FROM his perch, aware that Kara's men were hosing full-auto rounds to the north and east. The noise would have been deafening under other conditions, but audio exclusion had kicked in. The lead Citroën was within fifty meters of Kara's Mercedes. The Druze driver was attempting a two-point reverse but there was little room owing to other vehicles parked on the street. The bodyguards in the BMW had bailed out, racing to provide close support until the limo could evade.

A bright flash erupted to Breezy's left, scaring him out of his wits. He turned to see a sentry lowering an RPG launcher, immediately beginning to reload. The projectile seared downward into the concrete canyon, impacting near the Citroën's right rear bumper. *Not a bad shot,* Breezy thought, but there would be no time for a second.

Seconds from impact, the Citroën was taken under automatic fire by three guards on the street. One of them was Walid, the youngest son, gamely but ineffectually firing his 9mm submachine gun.

Glass erupted from the gray hatchback, but it barely swerved in response to the gunfire. Breezy watched in frozen fascination as the suicide vehicle smashed almost head-on into the Mercedes.

Seconds ticked off, each with a beginning, middle, and end.

One person tumbled from the limo, then another.

Then the Citroën exploded.

MOST OF THE SENTRIES expected the Peugeot to double up on Kara's limousine or to collide with the BMW. It did neither. Abreast of the grilled entry, it veered abruptly right and crashed through the wrought-iron gate. From there it accelerated across the courtyard, drawing sporadic fire from the roof.

The French machine slewed to a stop at the entrance to the main building and disgorged four men. Each carried an AK and one or two satchels. They sprinted inside, fanning out left and right.

FRANK LEOPOLE, PHIL GREEN, and Jack Jacobs were the first armed responders to arrive at the lobby. They saw Jeff Malten rolling on the floor, clasping his side as dark liquid seeped through his fingers. Jacobs glimpsed two men dashing down the halls on either side, saw the satchels, and knew what was coming. He dived on Malten, expecting an explosion.

In the lighted hallway Leopole had a clear shot at the man on the left. The former Marine raised his M-1A, placed the front sight between the shoulder blades, and pressed the trigger. Once, twice. Twenty meters away, the assailant stumbled, caught himself, staggered drunkenly, and collapsed against the wall.

Something rolled from the corpse's right hand.

Leopole shouted "Grenade!" and hit the deck, covering his head with his hands.

The explosion was smaller than Leopole expected but the concussion left his ears ringing. He rolled over, looking for Green.

Leopole sat up, bringing his rifle to low ready. *Fight your way to your feet.* He saw more SSI men emerging from the dining area. Wallender appeared and Leopole asked, "Where's Green? He was just here."

The former Green Beret hefted his folding-stock AK and pointed to the corridor on the right. "Down here, Colonel." He ran in that direction.

Before Leopole could get up, he heard semi and full-auto fire from the hall. The noise was painful, ringing off the walls and ceiling.

Moments later Green reappeared, exchanging magazines and smiling broadly. "There's more, Colonel. Let's find 'em!"

BEIRUT

Ahmad Esmaili turned to Mohammad Azizi. "That is all? A car bomb and four men to attack the compound?"

"If we killed Kara it is well worth the cost. The attack on the building is a bonus, especially if some Americans are killed. In any case, it will disrupt the Druze operations for a while. That is our larger goal for the greater cause."

A chill descended upon Esmaili. He could only infer that the greater cause had something to do with the planned missile sites, and precious little to do with his own survival. He stored that thought in the ready-ammunition locker of his mental arsenal and backed out of the observation position.

"Where are you going?" Azizi asked.

"To collect my men or to retrieve their bodies."

KARA COMPOUND

The situation was well beyond confusion; it bordered on chaos.

While the Druze fighters were drawn to the street where their leader's limousine had exploded, the SSI team and a few of Kara's men searched the main building. Sporadic gunfire erupted in both wings, which Leopole took as evidence of twitchy trigger fingers. "Recon by fire," he surmised to Wallender. The search expanded for the other two intruders.

In the dining hall, two Druze and Bob Ashcroft had remained with the dancing sisters. The doors had no lock, so Ashcroft and a Druze had pushed a long table across the entrance to prevent the doors from opening inward.

Moments later an explosion rocked the facility, knocking down one door and leaving the other askew. Almost immediately two gunmen leapt the ruined table, hosing searching bursts from their Kalashnikovs.

Ashcroft had been nearest the door when it imploded. Knocked from a kneeling position onto his back, he was temporarily stunned. Meanwhile, at dining-hall distance, two Druze and two Sunnis began shooting at each other.

The invaders had the advantage of shock from the explosion, shooting down one of Kara's men before he could get a decent sight picture. One of the attackers then saw the prostrate American and swung on him.

In the far corner, Bahiya took a round through her left arm and spun away, shrieking in pain. In response, Jasmine leapt to her feet, panic-stricken.

The first assailant was seriously devout. Where others saw a fetching costume of gossamer and jewels, he saw whorish attire and responded religiously. He shouldered his rifle, pressed the trigger, and held it down.

Fueled by a massive adrenaline dump, Bob Ashcroft scooped up his Galil, thumbing the selector to full auto. Despite a poor cheek weld, he started at the assailant's belt and rode the recoil almost to the chin. The man went down in a scarlet spray.

Abruptly it was quiet.

Ashcroft looked around and gawked at what he saw. The other Sunni and the remaining Druze held AKs with the bolts locked back. *They're both empty!* The former cop thought that he had rounds remaining in his magazine and directed them where they were urgently needed. A nine-round burst put four 7.62s into the target's right side. The Hezbollah fighter collapsed and began a clotted wailing.

Ashcroft raised unsteadily to his feet and watched

wide-eyed as the Druze reversed his rifle, raised it over his head, and used the butt to cave in the Sunni's cranium.

Bahiya's contralto voice split the silence. In a high, penetrating keening, she wept over her sister's body. The American approached her, placed a hand on her shoulder, then knelt beside her. She stopped wailing in preference to deep, throaty sobs. As the dancer leaned into him, Ashcroft touched Jasmine's bare feet. "She saved my life and she didn't even know it."

19

KARA COMPOUND

"Tell me." Leopole spoke to Major Ayash in a flat tone devoid of warmth.

The IDF Druze inhaled, held his breath, then blew it out. "Kara is alive. He's suffering from concussion and some burns but he should survive." Ayash shook his head in amazement. "That man has more lives than a litter of kittens."

"The others?"

"Well, he pulled his wife out just before the explosion but she absorbed some of the blast. Her body probably saved his life. Nobody else got out of the vehicle."

Leopole absorbed that information, nodding slowly. Finally he looked up. "Then his sons . . ."

"Salim was in the Mercedes. But Walid rode with the escort, as his father always insisted. He is unharmed."

"Okay. I'm going to debrief my people and I need your help. Malten is our best medic but he took a round and can't travel for a while. I'm detailing Jacobs to stay with him and provide liaison. Now we have to know, Major: can we stay here or do we need to move someplace else?"

Ayash raised a hand. "You may stay here, Colonel Leopole. Believe me, the Syrian Army would have trouble getting near this compound today." He tossed his head. "There are measures in place that are not apparent, and some of them are—exceptional."

"You're saying there's IDF forces nearby?"

The Druze liaison man did not try to hide his smile. "I am saying the measures are, ah, exceptional."

"Okay, I'll accept that at face value. But we still need to know: how did the Hezzies get on to this arrangement? There was some sort of security breach."

Ayash touched Leopole's arm and directed him away from the gathering crowd in the compound's conference room. "Frank, you will understand how sensitive this subject is. But . . ." His voice trailed off and his gaze went to the far wall.

"But, you deserve to know. I spoke with Rafix on the way to the hospital. He was nearly delirious with shock and grief. But in putting together a few things he said, here is what I suspect:

"He was taking two prescriptions for pain, including morphine."

"Yeah, I know."

"Well, he was sobbing all the while but he indicated that the medicine clouded his judgment and he thinks he might have told the caterers more than they needed to know. If so, it would explain the timing of the attack—immediately after dinner, as he was leaving."

The American almost reeled on his heels. "Oh, my God." Leopole's right hand went to his forehead. "He must be . . ."

Ayash gave a decisive thrust of his chin. "Yes. He is."

"So what's the current situation? We can't have people walking around who know about the setup in here."

Ayash's face went rigid, as if carved in granite. "As of this evening, I do not believe that any of them will be walking about, Colonel."

Leopole appreciated the sentiment but held doubts. "I can't believe that anybody who passed the word would stick around very long."

"It does not matter. We ask certain people certain questions, and make it clear that it is in their interest to co-operate with us. After that, it's mainly a detective story."

"Ending in a dark alley someplace," Leopole prompted.

Ayash pointedly looked at his watch. "It's time for the debrief, isn't it?"

MOUNT LEBANON GOVERNATE

Ebrahim Larijani was shaken but able to function. He had not seen Moshen Yazdi's body, and Esmaili was glad of that fact. The 168-grain hollow point had taken the boy just above the left eye. *At least he felt nothing.* Presumably in that microsecond Yazdi ascended to heaven to bask in the presence of God.

During the fifty-minute ride back to the Hasbaya area, Esmaili had time to reflect on the operation and his men's performance. Both of the budding snipers had executed their orders, though it was uncertain how many Druze or Zionists they had shot. There had been little opportunity to discuss details with Azizi's security men, and Esmaili was uncertain of their competence or reliability.

At least they had taken Yazdi's body, sparing Esmaili's cell the doleful duty of preparing it for burial. Far better to commit the earthly remains to the care of brother jihadists.

Remains. That's all he was.

Esmaili had seen uglier corpses in his career, but not

recently. Still, he marveled at the American's precision in what must have been a two-hundred-meter snapshot in the dark. *He put that bullet beside Yazdi's scope, almost through the left eye.* Esmaili cast a furtive glance at Larijani. *These boys have no idea what they are facing.*

SSI OFFICES

"Admiral, it's Colonel Leopole. Line two."

Derringer jabbed the button on his phone. He had received the e-mail from Beirut half an hour before.

"Frank! You all right?"

"Yes, sir. Malten's serious but I think he'll be okay. A couple of other guys got flash-burns and fragments." The former Marine's voice was low-pitched, controlled. The satellite phone connection was excellent.

"What about Kara and his people?" Derringer knew there had been losses.

"Mr. Kara's under guard in a hospital. He should be alright but as you can imagine he's shook about his wife and son. Two others were killed in his limo and there were two KIAs in the compound. A couple of the wounded are serious." He decided there was no point in mentioning Jasmine, nor Ashcroft's efforts to comfort her bereaved sister.

Derringer tried to visualize the situation and realized that he could not. "Frank, listen. It's pretty obvious that there was a security breach. What do you know about that?"

"Most of our intel is speculation, sir. But our IDF liaison says that Kara's medication probably overrode his judgment and he might have told the caterers more than they needed to know." His voice trailed off, then resumed. "It's almost midnight here. We're doubling the watch and waiting for more information in the morning."

Derringer found himself leaning closer to the speaker phone, almost as if he wanted to whisper in Leopole's ear.

"Listen. If things are that bad, we can't count on maintaining operational security in the villages. You guys will be even more exposed out there."

Leopole realized that Mike Derringer was opening the door to canceling the mission. "Yes, I know, Admiral. I discussed that with the guys during our debrief. There's some concern, of course, but they're willing to stay so far." He paused, recalling the tension in the room, the anger over the security breach, though so far none of the SSI operators knew of Kara's lapse.

"But, Admiral, the guys' collective dander is up. There's a lot of sentiment for payback, especially once we get to the Hezbollah op areas. I know: that's not a good mind-set, and I'm riding herd on them with Chris Nissen. We're reminding everybody that we're here as trainers, not shooters."

Derringer thought of Fred Dalton Thompson's line as Admiral Painter in *The Hunt for Red October*: "This business *will* get out of control."

"All right, Frank. You know the situation, and I'll back whatever you have to do." He squirmed in his seat. "Now look. It's almost closing time here but I'm calling an executive session of the board for tomorrow morning. We'll discuss options and our legal obligations in case it's desirable to reduce our training operation or even cancel the contract. You'll be hearing from me with a preliminary report by tomorrow evening, your time."

"Thanks, Admiral. I appreciate that, and so do the guys. But honestly, I think we can proceed with the contract as things stand now."

"You watch your back, Frank. That's an order."

"Aye aye, sir!"

The line went dead but Michael Derringer was still looking at his phone twenty seconds later.

20

NABATIYEH GOVERNATE

"Tell me what happened."

Imam Sadegh Elham had never been accused of subtlety. Though Esmaili thought that Azizi would have provided a preliminary report, the cleric demanded an immediate debrief. In fact, he was waiting when the truck arrived at the Hezbollah cell's headquarters.

Esmaili's feet had barely touched the ground. He was sore and tired, more focused on addressing his sniper trainees than dealing with the priestly commissar from Tehran. "Imam, I can only say that the attack went as planned. I do not have direct information on the results but surely Brother Azizi can provide that for you." He turned to go.

A bony hand extended from the white robe, clutching Esmaili's arm. "I have heard from Azizi. I would hear from you. Brother."

Esmaili shot a glance at Larijani. The boy was being hailed as a hero by his classmates, including Hazim, who apparently had recovered from his snit at not being chosen. *They need a dose of reality*.

The grip tightened on Esmaili's arm. He looked down, then raised his gaze to Elham's face. The imam saw the emotion there and released his grip. "Come, let us talk briefly."

Accepting the situation, Esmaili ordered his thoughts. "The coordination with Azizi's fighters was good. The timing went well, based on the information the Beirut organization provided. Our two snipers opened fire on schedule and Yazdi was killed. I do not know if they hit any of the Zionists."

"No matter. They did well enough." Thus did Sadegh Elham write the epitaph of Moshen Yazdi. Esmaili thought: *It is always so with these priests. They are willing to send others to Paradise soon enough, but remain here on earth to die naturally.*

"I did not expect Larijani to survive," Esmaili replied. Somehow, he felt a growing urgency in putting a name if not a face on those who made the sacrifices. *No, those who* are *sacrificed.*

Elham ignored the sentiment. "Your report taken with Azizi's pleases me, brother. The coordination between two units that had never worked together speaks well for everyone concerned." He almost smiled. "Tehran will be pleased as well."

Esmaili read between the lines. Dr. Momen will be pleased. It was all Esmaili could do to ask what relevance the recent operation had to whatever was forthcoming.

"May I provide anything else, Imam?"

Elham waved dismissively. "You may go."

SSI OFFICES

Derringer gaveled the meeting to order. It was a rarity, as SSI's directors normally maintained boardroom decorum, but the news from Beirut had goaded most of the attendees into unaccustomed excitement.

As the chatter abated, Derringer remained standing. He wanted to exercise some command authority, though a couple of the people in the room had outranked him.

"I will summarize," he began. "Last night an attack was made against the Kara compound in Beirut, presumably by Hezbollah operatives. Rafix Kara's vehicle was rammed by a suicide car, resulting in the death of his wife, one son, and two other people. A second car smashed through the gate and unloaded four assassins armed with small arms and explosives. They were all killed but they killed some of Kara's people and inflicted damage on the compound. One of our team members was seriously wounded."

Derringer looked around the room. The short-notice meeting had barely drawn a quorum but that was sufficient. "The question before us is how this attack will affect our training team's contract with the Israelis and the Druze militia. Our people were about ready to leave for the Hasbaya region but now they're forted up, consulting with the IDF liaison officers."

Marshall Wilmont spoke for many of those present. "Admiral, it seems this attack was aimed specifically at our team. I mean, as I understand it, there hasn't been an attack on Kara's facility in recent months. The timing just doesn't look coincidental."

"Yes, that's right. I'm in touch with Mr. Baram of the Israeli embassy, and he's trying to get more information for us. But I don't think we can expect any hard intel right away. Meanwhile, I promised Frank that we'd discuss the situation and let him know of any decisions sometime today." He looked around again. "Any thoughts? Corin?"

Corin Pilong was SSI's contracting officer. She was so slightly built that she barely qualified as petite, though her intellect more than offset her Filipina physique. "Admiral, it's as I expected when we talked last night. This was accepted as a high-risk assignment, to the extent that we acknowledged the chance of fatalities. In fact, we took out higher insurance premiums for that very reason." She paused a moment to consult her notes, then continued in her silky voice. "There is nothing in the contract that allows us to withdraw for . . . well, really, for any reason."

Derringer nodded. "Yes, that's what we expected. After all, it reflects the circumstances that pertained when we agreed to work with the Israelis. Now, George Ferraro isn't here—he's in Spain with his wife—but I contacted him. As VP and chief financial officer he says that we cannot afford to violate the contract." Derringer gave an ironic smile. "That's not exactly news to anybody in this room, but I'd like the record to show that George's input was received."

Wilmont wriggled his ample bottom in his chair, a sure sign that he wanted to speak. Derringer took note. "Yes, Marsh."

Addressing the board members, Wilmont revealed what Derringer already knew. "A few days ago I talked with Brian Cottle, who basically approved us for this job when others in State didn't want to hear the letters SSI. He indicated that since things have changed in Lebanon, there's more, shall I say, appreciation for what we do. He didn't come right out and say that we're off the hook for the Iranian yellow cake scam that the Israelis ran on Foggy Bottom and Langley, but that seems to be the way it's going."

Samuel Small, an erstwhile Air Force colonel, wrinkled his brow. "So how does that affect our Druze contract, Marsh?"

"Well, I mention it because if we're getting out of detention with State, maybe we don't have to rely on this contract for our corporate survival."

Small drummed his fingers on the table. "So are you saying that maybe we should pull out and let the chips fall?"

Wilmont sensed that he was being made the heavy: someone who would violate a contract and hope for better offers. "No, damn it! That's not what I'm saying!" He glanced around, realized that his voice had risen, and people were staring at him. "I just think that we're obligated to consider whether the increased risk to our people is worth the penalty for withdrawing unilaterally."

Derringer sought to retrieve the situation. "I concur with Marsh that we owe our loyalty to the men we send in harm's way. But I talked with Frank late yesterday and he says they want to stick to the mission, at least for now." He glanced at Sandra Carmichael. She was not a board member but she attended most meetings to provide information. "Sandy? Any thoughts?"

Carmichael raised a manicured hand to brush a blond curl. "From the operations side, Admiral, I don't have much to add. Frank's the one with his boots on the ground, and the guys trust him. If they want to continue with the job, it's their call."

"Very well." Derringer caught a gesture from Thomas Varlowe, chairman of the advisory board. "Yes, General."

The former three-star leaned forward, his chiseled features and gunmetal gray hair emphasizing his demeanor. "It seems that there's a consensus that we will proceed with the contract. That is as it should be, but I want to emphasize the point. If this firm is to retain its credibility, and therefore its future, it *must* complete any contract that it accepts. Now, everyone here is understandably concerned with the safety of our people. But if I must state the obvious, I will. Our operators are well-paid professionals. *Very* well paid. They understand the risk and they accept it. The day we forget that fact is the day we close the door on ourselves."

Michael Derringer declared, "This meeting is adjourned." He felt a tug at his heart as Marshall Wilmont slumped in his chair.

KARA COMPOUND

"We're staying," Leopole declared.

The SSI operators gathered in the lounge area murmured their approval. In the second row, Bosco and Breezy tapped fists in a hoo-ah sentiment.

Rob Furr and Rick Barrkman clearly approved of the news. Though he envied his partner's opportunity during the raid, Barrkman had kept his opinion under control. "You lucky SOB" was all he had said.

Furr shrugged it off. "Luck of the draw, man. Coulda been you as easy as me."

In the back row, Robert Pitney bit his lip. He was disappointed in himself more than he let on. He had allowed himself to relax behind the guarded walls of the compound and lacked a weapon when general quarters sounded. He vowed that it would never happen again. Never.

Leopole elaborated upon what he learned from headquarters. "The board of directors met this morning and decided that our contract does not allow us to pull out of this assignment. There was, however, some sentiment for releasing anybody who wants to go." He paused to allow that information to settle. When nobody spoke up, he continued.

"The fact that we apparently were targeted rather than Mr. Kara's people has been noted by the board. But there's no provision for extra hazard pay since we're already drawing hazardous duty and overseas bonuses." He shrugged. "Sorry, guys. The pot of gold is maxed out."

Chris Nissen's Barry White tones rose from the first row. "Colonel, I don't know about the rest of the guys but I'd sure like to get off the bull's-eye here. When do we go to our op area?"

Leopole shifted his feet and folded his arms. "Well, Staff Sergeant, you know the old saying: 'Be careful what you want because you might get it.' We're probably headed for the Hasbaya area day after tomorrow. But remember that if the Hezzies could pick us out of the crowd here in Beirut, they won't have much trouble IDing us in the villages where the militias operate. So keep that in mind.

"As we mentioned before, we'll try to blend in as much as possible, especially regarding clothes. I do not recommend carrying anything but AKs or Galils because that's what the locals are packing." He shifted his gaze to the snipers. "You guys with the precision rifles should keep them out of sight as much as possible."

Phil Green raised a hand. "Colonel, now that Mr. Kara's laid up, who's the Druze honcho?"

"Well, Mr. Kara never intended to operate with us in the field so nothing's changed in that regard. Major Ayash remains the senior IDF liaison officer, and we'll be working with him and his subordinates."

Wallender asked the obvious question. "Colonel, how is Mr. Kara? I mean, is there any solid info on his condition?"

"Well, he wants to talk to me so I'm going to see him before we leave." Leopole did not bother expressing the sentiment, but it was one visit he was not going to enjoy.

21

BEIRUT

The ward was well guarded. Kara's people appeared at least as professional as the police officers and possessed more daunting hardware. Frank Leopole had never seen an automatic weapon in a hospital before, but as Kara himself was fond of saying, "This is Beirut."

Pausing outside Kara's door, Ayash turned to Leopole. "He may still be sedated but he insisted on seeing you before you go. I have arranged for a doctor to interrupt us in about five minutes."

The American nodded. Then Ayash rapped a tattoo on

the door—three fast, two slow—and called something in French. *"J'ai voyagé loin."* Leopole knew nothing about traveling far, but followed him inside.

Rafix Kara lay propped up in bed, an oxygen tube to his nose. Leopole noted that it was a double room with the other bed removed. A Druze occupied a chair in the far corner, and with a start Leopole realized that it was Walid, the surviving son, wearing a ballistic vest. He cradled his MP-5 across his knees, a suppressor screwed onto the barrel.

Makes sense, Leopole thought. *Don't want too much noise in a hospital!*

Rafix Kara turned his head and focused on the visitors. The light of recognition illuminated his dark eyes. He raised his right hand, as his left had an IV inserted.

Ayash approached the bed and grasped the extended hand. Speaking slowly and clearly, he said, "Mr. Kara, Lieutenant Colonel Leopole is here to see you."

"My friend Frank." The voice was a croak, the words slightly slurred. Leopole stepped beside Ayash and laid a hand on Kara's arm.

"I'm here, Mr. Kara. I'm so glad that you escaped . . . and I am so sorry for the loss of your family."

With a start, Leopole realized that he may have insulted Walid but the young man gave no hint of resentment. Rather, he continued watching the door.

"Frank, listen." Kara managed a grip on Leopole's arm. It was surprisingly firm. "My family . . . it is the Druze people. You came to help them." He inhaled deeply, sucking in oxygen. "You can do it, Frank. Do not think about me. Just do your job with . . ." He licked his lips. "With the militias."

"Yes, sir. That's what we're going to do."

Kara inhaled again. "Promise me."

"Of course, Rafix. Of course I promise." An awkward silence fell across the room. Leopole was conscious of every passing second. Finally Ayash took advantage of the lull.

"Mr. Kara, I think that we should go. There is still . . ."

"Good-bye my friend Frank." Kara gave another squeeze. "I will not be seeing you again, but thank you for all you have done. And what you will do."

"Rafix, I am going to come back and see you before long. I'll give you a full report . . ."

"No. No, that won't happen, Frank. I'll be gone by then. I'll be gone." He looked up, directly into Leopole's eyes. "I deserve to die."

Frank Leopole, former lieutenant colonel of Marines, could not think of a response. He sought for the words and, finding none, conceded defeat. "Good-bye, sir."

In the hallway Ayash suddenly stopped. He turned and said, "Rafix Kara is a great man. But like all great men, he is flawed. In his case, it was not hubris but physical weakness that affected his judgment. The wounds he suffered over the years finally caught up with him, and he needed more and more pain relief. The morphine clouded his mind, and he unknowingly gave his enemies the information they needed to try to kill him. He survived the initial attack, but in losing his wife and one son he lost his will to live. So you see, Frank, they did kill him after all."

NABATIYEH GOVERNATE

Esmaili had a problem.

Ebrahim Larijani had left for Beirut as a subdued, visibly frightened young man. He returned with the aura of a blooded veteran despite the fact that there was no indication he had spilled any blood at all. Nevertheless, his colleagues accorded him deferential treatment that had been notably lacking before. After all, his rank in the class pecking order had only been superior to the departed Yazdi, blessings be upon him.

The exception, Esmaili noted, was Hazim. Still the best shooter in the class, he had welcomed Larijani upon return from Beirut but otherwise maintained coolly cordial relations.

Esmaili decided on a cell meeting in the truest Marxist sense.

Gathering his shooters well away from Azizi and Elham, the Hezbollah leader set up his unexpected star pupil for a lesson in humility.

"I have decided that we should sit down to study the lessons of Brother Larijani's experience in Beirut. Because he is the first of you to experience sniper combat, each of you can learn from his observations and take them with you when your turn arises." He turned to Larijani. "Brother, please describe your mission for us."

Larijani shifted his position. All the men were sitting on the ground, arrayed in a circle. Esmaili usually conducted such meetings in that manner to reinforce the perception of equality among the cell members. It also meant that every man could look at everyone else, with attendant psychological pressures for composure and veracity.

"Well, we deployed as Brother Azizi directed. I was on the north side of the Zionist compound and Yazdi on the east. We were both roughly two hundred meters from the target area. We arrived in daylight to see the details and study the enemy patrol patterns. Then as night settled, we took our positions and waited for the time."

When no one asked a question, Esmaili prompted with one. "How did you feel at that moment?"

"Teacher, I was ready to fill my mission."

"Yes, yes. But how did you *feel*? Were you nervous or calm? What was in your heart?"

Larijani looked down. Then he raised his gaze. "I was

afraid that I might fail to do my part." He swallowed. "I did not want to disappoint anyone."

Esmaili was taken aback. He did not expect so honest a response. He modulated his voice. "Yes, go on."

The novitiate seemed to relax a little. "When we got the order to fire, I was looking at a sentry on the far wall. I placed him in my sight and fired."

Hazim finally spoke. "What was your firing position?"

"I was sitting with my Dragunov resting on the edge of the wall."

"Did you hit your target?"

Larijani hesitated for two heartbeats. "I believe so."

Esmaili interjected. "You do not know? What about your spotter?"

"Well, I did not have a trained spotter. Just the security men from Beirut."

"How many times did you fire?"

The shooter thought for a long moment. "Four or five times."

Esmaili's voice held an edge. "A trained sniper should know if it was four or five. Which was it?"

"I . . . I think it was five. Yes, five."

Nobody believed him.

Hazim asked the obvious question. "How many targets did you hit?"

Larijani bit his lip. "It was dark and I had no spotter." He glanced away. "Maybe two or three."

Esmaili was pulled in two directions. He could further humiliate the boy by stating that a trained marksman could call his shots even without a spotter to confirm the hits. The steadiness of the sight picture and the precision of the trigger release would tell a good shooter all he needed to know.

On the other hand, Larijani had been selected to die and for whatever reason—fate, coincidence, God—he had been spared. Whether he had dispatched two or three enemies, or more likely none, he had done his duty.

"Perhaps we will receive more information from our brothers in Beirut," Esmaili purred. "But for the present, we can take the experience of Larijani and apply it to our own work when the time comes."

Before rising, Esmaili locked eyes with Hazim. For anyone who cared to notice, the status quo ante had been restored.

PART

IV

THE MISSION

22

HASBAYA, NABATIYEH GOVERNATE

Major Fahed Ayash provided the briefing almost before the SSI team had settled into temporary quarters.

"Welcome to Hasbaya, gentlemen. You will not be here very long but Lieutenant Colonel Leopole and I expect that some of you will be in and out of here, rotating from your militia areas. Therefore it is helpful for you to know something of the city.

"As you saw on the way in, Hasbaya is built on hills near Mount Hermon, sited around a tributary of the Hasbani River. The current population is about thirty thousand, and the local industries include grapes for wine and olive oil. Since you will be working with the Druze militia, you should know that a few kilometers northeast is the pilgrimage site of al Bayyada with its old praying halls.

"History is everywhere. Near Habbariye lie the ruins of a Roman temple with walls twenty-five feet high." He gave a sardonic smile. "It says something that one of the newest tourist spots is the mosque with a distinctive hexagonal minaret. It was built in the thirteenth century.

"Otherwise, there's the Chihabi Citadel from the Crusades in the eleventh century, plus the Chehab Palace.

"We're not far from Syria. Damascus is only about thirty-five miles east, and the border is much closer. That is why your training mission is so important. The militias in the area are under increasing pressure from Hezbollah elements backed by Syria as well as Iran."

Ayash turned to an easel with a map of the region. "Your primary operating areas are south and east of here, at the villages of Amasha and El-Arian. They are fairly small but their positions are important because they command obvious routes from the border, continuing farther inland to the south." He paused for effect. "Obviously, that means toward Israel."

Frank Leopole relieved Ayash at the front of the room, taking in the crowd of operators. He noted that most held rifles or carbines and some had sidearms as well. After the Beirut episode, he had recommended that everyone go armed everywhere, and the proliferation of AKs and Galils attested to the acceptance of his wisdom. Robert Pitney seemed content with his Springfield XD, but Leopole conceded that the speed shooter could do more with a pistol than many operators could accomplish with a rifle.

"Today we're going to split up into two units," Leopole began. "Partly that's so each team can start focusing on its specific mission, and partly for security." He did not have to elaborate. Bosco and Breezy exchanged hoo-ah glances, acknowledging that if one team was attacked before deploying to its village, the other would remain intact to accomplish its mission.

"I'll take Team One to Amasha and Chris will have Team Two at El-Arian. Major Ayash will float between them as needed, and coordinate with our IDF liaison out of this facility.

"My team includes Bosco and Breezy, Pitney, and Barrkman. Our militia contact is Rami Hamadeh, who some of you have already met.

"Chris has Ashcroft, Green, Wallender, and Furr with Salah-Hassan Fares. He will be here tomorrow.

"Now, Barrkman and Furr. I know you sniper dudes

would rather work together but we need to maximize our expertise so each of you can instruct the militia folks in your respective areas. If it becomes advisable to deploy an all-up team, we'll pull one of you to work with the other but I hope that isn't necessary."

Furr folded his arms and said nothing. Barrkman slumped in his chair, clearly displeased with the decision. Neither would protest—they were far too professional for that and were being well paid besides.

Leopole turned to the map and tapped the appropriate locales. "The villes are about ten or eleven klicks apart. Depending on transport, that means we can reinforce each other in maybe ten minutes, barring en route problems. As soon as we arrive we'll get on that contingency planning."

Chris Nissen raised a hand. "Colonel, what's current intel on the threat in that area?"

Leopole looked at Ayash for the answer. The Druze officer said, "It's been a hot zone, Sergeant. And it's likely to get hotter."

NABATIYEH GOVERNATE

Imam Elham summoned Esmaili and Azizi. "You have a mission."

Esmaili absorbed the sentiment. *We have a mission— he gives orders.*

The cleric eased himself into a sitting position against a stone wall. "Your task is one of deception. We know that the infidels expect Hezbollah to take action in this area. The geographic aspects are self-evident." He nodded behind him, toward the Syrian border fifteen kilometers away. "Therefore, you will begin a series of small actions across a broad front. Using mortars and snipers, your group and others in this area will cause as much confusion as possible, especially among the Druze villages that command terrain features or important roads. They will know that greater action is pending, but not when. And that will be our advantage."

Azizi ventured a question. "Imam, when *is* the time?"

Elham looked at Azizi for a long moment. "That will be revealed when you need to know."

Esmaili was thinking ahead of the game, trying to anticipate problems and requirements. "A few questions, if I may," he began. Without awaiting approval he pressed on. "Are we to conduct these deceptions as pinprick attacks to keep the enemy off balance, or on a scale large enough to desensitize them for the greater effort?"

The priest cocked his head as if studying a specimen under glass. "That is an astute question, brother. It shows that you appreciate the nuances of the endeavor." He glanced briefly at Azizi, who turned red-faced at the implication. "How would you distinguish between the two?"

Esmaili felt himself warming to the subject. It was a welcome relief from his usual relationship with the imam. "Mainly it is a difference of scale. As you say, with some snipers and a few mortars we can keep things unsettled with minimal effort almost indefinitely. But if there is to be a large ground offensive, we will need more men and equipment. Also more supplies."

Elham nodded. "Just so. For the present Tehran and Damascus have few fighters to spare. I can tell you that those available are either committed elsewhere or are being held in reserve. But this will be a multifaceted campaign, not limited to those who fight conventionally. You both know of the survey crews that have prepared possible rocket sites. There are also clandestine teams—special operations troops—who will use the confusion caused by the larger effort to accomplish their tasks."

Azizi sought to ingratiate himself again. "Whatever the assignment, we will do it, Imam. When should we begin the attacks, and what are our targets?"

The priest pulled a printed sheet from his robe. "These are your objectives and the schedule. But tomorrow would not be too soon."

NORTHERN ISRAEL

"You're wrong, Sol. It's going to be even harder than we expected."

Colonel Yakov Livni and Brigadier General Solomon Nadel had a peculiar relationship. Their respective duties—covert operations and conventional ground forces and logistics—necessarily overlapped on both sides of the Lebanese border. The irony was lost on neither officer that the colonel dictated his requirements to the general, but their mutual professionalism kept them on track.

Nadel was unaccustomed to colonels telling him that he was wrong, but in the freewheeling IDF such candor was not unknown. "All right, I said it would be difficult to provide support to the militia. If I'm wrong, tell me how it's going to be even harder."

Livni plunked his ample bulk into a straight-backed chair and jabbed a finger at the map. "From recent intelligence we know that Hezbollah is getting more direct support from Syria. Yes, the Iranians are the power behind Hezbollah but the geographic fact remains that they can't do much without Syrian cooperation. That means it's doubly difficult for us to keep track of their movements, let alone their intentions." He pushed his glasses up on his forehead. "Without more eyes and ears on the ground, we can only guess at what the Druze are going to be faced with."

Nadel paced a few steps away, then returned. "Look. That's what I don't understand. My God, Yakov, the Druze militias are already there. They *live* there! Surely they know the situation better than anybody in Jerusalem or Tel Aviv."

"Stay with me, Solly. Yes, *of course* the Druze know the local situation. We rely on their information to produce our intelligence estimates. But they're seeing the trees, not the forest. That's why I'm saying that the reports you receive are more pessimistic, and justifiably so. They include information from more sensitive sources, especially back-channel reports and what the politicians call 'technical methods.' Of course that means signal intelligence and decrypts, but nobody wants to say so."

Nadel threw up his hands. "All right, then. Quit trying to impress me with your high and mighty sources that you can't reveal. For the moment let's say that I accept them at face value. Just tell me what I need to know in order to support your Druze friends."

Livni smiled for a change. "Now we're getting somewhere. The American training teams are ready to move from Hasbaya to the first two villages. Amasha and El-Arian. There has already been sporadic Hezbollah action in that area. Nothing dramatic, just harassment. A few sniping incidents, some mortars and roadside bombs. But we expect that's going to increase, either as part of a bigger harassment campaign or as cover for something else."

"Cover? You mean something covert?"

An exaggerated shrug with raised hands. "It's too early to tell. But I need your boys to be ready to reinforce either of those places on short notice. If Hezbollah makes an overt effort to seize one or the other, it could signal the start of a larger offensive. In that case, we need to move fast."

"I agree. But in what strength?"

"General, I'm glad you asked."

23

"Well, what've we heard?"

Michael Derringer was never known as a microman-
ager but when an operation was under way he liked to
keep his thumb on its pulse. The impromptu meeting of
the SSI brain trust was evidence of his concern.

As the senior operations officer, Sandy Carmichael had
the conn. "Admiral, our teams are deploying to their operating areas. They'll be in position later today. Frank has
half the crew in a place called Amasha and Chris Nissen
is taking the others to El-Arian. Both are villages south
and east of Hasbaya."

"Very well. How's our comm with them?"

"So far, so good. Satellite phones work well, and for the
reliability it's worth two dollars a minute. Conventional
phone service is adequate, and we also have e-mail contact
but the server in that area seems somewhat erratic."

"What about Frank's contact with the IDF across the
border? I mean, in case he needs reinforcements immediately."

Carmichael nodded. "Sir, I was coming to that. Frank
confirmed that he has round-the-clock contact with Northern Command. But if our guys were targeted in Beirut, it
stands to reason they'll be in the crosshairs out in the countryside. I'd like to know what we can do to extract them if
necessary."

Derringer turned to the visitor. "Mr. Baram?"

The Israeli diplomat leaned forward, hands clasped on
the table. "I am glad that you asked me to this meeting,

Admiral. Our Druze liaison officers are, of course, aware of the situation, and best positioned to provide timely assistance. Their counterparts in the IDF also will lend whatever assistance they can, and I understand that air evacuation is the best option.

"However, I agree that it would be helpful to have prior consent of, ah, certain U.S. Government assets in the region. I am making that request both to your State Department and Department of Defense, though it may be some time before I receive a response from either one."

Derringer squirmed in his chair. "I'd feel better if that had been settled before our teams arrived in Hasbaya but I recognize the urgency our clients feel in getting the training started. Now, I'd like to think that we can rely on the IDF to extract our people on short notice. If there is any doubt about it, we need to know. Today."

Baram looked into Derringer's face. "Admiral, at present there is no doubt about our willingness to do so, and currently there's not much doubt about our ability. I have dealt with the colonel running covert operations in Lebanon, and he is a good man. A very good man. If he says something will be done, it usually gets done."

The SSI president swiveled his chair side to side. "Very well, then. I'll accept that at face value." He turned to Carmichael. "But I'd like to see if we might tap our Sec-Nav or even DoD contacts. It'd be the long way around, but the amphibious group in the eastern Med could get some choppers in there."

"Yes, sir. I've already staffed it. Depending on specifics, it's about twenty-five to thirty miles from the coast to our op areas. There are terrain features that would be helpful during ingress and egress, but until we know something about threat levels it's too early to say whether H-46s or 53s would be able to operate in that environment."

"Oh, how's that?"

"Well, sir, the situation might not be very permissive,

at least not for helos. I understand that SA-7s are about as common as RPGs in that area. Likely even some double-digit SAMs . . ."

Derringer cut off the explanation. "Who has the 'phib gru out there?"

Carmichael congratulated herself on her prescience. "Rear Admiral Millikin. He's . . ."

"Bill Millikin," Derringer interrupted. "Good man. He has experience in dustoffs on a hot LZ." He paused, as if lost in reverie. "Evil Hyphen . . ." The statement brought uncomprehending looks from the other staffers so Derringer added, "A covert op in Africa about fifteen years ago."

Marsh Wilmont had kept a low profile after his previous showing, but Lieutenant General Varlowe was blessedly absent today. "Mike, are you thinking of going back-channel to talk to Millikin?"

Derringer drummed his fingers on the table. Finally he said, "Actually, I hadn't thought about that. But if neither we nor Mr. Baram can get some commitments from State or the Pentagon, I'm not averse to it."

Before Wilmont could reply, Derringer nodded to Omar Mohammed. "Omar is here because he consulted on the training syllabus for the Druze militias. I think we should hear from him about prospects for fulfilling the contract in case we have to withdraw some or all of our people."

Mohammed stroked his immaculate goatee. "It remains to be seen whether we would collect full payment for a good-faith effort to train the militias in that area. Our legal department would have to make a judgment, and Ms. Pilong is out today. But as far as the operational end, at the very least we have provided a detailed training program that the IDF liaison teams could follow."

Carmichael had a thought. "What if we were able to continue training Druze cadres someplace else? Maybe even in the Beirut area?"

Mohammed cocked an eyebrow and looked at Derringer.

"That is an excellent suggestion. I think we should pursue it."

Derringer scribbled some notes to himself. "Very well, then. I'll see about the old boy network in the Med and you folks coordinate with a fallback plan for returning to the Beirut area." He jabbed his notepad with his pen and smiled. "Nice to have options, isn't it?"

EL-ARIAN, NABATIYEH GOVERNATE

The El-Arian militia was reasonably well organized and possessed a degree of experience. The group leader, Salah Al Atrash, had placed his newest members on sentry duty, a compromise between breaking them in as quickly as possible with minimal risk. He had found that issuing automatic weapons to earnest young men eager to prove themselves before their neighbors and kinsmen yielded one of two results: early maturity or premature death.

The sentinel called Talea was twenty-three years old, generally popular with some promise as a potential leader. As he paced beside the stone wall leading to the village entrance, he paused to scan the surrounding terrain. Al Atrash had worked his men diligently in recent days, clearing away tree trunks and debris, and clipping grass that could conceal anyone trying to approach unseen within 250 meters.

Talea had just turned to resume his patrol when a ballistic crack rent the morning air. Fifty meters away, a youngster going about his chores looked up at the unexpected sound in time to see the guard collapse in the road.

A pair of finches broke cover at the noise, but otherwise the area remained calm. Several moments passed before concerned citizens ran to the spot and turned over the sentry's body.

Some 315 meters away, Ahmad Esmaili patted Hazim on the shoulder and motioned backward. They eased away, keeping low to avoid profiling themselves against the skyline.

Hazim reached out and retrieved the expended 7.62×54mm cartridge case. Feeling as good as he could ever remember, he wanted a souvenir of his first kill.

AMASHA

Frank Leopole surveyed the topography around Amasha. As a professional infantryman, he had never looked at ground the same way after Basic School. Where most humans saw rolling terrain or picturesque hills, he saw dead ground, defiles, and crests. Danger, safety, opportunity.

Major Fahed Ayash and militia leader Rami Hamadeh accompanied the SSI man on his tour of the village. He noted that two hills provided an overlook of perhaps twenty meters advantage. "I wonder why the founders of this place located here rather than over on the high ground."

The two Druze exchanged knowing looks. "Colonel Leopole," Ayash explained, "four hundred years ago, access to water was more important than military concerns." He pointed to the stream a long pistol shot away.

Leopole felt his cheeks redden. "Well, that's as good a reason as any and better than most." He laughed self-consciously. Then, seeking to retrieve the situation, he observed, "Either of those hummocks would be useful for forward observers or some decent snipers." He gauged the distance. "Must be five to six hundred meters."

Hamadeh chuckled. "It is 560 meters to the nearest and 620 to the other. I have paced it myself. You have a good eye, Colonel."

The American grinned self-consciously. "Well, I spent a lot more time on rifle ranges than looking for water." Seeking to change the subject, he asked, "What are your security arrangements for those hills?"

Hamadeh spoke French-accented English. "We patrol the area and one time had guard, ah, post, there. But not enough men to keep on there so we did some nights." He paused, seeking the words. "Then Hezbollah took two men and killed another. We never see them no more so we cannot put men on hills after dark."

Leopole turned to Ayash. "Couldn't the Lebanese army help with some people?"

The Israeli Druze shook his head. "This is a small place, Colonel. The national army is occupied all over the country. That's why the militia receives as much support as it does."

"Well, we'll do everything we can to help make up the difference." He turned to Hamadeh, speaking slowly. "In our briefings we were told that you do not have facilities such as shooting ranges. Is there someplace we could use for that purpose? Maybe with a backstop?"

The commander nodded enthusiastically. "Yes, yes. Old quarry behind town. Maybe seventy-eighty meters."

"All right, we'll make do with that." He began walking. "Gentlemen, let's get started."

24

AMASHA

"How are they doing?" Leopole asked.

Bosco was inhaling half a bottle of water. He nodded while swishing out his mouth, then swallowed. "Pretty good, Boss. Pitney really helps."

Leopole stood behind the firing line, watching the former policeman with some of the militiamen. Robert Pitney was leaning over a shooter who had assumed a rough sitting position, demonstrating where knees and elbows belonged. The American was speaking animatedly, with apparent authority.

Bosco wiped his mouth on his sleeve. "I don't know how you say 'cheek weld' or 'sight picture' in Druze talk, but Robert seems to have it dialed in."

"Well, it's preferable to have a native speaker, of course. But you guys seem to do okay working with translators."

"Yeah. Rami and Hamdam speak enough English for us to get the point across, but something's gotta be lost in translation. Like, you and I know what we mean when we talk about seating the butt in the pocket of the shoulder, but imagine how that comes out in Arabic!"

Leopole allowed himself an appreciative grin. "Hey, if it works, it works. The groups are tightening up at twenty-five meters and some of the militia are getting faster hits."

Bosco set his bottle down and prepared to return to the line. "Boss, it's not my call, but you might tell Robert not to shoot up to speed when he's doing drills by himself. Some of these studs see him rip off six aimed rounds in a second and want to shoot as fast as he does. It don't occur to them that he shoots like this"—he cupped his fingers into a two-inch circle—"and they shoot like this." He raised his hands in an expansive gesture.

"Like Jeff Cooper always said: slow is smooth and smooth is fast. Keep 'em smooth, Bosco."

As Bosco resumed his duties, Pitney came off the line for some water. He removed his ball cap and wiped his forehead. "Kind of hard to stay hydrated in this heat, Colonel. But these guys need all the trigger time they can get."

"Well, as soon as they're safe in daylight we'll introduce them to twilight and then full dark. But that's likely to be a slow process because we'll have to do a lot of dry runs before I'll trust them with loaded weapons at night."

"Yes, sir. I think we can do better if we keep the night relays smaller. It'll mean more range time, of course, but we'll have better control of them."

Leopole considered the suggestion and found it had merit. "That's not a bad idea, Robert. Have you done that before?"

Pitney raised a bottle from the ice chest and took a long pull. His Camelbak had gone dry fifteen minutes earlier. "Yeah. But that was with a group smaller than this so it wasn't as hard. Besides, it was an indoor range where we could control the lights. Worked really well." He chuckled. "Besides, those were cops and some of them actually could look at the sights and press the trigger. These guys . . ." He shook his head. "On the first day I just about bought myself a ticket home. The gun handling was . . ."

"Atrocious?"

Pitney laughed again. "I don't know. What's worse than atrocious? Awful isn't bad enough."

"Abysmal?"

"Somewhere in the first part of the alphabet. But you know, it's odd. The main problem was muzzle awareness. Everybody sweeping everybody else. It's hard getting across to these guys that you're supposed to treat every gun as if it's loaded, even if you just unloaded it. Some of them just don't get that. But then I noticed that nearly all of them followed Rule Three."

"Finger off the trigger?"

"Right. Rule One and Two went out the door but I guess the militia have seen enough movies and news reports that they kept their fingers alongside the frame."

Leopole conjured up his recent discussion with Bosco. "How's the language situation?"

Pitney shucked his Camelbak and began refilling it. "Oh, not bad. My basic Arabic is still pretty good. It took me a little while to get used to Druze pronunciation. They speak kind of an archaic Arabic with what we'd call a soft D and a strong, throaty K. But if they slow down just a little I don't have much problem."

"Good job, Robert. Keep it up and maybe we can go home early."

"As Breezy would say, 'Hoo-ah that, sir.' "

NABATIYEH GOVERNATE

Esmaili saw Azizi conferring with some new arrivals but kept his distance. The strangers were unloading mortar tubes and base plates from a truck with Syrian markings and seemed intent on talking only to the man from Tehran. The imam was nowhere to be seen, which meant he was either plotting or praying.

At length Azizi left his friends to their own devices. Esmaili intercepted him.

"Brother, may I ask what do your mortar men have?"

"Oh, mostly old Soviet equipment, the 2B14 Podnos and M31/M68. Both are 82mm. We find that it is a good compromise between the 60 and 120mm weapons. The Podnos fires a three-kilogram bomb with a range of four kilometers. They weigh only forty kilograms so we can move them and some ammunition with four men."

"They have experience in operations?"

A faint smile. "Oh, yes. Considerable experience."

Esmaili conceded the advantage of portability but recognized the limitations. "I only ask because it may be difficult to displace from the firing position once the Druze learn to estimate the location. Their Zionist friends may provide aerial drones for surveillance."

"Yes, that is always a possibility. The aircraft also may have thermal imagers once our night attacks become evident. It is also thus, brother. The tide comes in and the tide flows out. But Islam's tide is inevitable."

Esmaili thought: *You have been spending too much time with Elham, brother.* Then he said, "So it always has been. And so it shall be here, God grant us the strength to do our part."

"Our strength is in our arms and in our hearts. And the greatest of these is our hearts, for there faith abides."

Esmaili inclined his torso in a slight bow. "Truly said."

Walking away, Esmaili felt a spasm in his shoulder muscles. *Azizi used to be halfway rational. Now he has absorbed the imam's zeal, and that bodes ill for anyone involved with him.*

With a start, Esmaili realized that Azizi must have some additional information that he had not yet shared. The cell leader quickened his pace, seeking a solitary place where he could sit down and think before afternoon prayers.

EL-ARIAN

In his Special Forces career, former Staff Sergeant Chris Nissen had seldom dealt with snipers, either incoming or outgoing, but now he was faced with both.

The SSI team had barely arrived when the local militia explained the situation. The Druze leader, with the unlikely name of Ayoob Slim, had been taken aback when he met the American, apparently surprised that a black man would command the training team. But Slim, an intense individual of some forty years, seemed capable of objectivity. Upon consulting with his IDF liaison, Captain Salah-Hassan Fares, he quickly got down to specifics.

Fares translated. "Sergeant, there are Hezbollah snipers

here. They have come before but mainly just to shoot at the village. This new one, he hits what he sees."

Nissen thought for a moment. "Are you sure there's just one?"

After some back and forthing with Slim, Fares raised his hands. "I am not certain. The local men seem convinced because there is usually just one shot. But they cannot say where it comes from, so there could be more than one, or perhaps just one who moves and shoots again."

"Well, we can't let one gomer with a rifle stop us from training. Let's have my team meet with Mr. Slim and his folks and explain the lesson plans. Then I'll have a word with my precision rifleman."

Robbie Furr had a goodly opinion of his professional abilities but he did not relish odds of two or three to one.

"I'll see what I can do, Chris, but I'll need a spotter. I mean, somebody who knows what he's doing."

"You'd like to have Barrkman back."

Furr nodded, rubbing his balding head. "He's about the only game in town. I could work with Green or Ashcroft because Wallender has some language ability that you need. But Phil and Bob aren't sniper-trained. If I'm going up against some semipros, I want the best I can get."

Nissen appreciated the shooter's sentiment, having had to go to a couple of bad places with goody-good people on occasion. He knew that Leopole would be reluctant to place all his sniper eggs in one basket but saw no harm in asking. He looked at Furr and said, "I'll see what I can do."

25

AMASHA

The sound was distinctive: a hollow, metallic *plunk*. The mortar shell landed well short of the village but the defenders knew there would be more.

Bosco perked up. "That sounds like an 81-mm tube."

"How'n hell can you tell, man?" The paratrooper in Breezy was skeptical of anything that a soldier could not hump on his own.

"Hey, dude, Rangers use mortars, you know? I was A-gunner on a 60mm for a while. Got so I could hit Pierce County. Thing is, I don't think the Hezzies would have 81s. Prob'ly 82s."

"Well, how far does that thing shoot? It's gotta be pretty close if we can hear it."

"The M224 is good for over three thousand meters, but this one's closer."

"Well, 82s got more range."

"I know, Breeze. But most all the ammo is three–four pounds. You can only chuck one of those so far."

"Well, if it's only fifteen hundred meters out, that's a hell of a hike in injun country."

Bosco shook his head. "No, man. You don't gotta find the tube. All you do is find the FO and pop him."

"Man, that's a needle in a Lebanese haystack." Breezy swept his hand generally eastward. "How'n hell do you find somebody in all that territory?"

"I think we should talk to the sniper dudes. They know about skulking and snooping and stuff."

As if to emphasize the urgency, another round topped

out of its parabolic arc and descended toward the village. Bosco jumped left as Breezy dived right. The projectile landed thirty meters away, dropping rocks and debris in the area. Breezy poked his head up, cocking a wary eye at the sky, and scrambled on hands and knees to his partner. "That does it, man. If our snipers are going after that FO, then I'm goin' with 'em."

Several minutes later Bosco and Breezy consulted with Rick Barrkman. The sniper said, "It's not as hard to find an observer as it seems. At least you can narrow down the area. I mean, he needs a good view of the target and that usually means elevation. Now, most people would assume he's somewhere in line between the tube and target but that's only for amateurs. I think these Hezzies probably have some experience, so let's scope out the geography."

The trio adjourned to the roof of the Yousef family and surveyed the terrain within three-quarters of a mile.

At length Barrkman said, "If I was an FO, I'd take my radio to that bluff to the northeast. It has a decent view of this place, it's off axis from the tube, and it's far enough out to discourage intruders." He looked at Bosco.

Jason Boscombe looked back. "Let's intrude, dude." He smiled broadly.

Frank Leopole was skeptical. "If I let you three yahoos go traipsing through the boondocks, I'm not likely to get all of you back, and I need you." He thought for a moment. "Brezyinski, you stay here. Barrkman, you and Boscombe take two Druze who really know the terrain. Check with Hamadeh for his recommendations." He paused for emphasis. "In no case will you return later than sunset. Even with night vision, when you're on the move after dark the advantage goes to the home team. Got it?"

Barrkman nodded. "Got it. Sir."

As the sniper and the former mortar man strode off in search of the militia leader, Brezyinski entered a visible sulk. Leopole was tempted to ignore the youngster's pout but decided to humor him. "Relax, Breezy. You're staying here because I can't spare you."

"Well, sir, I dunno. Like, does that mean that you *can* spare them?"

"Don't push it, son." Leopole unzipped a patented Marine O-5 type of smile. "Look, it's a big-picture situation." Seeing that he had made no dent, he tried a different approach. "It's like this, Brezyinski. I'm the forest. You're a tree. You receiving me, son?"

"Five by, Colonel. Five by."

OUTSIDE AMASHA

"I can't believe they're that dumb."

Barrkman rubbed his stubbled chin and pondered the situation. The Hezbollah mortar team had fired six rounds in the past forty minutes, almost inviting retaliation.

"Maybe they're moving between shots," Bosco suggested. "There's several minutes' delay after every couple of rounds."

"Yeah. Or maybe the FO is moving. They wouldn't expect us to go deep, looking for the tube."

Bosco nodded. "Well, I sure don't want to go tromping around out here a mile or more looking for something that's bound to be guarded. Now, the observer . . ."

"He could move fast. He'd only have one or two guys with him."

Barrkman turned to Rami Hamadeh, who had insisted on going with the Americans. "Rami, like we discussed: we can ignore the most obvious spots and back off from there. Since the observer probably is not on top of the nearest hill, where would be the next best place?"

The Druze chieftain pointed to the southeast. "Next hill, farther away but still good look at my village."

"Okay. That makes sense. We'll try it." Before Barrkman could say anything else, Hamadeh and his friend took the lead, moving fast and low. The SSI men trailed at a decent interval.

Twenty-five minutes later Hamadeh held up a fist. The group went to cover, having flanked the far hill. Hamadeh had his compact binoculars out, scanning the terrain. Barrkman was using his Bushnell while Bosco and the other Druze maintained a 360-degree search.

Another 82mm round arced overhead, inbound to Amasha. It exploded near the village square.

Hamadeh stopped his sweep, lowered his glasses, and stared at the hillside. Then he raised the optic again. Moments later he turned to Barrkman. "Two men, moving this way. Maybe three hundred meters."

Barrkman looked hard at the area indicated. He shook his head. "I don't see them, Rami."

"They are in grass. You see gray rock?"

The sniper quickly found a four-foot boulder sunk into the slope. "Yes, a little over three hundred meters."

"Watch that. Get ready."

In the two-foot grass Barrkman assumed a sitting position. He steadied the Robar QR-2 with his ankles crossed, elbows braced inside his knees. Satisfied, he removed the cap from the elevation dial and added three minutes of angle from his two-hundred setting.

Bosco took the shooter's Bushnell and assumed a spotter's position behind him, ready to call the shot.

"Wind's quartering from the left," Barrkman whispered. "Not enough to worry about." He thought: *Shooting uphill so the round will go a little high. Torso hit will be no problem.*

He chambered the first cartridge from the ten-round M14 magazine.

Minutes passed. Barrkman felt a cramp building in his right leg but willed it into submission. He had held the same position for longer periods.

"Tango," Bosco said. "Make it two."

Two camouflaged forms appeared from the left edge of Barrkman's scope. Both had AKs; one carried a field radio. They settled behind the boulder as if conversing.

"Which one you gonna dump?" Bosco asked in a hushed voice.

"Maybe both. Otherwise the guy with the radio, of course."

"Hey, the FO could be the one without the pack. He'd be senior."

Bosco's logic made sense. Especially in the rank-conscious Muslim world, the lesser man would likely be the mule. It was contrary to Soviet doctrine when platoon leaders often carried their own radios for better command and control. Even if it marked them as priority targets.

Barrkman looked to Hamadeh. "Rami, what do you think?"

"Shoot radio man, the other no can talk."

Barrkman acknowledged the logic but realized that if he only got one shot, the observer could escape to ply his skills another day. Finally he set his mental trigger. *I'll take the first one that gives me a decent shot.*

He inhaled deeply, expelled the breath, and repeated the process.

In the slanting evening sunlight, the two forms reappeared. One clambered atop the rock, allowing him to peer over the crest of the hill, looking toward Amasha. The man with the radio stood nearby.

Barrkman crosshaired the man atop the rock. *Hello, Mr. FO.*

He thumbed the tang safety forward, then settled into the physical-mental condition that he called "The Zone."

The world went quiet around him, narrowing to the crosshairs and the pressure of his right index finger. A life balanced precariously upon the thin edge of the sear.

The trigger broke cleanly, the firing pin snapped forward, and the round went.

The ten-pound rifle recoiled straight back. *Center left!* As the barrel came level again Barrkman had cycled the bolt and resumed his hold. The rock was barren but the radioman was stooped over, looking at something in the grass.

Barrkman did a compressed breath, held it, and put the crosshairs on the second Hezbollah fighter. The round went before he was ready. *Damn it! Low left!*

By the time he ran the bolt again, the second target had disappeared.

"Tango two ran downhill," Bosco reported. "Nice job on the first one, though. He dropped like a sack of wheat."

Barrkman realized that his pulse was elevated. "Damn it to hell! I got on the trigger too soon." He lowered the QR-2. "That's the first time I wish I had a semiauto. Just a smidgen faster and I could've got him too."

Rami Hamadeh smiled broadly. "You do well. You shoot the one who calls down the bombs. We go look."

Bosco glanced at Barrkman, who rose to his feet. "I don't know, Rami. There could be other gooners out there."

The Druze shook his head. "Gooners?"

How do I explain Gomers and gooners? "Like, bad guys. Hezzies."

"No, it is okay, yes? You go back. We get dead man's papers, maps, yes?"

Barrkman nodded his consent. "Okay, but don't take too long. It's getting dark."

Walking back to the village, Jason Boscombe shot a glance at his newfound partner. *I just want to get back to town but maybe he doesn't want to look at the corpse.*

Returning with a confirmed kill, verified by three witnesses, Rick Barrkman felt no need to score and paste the target.

When they reached the village Leopole asked, "How'd it go?"

Barrkman nodded toward Hamadeh. "Rami called it right, Boss. He figured where they'd be and they walked right into the scope."

Hamadeh and his partner came around the corner, carrying a satchel and some Hezbollah equipment. The Druze leader hefted the satchel. "Maps and military papers. Radio fre . . . freq . . . channels. Yes? I translate them soon."

"That's excellent, Rami," Leopole replied. "What else did you see?"

Hamadeh turned to Barrkman. "You not miss second shot, Meestair Barrkman. Blood on the ground, yes. We followed south to southeast." He patted a leg. "You must hit him low. Dragging one foot, yes."

Bosco gave Barrkman a comradely hoo-ah punch on one arm.

26

EL-ARIAN

"And the Ranger's aim was deadly with the big iron on his hip. Big iron on his hiiiip . . ." Phil Green was an Arizonan down to his boots. Though something less of a singer, he mouthed the lyrics to the classic gunfighter ballad.

"Marty Robbins sang about six-guns but *this* is my idea of Big Iron!" He ran an admiring hand along the barrel of the 12.7mm DShK machine gun. Ironically, the Dashika had become an icon both of the Soviet Army and the Afghan mujahadeen who ousted the Russians from their country.

Captain Salah-Hassan Fares of the IDF Druze contingent was pleased with his coup. But no more so than Ayoob Slim, whose militia benefited from the acquisition. His men had unloaded the seventy-five-pound weapon from the truck and set it on its tripod mount.

"Wish we had another one," Nissen said. "Cross fire's the best way to prevent trespassing." He smiled broadly, pleased with his down-home wisdom.

Wallender was unconvinced. "It's an old design from the 1930s, isn't it?"

"Hell yes, it's an old design," Green replied, "even with the postwar mods. But so's the 1911 pistol and the Ma Deuce .50 cal. Let me tell you, friend: if something's still being used seventy or eighty years later, there's a good reason for it!"

Nissen stood back and scrutinized the Dashika. "I'd like to get one or two of these on wheels. You know, like the Russians used. I wouldn't care so much about the shield. But if we have to defend this place, it'd be nice to have some mobility for our heavy weapons." He tapped the antiaircraft sight. "We don't need all the baroque accessories, but we can keep the recoil damper."

While the militiamen set up the gun under Slim's direction, Fares pointed out the features. "This weapon is fed by a fifty-round belt at six hundred rounds per minute. There is a three-position gas regulator, and we will find the best setting according to what ammunition we receive. The muzzle velocity is 850 meters per second, a little less than your .50 caliber."

Nissen turned from the DShK to the surrounding terrain. "Captain, where do you recommend placing this gun?"

The Israeli Druze looked around. "Your idea of a wheel mount makes sense. We should be able to move it quickly depending on where an attack comes from." He rubbed his chin as if pondering a philosophical point, which in a manner of speaking was the case. Then he looked up and behind him. "There." He pointed to a flat-roofed building. "Best field of fire for a fixed position."

The American gauged the geometry and agreed. "Okay, that looks good. Assuming the home owners don't mind."

Fares gave an ironic grin. "Believe me, Mr. Nissen. They will not object."

Green wondered where the conversation was headed. "If we're going to defend this place, shouldn't we be building more walls and clearing better fields of fire?" His blue eyes took in the surrounding terrain, which included a goodly amount of scrub brush.

Fares called to Slim, who trotted over to the group. After some fast Arabic, the militia leader nodded and turned to his men, talking animatedly.

"What'd he say?" Nissen asked.

"He is asking for volunteers to cut the brush and carry stones to build a new wall on this side of the village."

Green folded his arms and looked skeptical. "Who's gonna volunteer for work like that?"

Fares suppressed another smile. "Mr. Green, these people know that if they want to keep their homes they must be willing to defend them. The Druze have a long history of fighting to protect their culture." He inclined his head toward the town. "If the militia want it done, it will be accomplished. The only question is how soon."

"Outstanding," Nissen exclaimed. "Now if we could find another machine gun."

Fares replied, "This one is Russian but I know of another from China. Or maybe Pakistan. Either will do."

Nissen clapped Green on one arm. "Hey, bro, don't you love it when a plan comes together?"

NABATIYEH GOVERNATE

Azizi convened a meeting with Esmaili and the leader of the mortar section, another Iranian known as Abbasali Rezvani. Esmaili was experienced enough to know that the man probably was born with another name.

"We have made a good beginning," Azizi opened. "Now is the time to increase pressure on the enemy."

Rezvani seemed immune to concern. He was a spare, slender jihadist in his late thirties. Not the type of man accustomed to lugging a forty-kilogram tube and base plate around the countryside, though it was a near certainty that he seldom conducted such exertions himself. "We can operate both day and night," he replied. "But it will be necessary to provide more security to my teams."

Azizi nodded. "Yes, brother. It is advisable to alter our attacks in order to prevent the militias from recognizing a pattern. As for more security . . ." He looked to Esmaili.

"Some of my men can accompany the mortar teams, but that will mean fewer snipers to harass both villages."

"We still have work for your snipers, my brother. But Rezvani lost an experienced observer who was killed by an enemy sniper. The radioman was fortunate to escape with a wound."

Esmaili rubbed his chin, mentally allotting assets. "If you begin shelling the Druze at night, you might escape the first two times or so. After that, the Jews and the Americans will supply them with night vision. In fact, they probably have such equipment now."

He decided not to mention that Hazim had inherited just such an item from the Israeli marksman killed in what now seemed a long-ago ambush. Instead, he changed the subject.

"What information is available on the Zionist mercenaries working with the militias?"

Azizi was prepared. "They have established training programs in both Amasha and El-Arian. Their facilities are meager but evidently adequate. So far the emphasis seems to be on small arms and defensive measures."

"What about heavy weapons?" Esmaili thought that surely the defenders would upgrade their defenses in the face of the new threat.

"There is no information as yet. But we should expect that they will add more as the situation develops."

Esmaili fidgeted and eyed Rezvani. The man seemed capable enough but he spoke little and asked no questions. Apparently he was willing to conduct operations exactly as ordered—the perfect soldier to some minds. "My brother, I ask about the militia's weapons because I believe we need to plan ahead of events. For example, if we are expected to seize one or both villages, we will need more information. And more men."

The statement carried implicit questions that Azizi recognized, even if he was unwilling to answer them. "At present we have no such intentions. Our part in the overall plan is to occupy the defenders of both places while our brothers expand their control over the surrounding territory. Meanwhile, we continue as directed. We will keep the Druze occupied with sniping and mortar attacks, day and night." He paused, seemingly pondering whether he should elaborate. Then he stood. "I leave you both to continue your work."

Ahmad Esmaili knew when he had been dismissed. He returned to his subordinates, musing whom he should next send within range of the sharp-shooting mercenaries.

AMASHA

The rock exploded with abrupt violence, sending shattered stones in all directions.

Everybody hit the deck.

Breezy found himself cheek by jowl with Rami Hamadeh, the IDF liaison officer for the Amasha militia. The American raised his face from the sandy soil. "Welcome to the war, Lieutenant."

Hamadeh crayfished several meters along the base of the rock wall, then raised his head for a quick look. Breezy was quick to offer an opinion. "Nothin' to see out there?"

"The sniper could be anywhere. He will keep up a harassing fire until he tires of the game."

"Or until we nail his sorry ass." Breezy looked around for Leopole or Barrkman. "That's the trouble with countersnipers. They're like cops. Never one around when you want one."

Lacking an appreciation for American humor, Hamadeh ignored the flippant statement. Instead, he rolled onto his back, cupped his hands around his mouth, and shouted to the Dashika crew atop the nearby house. The gunner replied with a question while his loader and spotter seemed awestruck. In moments it was apparent why.

Pointing to their right, Hamadeh said, "Go there, ten–fifteen meters and watch for snipers. Anywhere that looks possible."

Once Breezy was in position, the Druze officer stood and pulled his binoculars from their case. He began scanning the terrain, seemingly looking for the offending Hezbollah shooter or shooters. In a few seconds he lowered the glasses and began walking along the wall.

Mark Brezyinski had seen enough displays of bravado in his life to recognize genuine courage when he saw it. He thought: *Great big brass ones. Those gomers got the windage dialed in. All they need is a little elevation and this guy's bore-sighted.* Then he returned his scan to the surrounding terrain.

Hamadeh stopped, turned around, and jogged back. He

passed behind Breezy and went several more paces in a long, slow lope, then halted again.

Another rifle shot split the air. It passed somewhere above the living decoy.

Hamadeh remained in place, peering through his binoculars again. He remained until another round snapped out, apparently from a different location. The IDF man went to his knees and turned toward the elevated machine gun. At that moment the Russian weapon pounded out an authoritative tattoo: six- and eight-round bursts traversing a couple of likely spots.

Breezy crawled on hands and knees to join the officer. "I couldn't see anything. But, Lieutenant, you're gonna check into a Dragunov round one of these times."

Hamadeh unzipped an ironic grin. "Ah, yes, yes. Your special forces men say, 'Rami, you will swallow a 7.62 pill.'"

"Fershure, dude."

"Pardon?"

Breezy returned the smile. "It means, my green beanie colleagues knew what they were talkin' about."

Hamadeh shook his head decisively. "No, no. I will die in bed many many years away. My mother's mother read my hand when I was born. She was never wrong."

The former paratrooper absorbed the serious sentiment from the officer who appeared so supremely confident. "Well, I loved my grandma but I wouldn't let her place a bet in Vegas for me, let alone set the odds on a freaking sniper!"

"Well, yes, Mr. B. Your grandmother, she was not a Druze!"

27

Essam Tawfiq was an experienced fighter but he had little
knowledge of mortars. Consequently, Esmaili sent him to
learn by observing so he watched closely while Rezvani's
number-two team set up its 2B14 weapon. The four men
worked quickly, obviously well drilled in the process. The
gunner and his assistant had established a prominent tree
stump on the near horizon as their marker stake, and they
could shift aim from there.

The A-gunner was friendly, apparently proud of his
weapon and his role. "We can traverse a total of eight degrees, which is adequate for our need. The elevation varies
between forty-five and eighty-five degrees."

"Why is this called the 'Podnos'?"

"I am told that it is the Russian word for 'tray.'" The
man pointed to the base plate which in fact resembled a
circular serving tray.

In the gathering dusk the crew set out a pile of 3.1-
kilogram shells. Meanwhile, the lead gunner consulted
his compass and a topographical map of the area. He was
satisfied that he had identified his firing position within
several meters and felt confident of putting the first round
close enough to hit with the second or third. After that he
would fire three for effect, dismount the tube, plate, and
tripod, and be gone in the Toyota "technical" in a matter
of minutes.

As leader of the security element, Tawfiq was responsible for getting his flankers and the forward observer back
to base. It was not a cheery prospect. He sidled up to

Hazim. "Be prepared to move as soon as the weapon is loaded in the vehicle."

The youngster nodded silently, fondling the case containing the dead Israeli's night scope. The sky was still too light for the specialized optic, and much as he relished the thought of using it on a genuine target, he did not want to use up valuable tube life unnecessarily.

NORTHERN ISRAEL

Yakov Livni was about as grumpy as a colonel can be in a general's office. After twice insisting to Solomon Nadel's chief of staff that a meeting was urgently required, the visitor from special operations was politely invited to cool his heels until the staff meeting was over.

Ninety-five minutes later the officers began filing out of the inner sanctum, bringing Livni to his feet. Since he outranked most of the conferees, Livni felt little reluctance in bulling his way past the juniors and barely excusing himself when he collided with other colonels. He reached the door of Nadel's office to find the brigade commander engaged in conversation with a lieutenant colonel and a major, neither of whom took much notice of the interloper. From the murmured conversation, Livni inferred that the subject was less important than his own, so he barged ahead.

"General, thank you for seeing me on such short notice!" Livni stomped into the room, displacing the light colonel en route, and plunked a manila folder onto the desk with a resounding thud. "Since we both know that time is short, I'll get right to the point." He helped himself to the nearest chair, still warm from recent occupancy, and flipped the folder.

The major craned his neck, trying to assess the import of so rude an entry, but Livni slapped the folder shut. Looking up, he declared, "I'm sorry, gentlemen, but you will have to excuse us. This material is for Sol's eyes only."

Nadel's expression turned from displeasure to indulgence as he nodded to the officers. "I'll see you tomorrow morning, boys."

When the major closed the door behind him, Nadel leaned across the desk. "Yakov, what in the hell is so damned important that you have to . . ."

Livni held up a reconnaissance photograph. Nadel took it, examined it, and handed it back. "Where was that taken?"

"Twelve kilometers south of Hasbaya. You recognize the layout."

"It looks like an excavation for a missile site."

The smile was back on Livni's moon face. "You missed your calling, Solly. You should have been a photo interpreter instead of a general."

Nadel tapped the folder. "What else do you have in there? And where did you get this material, anyway? That sort of intelligence is supposed to come . . ."

"Oh, never mind. You would see this information eventually, but because of my uncommon intellect and special connections, sometimes I get interesting items ahead of some important people. Even generals."

Nadel sat down and opened the folder. It contained other photos and some intelligence summaries. At length he looked up. "Yakov, you're not telling me something. This is all very interesting—even important. But it's beyond my area of operations unless we're about to invade Nabatiyeh Governate. And unless you just got a huge promotion, you don't give that order."

"Sol, let me tell you what I think."

"As if I have a choice."

Livni ignored the good-natured quip. "These recon images show at least two sites within several kilometers of Hasbaya with evidence of surveying a third. Now, of course Hezbollah has long-range missiles, and certainly is willing to use them. But to what purpose? I mean, unless they're content just to lob some occasional rockets at your headquarters and the surrounding area, what's the point? They know it will invite retaliation."

Nadel frowned in concentration. "Well, depending on the type of missiles, basing them there, they could hit as far south as—"

"A Fajr 5 wouldn't reach Haifa but a Zelzal could hit Nablus, or even farther depending on the model."

The general stood up and began pacing, as he often did when he wanted to think. "Yakov, it just doesn't make much sense. Hezbollah doesn't telegraph its blows like this. There's not even any attempt at camouflage."

"Correct."

Nadel pulled up short. "Well then?"

"Well then, I think your boys should be more worried about what's not evident in these pictures than what is."

"You believe this is a deception? Something to move our focus elsewhere?"

Livny slapped the desk. "General, you show real promise. Remind me to recommend you for a promotion the next time I dine with my cousin, the deputy defense minister."

"All right, all right. I'll put the brigade on enhanced alert. We'll increase patrols, looking for more infiltrators, that sort of thing."

"It's a good start, Sol."

"Sure, but it's only a start considering I don't know what I'm looking for."

Yakov Livny picked up the folder and prepared to leave. "That makes you a member of a big club, my friend."

EL-ARIAN

Two groups of men hunted through the Lebanese night, each seeking its prey without full knowledge of the other.

Using a commercial GPS unit purchased in Beirut, Tawfiq directed Rezvani's mortar team to its predetermined firing position almost three kilometers from the village. The experienced crew needed only minutes to set up and prepare to fire, but establishing radio contact with the forward observer took longer. That vital member of the team had carefully selected his vantage point well away from the weapon site.

After ensuring that his security element was properly positioned, Tawfiq hastened back to the firing point. He found Rezvani on the radio to his FO.

"Jinn, this is Dancer. Reply." Rezvani double-clicked the transmit button to ensure that the listener knew the message was ended. He pressed his earphones with his left hand, as if squeezing more performance from the set. Finally he looked at Tawfiq. "He was preparing himself just a moment ago."

TWO KILOMETERS TO THE west, a Litton night-vision scope was put to use. The image glowed greenly on the CRT, showing a human form via infrared heat. The viewer tweaked the focus knob. Finally Josh Wallender turned to Captain Fares. "They came where you said they would. Confirmed hostile. He has a radio and a guard."

The Israeli Druze nodded in silent acceptance of the compliment. In truth, however, he did not consider his coup a significant achievement. Once it was known where FOs had operated previously, it was a safe bet that they would not return to those spots very often. Then it was a matter of deducing which new vantages were most useful and assigning the other two teams accordingly.

"We will wait a little," Fares whispered. "Ayoob Slim's team might find something as well, and we could take two observers."

The American rolled his shoulders to ease the muscular tension. He was accustomed to hunting humans in the dark, but the stationary position led to cramps. "It's up to you, Captain, but the longer we wait the more likely they'll drop some rounds on the town."

"Yes. But the first shells are almost always off target. That gives time to decide the best course."

"But how do we know where the first rounds hit? We can't see what the observer does because he's always in position to do just that."

A gunshot shattered the night. Wallender's pulse spiked at the sonic blast. Its piercing decibels startled everyone in the group, all of whom would have dived for cover if they were not already prone.

Fares turned, immediately grasping what had happened. He asked if anybody were injured. Receiving negative replies, he loosened a stream of heartfelt invective at the militiaman who had carried a rifle with a round chambered, safety off, and finger on the trigger.

The offender was simultaneously appalled at his slovenliness and the humiliation heaped upon him. Belatedly he complied with the Israeli's order to lay down the AK and step back. Despite the darkness, in one fluid motion Fares scooped it up, pulled the magazine, and cycled the bolt. A cartridge was ejected from the chamber, tumbling to the ground.

Fares handed the empty rifle to another Druze, then turned to Wallender. "We cannot stay here very long. Do you still see the men?"

Wallender returned his attention to the Hezbollah team's previous position. He scanned left and right. "Nothing. They're gone."

THREE HUNDRED METERS AWAY, Rob Furr and his companions heard the shot. He knew the hunter's conventional wisdom: One shot, meat. Two shots, maybe. Three shots, none. He thought: *Somebody just got whacked.*

In moments Wallender's baritone was on the tactical frequency. "Trigger, this is Scope, over."

Furr keyed his mike. "Scope, Trigger. Go."

"Ah, be advised. We had some tangos but one idiot just had a November Delta here. We're moving. Over."

Furr indulged in some heartfelt blasphemy, angry at missing an opportunity. He forced himself to concentrate. "Roger, Scope. We'll stay put for a while in case something comes this way. Out."

The sniper turned to Ashcroft and the English-speaking militiamen. "One of Josh's people just had a negligent discharge. They're moving to the fallback position."

REZVANI HEARD THE CARRIER wave and concentrated on the cryptic message. Then he looked at Tawfiq. "There was a shot somewhere near the observer position. My men are taking a circular route back. We will fire a few bombs on the approximate azimuth and displace."

Before Tawfiq could reply, Rezvani was hissing orders to the mortar team. The gunner spun the traverse wheel, checked the elevation, and nodded. The A-gunner had prepped three rounds and had them close at hand. All three went down the tube in less than five seconds. Before the last one had landed, the tube was being dismounted from the base plate. Thirty seconds later the bipod was disconnected and being carried to the vehicle.

Rezvani grasped Tawfiq's arm. "I will take one security man to help guard the weapon. You take the other and meet the observers at the alternate point. They do not know the terrain like you do. We will drive there and return you to the base."

Tawfiq was unconvinced of the wisdom of separating the team in the darkness, let alone possibly near an alerted enemy, but there was no time to argue. Rezvani was on his way, leaving Hazim with Tawfiq. The commander and his lead sniper set out cross-country.

JOSH WALLENDER HAD THE point with the best night-vision optic. He moved steadily but cautiously, stopping occasionally to allow the rest of the team to keep up with him and maintain proper interval. Fares was next in line, better to communicate with the Arabic speakers. Since he could not read a compass with the NVG in place, he navigated by guesstimate.

Without realizing it, en route to the alternate position, Wallender took a wrong turn. He moved more northerly than intended, owing to a stony crag that blocked the direct line. Though he intended to resume his previous route, the erratic outline of the crag conspired with darkness and poor footing to put him thirty degrees off track.

Salah-Hassan Fares knew the area far better than the American but had seldom ventured out at night. Using a red-lensed penlight, he took occasional compass readings to their direction but could not consult his topographic map on the move. He made a mental note to bring Wallender back on course once the terrain evened out.

Half an hour later there occurred what military professionals call a meeting engagement.

ESSAM TAWFIQ NEVER WOULD have admitted that he was lost. But beneath a quarter moon, the ambient light was insufficient to find his way visually, and the often rough terrain had forced several detours. When he realized that he could not recognize any landmarks, enough time had passed that he knew he had missed the forward observer team.

Tawfiq stopped, gesturing Hazim to keep back. The leader then knelt behind a tree and pressed the transmit button. "Jinn, this is Tawfiq. Reply."

When two other attempts produced no response, he

switched frequencies and made the call he did not want to make. "Dancer, this is Tawfiq. Reply."

The response came through muted but legible. "This is Dancer. Where are you? Reply."

"I am looking for Jinn."

"He called ten minutes ago, looking for you!" There was an insistent pause. "Reply!"

Tawfiq considered his response before keying the mike. "I am . . ."

"TANGOS! LEFT FRONT!"

Wallender saw one human form in his goggles and another heat source behind it. It was usually difficult to estimate distance with NVGs, but surely the strangers were within the two-hundred-meter zero of his sights. He went to kneeling, aware that Fares and Ashcroft had deployed either side of him.

"No joy," Ashcroft said.

"I'm on 'em." Furr assumed a braced standing position, leveling his Robar custom rifle in the notch of a tree. The night scope's reticle settled on the nearer form.

Wallender's mind raced. The odds that two or more friendlies would be somewhere ahead of his group approached absolute zero but he could not afford to take chances. He spoke into his headset. "Slim, this is Josh, over."

Phil Green replied. "Slim Six actual is nearby. You need him?"

"Negative, Phil. I need to know your posit, definitely. Over."

"We're still at our briefed position. No joy here."

"Roger that. We got bogies in front of us. Over."

Seconds ticked past. "You need help?"

Wallender shook his head, as if Green could see him. "Negative. Will advise, out."

He turned to either side. "Tangos are hostile. Repeat, tangos are considered hostile."

Ashcroft asked, "Shall we flank 'em?"

"No, keep everybody together. It's bad enough in the dark."

HAZIM SCANNED THE AREA while Tawfiq talked on the radio. On the second sweep his captured Galil with the night sight picked up two or three human forms. He rode the adrenaline spike, then relaxed slightly. *The observer team at last!*

The youngster took several steps forward, tapped Tawfiq on the shoulder, and pointed into the dark. "I believe the observers are less than seventy meters ahead." He assumed a sitting position.

"What? Where?"

Hazim was tempted to hand the Galil to his superior so Tawfiq could look for himself but thought better of it. "Call them, brother."

It was the best news Tawfiq had heard all night. He stood up and keyed the mike. "Jinn, I think we see you. Reply. Now!"

When no response came, Tawfiq began feeling more anger than caution. He took several steps forward, raising his voice. "Jinn! Reply!"

THE FIRST ROUND FROM Furr's rifle took the leading Hezbollah man almost on the notch of the sternum. The impact drove him to the ground, where he rolled over and muttered liquid syllables.

Hazim immediately put his scope on the most prominent target, remembered to control his breath, and pressed the trigger. He repeated the process five times, each aimed at a different shape.

ROB FURR WAS AN expert rifleman; he could cycle his bolt-action weapon almost as fast as he could produce aimed fire from a semiauto. But the volume of incoming Dragunov rounds provided a temporary advantage to the Hezbollah sniper.

Hazim's first round had missed its mark but struck the disarmed militiaman several meters behind its intended target. The youngster cried aloud, grasped his shoulder, and fell to one side. The second round destroyed Josh Wallender's night-vision device, sending metal fragments into his face. The third and fourth rounds struck Furr's tree, forcing him to seek cover.

The fifth round killed Salah-Hassan Fares. The sixth went somewhere into the Nabatiyeh darkness.

With a last wide-eyed look at Tawfiq's body, Hazim scrambled across the rocky ground, fleeing that dreadful place.

28

SSI OFFICES

"How bad is it?" Derringer knew only the basics of the previous e-mail from Lebanon.

Sandra Carmichael checked her scribbled notes. "I just talked to Frank on the satellite phone. Our El-Arian team—that's Chris Nissen's—was involved in counter-sniper and security operations last night. They were out with some militia looking for a mortar that had been dropping rounds in the area lately. Apparently they ran into the Hezbollah security element and there was a fire-fight. Josh Wallender took a round to his NVG and may be blind in one eye. Anyway, Terry Keegan is going to bring him home from Beirut."

Marsh Wilmont asked, "What about the other casualties, Sandy?"

"One of the Druze leaders was KIA and another militiaman was wounded."

"Who was the leader?"

Carmichael squinted at her handwriting. "Fares. Salah—something—Fares. He was the IDF contact for the El-Arian unit."

Wilmont expelled his breath, drumming his fingers on the table. "Not that it really matters, but any word on hostile casualties?"

"Rob Furr got off the first round and apparently that guy's a KIA though nobody went looking for bodies. As Frank said, there wasn't time to score and paste targets. After that, the hostile sniper or snipers opened up and achieved fire superiority. Then they broke contact and disappeared."

Derringer was clearly troubled. "If that's an accurate report, we finished on the short end of a three-to-one score." He shook his head. "How did that happen? We're supposed to be better than that."

Carmichael's rebel blood began stirring. "Excuse me, Admiral. But this was a collision of two maneuvering forces at fairly long range in the dark. Frank's not making excuses but he says the whole thing lasted about fifteen seconds, if that. Furr was the only one to make an aimed shot because only he had a night scope. The opposition had semiautos, probably Dragunovs, and they throw more lead than a bolt gun."

The SSI president saw the fire in the blue eyes and backed off. "All right, Sandy. All right. But if we understaffed this job, we need to send more people." He thought for a moment. "Can we send a replacement for Wallender?" He looked at Jack Peters, head of scouting and recruiting.

The former Green Beret almost smiled. "Admiral, I'd be

willing to go myself! But since that's not why I was hired, I should be able to turn up a couple of guys. However, you understand, neither of them are going to be as well quali-fied as those we already have over there. We really did send the first team, especially where language is concerned."

Marsh Wilmont leaned forward. "According to Morde-cai Baram, everybody's happy with the progress the Druze are making with our instructors. But we did expect casual-ties on this contract. That's why we have a few guys suited up, sitting on the bench."

"How soon can they get over there?"

Peters frowned in concentration. "I'll have to check, but probably not before the end of next week."

Derringer turned to Carmichael. "Sandy, let Frank know that we're lining up two replacements. Obviously one will fill in for Wallender, then Frank or Chris can decide where to put the other. But with things heating up, it's probably best to have another man there right away."

The blond head bobbed. "Concur, Admiral. The new guys will need some time to get up to speed in any event."

"Speaking of Wallender, I want him to get the best pos-sible care. If we have to pay some out-of-pocket expenses for the best specialist, so be it." He looked at Wilmont.

"I'll make it happen, Mike."

NABATIYEH GOVERNATE

Esmaili sat with Azizi, considering tactical options within the context of the emerging strategic plan.

"Tawfiq will not be easy to replace," Esmaili said. "He was my best and most experienced man."

The liaison man from Tehran slightly cocked his head, studying the Hezbollah leader. "You fought together for a long time."

A quick nod. "To lose him in a relatively minor mission is . . . regrettable." Esmaili managed to keep an even tone in his voice.

"Well, he now sits in Paradise. Allow your sorrow to be eased with that knowledge."

For an ephemeral moment Ahmad Esmaili felt himself warming to the go-between. Then he caught himself. *Show no weakness. It can lead to mistakes. And mistakes can be fatal.*

"Truly." After a suitable pause Esmaili asked, "How shall we proceed?"

Azizi relaxed. "As much as Brother Tawfiq will be missed, we are to continue our operations. Your young marksman, Hazim. He did well."

"So it seems."

The cocked head again. "There are doubts?"

"Brother, there are always doubts after combat. Especially after a fight in the dark. I do not doubt Hazim's belief in what he told us. But with no one else to describe the action, it is impossible to know for certain."

"Yes, of course. That is why I have sent agents to El-Arian. They may learn something in addition to what our signals branch reports on militia radio intercepts."

Esmaili frowned despite himself. "Why the concern? As I say, it was a small incident except for the loss of Tawfiq."

"I remember what you said about the phantom sniper in Baghdad. Juba?"

"Yes, I discussed that with Tawfiq. It's not certain that he was real. Why?"

"We might make use of young Hazim. Build up his reputation, perhaps even using his real name. It could cause fear in the militias while we continue sending your other snipers to harass them."

Esmaili realized that he may have condemned the youngster by a casual discussion with the now-deceased instructor. "If he gains enough of a reputation, he will certainly be hunted down and killed."

Azizi rolled his shoulders. "We all serve God in our own way, brother. Meanwhile, I have sent for help."

"What kind of help?"

"A Chechen sniper, vastly experienced. You know that Chechen Muslims are mostly Sunni. Well, the fighter known as Akhmed grew up sniping Russians and has trained resistance fighters in Afghanistan. He has more than two hundred hits to his credit."

Esmaili was tempted to smile. "There are claims and there are results. They are not always the same."

With a wave of a hand, Azizi placated his colleague. "It does not matter. The important thing is that Akhmed has skills well beyond any of your . . . er, our men. His identity will be kept secret but his deeds can be publicized to our benefit."

"In other words, to Hazim's detriment."

"As I said, we all serve God in our own way."

NORTHERN ISRAEL

For a change, Brigadier General Nadel went looking for Colonel Livni. Not surprisingly, the senior officer found his nominal subordinate engaged in a shouting match with a sergeant. The colonel won, not from a position of greater authority, but the ability to summon greater decibels.

The NCO offered a perfunctory salute and stalked away.

"What was *that* about?" Nadel asked.

Livni waved dismissively. "Oh, Feldmann throws occasional tantrums. He can't stand the thought that somebody else might know as much as he does."

Nadel arched an eyebrow. "A sergeant resents a colonel's level of knowledge? That's one for the record book."

"I've known Feldmann for ten years or more. One of the smartest people I ever met but he's a victim of his own intellect."

"How's that?"

"Well, he's turned down a commission at least twice. His family are all fervent socialists, some from the old school. They equate officers with snobbery and privilege so he wouldn't ever consider joining the 'elite.'" Livni etched quote marks in the air with both hands.

"So why keep him around? Is he so bright that he's worth the effort?"

"Mostly he's just a pain in the ass, but now and then he comes up with something really useful. Sometimes it's a fresh way of looking at an old problem."

Nadel leaned forward. "Yakov, you always pique my curiosity. May I ask what's the problem this time?"

"Peanut butter."

The general's face betrayed incredulity. Before Nadel could respond, Livni explained. "There's a big dispute in some orthodox communities about whether peanuts can be used during Passover. You know, like other legumes. I told Feldmann that the Ashkenazi don't allow peanuts but do allow peanut oil, which is true. And presumably kosher peanut butter should be allowed. Since he's not Ashkenazi it's not really a concern but he disagrees." Livni shrugged. "Feldmann often disagrees just to be disagreeable."

While Nadel absorbed that revelation, Livni folded his arms and tapped his toes. "What can I do for you, General?"

Nadel shook his head as if avoiding a pesky gnat. "Get rid of that damned sergeant. He's undermining your morale and the national war effort."

"Well, as long as I run special operations, I'll keep some special people around me. Now, what's on your mind?"

"I got your message about the militia situation in El-Arian. I agree they're going to need a Druze officer to replace Captain Fares."

Livni nodded slowly, pondering options. "Do you have anyone in mind?"

"I'm thinking of Hussain Halabi. A bright, energetic lieutenant. Do you know him?"

"I've heard of him." The colonel unzipped a wry grin. "But God deliver us from bright, energetic lieutenants!"

"Well, he has some experience over there and I think he would fit in. Besides, he's the best English speaker among the likely candidates, and that's important."

"Agreed. The militia is asking for more American instructors but that's going to take a little time. The way things are going in that area, they might not arrive soon enough to make a difference."

Nadel inclined his torso, obviously interested. "Why? What have you heard?"

"I don't think I've heard much more than you have, Sol. But the way I see things, there's likely to be more Hezbollah activity than before. It could lead to something bigger than we've seen in quite a while."

"All right, then. I'll make sure that my boys keep their contingency plans updated." He wagged a cautionary finger. "Just don't let me be surprised, Colonel!"

29

SSI OFFICES

"Okay, who can we send? I have to let the admiral or Marsh Wilmont know today." Sandra Carmichael did not like to lean on a colleague, but time was short and getting shorter.

Matt Finch of SSI's personnel department was ready

for the inquiry. "Ken Delmore's ready to go and Steve Lee says he'll commit to a couple of months if we really need him. But that's going to cause problems."

"Yes, I know. Wallender was committed to the full contract, so if Steve only signs on for sixty days we'll end up short again."

Finch nodded. "Yes, but there's more than that. I mean, he's a former major and a Ranger to boot. How's he going to fit in with Nissen's team? They don't know each other very well, and I just don't see Staff Sergeant Nissen rolling over for a new guy O-4." He shrugged. "It could cause more problems than it solves."

Carmichael leaned back and examined her manicured nails. "Well, one thing's for sure. We can't tell the operators in the field how to do things. I'll get hold of Frank and see what he says. Maybe the best bet is to reshuffle the deck. Send Delmore to Nissen and transfer one of Frank's people as well. Then Lee can understudy Frank—maybe work as his exec."

Finch gave a toothy grin. "Colonel, did you ever consider a career in the personnel field?"

Carmichael speared the human resources dweeb with her blue gaze. "Negative. Not once. Not ever."

NABATIYEH GOVERNATE

Hazim was the man of the hour. Though trying to maintain Muslim decorum, he simply could not suppress the soaring feeling of ego gratification.

It was delicious.

Azizi added spice to the taste by openly lauding Hazim. "Our sources are clear, my brothers. Hazim fearlessly engaged a superior number of the enemy and killed or wounded three of them. He is our lion! Learn from him and become lions yourselves!"

Sharp male roars erupted from the jihadists, reducing in the end to a rhythmic chant. "Ha-zim! Ha-zim!"

Standing behind the crowd, Esmaili permitted himself a sardonic smile. He recalled the debriefing after Larijani returned without Beirut.

"How many rounds did you fire?"

"Ah, five or six."

"And how many hits did you gain?"

"Ah . . . I do not know, Teacher. It happened so . . ."

"A good sniper knows where the sights are when the bullet fires. That tells him whether he hit or missed."

Now all that was suppressed, never to arise.

Azizi waved down the cheering fighters. Esmaili actually thought that the man seemed to believe everything he was declaring. "Hazim has spilled the blood of our enemies before, and now he adds to the count even at night. He should be the model for us all, and I promise you, brothers—he will have every chance to do so again!"

More cheers erupted from the crowd. Even Ebrahim Larijani joined in the chorus, seemingly recovered from his lesser notoriety at surviving the Beirut mission.

"Learn the lesson, O my brothers!" Azizi's voice rose in pitch as the spirit came upon him. Or, as Esmaili cynically surmised, as the manipulator arose in him. "The product of slaying the infidel is not merely reducing his numbers. It is instilling fear in the black hearts of the survivors. We shall multiply that fear by making known the names of our finest warriors. I promise you, the name of Hazim is being known and feared by our enemies!"

AMASHA

Frank Leopole convened his team members on short notice. "There's been some developments that you guys need to know about. Rather than recycle the intel, I'll have Captain Hamadeh fill you in."

The Israeli Druze officer stepped to the head of the room. "You know of the incident a few nights ago when Captain Fares was killed and Mr. Wallender was wounded. We are hearing from believable sources that it was the work of a particular sniper with a Hezbollah unit in this area. He is called Hazim. We do not know much about him, other than he is young and apparently experienced. The fact that his name has been released indicates that Hezbollah places considerable faith in him. It is not entirely unknown for particular fighters to receive such attention, but often it turns to a propaganda ploy."

Rick Barrkman took a special interest in his opposite number. "Captain, you say that he's young and experienced. How do we know that?"

"There have been two radio broadcasts extolling this Hazim. They were monitored by our signals intelligence."

"So we really don't know how authentic the info is."

"No. As I said, it could be propaganda, but the details of the latest incident indicate otherwise. My special operations contacts treat Hazim as a genuine threat."

The other Americans were serious, silent, and focused. Leopole took them in: Bosco and Breezy plus Robert Pitney. At length Breezy asked, "So are we gonna hunt for this guy or what?"

Leopole interjected. "We are not. It's possible that's what they want us to do. Otherwise there's not much reason to put some shooter in the spotlight—distract us with a stalking horse."

Hamadeh cocked his head. "Stalking horse?"

"It's a deception. Goes way back to the early days of hunting when animals were scared off by humans but a horse or cattle distracted the game's attention from the hunter. In this case, Hazim or whoever he is could be intended to make us look over our shoulders when something's coming from another direction."

While the Israeli absorbed that esoterica, Barrkman pursued his own line of thought. "Hezbollah definitely has more than one shooter. This Hazim might be their star but he can't be everywhere. I wonder if he's really doing the job or maybe taking credit for everybody who gets lucky."

Leopole unzipped a wry grin. "Why, Mr. Barrkman, you sound downright cynical."

"Guilty, your honor." The sniper laughed. "But I was just thinking, there's examples from history of super snipers who probably didn't exist. At Stalingrad the top Russian shooter supposedly had a duel with the top German and finally killed him. But it turned out that there was never a German sniper with the supposed name—Thorvald or Koenings. Just Communist propaganda."

"So how would you like to proceed?"

"Let's see if this Hazim dude turns up again. If so, Rob and I can whack him."

Leopole shot a glance toward Hamadeh. "Maybe that's what they want us to do. Commit our first team."

"Well, maybe so. But I'd like to talk to Rob, Colonel. He's the only one we know of who's tangled with this turkey, and he might have a take on him that only a sniper would know."

The SSI leader realized the wisdom of Barrkman's approach, and decided to concede. "All right. You can huddle with Furr, but I do not want both of you operating together without a solid plan. Keep me informed."

"Gotcha, Boss."

EL-ARIAN

As a Special Forces NCO, Chris Nissen had become accustomed to losses and to changes in plans. Now he tried to juggle both while working above and below his level of authority.

He pulled Green and Ashcroft off the morning's training cycle to impart some information and seek advice.

"I just heard from Colonel Leopole. The office back home is sending two standby guys in a few days. Neither of them have language ability that's useful but they're experienced operators. So I'll continue translating here."

Green chewed his mustache for a moment. "Well, we sure can use some help, but mainly I wonder about the Druze situation. Since Fares got whacked, who's going to replace him? I mean, obviously we can't operate very well without a bilingual liaison officer."

Nissen glanced over the operator's shoulder. Rob Furr was working with Ayoob Slim's people thanks to a militiaman who spoke passable English. "We're about to get more shorthanded. Frank's pulling Furr out of here to work with Barrkman on some countersniper job. He leaves tomorrow."

Bob Ashcroft resorted to mental arithmetic. "The way I count it, that leaves us with three and—what? Thirty or thirty-five militia?"

Nissen rubbed the back of his neck, grateful that his African DNA had prepared him for an oppressive, overhead sun. "About that. Slim there says it varies from day to day, depending on duty rotation and personal or family matters." He shrugged philosophically. "It's an old story. Goes with the militia lashup."

"How's that?" Ashcroft asked.

"Well, that's the thing about a militia, you know? It's not a standing force, which means that you go with whoever's suited up at the kickoff."

Green chuckled. "Like the Minutemen who'd fire one or two shots and skedaddle when the redcoats approached. Or the Continental militia who went home to harvest in the summer."

"You got it, bro."

Ashcroft looked behind him again. "Are these guys ready for prime time?"

Chris Nissen unzipped a toothy smile. "That's what's so damned fascinating about this business. You never really know until it's showtime. And then it's too late."

30

NABATIYEH GOVERNATE

The visiting dignitary was known as Akhmed. The Chechen sniper arrived with two packs, a custom rifle case, and a significant reputation. In his travels his score was said to run upward of two hundred Russians, treacherous Afghans, collaborationist Iraqis, invading Americans, and assorted other infidels. It was said that he never missed.

Esmaili did not believe it; neither did Hazim, who now admitted that he missed fairly often.

Nevertheless, Esmaili and Azizi were present to greet Akhmed when he stepped out of the truck. Azizi took the lead. "Brother, welcome! Your presence here honors us all."

Akhmed bowed his head in deference to the homage paid him. He muttered a perfunctory response that was barely audible and shook hands without conviction. Esmaili would have dismissed him as a dilettante but for the eyes, dark and peering. Many Muslims avoided direct eye contact. Not the Chechen. He looked directly at each Hezbollah officer, as if trying to see what lay behind their own eyes.

The three quickly got down to business.

Settling in a secluded cabin, Azizi and Esmaili briefed the master sniper on their plan. "We know that your time here is limited," Azizi began. "Therefore, we will make it as useful and . . . profitable . . . as possible."

Esmaili shot a look at his colleague. Nothing had been said about payment for Akhmed's services. The Iranian looked at the Chechen with surging ambivalence: respect for his record and questions about his motives. *Well, he has to eat like the rest of us.* But Esmaili wondered how so devout a fighter as Azizi got his philosophical fingers around the notion of a mercenary who was well paid for slaying God's enemies. Let alone Imam Elham.

Akhmed nodded his appreciation. He was a tall, spare man in his late thirties or early forties. He moved smoothly, confidently, and seemed to expend his words as economically as his ammunition. "I shall want to see the ground as soon as possible. Today, even. After that we can talk again and make more definite plans."

"Yes, of course," Azizi replied. "Brother Esmaili is completely familiar with the area around both villages."

Akhmed turned to Esmaili and focused on him. The Iranian was mildly upset to discover that he found the attention unwelcome. *He looks at me as if through a scope.* On the other hand, Akhmed the Sniper probably looked at everyone that way. Esmaili tried to envision two hundred kills, or merely two hundred hits. Never a scorekeeper, he acknowledged that most of his victims had been killed at close range from his early days on the firing squads.

Close range—what range does this Akhmed prefer?

"Brother, the terrain around Amasha and El-Arian is similar. We can insert you into favorable positions from two to perhaps six hundred meters."

"I usually fire from two hundred meters for head shots,"

Akhmed responded. "On a standing man, between four and five hundred."

Is that all? Esmaili hoped that his disappointment was well concealed. "What rifle do you shoot?"

"A modified Dragunov. It is not my first choice, but the British AWC that I prefer was ruined in a recent operation. With that, I was confident out to seven hundred meters."

Esmaili merely nodded. He knew that the AWC PM was effective well beyond seven hundred. Rather than press the matter, he concluded, "You should have something to eat, then we can examine the terrain."

Leaving their guest to have lunch, the Hezbollah men stepped well away. "I did not know he shoots for hire," Esmaili began. The tone in his voice said, *As you failed to tell me*.

Azizi took no offense. "It is his way, and his services are invaluable. God will know Akhmed's heart and his worth at the proper time."

Esmaili was disinclined to discourse on religious matters. "I can understand his concern with the Dragunov, but the British rifle is capable of far more than seven hundred meters. Certainly nine hundred—with a capable marksman."

"Oh, Akhmed is certainly capable. But he only shoots when he is confident of a kill. That is part of his fee: a bonus for every observed hit. Therefore, he seldom works with a regular spotter. Whomever we assign to him will also serve as . . . how would you say it? A tabulator?"

Esmaili folded his arms, assuming a petulant posture. "And our man? What does he receive for his services?"

"Let us hope he does not receive a bullet through his head. But to answer your question, brother, our man will have the knowledge that he serves Allah."

"Of course, my brother. Of course."

AMASHA

"Your mission is this Hazim character. He's out there. Find him, shoot him, and don't get hurt."

Rob Furr and Rick Barrkman absorbed Frank Leopole's directive. But their pleasure at being reunited was marred by the onerous chore of locating an elusive shooter who devoutly wished to remain hidden. Both snipers knew how tediously dangerous their job could become.

Furr was smart and capable but also cautious. "Colonel, isn't it possible that the Hezzies want us to go looking for this guy? They probably know there's only two of us with this training team."

"Rick and I have already discussed that. In fact, we talked to Captain Hamadeh about it. So, yes, this Hazim or whoever he is might be a stalking horse to draw us out. But apart from the Hezzies' propaganda, we know that somebody out there is a decent shot, and I believe in preventive medicine rather than trauma treatment."

Barrkman had studied the area topographic maps and narrowed the likely hides near both villages. "Skipper, we'd double our chances of tapping this guy if we split up and work with other spotters. Rob and I might be willing to do that, but there's no reason to think Hazim works alone. If it comes to a real sniper duel, it could be more of a tag team event than one on one."

Leopole's square jaw was thrust outward. "Concur. That's why I brought you guys together again. We'll go with our strength for starters and see what turns up. If there's no definite results after a few days, we can split up."

Furr squirmed slightly, shifting his feet. "So, how do we know if we bag this bird? I mean, even if we get the body he probably won't have ID on him. It's not like there'll be a big sign saying, 'Congratulations, you just snuffed Hazim.'"

"Good point. I guess we'll know if their sniper activity falls off. If not, it means it's not him or they have other talent. In either case, we're ahead if you whack one of their shooters."

Furr and Barrkman gave each other approving glances. The personal nature of the contest appealed to their competitive spirits.

"Another thing," Leopole added. "This isn't like the usual sniper or even countersniper operation. Basically, we've been called out and it's high noon on Main Street in Dodge City. In other words, it's a duel. But there's more riding on this than just who walks away. Hezbollah will learn something about us depending on whether we accept the challenge or not. So the fact that you guys are out there hunting Hazim tells the opposition that we're not playing safe. We're here and we mean to stay."

"Don't worry, Skipper," Barrkman chirped. "If we find him, we'll kill him."

Leopole tipped his cap back on his head and rubbed his chin. He thought for a moment, then looked both shooters full in the face. "That's the way to think of it, you're the hunters, but you're hunting other predators. They may have more experience than you do, and presumably they know the land better. But I'm confident that you're both more proficient, and I think you're smarter." He grinned. "Guys, just don't get wrapped around your egos. Keep your heads in the game without worrying about what the Druze or I or anybody else thinks. At the same time, realize that you're going up against a specific individual who's proven that he's dangerous, day or night."

Furr recited something he had heard long ago. "Colonel, I respect my enemy but I don't fear him."

"Who said that?"

"Me!"

Leopole snorted. "Like hell you did!"

Furr toed the ground, glancing into the dirt. Finally he conceded, "I think it's from an old samurai movie."

"Well, you don't look like any samurai I ever saw. But forget that bushido bullshit. There's no warrior's code out there, guys. There's only winners and losers."

31

NABATIYEH GOVERNATE

The imam was back from Tehran. He beckoned, and Esmaili resented the gesture to the core of his soul. The Hezbollah commander also detested the sentiment behind the come-hither motion, for it screamed a tacit message: *I command and you obey. Or else.*

Esmaili approached the cleric, who turned and walked into the house that served as the cell's headquarters. With a dismissive flick of the hand, Elham ordered the building emptied. In seconds Azizi appeared and the three sat down around the wooden table.

"I have received our final orders," Elham began.

Esmaili and Azizi locked eyes for an ephemeral moment. *Our final orders.* Not only did the phrase have the ring of finality, but it implied that all three jihadists were about to set foot upon their final venture. Esmaili knew from experience and a well-honed skepticism that wherever the trail led, Sadegh Elham would remain alive to tell the tale.

"We are to launch simultaneous attacks on the villages of Amasha and El-Arian. It is a maximum effort, without concern for casualties."

Esmaili's glance at Azizi said it all: *I told you so!* He wondered how long the liaison man's devotion and enthusiasm would remain intact.

Then Elham added, "That is, except for a handful of faithful fighters."

Azizi did not seem overly relieved or concerned. He merely mouthed the expected phrase, "However we may serve, Imam."

Unfolding a map, the priest spread it on the table. "Our instructions from Tehran require attacks on the villages mentioned. But they are diversions, which is why heavy losses are acceptable. The main attack will be directed elsewhere, and you will be informed when the time is right. The time will depend upon weather to cover us from enemy aircraft."

Esmaili realized that the explanation was intended for him. Apparently Azizi already knew the full plan, and that perspective did not sit well with Ahmad Esmaili. *They are close—at least far closer than I am to either of them. Therefore, I am likely expendable.*

"Imam, if I may point out something. If the main attack goes in another direction, we will have to know its strength to allocate men and supplies. Otherwise the two diversions could soak up assets that will be needed elsewhere."

Elham cocked his head slightly, scrutinizing the Hezbollah leader. The cleric's steady gaze made Esmaili infuriatingly uncomfortable. At length Elham said, "Brother, you state the obvious. *Of course* the main mission will require men and . . . special equipment. That goes without saying. You should give us credit for competent planning." Before Esmaili could respond, the priest added, "All has been considered long before now, my brother. I ask only that you place your trust in us, as you would in Allah."

Esmaili's mind raced. *They are mad: they equate their own judgment with God's!* But then he remembered his childhood instruction: certain imams were especially beloved of God, as evidenced through religious scholarship and good works. Though not equal to a caliph, whose word could not be questioned, the leaders of a defensive jihad possessed special status in The Faith.

Esmaili inclined his head. "Imam, my apologies if I seemed doubtful. But you will understand my concern for seeing to the success of whatever my part of the mission may involve." *A nice recovery,* he told himself.

Azizi sought to defuse the tension. "Brother Esmaili, it can be stated that you will have an important, even a crucial, role in the main attack. The unit you lead will be small, and therefore will not detract from either of the diversionary actions."

"And the special equipment?"

"It will be provided at the appropriate time. There will be technicians to deal with it, so that aspect should not worry you."

Esmaili rolled his shoulders, evidence of the strain he felt building inside. But as long as the commanders were talking, he decided to risk further questions. "As you wish, brother. But again: I am concerned about proper execution of the full mission. If I am to lead the main effort, who will direct the attacks on the villages?"

Azizi unzipped a smug grin. "I will. Therefore, your more important role will not be burdened with other concerns."

Esmaili felt himself blanch. Now he knew: the "main attack" would almost certainly be a suicide mission, leaving Mohammad Azizi to supervise the covering forces in relative safety.

Esmaili heard his voice say, "As you wish, brother. I am yours to command."

EL-ARIAN

"Okay, here's how it shakes out," Nissen began. Phil Green and Bob Ashcroft paid close attention: their ex-cop antennae had sensed the atmosphere and picked up the growing tension.

"HQ is sending Steve Lee and Ken Delmore. They'll be here in a couple of days. We're getting Delmore directly and Frank will send us Pitney."

Green's blue eyes lit up. "I know Ken. We worked with him in Afghanistan."

Ashcroft laughed. "Yeah, he looks like Mr. Clean on steroids. Bald as a billiard ball with twenty-inch biceps. He can prob'ly bench-press a Yugo without breaking a sweat."

Nissen almost laughed. "Well, that's fine, but I don't know him. What's his background?"

"Eighty-second all the way. Jumped into Grenada and landed on the runway. Says he was flat on the concrete with blue tracers flashing overhead and he thought, 'I spent all that time building myself up and now I just want to get small!' "

Nissen chewed on that information and was pleased with the taste. "Well, nobody mentioned any language ability but apparently he has instructor credentials."

"Sure does," Ashcroft replied. "He's been to a bunch of armorers schools and prob'ly knows more about the M16 and M4 than anybody I've ever met."

"Okay, that's fine. I'm really glad to get Pitney because of his Arabic ability because I can't do it all."

"So what's with Lee?" Green asked.

Nissen shifted his feet. "He's going to work with Frank. Nobody said so but I think the front office thought it'd be awkward to have somebody senior to me move in here. Personally, I can work under anyone who's competent but

Lee will be brand-new in-country and things might pop pretty soon."

Ashcroft nodded his agreement. "We worked with Steve in Afghanistan and Pakistan, too. In fact, he led one of our teams hunting the al Qaeda cell that was spreading that virus. He did a good job."

Chris Nissen was increasingly aware that he was relatively junior with SSI, leading men who had served together on other contracts in other climes. "Well then, Frank and headquarters called it right. I'm used to working with local indigenous personnel because that's what green beanies do. Apparently Lee's a door-kicker at heart, and his admin experience can be useful at Amasha."

"Okay," Green replied. "How do you want to work Pitney into our band of bros?"

Nissen laughed aloud. "Hell, it looks like I'm gonna be the El-Arian chief of police! With three ex-cops on the job here maybe I can even sleep in once in a while."

"I've talked with Robert a few times," Ashcroft said. "Obviously he's a tremendous shooter, and evidently he does well as an instructor, speaking the lingo and all. Personally, I'd rather work through him than most of the militia dudes who sort of speak English."

"Concur," Nissen responded. "But let's keep pushing these guys on the basics. The first time a round cracks past their ears they're likely to dump half of what they ever learned."

Green smiled. "Makes 'em a member of a real big club, don't it, Staff Sergeant?"

32

Rob Furr fidgeted again. Finally he whispered, "Damn, I gotta piss."

Rick Barrkman barely turned his head. "You should've thought of that before we crawled clear out here."

"I did, damn it! I drank more water tryin' to stay hydrated."

Another rifle round cracked across the rocky terrain. Barrkman's scan went to his left front. "That was about three, maybe four hundred yards. This gomer must not be Hazim because he hasn't moved much the last three shots."

"Well, maybe Hazim isn't the sniper stud he's supposed to be." Furr temporarily forgot about his bladder. "What's he shooting at now?"

Barrkman glanced to his right, squinting in the sunlight toward the village a quarter mile away. "Can't tell. It's probably just more harassing fire. I think they're trying to draw us out."

"Yeah. Nissen said there's no activity over at El-Arian so maybe they're setting us up for a fall there by decoying here."

Furr nodded. "Makes no sense to telegraph their punches here. Unless maybe they just want our attention in this area to cover something bigger."

"Well, that's strategy and we're tactics. Take another look, will you?"

Furr raised himself slightly from his position directly behind Barrkman, clearing the grass while glassing the open ground. Both men were sweating beneath their ghillie suits in the midday sun. They had chosen a shaded position partially covered by flat rocks that broke up the terrain and rendered them less visible to a knowledgeable observer.

"Nada." Furr looked upward through his veil. "Sun angle's changing, amigo. We should think about moving before we lose the shadows of the trees."

"Okay. You back out. Give a bird call when you're set and cover me while I move."

While Furr retrenched, Barrkman kept his eye to his bipoded rifle. He continued scanning slowly, methodically, hoping for a glimpse of movement or a careless reflection. Nothing emerged.

Two minutes later Furr's call chirped out, a two-tone baritone warble. Barrkman folded his bipod and began inching back. In a few meters his left foot wedged between two rocks and he tried to dislodge them. Unsuccessful, he raised up for better leverage and kicked with his right foot.

A gunshot split the air, impacting two meters in front of him.

Barrkman ducked reflexively. "Damn! That was close!" He kicked hard, felt one rock move, and scampered backward on hands and knees.

Another round split the air, passing overhead.

Furr edged laterally eight to ten meters, then risked a quick peek over the weeds. "Nothing out there much closer than four hundred yards."

Barrkman brushed the sand from his face. "What did it sound like to you?"

The spotter thought for a moment. "It sorta sounded like the ballistic crack you hear in the pits during a five-hundred-yard string in a high power match." He shrugged. "It's sure not that two-hundred-yard *snap*."

"I've got an idea."

Furr shook his head. "Uh-oh. That means you want me to get shot at."

A knowing smile creased Barrkman's tanned face. "Not this time. I'm going to move off to the left and poke my hat over the top with my binoculars to catch some sunlight."

"Those are real nice glasses, Rick." He eyed the Steiners covetously.

Barrkman grinned again. "Hey, if that raghead can put a round through my optic, it's a lot better than through my head." He motioned his partner into position. "You do two things: watch for something, and notice the interval between the impact and the sound."

"You know if he's smart he won't shoot again. Not for a while, anyway."

"Hey, dude, just 'cause he's accurate don't mean he's smart."

EBRAHIM LARIJANI ALLOWED HIS adrenaline to peak, then remembered to control his breathing. He turned to his spotter, Fahed. "Well?"

"I saw dirt from the bullet strike. It was short of the camouflaged form."

Larijani frowned, visibly unsettled. "Surely it was a hit. I had a steady rest."

"The first shot was low. I could not observe the second."

"Well then, it must be a hit."

Fahed had been warned about Larijani's ego. Esmaili had confided that Larijani was eager to redeem himself after the Beirut episode. "It could have gone high, Ebrahim. Now come, we must displace."

Larijani shook his head, returning to his Dragunov's scope. "No. This is a good position. If we displace we will lose sight of them." He thought for a moment. "Besides, the Chechen said if we locate them we should stay to keep them pinned down."

They will certainly move by now! Fahed laid a hand on

his partner's arm. "Brother, remember what the teacher always says. Once you have taken a shot, you must move."

Larijani shot a glance at the spotter. "Enough! I command here, and we will stay!"

Suit yourself, Fahed said to himself. He began inching away from the sniper, conceding that survival had just trumped teamwork. As he rolled onto his back, he was unaware that his binoculars caught the slanting sun.

"TARGET! LEFT FRONT, ELEVEN o'clock, maybe four hundred." Furr's voice carried an edge of excitement.

"What've you got?"

"Reflection under those trees. Stand by." Furr raised the Swarovsky rangefinder and lased the suspicious area. He checked the digital readout. "Three sixty, Rick."

"Yards or meters, damn it!"

"Yards of course!"

"Just checking." Barrkman thought about the situation. "Okay, get on your rifle. I'm going to try the hat and glasses trick. You shoot whatever shows."

Furr slid the Robar Snout Rifle into position, resting it on his drag bag laid across a rock. He cycled the bolt, adjusted the elevation dial, placed his eye to the scope, and nodded. "Sniper on."

"THERE! FARTHER BACK," LARIJANI exulted. He looked to his right, expecting to see his spotter close by. Instead the wretch had moved two or three meters away. "You cannot see anything from there!"

"I can see what I need to, brother."

Disgusted, Larijani returned to his scope. If he was low before, he needed to hold a little higher this time, and settled the aiming point on top of the hat.

He took up the slack in the trigger, held his breath, and pressed.

When he came down out of recoil he regained the target's position in time to feel a sledgehammer blow at the base of his neck.

Fahed heard the unmistakable sound of a nearby bullet strike, then realized that the report of the shot followed it. Larijani was on his back, gurgling loudly and holding his throat with both hands. Bright arterial blood pulsed between clasped fingers. The shooter's mouth gaped wide, trying to suck in air but the esophagus was clogged with a hot, thick liquid.

Fahed was tempted to say, "I warned you," but there was no point. He edged around the dying man's feet, retrieved the valuable rifle, and made his way to safety.

BEFORE THE SOUND OF Furr's shot had died away, an inbound round overwhelmed it. The ballistic shock of the 7.62 bullet was enough to tell the Americans all they needed to know; the impact on the rock merely confirmed it.

Furr and Barrkman dropped to the earth, their heads nearly colliding. They performed an unintended chorus: "Holy shit!"

Barrkman looked at his partner, both men wide-eyed. "We were set up!"

"No shit, Charlie!" Furr wiped some dirt off his face. "Damn, that guy's fast on the trigger."

"Yeah. *That* must be Hazim!"

HAZIM LOWERED HIS BINOCULARS and turned to Akhmed. "It was very close."

The shooter returned to his scope and scanned the area. "The crosshairs were steady and the trigger released cleanly. It should have been a hit."

The spotter knew that other variables affected the end result but recognized this was neither the time nor the place to argue the niceties. "Well, we must assume they know we are here. We should displace."

"Yes," Akhmed replied. "Unlike young Larijani, I fear."

Pulling his rifle off the improvised rest he said, "But at least he served his purpose."

AMASHA

"Okay," Leopole said. "Now give it to me again, without the poetry."

Furr took another pull from his water bottle and wiped his balding head. Barrkman sipped from something that was not water and smacked his lips.

"Like we said," Furr began. "We staked out a good place east of town. Not too obvious but it had a decent field of view and we were in shadow most of the morning. We heard the harassing fire from time to time but couldn't spot the shooter or shooters." He squinted in concentration.

"I was on the scope and Rick was on the trigger at that time because we'd been trading off every half hour. We'd just pulled back into more shade when they sent one our way."

"How'd they spot you?" Leopole asked.

Barrkman owned up. "I was crayfishing backward and caught a foot between two rocks. I reared up to pull free and they saw me. The first round was just short. The second went high."

"How much wind?"

"What?"

Leopole inhaled, then expelled his breath. "How much wind was there?"

Barrkman fidgeted again, a sign of agitation. "Hell, I don't know, Frank. What's it matter?"

"My point is, gentlemen, if there was a decent wind, that was a good shooter to get the deflection right and the range so close."

The two snipers looked at each other. Finally Furr said,

"I was checking for mirage. There was hardly any. The trees were barely moving. Maybe five miles per hour."

"Okay, go on."

Barrkman took up the tale. "We got settled farther back in the shadows and let things settle down. Then we thought about the sonic crack and figured the shooter was inside five hundred yards. Then Rob caught a glint. So I edged off to one side and did the old hat and binoculars trick."

Leopole smiled despite himself. "The statue of liberty play!"

"Well, obviously these guys don't watch much football because Rob nailed him."

The SSI leader turned to Furr. "Tell me."

"I pegged the range at 360 and got on the gun." Furr raised his right hand alongside his cheek, left hand extended in front of his chin. "When Rick raised his hat and glasses, the gomer fired. I had a good sight picture and lit him up."

"You know you hit him?"

"Well, Rick couldn't actually spot for me, but believe me, Boss. That's a mort." He took another swig. "But before I could run the bolt another round hit the rock I was resting on. Scared the *hell* out of me. We both hit the dirt."

"Where'd that round come from?"

Barrkman thought about the geometry. "I think it was about 2:00 or 2:30 from us. Obviously they'd been waiting for us to shoot their buddy."

A polite knock of the door was followed by Ayoob Slim and his English-speaking aide. "Excuse, please."

"Yes, sir," Leopole said. "Come in."

Slim and the militiaman entered. The latter laid a knapsack on the table. It was half covered with dried blood. "We find this where you say," the acolyte explained.

Leopole looked in the bag and found nothing of interest. He grinned at Furr. "Like you said, Rob. That's a mort."

Barrkman punched his partner in the arm. "Way to go, pard."

Furr merely took another drink.

"Was there a body?" Leopole asked the Druze.

"No, sir. But much blood on ground. Dragged marks in grass. Two hours no more."

"Thank you, gentlemen."

When the militiamen had left, Leopole resumed the debriefing. "Okay, you nailed one because they sacrificed him for a chance at you. This Hazim character is smart and patient. That's worth knowing. So how do you want to proceed?"

The shooters exchanged knowing looks. Barrkman said, "Let us sleep on it, Boss. We'll talk to you in the morning."

"All right." Leopole clapped Barrkman on the shoulder and left.

As the door closed, Furr regarded his friend. "Man! How you gonna sleep after that?"

33

NABATIYEH GOVERNATE

Imam Elham convened a small select audience to hear the message from Tehran. "The moment has arrived," he announced. "We will begin in three days or less."

Elham glanced around the room. The other cell leaders were focused, attentive. Mohammad Azizi appeared to possess an excess of nervous energy. Clearly he was eager to demonstrate his influence.

"This mission has no code name," Azizi added. "It is simply 'The Operation.'"

Esmaili assessed the fighters' collective mood. Generally it was relaxed, though some of the men fidgeted. Perhaps they knew that The Operation would lead to their rendezvous in Paradise.

"We have received detailed instructions by messenger," Elham continued. "Radio communication has been kept to a minimum, and little information has been passed that way, even in cipher."

Esmaili felt a faint prickling between his shoulder blades, as if he sensed a sniper's crosshairs settling there. "Excuse me, Imam, but that seems to indicate that some information has been radioed. The Jews and their American lackeys undoubtedly can break any code."

Azizi was not pleased with the outspoken cell leader. While Elham had been away, coordinating other aspects of the forthcoming venture, Azizi became responsible for defending the operation's planning and execution.

Elham interjected, concerned about any possible rift in the organization. "Yes, my brother. Given the opportunity to retrieve two or three very brief messages from hundreds or thousands sent on our net, and given enough time, any coded message can be broken, especially with computer analysis. But rest assured, brothers, that our benefactors in Tehran have taken every precaution." He smiled indulgently, as if assuaging a classroom full of worried children. "Without going into unnecessary detail, I can say that what messages are sent by radio are done so in what is called a onetime pad. That means—"

"That the encryption method is used only for that message, never to be repeated." Esmaili felt testy enough and worried enough to commit a breach of decorum.

Azizi suppressed a scowl at his Hezbollah colleague, aware that some men in the room were astute enough to interpret the building tension. "Quite so. Your experience does you honor, my brother. And therefore, you will understand that even if our enemies should overhear one of our messages, they will have a very difficult time reading it and an even harder time making sense of it." He morphed his frown into a smile. "By then, it will be far too late for them."

Elham took charge again, returning focus to the overall plan. Using a map pinned to the wall, he said, "The attacks on the villages will provide cover for the special operations teams infiltrating the Jewish border and proceeding to specially selected targets." He pointed to the crossing points within a few kilometers of each other.

"And the method of attack?" Esmaili asked.

Sadegh Elham raised his stony gaze from the map to the questioner's eyes. "Dr. Momen has provided us with the greatest possible weapon. Carrying it to Paradise represents the greatest possible honor."

Esmaili grunted. "A suicide mission."

"Oh, no, brother. Not a typical suicide bombing. Rather, each weapon is the greatest suicide bomb yet available to us." He leaned back and actually smiled. It was a chilly, predatory smile with ice around the edges.

"We have two nuclear devices. Each of them can be carried by one man, and each bomber shall have at least three escorts. Their mission is to get him to his assigned target—at the cost of their lives."

EL-ARIAN

Phil Green stuck his head inside Nissen's small office. "Newbies are here."

Nissen laid down the map he was examining with the new Druze liaison officer, Hussain Halabi. The former NCO tapped the Israeli on the arm. "Come on, Lieutenant, let's meet the troops."

Outside, two men dismounted from the Land Rover. Robert Pitney was accompanied by a very large individual wearing green fatigues and a boonie hat that appeared half a size too small. Green exclaimed, "Ken, my man! You still using VWs for barbells?"

The two mercenaries exchanged comradely hugs and back slaps. Ken Delmore tweaked Green's mustache. "You're getting gray, amigo. Or did you just stop using Grecian Formula after Pakistan?"

Green reached up—it was a bit of a stretch—and pulled off Delmore's hat. "At least I still have hair!"

Delmore, a determinedly cheerful giant, retrieved the hat and looked around. "Colonel Leopole said that Bob A. is here. Where'd he get off to?"

"Oh, he's like, you know. Working." Green shrugged philosophically. "Some people insist on doing that." Sensing Nissen's presence, he made the introductions. "Chris Nissen, Ken Delmore."

The two shook, Nissen wincing slightly at Delmore's crushing grip. "Welcome to our humble AO," Nissen began. "You come well recommended."

"Well, thank you, Sergeant. I'm really looking forward to working with you guys. Just show me the area, let me check my zero, and put me where you need me."

"All right." Nissen looked at Pitney. "Robert, you're probably familiar with the general situation from your time at Amasha, but you might as well tag along while we show Ken around."

Before Pitney could reply, Nissen gestured to the IDF delegate. "Gentlemen, this is Lieutenant Halabi. He's our . . . ah, new . . . Druze liaison officer."

Halabi took three brisk steps forward and shook hands with the two Americans. "You are much needed here, gentlemen. Thank you for coming."

Delmore grinned hugely. "My pleasure, sir." Nissen and Green grinned at each other, and Pitney caught the meaning. The money's better than good, which always doubled the pleasure.

Nissen turned from the informal meeting and led the way down the main road running through the village. "As you can see, this is a defensible position, especially with the open areas on most sides. The militia has been working to improve the perimeter, and we have people on guard twenty-four/seven."

Delmore stopped abruptly and stood in his size twelve boots. "Good field of fire on this side of town, and it looked pretty much the same on the way in. Nearest cover must be—what? Three hundred meters?"

Halabi stood with arms akimbo. "It is 320 from here to that stand of trees. I suggested that we plant command-detonated mines in there but the militia lacks expertise and equipment in that area. I hope for some improvement before long."

Pitney usually was content to stand back and absorb information. But the Israeli's comment left an obvious opening. "Excuse me, Lieutenant. But just how long do your sources indicate we have until Hezbollah makes a move?"

Halabi arched an eyebrow. "My sources are no better than anyone else's most of the time. But I understand that some unusual measures are being taken for our benefit." His concluding smile said that no further details were forthcoming.

WASHINGTON, D.C.

The Lincoln Memorial was always crowded in the summer, which was exactly why Mordecai Baram chose that spot to meet Michael Derringer.

SSI's founder arrived a few minutes early and took the rare opportunity to study the monument. As a lifelong, rock-ribbed Republican, Derringer had been educated to revere The Great Emancipator, but some libertarian doubts nudged the usual GOP dogma out of alignment. Having read Lincoln's first inaugural, Derringer concluded that "Honest" Abe had been just as slick a politician as Bill Clinton—enforcing the Fugitive Slave Law while declaring secession illegal while conceding the people's right to amend their government or overthrow it.

Derringer turned from the pale icon—ironically, the marble had been quarried in Georgia—and scanned the crowd.

There was Mordecai Baram.

Stepping around a crowd of poorly supervised children—apparently the only kind America produced anymore—the Israeli made eye contact with his SSI colleague. They avoided shaking hands and gave only a modest indication of recognizing one another. They stood side by side, looking up at the nineteen-foot statue as if it were the subject of an impromptu discussion.

"What've you got, Mordecai?"

"This is close hold, Michael, for obvious reasons." The diplomat paused, looking left and right. "Intelligence sources have turned up something of possible concern for your people in Lebanon."

"Your sources or ours?"

"There's not much to go on, but decrypts mention three citations of something merely called 'the operation.' From context it appears to be aimed at southern Lebanon."

Derringer turned to face Baram. "Your sources or ours?"

"Michael, please. Ask me no questions and I'll tell you no lies. Isn't that how it goes?"

Two boys scrambled past the men, brushing the adults' suit coats. Derringer resisted the impulse to snag one of the offenders by the collar. "Very well. What else?"

"That's all, at least for now."

The retired admiral shook his head. "That's it? Come on, there has to be more. This . . . operation . . . could be anything. Hell, it might be a surgery!"

"Michael, believe me. That's all there is just now. You can make whatever you like of it. Tell your people or don't concern them, as you wish. But I thought you should be informed."

Derringer inhaled, held his breath, then expelled it. He found himself staring at the base of one of the thirty-six pillars supporting the Doric temple. "Very well, then. Thanks, Mordecai." He turned to go, then paused and looked back. "You'll tell me if . . ."

"I promise."

34

NABATIYEH GOVERNATE

The courier took a wrong turn in the dark. By the time he realized his error, it was too late.

Rounding the curve on the rutted pathway, the Toyota pickup lurched to a stop as the driver stomped on the brake. The fact that he was on that seldom traveled route was suspicious enough; running blackout lights was a giveaway to the militia manning the checkpoint.

A short firefight erupted at the junction of the Amasha–El Arian road.

While the driver lurched the battered vehicle into reverse, his passenger and the two escorts in the back opened fire. But they lacked a stable platform whereas the Druze sentries stood their ground, aimed just above the slitted headlights, and began shooting. At thirty meters most of the rounds went home.

The windshield erupted in a small blizzard of glass chips, turning darkly red on the inside. Struck by four rounds, the driver died almost immediately, and his foot slipped off the accelerator. The passenger, the most important man aboard, took two hits in the upper torso. He dropped his folding-stock AK and collapsed beside the driver.

One of the shooters standing in the back quickly recognized a no-win situation and bailed out. He sustained a grazing hit to one hip and staggered into the dark. His partner, more motivated or less experienced, braced himself against the rear of the cab. He lived long enough to empty his magazine and was gamely attempting to reload when unintentionally shot through the head.

Twelve seconds after it began, it ended.

Two of the militiamen approached the perforated pickup from each side, unaware that if either had to shoot, his partner would stand downrange. The third guard stood out of the subdued glare of the remaining headlight, covering their approach.

Leading with his muzzle, the left-hand searcher saw that the driver was dead, as was the gunner in the bed. Then the Druze leaned inside to turn off the engine. His colleague on the opposite side opened the door and allowed the passenger to slump partway out. The man was inhaling fast, shallow breaths. He muttered something unintelligible.

"What did he say?" asked the first militiaman.

"I do not know," his partner replied. "I think it's Farsi."

NORTHERN ISRAEL

The knock on the bedroom door came at an unseemly hour. Nevertheless, Yakov Livni had a standing order: far better to lose a little sleep than to snore through something important. As a military history buff he knew that Hitler's generals had deemed *Der Fuhrer*'s rest more important than Operation Overlord, and at Leyte Gulf, Bull Halsey's staff had allowed the admiral to sleep rather than inform him that Kurita was reported eastbound through San Bernardino Strait.

"What is it?" Livni called through the door.

"A priority radio report from Halabi," came the reply.

"Bring it in." Livni snapped on the bedside light and sat up on his cot.

The watch officer, an earnest captain wearing a yarmulke, stepped inside. He handed the scribbled note to the special operations chief, knowing that this time of day—or night—Colonel Livni would require an interpreter.

Playing an optical trombone, Livni extended the message form back and forth, seeking the best focal distance. He squinted, cocked his head, and gave up. "Something about an operation and special packages." He looked up at the messenger. "Read it for me."

The captain retrieved the form. "Lieutenant Halabi says one of his militia outposts intercepted a vehicle about 0215." He checked his watch. "That was about fifty minutes ago. There was shooting, two Hezbollah dead and one wounded. The wounded man seems to be a messenger with an important dispatch for the cells operating around Hasbaya. Halabi attributes that to security concerns about transmitting messages by radio."

Livni was fully awake now. "What else?"

"Well, the medics at Amasha treated the man, who is Iranian. They got someone to speak Farsi to him and evidently they overmedicated him. He began talking in random phrases. The one that kept recurring has to do with 'the operation' and something called 'momen.'"

The colonel leaned back against the wall, deep in thought. At length he asked, "Were there any documents?"

"Yes, sir. But Halabi says none have any bearing on special operations or this 'momen' reference."

Livni rubbed his face, felt the stubble, and decided to ignore it. He threw off the blanket and swung his feet onto the floor. "All right. I'm awake so I might as well get up. I want to talk to Halabi in ten minutes. Then I need to see Sol Nadel. Call his chief of staff."

The aide grinned wryly. "Yakov, you know what happens to captains who wake generals before 0600?"

"I have no idea. So let's find out, shall we?"

NABATIYEH GOVERNATE

"There is a problem," Azizi announced. It was still early, even before the *Salat-ul-Fajr* dawn prayer, but Esmaili was accustomed to working odd hours.

The imam's acolyte approached Esmaili, who threw back the blanket and stretched himself off his cot. "We have to hold a planning meeting immediately."

Esmaili mussed his black hair, nodded while stifling a yawn, and from instinct picked up his AK-47. He followed Azizi out of the room, trailing him to the headquarters building.

Inside, Sadegh Elham was already convening the session. Among those present were the mortar crews plus Akhmed with Hazim and two lesser snipers.

The cleric wasted no time. "Early this morning one of our couriers became lost in the dark. He foolishly continued rather than awaiting daylight and drove into a Druze roadblock. Again, rather foolishly, he attempted to force his way through and was shot to pieces. One man survived and made his way here, wounded.

"We do not know if any of our brothers survived, but we must assume that at least one did. Therefore, the security we expected from minimal radio communication may be compromised. I do not believe that any useful documents fell into hostile hands, but anyone captured by the Zionist entity will be tortured into revealing what he knows."

Elham delivered a scowl that scalded the audience with the heat of his disapproval. A few jihadists squirmed uncomfortably; they read the tacit message. *Far better to die fighting than to surrender.*

"We are attempting to determine what the militia forces have learned, because anything that comes to them will be shared with the Jews. So unless we receive reliable information fairly soon, we must assume the worst. That means a premature assault on the Druze villages, and an early launching of our main attack."

At that, Elham nodded to Azizi, who rose and faced the audience.

"We are requesting immediate deployment of our special operators as a contingency against updated enemy intelligence. The working details of the plan probably will not change, but the timetable undoubtedly will. You are all advised to hold yourselves in immediate readiness. Double-check your weapons and equipment. Meanwhile, our group leaders will remain to finalize plans and schedules." He surveyed the men before him, then nodded briskly. "You are dismissed."

AMASHA

Frank Leopole was up before dawn. So was everyone else.

"Okay, people, here's how it looks." The SSI leader wanted a closed-door meeting with his instructors before discussing plans with the militia.

"Last night the checkpoint down at the fork of the road had a dustup with a Hezbollah unit. There were four

Hezzies in a pickup, and apparently they were lost because they stumbled straight into our guys. There was a short fire-fight resulting in two hostile KIAs and one prisoner, WIA. Another one got away.

"The militia took the POW to El-Arian for immediate treatment. He's Iranian, and had some documents that Lieutenant Halabi says are somewhat useful. But the most interesting intel came while he was sedated for treatment of two GSWs. He was babbling in Farsi, so Halabi got a translator and stroked the POW. I am informed there's reason to believe a Hezbollah operation is imminent, and we are treating that as a serious threat. From now on we're maintaining a twenty-four-hour watch at thirty per-cent immediate readiness and thirty percent standby. We will maintain that schedule until further notice."

Steve Lee, now the de facto second in command, barely had time to adjust to his new surroundings. "Frank, what can we expect? Are we looking at an Alamo-type siege or more harassment?"

Out of earshot of the militia, Leopole permitted him-self some dry humor. "Well, Steve, if we're at the Alamo, I'm Bowie and you're Travis. The rest of you can fight over who's Davy Crockett but I don't relish the prospect for any of those roles."

Picking up on the unaccustomed levity, Bosco rasped to Breezy. "I saw the Disney reruns. Guess I'm Georgie Russell. 'Give 'em whut fur, Davy!' "

35

The Mercedes truck had seen better days, but its battered exterior was an advantage to the owners. Its obvious hard use over the years helped conceal the exceptional cargo it carried.

The brakes squealed as the vehicle slid to a halt. Mohammad Azizi quickened his pace across the courtyard, smiling in anticipation while the driver and four passengers dismounted.

"Friends! My brothers! Welcome, welcome to you all." He indulged in a round of hand shaking and cheek kissing, especially with the senior man. When Elham materialized behind him, Azizi was quick to make the introductions.

"Abbas Jannati, I believe you know the imam."

Jannati inclined his head, grasping hands with the cleric. "It has been many months since our meeting with Dr. Momen."

"You traveled safely?" Elham asked.

"Oh, yes. Our Syrian friends were most helpful, even though they did not know our exact mission."

"That is as we planned it," Elham replied evenly. He eyed the other jihadists. "And these are our messengers to the Zionists?"

"Chosen by the doctor himself, Imam. They are pledged to deliver the, ah, packages, just as you stated."

Elham eyed the volunteers from Tehran. He decided that he would spend some time with each in order to confirm their devotion, but if they passed Momen's scrutiny, they were committed.

"Brothers," he declared. "Welcome. You may consider this place the portal to Paradise."

NORTHERN ISRAEL

"Come with me."

Few colonels give orders to generals, but Yakov Livni and Solomon Nadel had an unusual relationship. Livni led Nadel well away from the operations block, stopped at an M113 armored personnel carrier, and motioned the general inside. The vehicle was empty.

"What do you know about an Iranian scientist named Momen?"

Nadel's eyes widened. "The physicist? That's a bad one, I think. A hard-liner."

"So you know of him."

"He's involved in their nuclear program." Nadel almost visibly shivered. "Yakov, you're making me nervous."

"Well, misery loves company. Otherwise I wouldn't be talking to you inside an armored vehicle when my office has furniture and air-conditioning." Livni glanced around the interior of the American-built APC. "Now, I'm mainly here to see if you're hearing what I'm hearing. So—"

"So," Nadel interjected, "if your sources come from beyond mine, then something's afoot that can only mean bad news."

Livni nodded. "It's all coming together, Sol. The radio intercepts, some documents we have, ah, acquired. And now the fortunate acquisition of the Hezbollah courier near Hasbaya." He gave his colleague a playful nudge. "You've been to school. What do two and two amount to?"

The general gave his colleague a grim smile. "I've learned that it's not four, because in this business things are seldom what they seem."

NEAR AMASHA

"You see it? About ten-thirty, maybe four-fifty."

Furr slowly raised a gloved hand and pointed for Barrkmann. The sniper team had not been in position long enough to prepare a range card, and besides, the terrain was largely featureless.

Barrkman put his Leopold rifle scope on the area indicated to the left, raising his elevation setting to 450 yards. "Nothing."

"Okay," Furr whispered. "From the large, light-colored rock at about three hundred, look uphill and slightly left."

After several seconds the shooter emitted a low whistle. "Moving shadow where there's no trees." He grinned without taking his master eye from the optic. "Damn, you're good, Rob."

"You're just lucky it's your turn on the trigger."

"Well, you've done most of the shooting so far. Only fair that I get another shot." Though not usually envious, Barrkman rued that so far the score stood at two-one, Furr.

"We can't get overeager," Furr cautioned. "Remember, Frank said the militia had seen movement out here this morning but that don't mean it's hostile."

"What I remember is the way that other bastard's shot came out of nowhere. This might be another setup."

Furr shrugged beneath his ghillie. "If so, they're in for a surprise. Captain Hamadeh confirmed his reaction force is in position, seventy meters back. I just got the word on Baker channel." He double-checked the frequency on his tactical set and adjusted the earplug for more comfort.

"Okay, bwana. Now what?"

Furr returned to his spotting scope. "I make it a boiling mirage, midrange. Call it three minutes."

Barrkman studied the visible air, moving slightly right to left. "Concur." He rotated the windage knob four clicks right, then back one. He looked at his partner. "Now we wait."

Furr continued watching the suspect area, letting the shooter rest his eyes. If nothing happened, they would trade off in twenty minutes.

At length Furr muttered one word. "Movement."

Barrkman was back on the rifle, snuggled up to the SR-90. "I see grass moving but no target."

"Wait a sec." As the spotter stared through his optic, he caught an unnatural motion. "Rick, there's something moving above the grass, like maybe an antenna. See it?"

The wind caught the long, thin object, causing a reflection. "Got it. I think you're right. They must be recon rather than snipers."

"But there's nothing to see out here. The ville is hardly visible down the slope."

Behind his veil, Barrkman chewed his lip in concentration. He turned to Furr again. "Give the Druze a call. See if they can send a couple guys up here."

"You mean, like, to draw fire?"

"Yeah. But don't let 'em get within a hundred meters of us."

Furr keyed his mike. "Delta, this is Sierra. Copy?"

Five seconds passed. "Sierra, Delta. Copy." The Americans recognized Hamadeh's voice.

"Ah, Delta, we have movement to our front. Recommend you send two men to scout about 150 meters to our east. And be careful. Over."

"On the way. Out."

Furr looked at his partner. "This better work or they'll lynch us."

Barrkman gave no reply. He adjusted his prone position behind the modified Remington 700, seeking his natural point of aim. By flexing his right toes and bringing his left leg forward, he got the most comfortable elevation on the bipoded rifle. Then he told himself: *Breathe*.

"Friendlies, three o'clock."

Barrkman accepted the spotter's assessment while keeping his eye to the scope. The antenna was no longer visible.

Crack!

Furr swung his gaze to the right. He saw one of the two militiamen stagger and fall as the man's partner dived for cover.

"Where was that?" Barrkman swung his rifle side to side, desperately seeking a sign of the shooter.

"I think it's from the right front. Maybe one o'clock."

"Keep looking there. I'm staying on . . ."

Barrkman's voice shut off like a switch. He snugged up the Robar rifle, muttered "Round out," and fired. Immediately he cycled the bolt and fired again.

"Shit, Rick! What're you shooting at?"

The sniper cycled the bolt once more and fired a third round. Then, leaving the action open, he inserted another cartridge into the box magazine and closed the bolt. Now he had three rounds loaded.

"Two tangos, both down at the first position. Call the Druze. Have 'em sweep in that direction."

"Hell no! Damn it, somebody else just popped one of the scouts."

"They can flank the shooters from this side. Hurry!"

Without further delay, Furr was on the radio. "Delta, Sierra. Send your team out to the northwest. They should be able to flank the shooters."

"On the way. What is your situation? Over."

"Two tangos likely KIA. Out."

Furr crawled alongside the shooter. "Damn it, I didn't see a thing. What happened?"

"Just after the shot, I saw the head and shoulders of somebody in the grass. I realized we're looking at the backup team, like the one that almost nailed us before. Hell, maybe the same ones. Before they could shoot, I sent one and his partner raised up to pull him aside. So I shot him, and put in an insurance round."

Furr shook his head in wonder. "So you think you nailed Hazim?"

Barrkman grinned widely. "I sure nailed somebody, dude."

AMASHA

Captain Rami Hamadeh was pleased with the SSI team. "We have one man wounded but he should live. Though we did not find the other snipers, you did well, gentlemen. One enemy sniper killed and one captured."

Frank Leopole stood with arms folded. He suspected that Furr and Barrkman had hung out some Druze as live bait, but for the moment he was willing to cut them some slack.

Hamadeh sat down with the dead sniper's tally book. "This appears to be Cyrillic but I think it is not. If I had to guess, I would say it is Chechen. I will ask the prisoner."

Barrkman furrowed his brow. "Chechen? That's possible. I mean, there's reports that they send people to fight in Iraq."

"This was a man who took much pride in his work. See, without knowing the words, it is possible to tell the meaning of most entries. Obviously there is the date, the time, and undoubtedly the distance. All those last entries are three digits. The other columns might be the location, type of rifle, hit or miss, and number of shots fired."

Furr leaned over the Israeli's shoulder. "How many did he hit?"

Hamadeh flipped the pages. "I cannot tell. But there are about two hundred entries, apparently dating from 1999." He looked up at the American. "He was very good."

Barrkman was still giddy. "*Was* is the operative word."

Leopole interrupted the mutual admiration society. "Let me get this straight, Captain. You think that our guys hit their first team? The ones that got away were there to lure us out?"

Hamadeh nodded. "Yes, Colonel. That is how I see it. Of course, we will know more once I interrogate the survivor." He turned to Barrkman. "You hit him high in the shoulder. He lost quite a bit of blood but he can talk."

Barrkman absorbed that information. "I guess the third round went into the shooter."

"Yes, I saw the body. Two hits through the torso." He smiled broadly. "The sniper who outsnipes Hazim will be famous."

Robbie Furr did a high five with his friend. "Three for three at 450 yards in—what? Maybe eight or nine seconds? Way to go, pard!"

"Nobody's going to be famous," Leopole interjected. "The last thing we need is for every Hezzie fanatic to come gunslinging for the fastest sniper in Dodge." He lanced Hamadeh with a parade-ground stare. "The less said about this the better, but if anything does get out, your people did it."

"Understood, Colonel."

NABATIYEH GOVERNATE

"Akhmed is dead?"

Hazim stood immobile in the small room. Esmaili could read the disbelief on the boy's face. "He and Basaam have not returned. And you saw nothing of them?"

Hazim shook his head. "No, Teacher. After I shot the militiaman, we were going to displace when we heard three shots, close together. We moved back to the planned rendezvous but Akhmed and Basaam were not there. With more Druze in the area, we thought it best to return."

Esmaili almost laid a hand on the younger man's shoulder. "You did the right thing." He thought for a moment. "If Akhmed had not wanted to spread his experience among our shooters, you would still be with him. Be thankful for that, and remember the lesson."

Hazim went off to prepare for afternoon prayers while Esmaili and Azizi took a walk. The liaison officer spoke first. "You know, of course, that we can only pray that both are dead."

"I know, brother." Esmaili nodded toward the newcomers. "Both of them knew of our . . . visitors. But they had not been told the details."

"We shall have to discuss this situation with the imam, but I believe the plan must proceed, especially with the weather in our favor." He stopped and turned to his colleague. "And you, brother, will play a most important part."

36

NABATIYEH GOVERNATE

Imam Sadegh Elham determined that the time was right. Facing the nine selected men he had assembled, he spread his hands wide.

"My brothers, my warriors, I must beg forgiveness from some of you." He allowed the sentiment to hang suspended in the evening air. As a priest and an orator he had long since learned the emphatic benefit of silence.

"I confess before God that I have been required to deceive you as to your true mission. And security requires that all of us keep secret what I am about to reveal, even from the fighters who will attack the Druze villages. But I have consulted with the learned scholars in Tehran, and they tell me that a deception in advancing the jihad is permissible under special circumstances. To do otherwise would have placed our holy mission in serious jeopardy. Nonetheless, I accept whatever judgment God holds against me."

Seated in the front row, Esmaili thought: *As if there is a way to reject the judgment of God!*

Elham unrolled a map of Lebanon and extended it at arm's length. One of his acolytes accepted the paper and held it for the audience.

"You have been led to believe that we were planning for a long-range rocket attack against the Zionist state. Much of our work has been seen in that light, without actually saying so. That was part of the plan drafted by our Islamic leaders, commanders, and scientists. Many of you provided security to the surveyors who seemed to be preparing launch sites for rockets to destroy the putrid Jewish nation. Others prepared storage places safe from aerial observation. All of that work was what our Russian friends call 'disinformation.' In its own way, it represents as righteous a contribution to the global jihad as the martyrs who carry explosives strapped to their bodies."

Esmaili glanced to either side, curious as to how the rhetoric was being received. He noted that more of the youngsters paid strict attention than the older, presumably more cynical men.

Elham got down to details. "The deception and actual mission were both conducted by the planners in Tehran, blessings and peace be upon them. They felt it advisable to show some degree of activity in this area to justify the effort to secure additional ground. The Zionists and the Americans would inevitably see some activity here, from their airplanes and satellites, and draw the obvious conclusion—we were planning rocket or missile attacks sometime in the future. But all the while, the true mission went forward.

"The weapon of holy vengeance is not borne upon any rocket, my brothers. In fact, some of you shall have the high honor of escorting the device." He turned to Modarresi Ka'bi, one of the latecomers from Tehran. He was a slightly built man, apparently in his early thirties. He reached into a large duffel bag and, with difficulty, produced a rectangular shape. Murmurs coursed through the audience—some jihadists knew what they were seeing.

Ahmad Esmaili had already guessed.

Elham was speaking again. "This is our weapon, my brothers. It is one of two purchased at considerable cost in blood and treasure, and its useful life is limited. But when it is delivered to its destination, it will destroy the target in an atomic fireball!"

The room erupted in shouts and barks. Men leapt to their feet, dancing with joyful surprise. They seized one another and embraced excitedly, screaming *"Allahu akbar!"* Three minutes passed before Elham restored order.

Ahmad Esmaili played his part, singing the praises of all involved while taking in the scene. He tried hard to appear as elated as the others, but doubted that he convinced any skeptics.

Elham waved down the celebrants, most of whom now realized they had been selected to die. The couriers from Tehran—K'abi and Jannati—already had made that leap of faith.

The cleric expounded upon the jihadists' weapon. "A one-kiloton yield can destroy most of an area seven square kilometers. Therefore, your targets have been chosen with that fact in mind. Azizi and I shall brief each team independently to further preserve security. But some things will be obvious to you now: the attacks on the Druze villages will deceive the Zionists into focusing their attention there, while our teams make their way to the frontier.

"Each weapon has two specialists assigned to it. If something befalls one, the other can still activate it. Though these devices have timers for delayed detonation, we dare not trust them. Therefore, our four technicians have already pledged themselves to die in the certainty that each bomb explodes."

Elham turned his gaze to the other five men. "Those of you honored with the task of escorting the weapons to their targets also are known for your devotion to God. You will stand here tonight in the presence of your comrades and pledge your own devotion to the task, as befits a warrior selected for so critical a mission. You are to accompany your assigned specialists to the site selected for destruction, and no doubt most of you also will enter Paradise."

The imam pointed to Fida, whom Elham had not seen in weeks. "Fida, my brother, stand."

The veteran jihadist quickly stood, hands at his sides.

"Do you swear before these men and before God that you will ensure the success of this mission with your life?"

"I do!" The voice was strong and clear. The face bore a tight smile.

"Esmaili, stand!"

The Hezbollah veteran rose to his feet, striking a confident pose.

"Do you swear before these men and before God that you will ensure the success of this mission with your life?"

"Imam, I swear it!" A decisive nod of the head added emphasis.

Elham proceeded down the line, man by man.

Ahmad Esmaili remained standing until the last fighter was sworn. When the ritual was ended, he was pleased. *I would almost believe my oath myself!*

He looked outside and noted the lowering gray clouds. It was not hard to interpret the meaning: the attack would come before the weather improved.

COURTHOUSE METRO STATION
ARLINGTON, VIRGINIA

Mordecai Baram made no pretense of subtlety. He walked up to Michael Derringer and handed him a newspaper with an article highlighted:

> Reports from reliable sources indicate that Hezbollah has sought Iranian assistance in obtaining "suitcase bombs" capable of producing small nuclear detonations. Speaking anonymously, military spokesmen said that entry into Israel from southern Lebanon is the most likely approach. A well-placed Tel Aviv source stated that the situation is viewed with concern at the cabinet level.
>
> However, opposition cabinet ministers note that similar, though unfounded, concerns have arisen before, and polling indicates little public enthusiasm for committing Israeli forces to Lebanon again. Observers in Tel Aviv generally believe that further action will await more of a national consensus.

Derringer looked up from the paper. "Yeah. I've heard about this. After the Soviet Union collapsed, apparently a lot of backpack nukes were missing. But what's SSI's connection?"

Baram retrieved the paper and tucked it in his raincoat. He waited until a train rattled by on the opposite track. "Your team might be in danger."

Derringer's gray eyes widened behind his Navy-issue glasses. "You're saying that there are portable nukes in Lebanon?"

"We believe so."

SSI's founder looked left and right. No one stood close enough to hear. "Then what do you recommend?"

"We want you to find them."

AMASHA

Captain Rami Hamadeh hung up the satellite phone and turned to Frank Leopole. "That was Northern Command, General Nadel's brigade. We are alerted to expect a major Hezbollah effort within twenty-four hours. You should contact the El-Arian team right away."

Leopole sorted priorities in his mind. "All right, I'll call Chris on the command net. The scrambler should provide the security we need. But what does Northern Command mean by a 'major effort'? And how much support can we expect?"

Hamadeh stood up and consulted his notes. "Enemy forces: estimated at company strength or better. Intentions: apparently to seize this place and possibly El-Arian. Enemy ability . . ." He looked at the American. "You know that already, Frank. Mortars and probably automatic weapons. They seem to respect our night vision so I'd plan for a dawn attack but be ready for anything."

"They probably can't take both places with a single company, at least not at the strength of about 150 men. So that tells me they'll concentrate here or there unless they just want to divert our attention from someplace else." He shrugged. "Too many unknowns, Rami. They could just as well have a battalion out there."

The Israeli Druze officer nodded his agreement. "That may be. In any case, the background seems consistent: they're been surveying and leveling sites in this area, apparently for new missile or rocket batteries. They probably want to control this entire area before their next big barrage, and that means they'll come at us in whatever force is needed."

"Which takes me back to my other question. What kind of support will we get from Nadel's brigade?"

"The operations officer says a reaction force is standing by, capable of ground or helicopter transport. Believe me, Solomon Nadel will support us as much as anyone. But he can't launch a relief effort without approval from the defense ministry because of public concern about more involvement here."

"You mean, it's politics."

"Frank, I don't know about America, but in Israel, everything is politics, and it's *all* local."

Leopole rubbed his chin, staring at the floor. "I can understand those concerns, Rami, but does the ministry understand our situation? If we get pushed hard—really hard—we can't survive outside this village. There's nowhere to go; we'll get chopped up if we're driven out in the open."

"Well, between you and me, I'm reliably informed that some air support is possible. It depends on weather, of course, and the way things are looking, the attack is likely to come with low cloud ceilings."

"What about comm? I mean, somebody to direct air attacks."

The Israeli gave a knowing grin. "It so happens that I attended the close air support course when I was promoted to captain. I can direct gunships or jets."

"Well, let's hope it doesn't come to that. And let's hope these militiamen can do what we've trained them to do."

Hamadeh folded his arms and leaned against the deck. "Frank, where do you live? In the States, I mean."

"Arlington, Virginia. Why?"

"Well, if a bunch of heavily armed fanatics attacked Arlington, Virginia, wouldn't your citizens fight like hell to defend their homes?"

A tiny prickling sensation crept up Frank Leopole's spine. He thought: *Some would and some wouldn't. Some libs would make excuses for the attackers and then ask why the government didn't do more.*

Rather than confess his doubts, Leopole said, "Everybody I know sure would." *Especially a redneck, tobacco-chewing ex-gunnery sergeant named Dan Foyte.*

"Well, there you go. It's the same here, where everybody knows everybody else—and has for four hundred years."

SSI OFFICES

Derringer took Baram back to the office and immediately convened a meeting. Everyone remotely associated with the Lebanon contract was needed, and those not present were summoned.

Marshall Wilmont shook his head. "This makes no sense, none at all. If the Israelis themselves can't agree on the suitcase threat, why send us chasing all over Lebanon for something that likely doesn't exist?"

Baram permitted himself a chuckle. "Politics, my friend. That is, Israeli domestic politics. Did you see the musical *1776*? There's a funny scene where the New York delegate to Congress is asked why he never votes for or against anything. Finally he throws up his hands and bemoans the workings of the New York legislature. He says that everybody talks very fast and very loud and nobody pays any attention to anyone else so nothing gets done."

"You're saying that sounds like the Israeli government."

"No, I am saying that *is* the Israeli government!"

Wilmont appreciated the humor. "But it doesn't take an invasion to deal with some backpack nukes. Why not send some covert spec-ops teams?"

"Well, let us just say that recent efforts along those lines led to your contract."

As SSI's legal director, Corin Pilong knew about contracts. "Excuse me for interjecting business at this point, but if we're going to do more than training, it should involve an amendment to the contract."

Baram blinked in response. He appeared surprised at the no-nonsense comment from that baby-doll face.

"Corin's right," Derringer interjected. "We have a separate fee scale for training and for operations."

Recovering his composure, Baram waved a hand. "Given the very serious nature of the new threat, I cannot imagine that finances will be a problem. I will consult with Tel Aviv today. But I will need more information."

"Very well," Derringer said. "Mordecai, if you'll consult with Corin, I think the rest of us have a lot to do this afternoon."

DOWN THE HALL, SANDY Carmichael huddled with Matthew Finch of Personnel and Jack Peters, who usually handled SSI recruiting.

"If we're going after nuclear stuff again, we couldn't do better than Bernie Langevin," Carmichael began.

Finch nodded. "Concur. He stuck it out all through the Chad episode and the chase for the *Tarabalus Pride*."

Peters was out of the scientific loop, and did not mind saying so. "I've not dealt with him. What's the story?"

Carmichael knew the details. "Major Bernard Langevin, PhD, USAF Reserve (Ret), has his feet in three worlds: scientific, military, and diplomatic. He's been around the block. Got started as an undergrad physics student and went Air Force ROTC to help with tuition. He got a master's almost for drill and could've stayed for twenty. But the Air Force tried to nudge him into weapons design when he was more interested in the operational end, and became a NEST officer."

"NEST?" Peters asked.

"Nuclear Emergency Search Team. Or maybe it's Support Team. Anyway, the 'broken arrow' guys. But there wasn't much work along those lines so he went with the reserves for longevity and was offered a job with IAEA. Once in a while, if he has enough Merlot, he'll tell you he wasn't thrilled about the U.N. but the job got him to interesting places with a chance for some excitement."

Peters slowly shook his head. "A nuke who wants excitement? Nooo thank you. I remember a bubblehead friend of mine who said, 'I don't want to hear 'Oops' around nuclear reactors or submarines.' "

Finch knew Langevin's dossier almost by heart, and clearly admired the scientist. "As a onetime IAEA investigator, he's seen the best and worst of United Nations operations and eventually he left in disgust. As he said late one night, 'I might as well get better paid for what I know because I've already been ignored for it.' "

Peters accepted his colleagues' assessment. "Okay by me. But is he available? And what if he's not?"

Carmichael's mouth curled at the edges, producing the dimples that Peters secretly admired. "Oh, Bernie's available, trust me on that. Whatever he's doing, he'll jump at the chance to get his boots dirty."

Finch's Rolodex memory for personnel matters did a quick shuffle. "We don't have anybody else remotely like him, which is why he's on retainer. If Bernie can't go for some reason, we'll have to get the admiral to call in some DoD markers."

"Okay," Peters replied. "So who else do we need?"

Carmichael almost hated herself for what she was about to say. "I've been thinking about the language situation. We don't have anybody over there who speaks Arabic, Hebrew, and Farsi. But Hezbollah is heavily Iranian."

Finch's eyes widened as realization dawned. "Oh, no . . ."

" 'Fraid so, Matt. I'm going to ask Omar if he'll go."

Peters realized the implication. "Dr. Mohammed? I know he's a fine training officer, but how would he do in the field? I mean, he's . . ."

"Overweight, out of shape, and enjoys restaurants and museums. I know. But he's the only game in town."

Finch shrugged. "Well, all we can do is ask. So, who else?"

Carmichael thought for a minute. "With the guys we already have over there, probably nobody else. If there's extra security needed, I don't know why the Druze couldn't help."

Finch shook his head. "On something this sensitive? I'd think the Israelis would insist on people trained for the job."

Carmichael almost patted the recruiter's hand in sympathy. "Matt, I'm not going to say that Mr. Baram's lying to us. But if anybody thinks the Israelis are going to pass this off to some hired mercs, hoping they'll get lucky looking for a real small needle in a really big haystack, they're crazy."

"So . . ."

"So," Carmichael replied, "I'd bet next year's retirement checks that we're a backup. The Izzies probably have people in place right now. Then, when and if the nukes are found, if there's any publicity, Tel Aviv can deny their people were in Lebanon. They'll say . . . 'Ta-da! Our friends from SSI did it.'"

Peters caught the drift. "More deniability."

"You got it, cowboy."

Peters and Finch looked at one another, then at the diminutive ops officer. Their faces asked the tacit question: now what?

Carmichael reached for the phone, put it on speaker, and consulted her PalmPilot. After three rings someone answered.

"Langevin here."

"Bernie! Sandy here."

"Ah, Sandra my sweet! When do we leave? I have a week's worth of condoms."

She blushed visibly while stifling a giggle. "Dr. Langevin, you might like to say hello to my colleagues here with me: Jack Peters and Matt Finch."

"Uh, oh. Hello, gentlemen. Matt, I hope you are not going with Sandra and me. Threesomes are so passé these days."

Finch's brown eyes gleamed while he bit his lip. Peters mouthed the words: "Is he drunk at four o'clock?"

Carmichael waved him down, still chuckling. Then she tried to regain control of the conversation. "Bernie, you're right about taking a trip. How did you know?"

"Because, my sweet, you only call me when you want me to go somewhere, and it's never with you. So what is it this time?"

"Is your passport current?"

"Forever and a day."

"Good. We need you here approximately at noon yesterday. Time is very short, Bernie. *Very* short. To be safe, I'd recommend you pack a bag and bring all your travel documents and whatever references you need. We'll be working late, and you could be wheels in the well tomorrow."

"Where to?"

"For now, just the Middle East."

"All right. And, ah, what references?"

Carmichael thought for a moment; it was an open line. "Bernie, that suitcase you're going to pack?"

"Yes?"

"Well, this job could involve suitcases that radiate."

"On the way, Sandy."

The line went dead.

37

AMASHA

"It's coming. I can feel it."

Frank Leopole stood at the front of the room with the SSI team and Druze officers arrayed around him. He had sketched a rough topographical map of the area on the schoolhouse blackboard, using colored chalk to define various positions.

"Why now, Colonel?" militia leader Azzam Hamdam asked through his interpreter, a youngster with financial ambitions in Beirut—or Washington, D.C.

"A combination of factors. First, the timing. The harassing fire has dropped off since our snipers got a handle on things, but I don't know if that's an indication of Hezbollah intent. There's more activity over at El-Arian, so I've warned Chris Nissen's team to go on high alert."

Breezy raised a hand. "Boss, where'd our sniper dudes go, anyway?"

"They're conducting another surveillance of the area. At least Furr will return to El-Arian in a day or so but Barrkman might go with him. We'll see how things look tomorrow.

"Beyond that, the weather's clamping down. I understand we'll have low ceilings and maybe some rain the next couple of days. Even though we're supposed to have close air support, it's unlikely that Northern Command can arrange fast movers for a while. As for helo gunships, that remains to be seen."

Leopole nodded toward Rami Hamadeh. "Captain Hamadeh has some information to share."

The Israeli Druze took two steps forward and turned to face the group. "General Nadel's brigade is fully briefed to support us, and Colonel Livni's special operations detachment can insert some teams on fairly short notice. But I am told that the political situation is considered tense, and we should only expect outside help in extreme circumstances."

Steve Lee shuffled his feet and cleared his throat. "Captain, I understand that concern. But hasn't it occurred to anybody that if we wait for 'extreme circumstances' it'll probably be too late? After all, we're twelve miles from the border, and that's a long way if choppers can't get in."

Hamadeh had to concede the point. "It's the best compromise that Northern Command could arrange with the ministry."

Bosco sensed that something was missing. "Excuse me, gents. But where's the Lebanese Army while all this is going on?"

The Israeli raised his eyebrows, as if hearing an unwelcome question. Finally he said, "The army is stretched thin right now, especially in the areas around Beirut and Sidon. We have liaison with their headquarters but we cannot count on much help, at least on short notice."

Leopole turned to the blackboard. "All right, then. I've designated these points in white for twenty-four-hour defense, and these in blue for daylight. With Mr. Hamdam's permission, I have suggested manning levels until the crisis passes. That means an interruption of daily life in the village, but there's no way around it."

The militia representatives voiced their assent and Leopole politely dismissed them. Once they left, he shut the door and spoke in subdued tones.

"All right, listen up. I got an encrypted e-mail from Arlington, and Captain Hamadeh confirmed it from his spec-ops sources. There's serious concern about Hezbollah smuggling backpack nukes through this area."

"Ho-lee shee-it." Breezy's voice was hushed, fervent.

Bosco added, "Oy vay!"

"It's a short-notice alert, and we'll just have to hope for the best for a while," Leopole added. "But HQ is sending Omar Mohammed and Dr. Langevin to us ASAP. They could be here in a couple of days. If we have to shift gears and go after the nukes, the militia will simply have to look out for itself." He glanced at Hamadeh. "I imagine that the IDF will have people on this side of the border as well, but there's no word on that."

Hamadeh felt the pinch. His immediate fate rested with the militia and the SSI team; his ultimate allegiance lay with the State of Israel. "I'll see if I can get clearance for more information. It will be necessary if a nuclear threat actually develops."

EL-ARIAN

Chris Nissen beckoned to Robert Pitney. They paced several yards before Nissen spoke. Pitney thought he knew what was coming. "Robert, I take it that you've never been shot at."

"No. At least not intentionally." He grinned but the joke fell flat.

"Well, that's about to change. I've heard from Frank. The Hezzies will probably try to take us in the next couple of days. I just thought I'd give you some time to collect your thoughts if you like."

Pitney shook his head. "No thanks, Chris. I'm cool."

The former Green Beret regarded the former cop in the gathering darkness. "Yeah, I can see you're calm and collected. But . . . Robert, it's just never like anybody thinks it'll be."

"Yes, I know that. I've trained operators who've done the deed, Chris. We talk about the psychological aspects.

And I'm telling you, I'm ready for whatever's coming down."

Nissen shifted his feet and folded his arms. "Well, then you're a member of a big club. I thought I was ready, too. The first time, I mean."

"Oh? What happened?"

"Well, it was . . ." Nissen's voice trailed off. "It turned to hash." He snapped his fingers, loud and clear in the night air. "Just like that."

Pitney realized that Chris Nissen probably did not admit such things to many people, and accepted the NCO's candor as a compliment. He thought, *Maybe this is the ultimate time for candor.* "What about the other guys? Are they worried about me?"

"No. Not that I know of." Nissen hastened to reply, hoping to cut off any doubt that his top shooter might entertain. "But, Robert, they've all been to the show before. They pretty much know what to expect. I just don't want you to enter a combat situation with unrealistic expectations."

"Chris, I think I'm pretty damned realistic." The mild obscenity was unusual for Robert Pitney, who used it for effect. "It's going to be loud and scary and confusing. I've read about the loneliness of the battlefield: S.L.A. Marshall was way off base about firing ratios but he was right about that." He stopped to gather his thoughts. Finally he said, "Staff Sergeant, I'll do my part. You can take that to the bank."

Nissen nodded. "Okay then. Listen, you're one of only three Arabic speakers on either team. I'd like you to direct traffic for me. I'll tell you where I need people to go. There'll be less confusion if you tell them."

"Chris, I'm not just the best shooter in this ville. I'm almost certainly the best shooter in this country right now. I'll get more hits with fewer rounds than anybody, including your snipers—wherever they are. Just put me where you need the most hits."

The team leader leaned back, stretching his lumbar muscles. After a moment he said, "Tell you what. Under your contract I could order you to do just what I said. But I guess I can consider you a force multiplier. So here's the deal, Robert. You put your guys where I tell you to put them, make sure they're well set, then have at it. Shoot 'em up. But between reloads, check with me because comm is likely to go south. If you have to be a runner between your guys and me, that's how it's gonna be."

Pitney did not know it but he grinned. Extending a hand, he said, "It's a deal, Sergeant."

They shook, then parted.

On the way back to the HQ building, Nissen was intercepted by Bob Ashcroft. "How'd it go? Is he gonna be okay?"

"Well, I think so, Bob. He's a little hard to read. Either he's one of the coolest cookies I've ever come across or he's sitting on something inside."

"Maybe he figures that anybody who can shoot like him is golden."

Nissen rubbed his neck, kneading the muscles. "Yeah, I thought about that. But Pitney's too smart to take that for granted." He massaged his neck again. "If I had to guess, I'd say that after all his trophies and his training classes, he's finally got a chance to do the job, you know? Maybe he's looking to prove something to himself."

"Oh, Lord."

"Yeah. You said it."

NABATIYEH GOVERNATE

"The operation will proceed like this," Azizi began.

Facing his jihadists, he referred to a rough map drawn on a sheet of butcher paper, taped to the wall. "We are assigning two-thirds of our fighters to the attack on Amasha.

If we are able to occupy the village, so much the better. We may or may not try to hold it, depending upon government reaction. Meanwhile, one-third will attack El-Arian and keep the defenders occupied there. If we can force some people out of the villages, onto the roads and across the countryside, so much the better." He paused for effect. "You will not attempt to stop unarmed people from fleeing either area. Is that clear?"

Abbasali Rezvani, the head mortarman, ventured a question. "May I ask why, brother? It would seem preferable to prevent anyone from escaping and opposing us later."

"Ordinarily that would be true, but not now. The more refugees we have in the country, the better our special operations teams will blend into the scene. We want both teams to get as close to the border as possible before they break away from the crowds."

Rezvani accepted the logic of the argument, but pointed to the map. "Would not the refugees more likely go east or north, toward Hasbaya?"

Azizi smiled. "Not if there is fighting and frequent mortar shells exploding in that direction."

Sitting in the front row, Ahmad Esmaili glanced around. None of the special operators gave any indication of concern for the deception aspect of the plan. That was as it should be. None of the men attacking the villages knew that their casualties would be considered the cost of doing business as long as at least one of the suitcases reached its ultimate destination.

38

BEIRUT

The embassy staffer spotted the SSI men as soon as they appeared from the jetway. "Dr. Mohammed and Dr. Langevin?"

Omar Mohammed set down his briefcase to shake hands. "Yes. We didn't know who would meet us . . ."

"Jim Bassinger." He greeted Langevin as well, showing his ID. Then he said, "I'll get you through customs as fast as possible. Follow me, gentlemen."

Mohammed and Langevin exchanged knowing smiles. "Mr." Bassinger wore civvies but he looked West Point, which in fact was the case.

Safely in the embassy limo, Bassinger immediately got down to business. "I don't know what you heard before you left, but things are pretty tense here. There's two or three bombings a week and the army and police have their hands full. I know that your situation is compounded because there's no official Israeli presence, and I understand that SSI is contracted to the Israeli government. We've been tasked to support you as much as possible, but it's limited."

"How so?" Mohammed asked.

"Hezbollah and probably a bunch of other Islamic outfits have most of the embassies and consulates under constant surveillance. Your people, the Druze militia, are especially of interest. You probably heard about the attack on Rafix Kara's compound a while back."

Langevin nodded. "It was mentioned in our departure briefing."

"Well, Kara died yesterday. The news hasn't been released yet, probably because it's still uncertain who will replace him. Frankly, I'm not sure that anybody can."

Mohammed absorbed that information and filed it for later reference. "Mister . . . ah, it isn't really *Mister* Bassinger, is it?"

The staffer's mouth curved slightly at both ends. "Dr. Mohammed, it's not even Bassinger, but it'll have to do. I know you'll understand."

Langevin appreciated the fact that he was dealing with a professional. The State Department ID had shown that the bearer was James L. Bassinger. "So, what can you do for us, sir?"

"We'll put you up in a secure facility tonight and see about getting you down to Hasbaya tomorrow. You'll have an armed escort but there may be a delay. It looks as if Hezbollah is going to attack Amasha or El-Arian. Maybe both."

The physicist had suspected as much. "In that case, I would like to have a weapon myself."

Bassinger almost grinned at the sentiment. "Dr. Langevin, you will understand that the United States Department of State does not issue firearms to visiting citizens." Before either SSI man could reply, Bassinger added, "However, your Druze escorts undoubtedly will have a fine selection for you."

Langevin noticed the telltale bulge of Bassinger's suit coat. "What do you carry, James?"

The staffer kept a straight face. "I don't understand the question."

NABATIYEH GOVERNATE

Imam Sadegh Elham returned from the evening prayer and made the announcement. "It came to me during

Salat-ul-Asr. The weather remains favorable so we will attack tomorrow."

Esmaili knew what that meant. "Then the weapons teams will leave the day after, to take advantage of the confusion in the area."

"Just so," Elham replied. He turned to Azizi. "Brother, the attacks on the villages are in your hands. As we planned, do everything possible to draw attention on the local area. Keep up the pressure, regardless of casualties." After a short pause he added, "We can always find more recruits for the jihad."

The cleric returned his attention to Esmaili and Jannati. "My brothers, your service has been long and hard. At the end of this mission, you will finally be able to rest."

For the moment, Esmaili decided to ignore the religious significance of that sentiment. But the meaning was clear enough. He glanced at Jannati, who would carry the package with an assistant. The nuclear jihadist appeared calm and composed. *He has already decided to die.*

NORTHERN ISRAEL

Yakov Livni walked into Solomon Nadel's quarters unannounced. When the duty noncom intercepted him in the foyer, he waved her down. "Tell Sol that I need to see him."

Nadel appeared several minutes later, buttoning a checkered shirt, noticeably disheveled. "This had better be *damned* important," he growled. "My wife got a rare attack of libido half an hour ago."

"Well, that should be plenty of time, even at your age," Livni quipped. "Besides, aren't nuclear weapons in Lebanon pretty damned important?"

The brigadier detoured to the kitchen and returned with two beers. He dismissed the housekeeper with a nod.

"Tell me."

"Solomon, I'm sticking my neck out—way out. The information we discussed before has been confirmed again so I'm sending some small teams across the border. But if any of them run into the kind of trouble you'd expect with backpack bombs, they're going to need help." He paused, staring into his friend's face. "The kind of help only you can provide."

Nadel's response was a long stare. Finally he took another sip from his bottle and set it down. "Who else knows?"

"You, me, my chief of staff, and the operators. Twelve men in three teams."

"Nobody in Jerusalem or Tel Aviv?"

Livni grinned. "I'm old and bald, Sol. I'm not slow and stupid."

"Well, if we're lucky—really lucky—nothing will come of it. After all, it's still not certain that the backpacks exist, just that there's a plan. But if something does turn up, and we intercept the bombs, then everything is all right. Nobody will get a medal or anything, but the heat will be off."

"My God, Sol. You're talking like a politician!"

Nadel tapped his shoulder, where an epaulette would rest. "It comes with the position. As you well know." He leaned forward, sliding the beer aside.

"Look, if I have to send my people in to get your people, I'd be obliged to notify higher command. I'd have to inform headquarters even if I didn't wait for permission. Besides that, there's no keeping a secret with this sort of thing." He smiled. "As you well know."

Livni finally reached for his own beer and sampled it. "Hmmm . . . not bad." He regarded his nominal superior across the table. "I'll tell you what I know, Solomon. I know that your main concern is that I've started an operation that may result in some of your boys having to cross the fence, and some of them may not come back. I'm sorry for that—as sorry as I can be. But how in God's name can we allow portable nuclear bombs along our border, let alone risking their getting inside?"

"What about your Druze contacts? Can't they help?"

"Some of them are aware of the situation, but I don't control them." He bit his lip in concentration. Then he said, "You know that Rafix Kara died?"

Nadel leaned back, as if nudged. "No. My God, when?"

"Just the other day. There was no question of him making a full recovery but I thought maybe . . ."

"Maybe you could talk to him again?"

"Well, that would have been nice."

"So who will take over?"

Livni gave an eloquent shrug. "Who knows? His surviving boy, God love him, he's a fine youngster. But he's too young to fill his father's shoes, and I don't know who else might step up." He exhaled, almost a sigh. "I'm afraid it will degenerate into a power struggle, Sol. All the time and effort in building up a really useful, reliable organization. Now . . ."

Solomon Nadel finished the sentiment. "Now we need them more than ever."

39

AMASHA

The mortars began at dawn, falling on the perimeter defenses.

Frank Leopole was already up, supervising the dispersal of the militiamen. He warned two groups to spread out, but had language problems. Finally he grabbed Rami

Hamadeh and shouted over the explosions. "Tell them to keep their interval! One round could take out four or five of 'em!"

The Druze officer nodded, already having noted the problem. It was understandable, really. New troops—or at least men unaccustomed to combat—tended to bunch up for moral support. It was just what artillerymen and machine gunners counted on.

With low clouds hanging in almost a ground cover, the sun was obscured in its effort to break through from the east. Leopole conceded that even if he got approval for helicopter gunships, they would not be available until later in the morning. By then the issue was likely to be decided.

He sprinted back to the command center and picked up the satellite phone. After an interminable wait—it must have been twenty seconds—he heard the voice he wanted. "Nissen."

"Chris, it's started here."

"Yeah, here too, Frank. Harassing fire so far but our recce team reports large movement on the reverse slope."

"All right. I'm coordinating with Captain Hamadeh. He'll see about getting some choppers but with the clouds on the ground it'll be a while."

"Affirm. Good luck, Frank."

"You, too, guy."

Leopole scooped up his AK and walked briskly from the HQ building, then stopped. He realized that he had left his helmet inside.

An 82mm round exploded twelve meters in front of him.

BUCKETS OF COLD WATER in the face and all down his front. That's what it felt like. He could see nothing, and hoped that it merely meant he had blood in his eyes. He needed to swallow but had difficulty. Something was tightening in his chest and he opened his mouth wide, sucking in as much air as possible.

It was the damndest thing: he smelled brownies in the oven after school.

Someone was calling his name, as if from far off.

It sounded just like his mother.

"FRANK!" BREEZY SHOOK HIS CO by the collar, trying to get a response. "Frank! *Damn* it!"

Mark Brezyinski pulled his medic's kit closer and grasped for . . . what? *What do I need? Frank's so messed up.* "Oh, my GOD!"

Another round landed thirty meters away, dropping dirt and stones all around. Breezy hardly was aware.

A, B, C. Airway, breathing, and circulation. He leaned over Leopole, feeling for a pulse and finding none. He lifted an eyelid, seeking life . . . and found none.

Brezyinski realized that he was crying. Bawling like a damned kid. Almost, anyway. The hot tears left tracks down his cheeks, creasing the grime. He wiped his sleeve across his face, smudging the tears and the dirt. He forced himself to look around, regaining control. *C'mon, man. Ruck up. Stay in the fight.*

Steve Lee was alongside. He took one look and nudged Breezy. "He's gone, Breeze. Come on, there's others who need help."

"Hos-tiles to the front!"

Bosco was on the wall, shoving militiamen to better firing points as the Hezbollah infantry advanced. The fighters came on in two waves, dodging and weaving, a few firing ineffectively from almost three hundred meters. For a moment he thought, *Sure wish we had the snipers, but they're on the way to El-Arian.*

In the next moment he was shouting. "Pick your targets, hold and squeeze!" Bosco knew that only a few Druze could understand him, but he made the effort anyway.

Finding a good rest, he set both elbows atop the rocky wall, stared a hole in his rifle's front sight, and began squeezing off aimed rounds in the subdued light.

Mortar rounds continued falling, adding noise and confusion—and cover—for the attackers. Some militiamen ducked behind the wall, avoiding the worst of the fragments. Hamadeh sent their leader, Azzam Hamdam, to kick them back into position. Meanwhile, the Israeli officer went in the other direction, ensuring that the active shooters—which were most of them—spread their fire across the frontal assault.

ON THE WAY BACK, Hamadeh saw a militiaman blown off the wall by a mortar round. The Druze landed with a thud, rolled over two or three times, and tried to get up. The IDF officer knelt beside him, ran a quick assessment, and saw that he could be saved. Hamadeh waved to Breezy. "Over here!"

Though previously trained as a medic, Breezy was a shooter by choice. But in a curious way he welcomed the chance to work on somebody. He forced the image of Frank Leopole from his mind, examined the Druze, and exclaimed, "Dude! Don't you know a sucking chest wound is nature's way of telling you to slow down?"

With the help of another Druze, Breezy dragged the casualty around a corner, temporarily out of harm's way. He leaned down, ear to the man's chest.

"Can you help him?" the militiaman asked.

Breezy nodded. "It's a pneumothorax—air in the pleural cavity. His right lung collapsed. I can hear the air whistling through the hole." He found the medical terminology oddly comforting; never mind that his impromptu aide could not understand the argot. He grabbed the casualty's right hand and laid it on the wound. Then he had the other Druze press down with his own hands. "Keep pressure on the bleeding, okay?"

While the second Druze did as ordered, Breezy pulled a dressing from his kit. He tore it open with his teeth and pulled off the plastic wrapper. He talked himself through the process. "The wrapper of a field dressing is great, but you can use cellophane like from a cigarette pack or aluminum foil, or even duct tape. You want a big enough patch to keep the material from getting sucked inside, so make it, like, two or three inches around the hole."

The militiaman looked down at his fellow citizen, who seemed surprisingly calm. "Yes, yes. Is good!"

Breezy taped three sides of the patch, explaining, "That lets him breathe better. Now roll him onto his wounded side if you can. The extra pressure can help prevent more bleeding. Okay?"

Again the nod, accompanied by almost a smile. "Yes, good. Thank you, American. Thank you!"

Breezy patted the man on the shoulder, wiped more tears from his eyes, and returned to the wall.

THE VOLUME OF FIRE increased. With the attackers inside one hundred meters, and the mortar shells beginning to abate, it became more a rifle fight. Breezy heard the clatter of full-auto fire and looked to his right. *Damn it! Wasting ammo!* He ran in that direction.

He almost tripped over a body.

Looking down, he became immobilized. "No, man, nooooo . . ."

The body belonged to Jason Boscombe, formerly of the United States Army Rangers. He had taken a round through the neck: more likely from blind luck than skill. But it had severed the spine and Bosco was just as dead.

Brezyinski sank to his knees. He felt numb, empty, and drained of emotion. He was still kneeling like that when the Hezbollah fighters reached the wall.

NABATIYEH GOVERNATE

"Hold it!" Barrkman held up a hand. The Druze driver did not understand American English but recognized the stop signal.

The Land Rover braked to a halt on the two-lane road, engine idling. Barrkman cocked an ear to the southeast. "I saw something. A light, kind of like an explosion."

Furr leaned forward from the rear seat. "Maybe it's just . . ."

An ephemeral eruption burst near the gray horizon, followed three seconds later by a faint *carrumph*.

"That's prob'ly mortars," Furr declared.

"Yeah, and El-Arian's catching 'em."

The Americans paused to consider their options. In that short interval, two more flash-*carrumph*s occurred. "That's not harassing fire," Barrkman said. "I think it's the real deal."

Furr stuck his head out the window, looking around. "If so, we sure as hell can't stay out here. We gotta find someplace to hole up. Or go back."

Barrkman rubbed his chin in thought. "But Frank said if the Hezzies hit one ville they'll probably hit both." He turned to the driver. "Bahjat, where can we hide this thing around here?"

Bahjat Hanifes spoke passable English but required time and patience. "Hide? This thing?"

"Yeah." Barrkman patted the dashboard. "This vehicle. Where can we keep it out of sight. From the road." He remembered to speak slowly and distinctly.

"Ah. Not many places." He swiveled his head left and right. Then, without further comment, he put the gearshift in reverse and began backing up.

At length Hanifes stopped and cranked the wheel hard over. He let out the clutch with a jerk and the tires slithered through some mud puddles. The Druze maneuvered onto some grass, then eased the Land Rover down a slight incline. He backed under a small stand of trees, set the parking brake, and switched off.

Barrkman climbed out, surveying the terrain. "Well, we're out of direct view of the road and I guess we can cut some foliage to cover the windshield. Other than that, I'm out of ideas."

Furr unlimbered himself from the rear and tugged at some bags. "We can't stay near the car. If the Hezzies see it, they'll come for a look." He set aside the custom AR-15 he had carried across his knees and picked up the drag bag with his precision rifle. "I have a coupla days' worth of MREs and some water but that's it."

Barrkman set aside his AK-47 and withdrew his own sniper rifle. He began taking inventory. "Bahjat, what do you have?"

Hanifes hoisted his personal weapon, a Romanian AK, and a chest pack full of loaded magazines. From his knapsack he withdrew some bread, grapes, and bottled water.

Barrkman looked at Furr. "I don't suppose you brought your night vision, did you?"

"I thought I'd be back by this afternoon."

"Well, I've got mine but it won't be much good for anything but surveillance. A fight's a losing proposition with just three of us. Best thing we can do is lay low and see how things go."

Furr walked over to the Druze. "Bahjat, do you have a radio? Contact with Captain Hamadeh or Mr. Hamdam?"

"No, sir. No radio. I never need."

Barrkman walked several yards from the trees and looked around. "There's plenty of daylight, maybe more. We could walk cross-country toward Amasha and see what's doing there. It's better than getting caught on the road."

Furr pulled his Glock 19 from its shoulder holster and chambered a round before replacing the pistol. "But if we get there and it's under attack, then what? We'd be on the outside looking in. Maybe between the Hezzies and town."

Barrkman returned to the vehicle, withdrew his rifle case, and faced northwest. "Like I said, we should find us a hole and sit tight. But someplace that's not obvious—no hilltops but with a good field of view."

Pondering his partner's suggestion, Furr saw no alternative. Without speaking, he pulled a roll of electrical tape from the glove compartment and tore off two thin strips. He applied one to the inside of each partly open door, the other end attached to the frame. Then he shut the doors. "What's that?" Barrkman asked.

"If somebody checks this rig before we return, the tape will be pulled off."

"You are one sneaky bastard, you know that?" Barrkman grinned appreciatively. Then he added, "But what if they booby trap the truck?"

Furr grinned back. "Then we'll know for sure somebody was here."

The senior sniper laughed at the gallows humor. "Okay, then. All we need now is someplace to hide."

Bahjat Henifes was a quietly competent militiaman. "I know place. You come we go." He stepped off with a purposeful stride, and lacking options, the Americans followed at six-meter intervals.

40

EL-ARIAN

Chris Nissen had a problem. Or, more accurately, he had one problem that outweighed all the others.

Ducking another mortar round, Nissen grabbed Robert Pitney by the flak jacket. "Listen! We can't hold the eastern perimeter. There's too many Hezzies. We're gonna have to pull back to the inner perimeter . . ." He turned his head to avoid more dirt and rocks thrown up by another 82mm shell. "I think we can hold there."

Pitney nodded amid the noise. "Gotcha. I'll start on it." With that, he was on the way, shouting in Arabic, pulling every second man off the firing line.

Nissen gestured to Bob Ashcroft. "Pitney's pulling the Druze back to the interior perimeter. You get with Lieutenant Halabi and establish those guys as a base of fire to cover the others when they pull back."

Before Ashcroft had sprinted twenty meters he saw Halabi consulting with Ayoob Slim, the militia leader. They went in opposite directions: Slim to the firing line and Halabi to the fallback position. Obviously they had a handle on things so Ashcroft went to a gap in the line and looked for somebody to shoot.

There was no shortage of targets. Ashcroft estimated eighty to one hundred Hezbollah fighters advancing on the village, and not many were taking fire. He reminded himself to breathe, settled down behind his FN-FAL, and began firing at attackers perhaps 150 meters out. He was jarred by occasional mortar rounds, and once ducked to avoid automatic fire, but he selected individual targets and shot at each until it fell. He was counting rounds rather than hits, and at eighteen he decided to reload.

Something nudged his shoulder. Phil Green's blue eyes twinkled in the gray light. "Is this a private party or can anybody play?"

Ashcroft completed the reload and stuffed the previous magazine inside his vest. "I'm just playin' through. Nissen wants some cover for the militia who're pulling back to the inner line."

Green pointed a thumb down the wall. "If you'll notice, you're practically the last one here." With that he leaned into the wall and shot the two nearest assailants, forty yards out.

Ashcroft glanced left and right. *How's he stay so calm?* He tugged on his new magazine to ensure it was seated, then looked at Green. "Set?"

"Set!" Green shouted.

"Go!"

Beneath a volume of covering fire, the two Americans scrambled across the open ground between the inner and outer stone walls. They heard the Dashika's distinctive *chug-chug-chug* pounding from atop the nearest building. Green had to jump two militia bodies but scooped up one of the men's AKs en route.

As Ashcroft and Green leapt the inner wall, the militia's Dashika rattled out a long burst, perhaps fifteen rounds. Ken Delmore, an automatic weapons aficionado, looked up in disdain. "They're wasting ammo. And I don't think they're hitting very much."

The big man turned and made for the external steps leading to the balcony where the Russian weapon was mounted. He was halfway up when an RPG round impacted near the top of the landing. The two Dashika gunners were wounded and Delmore was blown off the steps. He fell eight feet onto his back, landing with a discernible *thud*. He didn't move.

Pitney was first to reach him. The ex-cop ran the A-B-C assessment, then shouted, "He's breathing!" He looked back at Delmore. "Can you hear me?"

Delmore opened his eyes, trying to focus on something. "My back." It came out as a croak.

"Okay, don't move." Pitney called in Arabic, summoning a militiaman who spoke some English. He said, "Stay with him. I'll be back. But don't let him move."

Pitney scrambled along the wall until he found Nissen. "Delmore's down and I think the heavy MG is knocked out. But most of the guys seem to be shooting."

"All right. Keep directing their fire, Robert. I don't know why the Hezzies haven't flanked us but they seem set on keeping up the frontal assault."

Pitney almost smiled. "Suits me." He found a good position amid the Druze and began firing. Nissen watched for a moment, curious how the hottest shooter in Lebanon would handle the situation. He noted that Pitney appeared almost calm, certainly deliberate. He shot quickly but not fast. Undoubtedly the Hezbollah unit scaling the first stone wall was taking serious casualties.

Hussain Halabi ran up to Nissen, hunched over amid the gunfire. "I think we need more men here. Let me bring half of those from the south side. They have almost nothing to shoot at."

"Okay, go ahead. I still don't understand why they're not flanking us." Nissen patted the liaison officer on the shoulder and Halabi scampered off. He went twenty meters and fell flat. At first Nissen thought he had tripped, but when the Israeli didn't move, the American suspected the worst. "Oh, no." He grabbed Ashcroft again. "Help me!"

The SSI operators ran to Halabi, and without speaking, each grabbed an arm. They pulled him into the lee of a bullet-pocked building and knelt down. Nissen turned Halabi's head toward him. One look was enough for Nissen. "He's had it. Must be AP ammo through the vest."

Ashcroft turned to resume shooting when Nissen caught him. "Tell Pitney to go to the south wall and bring half those guys back here. Hurry!"

Nissen ensured that Pitney dashed away on his mission, then walked along the wall, stooped over to reduce his silhouette. Occasionally he stopped to double-tap an attacker but mainly he kept moving, watching for gaps, lending encouragement. When he turned back to retrace his steps he ran into Ken Delmore.

Nissen's brown eyes widened in astonishment. "They said you were a hard down."

Delmore leaned close amid the noise. "I was. Back hurts like hell." At that, he pivoted, shouldered his custom AR-15, and looked for targets.

Moments later Pitney reappeared with several militiamen in tow. He distributed them along the wall, but the firing had dropped off. Nissen waved to Ayoob Slim, hailing the militia commander. With Pitney on hand to smooth over linguistic difficulties, the SSI leader and the Druze chieftain reached an agreement.

"Okay," Nissen concluded. "We'll keep this layout but I want the reaction force to move closer to this position. They've been trying to push us from the east all morning."

"About time for a change, don't you think?" asked Pitney.

"No, I don't. These blockheads get something in mind and they stick with it. That's why I want the reaction force closer to us than to the south."

"Well, okay, Chris. But it's not much more than a squad."

Nissen nodded. "Yeah, I know. But we can't stay nose to nose with these bastards indefinitely. If they throw another human wave at us, some might get through. So we need to plug the gap right away."

Pitney exchanged a few words with Slim, who said something and nodded vigorously. "Ayoob says he understands."

"All right. You and him get things sorted out. And run

an ammo check. We may have to redistribute magazines between the lookers and the shooters."

"Okay." Pitney thought for a moment. "The Hezzies took a beating. You really think they'll try again?"

Nissen grinned. "Not a doubt in my military mind. But I'm gonna check with Frank to see what's doing at Amasha."

41

OUTSIDE AMASHA

Mohammad Azizi lowered his binoculars and rubbed his chin. Sprawled on a hummock half a kilometer from the village, he judged that the attack was progressing tolerably well. He accepted the handset from his radio operator and called his subordinate commander.

"Ameen, this is Baahir. Reply."

The RO glanced at the leader of the security element. They exchanged knowing glances. *Trust Azizi to select a grandiose call sign. Baahir* meant "dazzling" or "brilliant" while *Ameen* was merely "trustworthy."

The assault commander took ten seconds to respond. "We are heavily engaged in . . ." The sound of gunfire crackled behind the voice, which faded out. Azizi waited for clarification, and when it did not come he tried again.

"Ameen, this is Baahir. Reply."

"I am here."

"This is Baahir. Listen, I can see people fleeing the opposite side of the village. Keep up the pressure but do not prevent anyone from leaving. Acknowledge."

The carrier wave snapped and sputtered. Something high-pitched assailed Azizi's ear, ending in a screech. Nearly a minute passed. Then the voice was back. "Ameen speaking. My radio operator has been killed. But I am advancing. Reply."

Azizi pressed the transmit button. "Baahir responding." Long seconds passed. He tried again.

After two more attempts Azizi passed the handset to his RO. The operator shrugged. "It seems that he can transmit but not receive."

"Well, there's nothing more to be done here." Azizi levered himself out of the prone position. He picked up his rifle and began walking downhill. "We should get closer, anyway." When the radioman caught up with him, he added almost as an afterthought: "Try to contact the El-Arian commander. I want to know the situation over there."

AMASHA

Breezy didn't know how he got under cover. He only remembered looking into Bosco's dead face. He was hardly aware of the gunfire around him: it was nearly constant, almost atmospheric. Just part of the landscape. Becoming aware, he remembered to run a system check on his rifle: half-empty magazine, round chambered, safety engaged. One full mag remaining.

Steve Lee rapped on Breezy's helmet. "You okay? We can't stay here."

Breezy stared into the retired major's face. *Lee. Steve Lee. You pulled me away from . . . Bosco.* He nodded. "We . . ." *We what?*

Lee slapped the operator upside the head, hard. "Damn it, Brezyinski, snap out of it! We're in deep serious here. Get your damned head back in the game!"

The sharp blow got results. Breezy's grief-numbed brain

defaulted to shock, then anger. He opened his mouth to scream at his tormentor, then something settled in the back of his mind. *He's right. Gotta stay in the fight.*

He blinked, hard. "Okay, Major. I'm all right now."

"Hoo-ah!" Lee hefted Leopole's satellite phone. "I hope to hell this battery's good. Wasn't time looking for another." He glanced left and right before leaving cover, noting the growing confusion around him. Some militiamen were withdrawing slowly, firing and leap-frogging back upon each other as they had been trained. Others were scampering for cover, though none had abandoned their weapons.

Lee inhaled, blew out the breath, and said, "With me."

He lunged upright, driving forward with his weight lifter's thighs, and pivoted to cover the far end of the block. Breezy was close behind, swinging his muzzle to cover the opposite side of the street. They went ten or twelve paces when Breezy saw the projectile smoking toward them. He only had time to scream "RPG!"

The warhead exploded within feet of Steve Lee, and he went down in a tumble. He was screaming in pain and rage, holding his ruined right leg with both hands.

Breezy stopped, entertaining an ephemeral question: *Is he done? Should I run?*

He slung his rifle and grasped the stitched cloth handle on the back of Lee's ballistic vest. Hardly noticing the 240 pounds of man and gear, Breezy pulled Lee through an open door.

"The radio!" Lee yelled. "Get the radio!"

Breezy looked outside and saw the precious lifeline in the street. He glanced at Lee's bloody leg—what was left of it—and hesitated.

"Go, God damn it!" Lee shoved at him with one hand.

Breezy dashed into the street, scooped up the sat phone, and dashed back inside. He unslung his medic's kit and pulled out a tourniquet. He worked fast, almost glad to have something to occupy his mind.

He knew that he was feeling the rising tide of panic. With an effort of will he choked it down. "It's bad, Maje, but I can handle it."

Lee allowed his head to rest on the floor, not wanting to look at his severed limb. He was surprised at how little pain he felt so far. *But it'll come.*

Breezy finished tending the traumatic amputation and pulled Lee farther inside the room. Some family's breakfast had been violently interrupted. Looking around, he saw Lee's carbine and fetched it for him.

"Jim Bowie," Lee rasped.

"What?"

"That's me. Jim Bowie, propped up in bed at the Alamo." Lee emitted a giggle. "Mexicans over the wall. Gooks in the wire."

Breezy feared that Lee was descending into shock. In the dim light, it was possible to see his eyes dilating.

"Major, can you stand? I can help you outside and maybe we can get help."

Lee shook his head violently. "No . . . no. Wouldn't make it." He fumbled at his vest, seeking his notebook. As he patiently, deliberately wrote something, he said, "Gimme a shot."

Breezy reached into his bag. "You want morphine?"

Lee clinched his teeth, biting down the rising pain. "All you got."

Brezyinski recoiled at the implication. "I can't do that. You know . . ."

Lee's left hand was on Breezy's throat. "Listen! I'm not gonna make it. An' you can't get out with me. But we can't let them get the sat phone. Here." He shoved the paper into Breezy's hand. The ruled lines were crudely scrawled in black ink smudged with blood not quite dried.

Breezy focused hard to read the words. *Fatal wound, can't move. Ordering B out with radio. Love to family. Lee.*

"Now, gimme enough morphine!"

On by far the worst day of his life, before or after, Mark Brezyinski rolled up Stephen Lee's sleeve, found the vein, and complied with his friend's wish. Then the onetime happy-go-lucky paratrooper picked up the sat phone, walked through the door, and went over the wall.

42

NABATIYEH GOVERNATE

Something was different about Imam Elham. He looked pleased for a change, standing before Hezbollah's yellow and green flag.

Greeting Esmaili, Jannati, and the others, he almost smiled. "I have just received a message from Brother Azizi. The operation against Amasha appears successful. Our fighters should completely occupy the village before long. Many people are fleeing."

Esmaili asked, "What of the attack on El-Arian?"

"That too is successful, even with lesser goals. Our forces have prevented any reinforcement of Amasha, and the defenders are reported staying in place. Some residents also are leaving there."

Jannati, who listened closely and seldom spoke, ventured a question. "Imam, then when will we leave on our mission?"

"Tonight, when there is more confusion in the dark. With refugees spreading across the countryside, it will be easier for our two teams to conceal themselves among the rabble."

"God is great!" Ka'bi, Jannati's partner from Tehran, leapt to his feet. He led the others in the familiar chant. Esmaili was among the first to rise in response, mouthing the words with the others.

We are the nation of Hezbollah!
I shall sacrifice my life for Allah.
I am proud.
I am ready to sacrifice all the others in the same way.

As the meeting broke up, Elham made that same infuriating come-to-me gesture to Esmaili. "I want to add a man to your team. He may be useful in holding any pursuers at bay."

"Yes?"

"Your young marksman, Hazim."

Esmaili blinked in surprise, measuring his words. *Hazim may fit your plans, but not mine, old man.* "With respect, I prefer to leave him here with the security force. He is still learning the business of sniping and he could slow us down."

"Brother, his mission is to slow down those who might learn of your presence. After that, he can make his own way. If he survives."

Esmaili thought: *Another man thrown away.* For an ephemeral moment he wondered why he suddenly cared about preserving one life when he had willingly led so many others to their fate. Maybe because the firing squad dream had returned again recently.

"As you wish, Imam."

Elham rewarded the chieftain with a rare pat on the shoulder. "We all serve God in our own way. You more than most."

NABATIYEH GOVERNATE

Breezy found a depression in the ground and sat down, rifle cradled across his knees. He tried to prompt more water from his Camelbak but it was empty. He leaned back against a rock and closed his eyes, inhaling slowly, deeply.

He saw Steve Lee lying on the floor of that house, calmly waiting for the morphine to do its merciful work.

Breezy's eyes snapped open. His brain began to churn. *Why'd he make me do that? He could have shot himself. Maybe he's Catholic or something. Hell*, I'm *Catholic— sort of—and I would have done it. Everybody knows what happens to prisoners. Your family gets to watch your head being cut off on TV.*

Mark Brezyinski was not given to rationalization. Before Amasha, his world had been ordered, if frequently violent. He had relatives whom he saw on occasion, but mostly he had SSI and his work. And Bosco. Now there was nobody to fill that void, the once-in-a-lifetime friendship. Breezy knew instinctively that there would never be another, and he allowed himself to cry a little more, as much for himself as for his dead friends.

There's a reason I'm alive. It's not just a crapshoot. But what is it?

On an impulse, Breezy pulled the crumpled, bloody paper from his pocket. He looked at Steve Lee's dying declaration. *Fatal wound, can't move. Ordering B out with radio. Love to family.*

An electric tingle ran down Breezy's spine. *It wasn't fatal. He could have survived. He just couldn't move. So . . . he was, like, saving . . .* me!

In the pale gray atmosphere of midday, Breezy saw the dawn's reality. *I don't really understand the sat phone, and probably he knew it. He could have destroyed it. But he gave me a reason to go.*

So he wasn't in shock. He was thinking clearly right up to the end.

Breezy raised his hands to his head, grasping the paper that would prove he behaved decently. For the first time he wondered whether he would tell SSI the truth of Steve Lee's death, or whether he would put the best possible mask on an ugly face and say that the operator died before Breezy left that awful place.

He got up, looked around, and seeing nothing, began walking in the general direction of El-Arian, still rubbing the moistness in his eyes.

He had gone about a klick when he heard something that froze him in midstride. A vehicle, fast approaching. Breezy looked around, seeking a hiding spot, and found none. In desperation he sprinted downslope toward a tree but it was too far. He dived into the grass, flattening himself, rifle shouldered.

The engine sound came from a Nissan pickup with a Dashika mounted in the bed—a "technical" in Third World terms. The truck screeched to a stop about eighty meters away, off the road, with the engine idling. Two armed men dismounted. Breezy glimpsed at least two others in the cab.

The two men—surely Hezbollah—went to opposite sides of the tailgate and opened their flies. *Pit stop,* Breezy thought. He moved his front sight from the dismounted men to the seated occupants. He disengaged the safety, keeping his finger off the trigger.

When finished, the pair climbed back in the bed. The driver engaged the clutch and began to add throttle when the assistant gunner pounded on the cab.

He was looking directly at Brezyinski.

Amid excited jabbering and animated gestures, the jihadists focused their attention on the strange form. The primary gunner swung the snout toward Breezy and tugged on the charging handle.

Breezy shot him off the mount.

When the A-gunner stepped behind the weapon, Breezy got off two fast rounds, one of which connected. The gunner sagged into the bed, screaming in pain.

The driver accelerated, leaving one motionless body in the dirt. Breezy tracked the vehicle as best he could, but the grass blocked his view. For a moment he allowed himself to believe he was safe.

The pickup came back, stopped fifty meters away, and the passenger opened fire with the Dashika. The first burst went high. The second chewed up the grass and dirt around Breezy. He crawfished right, getting off snap shots that did no good.

Now the driver had his AK out and was firing semiauto.

Breezy rolled away again, knowing that the Hezzies had achieved fire superiority. He could not stop and take aim without giving them a better target.

He tasted raw heart, felt his urgent bladder. He had no choice—keep moving.

The next burst straddled him—rounds impacting left and right. *God, God. I'm gonna die!*

Abrupt silence.

Breezy moved again, saw the Nissan still there but no shooters in sight. He rose to one knee, rifle ready. *What the . . . ?*

Three men appeared from behind the tree he had tried to reach. They advanced at a jog, spreading out, moving professionally.

Breezy waved a joyous wave, breathing the air of the saved. One of the men waved back.

Rick Barrkman had a huge grin on his face. Breezy leapt on him and hugged his neck, pounding his tactical vest, almost crying in relief. "Man, I thought . . . I was dead." He choked down a sob, rubbed his eyes that were wet again.

Rob Furr and the militiaman checked the vehicle. There

was one gunshot, which told Breezy all he needed to know. After loading the bodies, the Druze got in the cab and drove the truck downslope.

Furr walked up to Breezy and placed both hands on his shoulders. "You lucky bastard! If we'd been thirty seconds later they would've toasted you."

"Shit, tell me about it!" He wiped his face, gleaming with perspiration and tears. "Where'd you guys come from?"

Barrkman turned and waved to the Druze, who was bringing the Land Rover. Then he said, "We holed up for a while this morning when we saw the attacks on both villes. We waited till things quieted down and came back to the truck, then saw you. We barely had time to get our scopes on these guys."

Breezy sucked in more air, aware that his heart was still surging. "I never even heard you shoot."

"Not surprising." Furr laughed. "With all that belt-fed noise."

Barrkman cocked his head. "Breeze, if you're out here all alone, what's happening in Amasha?"

Breezy opened his mouth twice. Finally, he told them.

EL-ARIAN

"It's a mess over there." Chris Nissen raised his hands in frustration. "Brezyinski's version is probably the most recent, but we've had Druze reports that the place is still holding out."

The erstwhile NCO paced in the room, rubbing his chin in concentration. The other SSI operators sat or stood, according to their state of fatigue. Nissen surveyed them for their current utility:

Ashcroft and Green appeared strong. Delmore talked a good game but he moved stiffly, slowly. Barrkman was composed; Furr obviously worried about his friends in Amasha. Breezy had definitely changed. The puckish, surfer dude persona was gone, probably forever. He sat against the wall, obviously brooding.

Pitney was outside, coordinating the defenses with Ayoob Slim. *He's doing good,* Nissen conceded.

With seven men plus himself, Nissen had to make a decision shortly, and there was no point delaying it.

"Listen up," he said. "I've been talking to Captain Hamadeh. He's hoping for aerial surveillance to look at Amasha later today, if the weather lifts. The fact that the Hezzies haven't hit us again leads us to think this morning's attack was a delaying action. Apparently they didn't want us to reinforce Frank's garrison, and now that they probably own it, they may be satisfied. Or they might come back to pick up the pieces."

"So what do we do, Boss?" Delmore's voice was lighter than his back felt.

"Hamadeh hopes that some of the Amasha militia will be able to get here, like Breezy did. If so, that's great. If not, we have to arrange contingencies on our own."

Barrkman asked, "What sort of contingencies?"

Chris Nissen inhaled, then blew out his breath. "Okay, here it comes.

"Hamadeh has heard from his special operations liaison with Northern Command. There's intel, considered good, that the opposition has one or more backpack nukes."

The NCO waited for the inevitable chatter to abate. "This is not, repeat, not for distribution. But there are clandestine spec-ops teams on this side of the border, looking for infiltrators who could have the nukes. We've been asked to deploy one or two teams, assuming we can spare the manpower. If so, Hamadeh will notify his people to look out for us."

Green raised a hand. "Chris, that's not what we signed on for. The contract is training and . . ."

"Yeah, I know. I'm going to discuss that with Arlington as soon as I can. It's still pretty early there—about 0300." He paused, looking at the far wall. "Besides, they need to know about Frank and . . . the others."

"There's lots of people out wandering around, you know." Breezy's voice caught most of the operators by surprise. He had hardly said a word since relating the news about Amasha. "I think the Hezzies want a lot of civilians in the countryside."

"Why's that?"

"Cover. If there's backpack nukes out there, it'd be easier to sneak 'em to the border with a bunch of refugees."

Nissen looked at Green, who nodded. "That's a good point, Breeze. I'll talk to Hamadeh about it." *Maybe he's getting his edge back.*

"Meanwhile, we're getting some help from headquarters. There was an encrypted e-mail last night that Dr. Mohammed is flying to Beirut with a physicist. They'll join us ASAP."

Ashcroft perked up. "That must be Bernie Langevin! Phil and I worked with him on the yellow cake smuggling."

Green's mouth curled at the edges, elevating his mustache. "Only PhD that I ever met who can strip a Beretta."

"Well, I'm sure that's not his main credentials," Nissen replied. "Anyway, Dr. Mohammed is coming because he speaks Farsi as well as Arabic and Hebrew. He can be a big help, especially if we tangle with some Iranians."

Furr roused himself and made a point. "Chris, if we send teams out chasing nukes, how many guys would stay here?"

"I don't know yet. But I think we want three or four men per team, which means no more than two teams."

When nobody else commented, he put his hands on his hips. "Okay, that's it for now. I'll let you know as soon as I hear more."

As the shooters filed out, Breezy held back. Finally he walked up to Nissen. "Sergeant, I have one thing to say."

"Yeah?"

"If you send out a team, I'm on it."

Before Nissen could reply, Breezy was headed for the door.

43

SSI OFFICES

Sandy Carmichael set down the phone and sat in stunned silence. Then she removed her reading glasses, laid her head on the desk, and allowed herself to cry.

Marshall Wilmont found her that way four minutes later.

The burly, unkempt chief operating officer felt even more useless than most males in dealing with weeping women. He patted Carmichael's back, awkwardly slipping an arm around her shoulder, and asked, "Sandy, hon. Please . . . what's wrong?" The only reply was more sobs.

At length she raised her blond head, eyes streaming tears, and croaked out the words. "Oh, God, Marsh. They're dead. I think they're all dead!"

Wilmont reached over his operations officer and flipped the intercom. "Mike, you there?"

When no response came, Wilmont buzzed Derringer's secretary. "Peggy, where's the admiral?"

"I think he was going to see you, sir. I can . . ."

"My God, Marsh, what is it?"

Derringer appeared at Carmichael's door. He took in the scene and reached the desk in four brisk strides. Leaning over, he grasped Carmichael by both shoulders. "Sandy! Come on, what is it?"

Retired Lieutenant Colonel Sandra Carmichael raised herself upright. She reached for a Kleenex and applied it to her ruined makeup. After blowing her nose, she found her voice.

"I just heard from Chris Nissen. He says the attack on El-Arian was a deception." She stopped, inhaled, and exhaled. "His guys wanted to reinforce Frank's team but couldn't get out. They found Breezy in the countryside and . . . and . . ."

Derringer motioned for Wilmont to fetch some water.

"Go on, Sandy."

She wiped another tear from her cheek. "Breezy said . . ." She looked into Derringer's face. "Oh, Mike. He said they're gone. They're all dead!"

Wilmont set down a paper cup, which Carmichael sipped.

"Who's gone?" Derringer demanded. "Who was with Frank?" He looked at Wilmont.

"Steve Lee went to work with Frank and one of the others moved to Nissen's team."

Carmichael swallowed carefully. "Amasha was Frank's job with Steve and Bosco and Breezy. Pitney went to El-Arian with the new man, Delmore. There were one or two snipers with Frank, too."

Derringer pulled up a chair and sat opposite Carmichael. He realized that he was into Shock, the first stage of grief, and began allowing himself to expect the worst. For the moment he would skip Denial, touch upon Anger, and default to Acceptance. Depression undoubtedly would come in its own time.

"If Nissen couldn't get out, it sounds like Hezbollah not only took Amasha but they're holding it."

"What's that matter?" Carmichael's Alabama accent was sharp, angry.

Derringer touched her forearm. "Sandy, we still don't know for sure if Breezy's report is accurate. But we can't start dealing with it until we know the local situation." He looked at Wilmont. "Marsh, see if you can get Nissen on the satellite phone. We need more hard intel."

As Wilmont ambled out, Carmichael eyed her boss. "That's *my* department, Admiral. I can still function, you know." Her voice was flat, accusatory.

"Not right now you can't, Sandy. You take a little while to compose yourself, then we'll get down to business."

She nodded and walked from the office, headed for the ladies' room.

Derringer watched her leave. *Not so long ago she killed two men in a shootout and it hardly fazed her. But now she's probably lost two or three friends and she can't shoot anybody.*

HASBAYA

Bernard Langevin looked out of place in the company of Type A door-kickers. Slim and balding, he stood five feet seven and tipped the scales at 136 pounds regardless of what he ate. The fact that he held an intermediate certificate from a cordon bleu school put him in rare company for a physicist. But for the moment he deferred to SSI's training officer.

Omar Mohammed began briefing the field team. "Gentlemen, I know that we have arrived at the worst possible time. It's especially hard for me since I knew and worked with Frank Leopole for several years. I also knew Steve Lee and Jason Boscombe, as we deployed to Afghanistan. But we are professionals, and I know that we will continue doing a professional job.

"First: organization. Sergeant Nissen remains in charge at El-Arian, with Delmore who has a back injury. It's a risk, but our priority is finding the backpack weapons. Chris and I talked by phone and agreed to field the most operators possible while the militia continues defending the village. Since there's been no further attacks, that looks fairly safe.

"Now, we're deploying two teams, each with a linguist. I'll have one with Ashcroft, Brezyinski, and Furr. Dr. Langevin goes with Barrkman, Green, and Pitney, who of course speaks Arabic. We will be in radio contact, and if one team makes contact, we hope the other can join up. But we cannot count on secure communications, so keep that in mind.

"A couple of you know Dr. Langevin from pursuit of the Iranian yellow cake last year. For the rest of you, let me say that Bernard has a superb reputation both as a scientist and an operator." The training director injected a wry smile into his introduction. "He is the only physicist I've ever known who understands the principle of the double tap and the elegance of the Mozambique Drill."

Getting the response he desired, Mohammed continued. "With his arms control background, Dr. Langevin is of obvious help in our search for the backpack weapons. Assuming we make contact with the Hezbollah agents, he will decide how best to proceed. Since I speak Farsi, I will provide any language help required.

"Now, I'd like to ask Dr. Langevin to tell us about what we're after."

Aware that he was subject to testosterone-fueled scrutiny, the lithe physicist held up a photo.

"The item of interest is the RA-115 special atomic demolition munition, better known as a backpack nuke or suitcase bomb. There are other models like the -155 with different weights and yields. We might find something that nobody even knows about. But functionally they're similar to the American Mark 54, both capable of yielding about one kiloton. The Mark 54 weighed 163 pounds while reportedly the Russian weapons are a lot less."

Phil Green asked, "Doctor, how many nukes are we talking about?"

"Well, that's the sixty-four-million-dollar question. Open sources are pretty consistent at about eighty 115s but I've seen estimates as high as two hundred fifty. When the USSR collapsed in 1990, tactical weapons were pulled back to Russia from all but three of the former republics: Ukraine, Kazakhstan, and Belarus. There's been reports that renegade KGB agents sold some backpacks, and that's possible because apparently some of the weapons were kept by the KGB's own commandos."

"So you're saying that both the KGB and the military had backpacks?"

"That's how it appears. You have to appreciate how bureaucratic things were in the Soviet Union. It's as if everybody wanted a finger in every pie: basically empire building. The main agency was called the 12th GUMO, the ministry of defense office that oversaw nuclear weapons. So you had both KGB and military *Spetsnaz* units capable of delivering backpacks, but the actual control and distribution of the nukes was fairly complex. I think that some were kept near operational units while others were in special depots for inventory and maintenance."

Ashcroft raised his hand. "How much damage could one of these things do, Doctor?"

"A one KT detonation could level an area of two, maybe three square miles. That may sound like a lot but actually it's not. Remember, these things are demolition devices, meant for sabotage rather than strategic or even tactical use. The effects could be heightened by adding radioactive materials to produce a 'dirty bomb' that would increase lethality, but that would take some expertise."

Langevin began pacing, warming to his subject. "Now,

we need to remember. The Soviets weren't slipshod or crazy. They knew the possibility that some of these things could get into the wrong hands. So they put PALs on each weapon—permissive action links. That means that anybody who had a nuke would need the correct codes to enable a detonation for that particular package.

"There's more. The shelf life of a backpack nuke is pretty limited in any case, but once the weapon is separated from its power source it relies on a battery. At that point the clock's ticking before the weapon goes flat line.

"Now, I already alluded to the maintenance problems. It's safe to say that as a general rule, a backpack needed inspection and probably upkeep twice a year—maybe more. So . . ."

Ashcroft interrupted. "So anyone who bought one of the damn things would need some know-how or support to make it work."

The scientist nodded. "Correct. Depending on the type of weapon, the operator needs four to ten minutes to detonate it."

Rick Barrkman's baritone arose from the back row. "Doctor, how in the world do we know where to begin looking for these things?"

Langevin arched an eyebrow and looked to Omar Mohammed.

"I was coming to that little item," Mohammed began. "Originally we were going to the field with IDR liaison, Druze officers who have worked with special operations command. But the recent casualties have made that difficult, so we're relying on direct radio contact with Northern Command. If we find anything, we notify them as soon as possible, but not at the risk of allowing a weapon to get away."

"Doctor, how secure is the comm?" Furr did not want to take communications for granted.

"Each team has a frequency-agile radio that has been

tested for compatibility with Northern Command. That's in addition to our own radios for talking between our teams and El-Arian. I speak Hebrew, but if for some reason I cannot communicate, the Israeli command net will have English-speaking operators on hand until further notice. The authenticator codes are on cards with each set. Before we leave, we will check out another operator on each team."

Green's lips curled beneath his mustache. "Gosh, Doctor, where'd we ever get such high-priced equipment?"

Mohammed returned the door-kicker's mirthful tone. "Let's just say that I have a very rich uncle."

Rob Furr still had concerns that he wanted discussed. "Dr. Mohammed, I don't want to play what-if all day, but there's just a lot that could go wrong and I'd like to know what sort of planning is involved. Like, what if we get one of these nukes and Dr. Langevin isn't available? None of us knows how to disarm the thing."

Langevin rose to his feet. "If I am KIA, you mean." Without awaiting a response, he continued. "In that sorry event, women around the globe will tear their hair in a frenzy of grief." He managed a straight face. "But of lesser concern, you should keep 'the thing' as secure as possible and call for help. Obviously, you do not want it to fall into the wrong hands again, and I will show you how to render it inoperable. I have written instructions with pictures." His message was implicit: *Even you knuckle draggers can understand them.*

"Another thing," Ashcroft said. "I like to think I can get out of trouble as fast as I can get into trouble. Are we gonna have to walk out through Indian country?"

"No, you will not," Mohammed replied. "Northern Command and the Beirut embassy both have helicopters standing by. As soon as they hear that you have recovered a weapon, the helos will be on the way."

Barrkman had sat patiently through the what-if session.

"Sir, I would like to ask my question again. How do we know where to start looking?"

Mohammed lowered his voice to emphasize the seriousness of his words. "The border has been divided into operating areas for us and for . . . other assets. That's as much as I can say for now. If necessary, some of those assets can be directed to you via Northern Command."

"So there's Israeli teams out looking, too," Barrkman replied.

Mohammed made a point of looking around the room. "Other questions?"

Pitney finally spoke up. He was getting fidgety with all the discussion. "Yes, sir. When do we leave?"

"Right after dinner."

NORTHERN ISRAEL

Brigadier General Solomon Nadel strode into the special operations office. It was past dinnertime but the watch officers were accustomed to seeing the brigade commander at odd hours.

"Sir, Colonel Livni is not here just now," the major said.

"That's all right. He's entitled to some rest." Before the staffer replied, Nadel nodded at the map of the operating area. "Show me the teams."

The major traced a finger across the border. "Aleph, Beth, Gimel, and Daleth, east to west."

"Three men each?"

"Yes, sir."

Nadel tracked his scan across the map. "How did you decide where to deploy them?"

The major grimaced. "Feldmann."

"What?"

"Sergeant Feldmann. Colonel Yak . . . Livni . . . places great confidence in his intuition."

"Sergeant Peanut Butter?"

A grin replaced the grimace. "You heard about that? Uh, sir."

"Heard about it? Hell, I was there!"

"Well, General, that's the thing about Feldmann. They say he's always right or he's never wrong."

Nadel shook his head, as if just awaking. "What's the difference?"

"Nobody knows, sir. But when the leader of Team Gimel saw the layout he said, 'If Feldmann thinks that's where we'll find them, that's the sector I want.'"

"God help us," Nadel responded. Then, looking closely at the map, he added, "And the others?"

"Sir?"

"The other teams."

The ops officer shifted his feet. *He doesn't want to discuss it,* Nadel thought. "Well, General, I don't know if . . ."

"Well, I know. *Major.* Yakov and I already discussed it."

"Ah, yessir. I'm sorry, sir. The Americans have two teams in this area." He traced the region north of the IDF zones.

"Are you in contact with them?"

"Yes, General. We ran a routine communications check about half an hour ago."

"Then we've done about all we can."

The major grinned. "For now, anyway."

"Yes, for now."

SSI OFFICES

Marshall Wilmont had nothing encouraging to say. "Right now it's doubtful that we'll recover any of the bodies. Officially they're all MIA, but Brezyinski saw Frank and Boscombe killed, and apparently Lee was fatally wounded."

Carmichael said, "Marsh, I'm not criticizing Breezy in any way, but you know there's always room for doubt. Eyewitnesses are wrong all the time."

Derringer rapped the table. "What about the other two? Furr and . . ." He checked his notes. "Barrkman."

"Breezy found them between the villages," Wilmont replied. "Apparently they saved his a . . . neck. A real last-minute rescue."

Carmichael's mind was clearing, sorting options. "Where's the Israelis in all this? I mean, we were contracted to them on behalf of the Druze. What happened to the backup we were promised?"

"I've asked Mr. Baram to see us this afternoon," Derringer explained. "He might have something more by then."

Carmichael rattled a printout. "Thank God we still have e-mail contact with Nissen. With our encryption it's more secure than the phone. He confirms that Omar and Bernie have arrived. Because of the local situation at El-Arian he sent most of his team to meet them in Hasbaya. The embassy arranged helo transportation and will get our people to the search area."

Wilmont ran the time zones in his head. "If they start now it'll be well after dark."

Derringer drummed his fingers in the rudimental pattern that said he was thinking again. "They might as well, because the opposition isn't likely to wait."

NABATIYEH GOVERNATE

It was time.

After the evening *Salat-ul-Maghrib* prayer, Imam Sadegh Elham raised his hands in a benedictory gesture. "Remember the words of the father of Ahmed Assil, the first suicide bomber, who said, 'What else is there for a man but to sacrifice his son for his religion?' "

The two special weapons teams knew they did not need to respond to the rhetorical question. Instead, they listened with growing impatience to be on their way. But the priestly commissar had more words of inspiration.

"We will not bow to the great Satan, the arrogant power-hungry tyrant that plans to rule the world. We will shout the slogan we learned from Imam Khomeini louder, higher, stronger: Death to Israel! Death to America!"

The jihadists joined the chant. "Death to Israel! Death to America!"

Fervently shaking his fist, Ahmad Esmaili shouted as long and as loud as anyone.

Then, map in hand and compass dangling from his neck, he led his five-man team into the Lebanese night.

44

NABATIYEH GOVERNATE

The two jihadist teams separated soon after leaving the Hezbollah base, but both headed generally southwest. Neither knew the route or the target of the other, but Esmaili could read a map. He reckoned that both units would try to penetrate the same six-kilometer front along the Lebanon–Israel border. It just made sense: it was one thing to toss off a phrase about "suitcase bombs" and quite another to hump that thirty-kilogram weight across broken terrain at night.

Esmaili was not surprised when Abbas Jannati ordered Modarresi Ka'bi to carry the device for the first part of the trek. Apparently neither was Ka'bi who, for all his undoubted devotion, lacked the younger man's athletic frame. He stopped frequently to hoist the load higher on his shoulders, and though he seldom complained, it was clear that he would be just as pleased to share the honor of carrying the RA-series weapon to its destination.

At length Ka'bi called a halt. "Brothers, forgive my body's weakness, but I must rest." Without awaiting approval, he slipped the harness off his back and sat down, leaning against a rock. He pulled a water bottle from his cargo pocket and drank deeply.

Esmaili gestured to his teammates. Hazim and his two partners walked about twenty paces away and faced outward, keeping watch. Ka'bi rubbed a shoulder. "We would make faster time on level ground."

"You state the obvious," Jannati hissed. "But we could be seen near the road and that must not happen." He turned to Esmaili. "How are we progressing?"

The cell leader consulted his map, using a red-lensed light. "We have come perhaps four kilometers. It is a little over ten to the border."

Jannati glanced over his shoulder at his colleague. "Perhaps it would have been better to come this far by vehicle."

Esmaili folded the map and tucked it in his shirt. "No, the risk is too great. The militia patrol this area sometimes, and they would surely stop any vehicle this time of night. That has already happened, you know."

The nuclear warrior nodded. "Yes, I heard. That was unfortunate. We can only trust that it did not betray our plans to the Zionists."

"Brother, do not worry so much. God will guide our path."

Jannati stretched out a hand and clasped his escort's arm. Then he rose and picked up the weapon.

As he resumed the march, Esmaili congratulated himself upon his growing ability to sound sincere on religious matters.

SOUTHERN LEBANON

It was blind, dumb luck.

The leader of Team Gimel called a halt to change batteries in his night-vision optic. He had used the device more than expected, because his tactical sense told him the men he hunted would keep to the depressions and shadows. Twice he had been startled by thermal images nearby, but neither were hostile. The first had been a group of four people, apparently a family settled for an uncomfortable night in the countryside. He had crept close enough to overhear their muted conversation and determined that they were more refugees from Amasha.

The second image had spiked his adrenaline because it moved. The lieutenant had flicked his safety off before he realized it was a stray goat.

While the officer installed a new battery, his NCO caught something moving toward them. In a hoarse whisper he called, "Alert. Right front."

The commandos went on point just as the strangers saw the Israelis. For a cloud-shrouded moment both teams looked at each other in the nocturnal grayness, less than twenty meters apart.

The Hezbollah team responded as briefed. Backing away, the leader called in Arabic, "Where is my daughter? Where is Fatima?"

When there was no reply, the Iranian concluded that the strangers were hostile. He ordered his men into a semicircle, weapons pointed outward.

The sergeant, who spoke fluent Arabic, responded convincingly, "We have not seen her." Immediately he berated himself: *I should have said I have not seen her. Now they know there are others.*

"What is your village?" the voice demanded.

The lieutenant was beside the sergeant. "Tell them you don't understand." Then he was gone, moving left. The third man obeyed a signal to flank right.

"What did you say?"

There was muted, rapid talk in the dark. The NCO thought it sounded agitated, perhaps an argument.

The jihadist asked again, "What village are you from? Have you seen a little girl?"

Seconds later the lieutenant's voice rasped over the tactical headset. "Four or five men, all armed."

"I see five," the corporal said from the opposite flank.

The Israeli officer recalled his initial doubts: three men were too few to handle a determined enemy but with only twelve operators, the fourth team afforded more coverage. Now came the crunch. "Moshe, ask them to come to us."

The sergeant opened his mouth to speak when the Iranians started shooting.

In the next fifteen seconds, eight men fired more than 130 rounds. The dank night was split by muzzle flashes from AKs and Galils, and both sides took casualties. As the focus of the Muslims, the Israeli sergeant had little chance. He took four rounds through the torso and crumpled to the earth.

The lieutenant and the corporal used their positions to advantage. They shot down three enemies before the other pair shifted fire to them. The officer was hit in the legs, fell prone, and kept shooting. The corporal fired an ineffective burst at a fleeing shape and another fighter eluded him.

The fifth man had the weapon.

The lieutenant called on the team channel. "Moshe, are you there?"

Moments ticked past; the pain began rising above his knees. Finally the corporal responded, "He's dead."

"Levi, I'm hit. I can't move. Can you find the package?"

"I'm moving."

The corporal executed a tactical reload and scampered through the area, littered with empty brass and bleeding bodies. He searched for several minutes when he heard a high-pitched scream: *"Allahu akbar!"*

Turning in that direction, the commando closed the distance, his pulse accelerated with physical effort and impending dread. Gunfire erupted ahead of him, scything, searching fire. The Israeli recognized the situation: the surviving gunman would hold off any pursuers while the weaponeer activated the device.

The nocturnal hunter swung wide to his left, seeking an opening from the flank. It took longer than he wanted, but he was the only remaining chance.

The next thing he heard was an incredibly loud explosion emitting a blinding, searing light.

45

SSI OFFICES

"There's a nuclear event in southern Lebanon."

Sandra Carmichael's hands went to her cheeks. "Oh, dear God . . ."

Derringer's voice came over the intercom. "It's on Fox right now."

Carmichael refused to have a television set in her work space but she knew where to find one. She threw off her high heels and sprinted to the briefing room. It was crowded when she arrived and getting more so.

The reporters were a serious-looking journalist in his mid-forties and a gorgeous newsreader in her early thirties. Carmichael was peeved when two visiting Pentagon types indulged in male bonding.

"I prefer Patti Ann Browne," said Manpower. "She is just plain beautiful."

"But Julie Banderas is hot," replied Plans and Programs.

Carmichael exerted some command presence. One ice-laden gaze of her baby blues was enough to silence the kibitzers. *They don't know,* she told herself. *Officially we're not even there.*

"The magnitude of the blast is still unknown," said the journalist, "but Lebanese, Israeli, and United Nations authorities are examining the evidence. However, it's feared that casualties will run in the hundreds if not thousands on both sides of the border."

"Yes, Jarrod," chirped the eye candy. "We have a report from Washington on emergency response teams, and here's Claren DeWild with some details . . ."

While most of the SSI staff absorbed the usual routine of such events—repetition of what little was known—Marshall Wilmont silently beckoned from the door. He led Carmichael and Matt Finch to Derringer's office and closed the door.

"We don't know about our people yet," Derringer began. "From what I've learned about the location, it's well away from the Hasbaya area."

"But, Admiral, our teams are undoubtedly along the border looking . . ."

"Yes, I know, Sandy. I know. We're trying to call Chris Nissen right now."

The intercom buzzed. "Admiral, Sergeant Nissen on the sat phone."

Carmichael's hands went to her cheeks. "Oh, thank God."

"Thank you, Peggy." Derringer punched the button. "Chris, do you read me?"

"Affirmative, sir." Nissen's baritone came through crisp and clear.

"Very well. What can you tell us?"

"Not much, Admiral. Everybody's all right here in El-Arian but we still don't know the full situation at Amasha. Apparently the Hezzies still own it. But as for the blast down along the border, we don't know a thing."

"No word from our people there?"

"There was a brief message from Langevin but it was garbled. I don't think they're in danger because he sounded cool. But I haven't had a peep from Dr. Mohammed."

"Chris, do you know where he was in relation to the detonation?"

"No, sir. I mean, we still don't know exactly where it happened. Just somewhere north of the border. If I had to guess I'd say south of Al-Khiyam."

Derringer scribbled a note with the obscure-sounding name. "Why's that?"

"Mainly a hunch. It's the biggest place near our search area and I think we'd know if the town had been nuked. The weapon we're looking for has a limited radius."

Carmichael leaned on the desk. "I thought there were two or maybe three nukes."

Derringer nodded. "Chris, our information was two or more weapons. What's your take?"

"Well, sir, I meant the type of weapon. But Dr. Bernie seems to think it was two max. Maybe the size of the explosion would tell how many backpacks went off, but I still think it's one. After all, if I was running their op, I wouldn't put all my eggs in one basket."

Derringer looked around the room. "Anybody else have a question?" Carmichael, Wilmont, and Finch shook their heads.

"Chris, thanks for your help. I know you'll keep us informed."

"Count on it, Admiral."

Finch unbuttoned his vest and began rolling up his sleeves. "It's going to be a long wait."

Carmichael nodded. "No lie, GI."

NABATIYEH GOVERNATE

Joyful pandemonium. Shouting, dancing, and gunfire in the air. Only one man stood apart from the celebration.

Imam Sadegh Elham watched on the sidelines; arms folded, face impassive. At length he turned to go to his quarters when Mohammad Azizi arrived.

"You heard?" Elham asked.

"Yes. Just now." He looked at his watch. "It must have been about forty minutes ago."

"What is happening at the villages?"

Azizi was surprised that the cleric would care about the diversions that made the nuclear surprise possible. "We control Amasha and keep watch on El-Arian. Whether we can hold Amasha, I do not know. The Lebanese Army is bound to respond sooner or later."

A dismissive wave. "No matter for now. As long as the situation is stabilized in this area, I am satisfied."

"But what about the special teams? Are both gone?"

"I believe that one was intercepted and followed orders. The other . . ."

Azizi blinked as if coming awake. "Followed orders? Imam, I did not know of any such orders. You mean, to detonate a weapon on Lebanese soil?"

The priest's dark eyes bored into the other man's face. "You did not need to know all the contingencies. But if you *think* for a moment"—he allowed the barb to sink in—"you will see the wisdom."

"Ah, I see. Better an explosion anywhere than to allow a bomb to be recaptured."

"Certainly. But there are other teams, brother. Ones

that I did not mention. They also probe the Jews' defenses and will draw some of the searchers away from our special operatives."

Azizi regarded the priestly commissar with renewed respect. The operation was more sophisticated and more complex than the Hezbollah man had realized. "Imam, I bow to your foresight and planning."

Elham's response was to turn back to the celebrants, watching their juvenile display for a moment. Then he walked away, intending to pray for better results with the second weapon.

NORTHERN ISRAEL

"Well, damn it to hell, what *do* we know?" Solomon Nadel's normal composure had abandoned him in the frustration and concern. "I have my brigade on full alert but not even division knows what's happening."

Yakov Livni gave a sardonic grin. "Solly, I doubt if even Mossad knows what's happening. All I can say is that I'm grateful the explosion happened up there rather than down here."

"Nobody I know will argue that point, but we have to assume there are other weapons. Whatever happened, we still need people combing the area looking for more infiltrators."

Nadel slumped against a desk, arms folded. "Yakov, what about your teams?"

"You mean the ones that officially don't exist?"

Nadel nodded.

"Well, it looks as if two of them actually do not exist anymore. There's no word from Team Gimel or Daleth, which I think were in the area. Aleph and Beth have checked in but they're farther from the blast."

"So we may never know about the other two teams."

"Depending on where they were in relation to ground zero, no. I expect overhead coverage fairly soon. Once I see the exact area, I can make a better guess as to our boys' location."

"Well, keep me informed, Yakov. But for now I have to get my brigade deployed. We really don't know what's coming, do we?"

Livni spread his hands. "Maybe more of the same."

NABATIYEH GOVERNATE

Jennati had seen more than a very bright flash to the west. He saw opportunity.

"Brothers! The premature explosion is a blessing from Allah. We can use the area to approach the border unseen."

Esmaili half expected somebody to object. When no one did, he found his voice. "That area now is contaminated with radiation."

Jennati hefted his load and smiled. "My brother, what does it matter? We are all pledged to die."

Speak for yourself, Esmaili thought. Instead, he said, "But the Zionists will be completely focused on that area. They will have aerial surveillance and probably satellites as well. We cannot hope to escape detection there."

The weaponeer erased his smile in a heartbeat. "I believe we can. The device probably devastated an area of several kilometers or so. That is more than enough to conceal so small a group as ours."

With that, Jennati abruptly turned right and strode toward the blast site. Esmaili went along for the moment, studying the terrain for a likely hiding place.

46

"Are you sure they had a backpack?" Langevin wanted to be certain before he committed either team to action.

"There's four or five," Green replied, pointing to the isolated house. "I just got a glimpse but yes, two had backpacks." He bit his lip. "Of course, they might have been ordinary packs."

The physicist mulled that over for three seconds. "I don't see any option, gentlemen. We must assume they're carrying a weapon." He retraced his steps deeper into the copse of trees and pressed the transmit button. "Alpha, this is Bravo, over."

Seconds later Omar Mohammed's cultured tones responded. "Bravo, Alpha here. Over."

"Omar, we have a sighting. Recommend you join us at these coordinates." He handed the set to Barrkman, who was navigating with a map and GPS.

Fifteen minutes later the two teams were united. They wasted no time.

"All right," Mohammed began. "Bernie stays here of course. I'll provide perimeter security with Barrkman and Furr. Ashcroft, Brezyinski, Pitney, and Green are the entry team." He glanced around. "Questions?"

There were none.

Approaching the house from the blind side, Robert Pitney willed himself to control his pulse, much as he did before a stage in a major match. He had visually checked his Springfield XD. He had a full magazine of .40 caliber Black Talons and one in the chamber. Thirteen rounds to get him through the door and across the room before a reload. A LaserMax sighting system had replaced the normal recoil spring assembly, affording an optical sighting plane nearly identical to the bore.

He thought deeply about what he was going to do. Then he nodded to Phil Green.

The shotgunner stepped back and shouldered the Benelli entry gun. He aimed at the lower door hinge and fired. The ounce and a quarter slug splintered the wood, separating the hinge from the door. Green rode the recoil upward, instantly shooting the middle and top hinges as well. Then he put the last two rounds either side of the doorknob, raised his right foot, and kicked hard.

The door collapsed inward, slightly askew. Breezy was first through the breach, closely followed by Pitney and Ashcroft.

Shooting erupted inside.

As his partners began the dash into the room, Green thumbed three buckshot shells into the tube magazine and followed the other operators.

Breezy was quick on the trigger but his MP-5 had only stuttered when he was knocked off his feet. His ballistic vest stopped a 7.62×39 round fired five meters away. He thought: *Fight your way to your feet.* He was forcing himself into a sitting position, raising his MP-5, when Robert Pitney opened fire.

Standing to Breezy's right, slightly in front of him, Pitney activated his pistol's laser and swept the room, left to right. Even through the Dillon electronic hearing protectors, the short-barreled, compensated pistol barked out a succession of rapid-fire rounds. Breezy heard the cadence almost as a submachine gun: *pop-pop-pop-pop-pop.* The muzzle flash was impressive.

Behind the sights, Pitney's sensation was different. He was aware of gunfire in the room, incoming and outgoing, but he ignored it. He had microseconds to discern the hostiles, place the orange-red dot above the eyebrows, and stroke the trigger. The first man—the one who shot Breezy—was kneeling behind a table. The third fighter was shorter than those on either side, requiring a fast adjustment of the dot's placement. When the muzzle aligned on the fourth man, Pitney double-tapped him before swinging back to where the first had stood. Nobody was there.

Move!

Pitney remembered to lateral away from his firing position in case somebody had time to draw a bead on him. Now he was aware of Ashcroft's FAL barking once, twice. Green appeared between them, shotgun at low ready.

"Clear!" Ashcroft called. He and Green advanced on the prostrate forms, kicking weapons away.

Breezy finally found his feet. Swearing fervently, he hoisted himself off the floor and leaned against the wall. He was breathing heavily but recovered his poise to scan the room, looking for somebody to shoot.

"Breezy, you okay?" It was Pitney.

"Yeah, I think so. This vest . . ." He fingered the hole in the nylon covering.

Pitney turned toward the others. "Bob, what'd you shoot?"

Ashcroft rolled a body over with his right foot. "This one was still moving."

Pitney exchanged magazines and took two steps toward the four corpses. He uttered something unintelligible.

"Man, that was fast!" Breezy exclaimed. He regarded the speed shooter. "You saved my ass, amigo."

Pitney looked at the cadavers on the floor, nodded, and holstered his pistol. Then he turned and walked outside.

Green opened a shaded window, admitting more sunlight. The three SSI men began a professionally detached postmortem on their opponents.

"Lookit," Breezy said. "The first three all checked into a round almost between the eyes."

Ashcroft leaned over the fourth Hezbollah man. "This one took a hit alongside the nose. He was still twitching so I finished him off."

"Well, that settles it," said Green. "Pitney can join my army anytime."

The ex-cop looked around. "Hey, where'd he go?"

Breezy stuck his head through the doorway. "Oh, he's outside having the dry heaves."

Green looked for the packs and found them leaning against the wall. He thought they were the right size for an RA-115 but they were mostly empty. "Guys, I think we've been suckered."

NABATIYEH GOVERNATE

It was time for a decision.

Esmaili waited until the group approached a small hill, then called a halt. He noted that the grass was beginning to resemble exposure to prolonged drought, and read the signs accurately.

Addressing Jannati, he said, "We are approaching the edge of the blast zone. I agree that we will probably meet no one ahead of us but we should beware of those who may chase us."

Jannati had allowed Ka'bi to resume carrying the weapon, freeing himself until the final push. The nuke-qualified leader turned and surveyed the terrain behind them. "We can see for two kilometers or more, brother. There is no need for concern as long as we keep watch."

Esmaili nodded, as if sagely. "I agree, Commander." He made a point of appearing deferential to the Tehran expert. "But why not post a man to guard our rear? He can catch up to warn us or he can delay them if necessary."

Jannati obviously cared little for the welfare of any of his jihadists. Which was to say, nothing. But without appearing indifferent, he accepted the Hezbollah veteran's advice. "Very well. Select one of the escorts." With that he motioned for Ka'bi to continue westward, deeper into the beaten zone.

Esmaili turned to Hazim. "Take a position partway up this hill to avoid exposing yourself on the skyline. Watch for anyone following us. If no one appears in an hour, follow our trail."

Hazim shifted his feet, apparently ambivalent. He seemed honored at the responsibility but nervous about being separated from the group. Finally he said, "I will, Teacher." He hefted the scoped Galil and selected a position behind a rock.

Esmaili merely nodded. *It's the most I can do for you, boy.* Then he topped the hill, seeking the place he knew must exist nearby.

NORTHERN ISRAEL

Yakov Livni knew there was no point trying to talk to Brigadier General Nadel for a while. The brigade's maneuver elements were spooled up, dispersing to avoid presenting a concentrated target for whatever was coming next.

As a Merkava raced past, Livni pulled a handkerchief and covered his mouth. His aide wondered why the special operations officer was standing in the open, watching the traffic. "Colonel, shouldn't we stay in the command center? There's bound to be intelligence updates."

"Until I can see something like satellite coverage, the rest is just gossip." He shot a quick look at the captain. "You're old enough to know that."

"But, Colonel . . ."

Livni cut him off with a raised hand. "I'm too old a bunny to believe every report that comes after something like this. There will be ten wrong reports for every accurate one, and later on nobody will be able to say how the ten got started." He shook his head. "No, I'm going for a walk while I still can. You tell the on-duty staff to sort out what seems to make sense. I'll look at those reports when I get back, then the others later on."

Without awaiting a reply, Yakov Livni stepped off in the direction he happened to be facing. He ignored the vehicles speeding past, unconcerned that he might not be seen in the swirling dust.

Teams Gimel and Daleth were likely just dust themselves.

47

NABATIYEH GOVERNATE

Omar Mohammed asked the obvious question. "What are we up against?"

Bernard Langevin rubbed his chin in concentration. "It's hard to say for certain, Omar. But we can make certain assumptions. A one-KT ground burst would scoop out a good-sized hole and blow radiated dirt and debris into the atmosphere. How far it would go depends on composition of the soil and current winds."

"How close can we approach the blast zone?"

"Well, a rule of thumb for a kiloton weapon is near or total devastation within eight hundred meters with radiation extending maybe ten square kilometers. But radiation effects are extremely variable. We can probably enter the obvious blast zone for a way but it's best to err on the side of caution. At least for a while."

Phil Green was looking over Rick Barrkman's shoulder, studying the map. "I have a question. If there's another team, which way would they go? Maybe they'd go through the blast zone to shake off any pursuers."

Barrkman looked up. "You know, that makes sense. It's not like they'd worry about their long-term health."

Mohammed and Langevin studied the sniper as if seeing him for the first time: The others read their expressions: *They don't expect shooters to think like that.*

Finally Mohammed spoke up. "All right. I believe we can have it both ways. We will proceed with our two teams as before. Bernie knows the nuclear effects and can tell when to turn back from the blast zone. I will continue on course more directly for the border." He looked at the grim-faced men around him. "Any questions?"

Furr asked, "What if nobody finds anything?"

"Then we will remain in radio contact. If we lose communications, we will regroup here at sunset."

Without awaiting comment, Langevin unlimbered his Geiger counter and started walking toward the detonation site. Barrkman, Green, and Pitney followed at a greater interval than usual.

NABATIYEH GOVERNATE

They had gone far enough.

"Brothers." Esmaili's voice was level, even friendly.

Jannati turned at the sound and saw the muzzle of Esmaili's AK, aimed at his chest. A single round took him off his feet as his brain registered the most important question in the universe: *Why?*

For Abbas Jannati, Planet Earth faded to a washed-out

pale color, dimmed to gray, blurred into invisibility, and went permanently black.

He barely heard the other shots, one- and two-round sequences.

Esmaili fired deliberately, almost calmly, from the shoulder. He had already decided his engagement sequence: the leader, holding an AK, then the two security men on either side.

Modarresi Ka'bi came last.

The thirty-six-year-old fighter carried no rifle because he packed the weapon. Without time to shed his thirty-kilogram load, he could only make a vain attempt to flee, and he got perhaps ten meters before two rounds knocked the pins from under him. He hit the rocky ground face-first, beginning to feel the pain in both legs. Esmaili ended the torment with an aimed round to the cranium.

Esmaili checked the other bodies, found no signs of life, and reloaded. Then he grabbed a folding shovel, picked up the weapon, and began walking west. He was headed into the blast zone.

NABATIYEH GOVERNATE

"Did you hear that?" Barrkman asked.

Bernard Langevin stopped in his tracks. "Gunfire?"

Green nodded. "Yeah, four or five rounds."

Barrkman pointed to his right front. "I think it was over there. Hard to tell how far."

Langevin pressed the transmit button. "Alpha, this is Bravo. Over."

"Alpha here."

"We just heard shots farther into the blast zone. Maybe a klick or so west of us. We're going to look. Over."

"Be careful, Bernard."

"Always. Out."

NABATIYEH GOVERNATE

When the grass turned from brown to dead, Esmaili stopped. He set down his burden beside what appeared a hurricane-blasted tree and looked around. He noted a prominent rock fifteen meters away and unlimbered the folding shovel. Digging in the earth beside the rock, he scooped out a hole large enough to accept the backpack and stuffed it in the hole. Then he filled in the hole, spreading the excess dirt far enough away to avoid notice.

Esmaili sat on the rock, sipping water. Then he took three compass bearings and wrote them on a pad, but he felt confident of finding the place again without map references.

Good, he thought. *Now I only have to find the Zionists. They will make me a wealthy . . .*

The rifle bullet slashed past his right ear. Before the sound subsided, Esmaili was flat on the ground, reaching for his AK.

He squirmed to the edge of the rock, searching for his assailant. He felt the bile rising from his stomach, more from disappointment than fear.

Hazim, you damned fool! I gave you a chance to live!

When no other shots followed, Esmaili sorted the possibilities. *He thinks I am dead and has left me for the jackals, which is unlikely. Or he is waiting to see if I move. Or he's moving to a better position.*

The Iranian reckoned that an ambitious, self-confident youth would not sit it out. *Patience is not a youthful virtue. Therefore, he is moving, probably to my left where he gains a better view.*

Esmaili low-crawled through the ruined grass, back a few meters from the trunk of the tree. In a few minutes a crouching figure approached from the west. *He circled farther out than I thought. Good for you, boy. But not good enough.*

From his prone position twenty-five meters away, Esmaili identified the rifle before the face. The scoped Galil told him all he needed to know. "Hazim!"

The young marksman spun at the sound of his name. Before he spotted his teacher, he felt the impact of a 7.62 round in his right shoulder. He dropped the trophy rifle and slumped to his knees, crying in anguish and in pain.

"Don't move!"

Esmaili rose high enough to check his surroundings. Seeing no one else, he swung to his own left and approached Hazim from the right side. The stalker had crumpled to the ground, holding his shoulder with his left hand. He moaned and sobbed, talking unintelligibly.

Esmaili knelt beside his pupil and tossed the Galil away. The Iranian regarded the young Lebanese as if he were a specimen under a microscope. Pale complexion, a sheen of perspiration on the face, eyes wide.

"You were a decent pupil at one time, but you never learned to call your shots. That one went to my right. And you could not have been more than 150 meters away." His voice carried a *tsk-tsk* quality.

Hazim raised himself on his left elbow. "Traitor! You murdered the brothers! I saw the bodies!"

Esmaili's left hand snaked out, quick and hard. The blow stunned the boy for a moment. Before he could react, Esmaili said, "Fool! I gave you a chance to escape. You would have been wise to take another direction. Now . . ."

"Kill me, traitor! You're going to do it anyway so do it now."

Esmaili slung his AK and pulled the marksman to his feet. "You damned, stupid young idiot!" He shook the boy roughly, causing a yelp of pain. "You can still get out of here." He shoved Hazim eastward and retrieved the Galil.

"You're . . . you're not going to kill me?"

Esmaili waved violently. "Go! Just go!"

Still disbelieving, Hazim forced himself to walk. Amid the pain and weakness, he tried to sort out the rationale for letting him live. Surely the Teacher knew that if Hazim recovered he would tell what the Iranian had done, where he had buried the weapon. But why send him away? Why . . .

Hazim looked back, saw Esmaili traipsing ten paces behind him. They had gone about two hundred meters and the Lebanese countryside lay before them. Israel was somewhere off to the right. Maybe the Teacher was going there . . .

The round from Esmaili's AK struck Hazim at the base of the skull.

Accelerating his pace, Esmaili barely looked down. *I couldn't leave a corpse so close to the weapon.*

48

NABATIYEH GOVERNATE

Ahmad Esmaili saw them before they saw him.

He went prone in the grass, now brown again rather than dead. He looked at them through Hazim's scope. *Four men, all armed, perhaps three hundred meters.* He decided to let them approach.

When it was obvious that the searchers would pass barely one hundred meters from him, Esmaili laid down his rifles. He stood up, raised his hands, and began walking. *It is worth the risk.*

Pitney saw him first. In Arabic he shouted, "Do not move!"

Esmaili froze in his tracks. He recognized the intruders as professionals.

While Barrkman and Green kept watch, Pitney and Langevin talked to the stranger who seemed to wander alone and unarmed in an extremely violent place. But first they searched and cuffed him.

"What was the shooting over there?" Pitney asked.

"Oh, four men were killed. Nobody else was there."

The cop in Robert Pitney began to surface. "What are you doing out here by yourself?"

Esmaili decided now was the time. "I have knowledge of a nuclear weapon and wish to sell that information to the Israelis."

Half an hour later Omar Mohammed arrived. He deployed Ashcroft, Brezyinski, and Furr on perimeter security, then looked at the man who gave his name as Ahmad Esmaili. Mohammed took a chance and asked in Farsi, "How is it in Tehran?"

Esmaili smiled, feeling increasingly confident. "There is much nuclear activity, my friend. I was with Dr. Momen recently." He raised his manacled hands. "I could show you." Mohammed uncuffed him, explaining, "He says he knows of a weapon."

Langevin was skeptical. "How can he prove that? And where is it?"

After the translation, Esmaili tore a page from his notebook and handed it over. Langevin recognized a reasonably accurate set of Cyrillic letters and numbers. "This is a serial number of a nuclear demolition device?"

Mohammed confirmed that it was.

"Where is it?"

Esmaili grinned self-confidently. "That information will cost the Zionists a great deal of money."

NORTHERN ISRAEL

"Colonel!" The captain ran to Livini as he entered the operations block. "Colonel, we just heard from the American team. They have a Hezbollah officer who claims he has hidden a suitcase bomb."

"Where?"

"Eight kilometers over the border, on the fringe of the detonation zone."

Livni absorbed that message, rubbing his stubbled chin. "Well, he's not going to give it to us for the asking. What does he want? Money? Asylum?"

The captain nodded. "Correct on both counts. Two million American dollars, a new identity, and a passport to anywhere on the planet."

"Well, I can't make that promise, and even if I did, he wouldn't believe it. So what does this man expect? We can't have him and the Americans standing around in the dark while Tel Aviv sends diplomats into the Lebanese countryside."

"The American scientist, Dr. Langevin, suggests that he and the head of the team come here with the Hezbollah man. We can keep them safe until Tel Aviv figures out what to do."

Livni rubbed his neck. "Meanwhile, what about the weapon? Anybody could find it and take it."

"Yes sir. That's why this Esmaili suggests that we make a deal—fast."

"All right. Bring them in. And see if the other Americans need a flight to El-Arian."

The aide raised a hand. "But, sir, what about approval to enter Lebanese airspace?"

For once, Livni actually smiled. "When I was in Washington I learned a wonderful philosophy: it's easier to ask forgiveness than permission."

SSI OFFICES

Derringer took the call from Nissen. "Yes, Chris! Talk to me!"

"Admiral, I figure you could stand some good news. Our guys found a Hezbollah operative who had another bomb. Evidently this guy snuffed his teammates and stashed the nuke. He wants to sell it. Now he's in Israel with Dr. Mohammed and Dr. Langevin. They'll stay with him until the Israelis figure what they're gonna do."

"Was anybody hurt?"

"Ah, no sir. For a change."

"What about the rest of the team?

Nissen chuckled. "They're back here, enjoying some MREs and local wine. Things have calmed down here, but with nukes in the picture, I think the Lebanese Army will kick the Hezzies out of Amasha."

Derringer forced the nuclear concern to the back of his mind. "So there's nothing new about Frank and the others?"

"Ah, no sir." After a pause, Nissen added, "I just don't think they made it, Admiral."

"Very well. I want everybody to sit tight. Don't leave the village, Chris. We're going to see about terminating the contract and bringing everybody home."

"Works for me, sir."

Derringer hung up and turned to the staffers who had been waiting for the call. He focused on Corin Pilong. "What do you think, Corin? Can we get out of the remainder of the contract?"

The Filipina's huge brown eyes gleamed in response. "Admiral, the first thing I learned is that it takes two willing parties to write a contract but only one of them to end it. Without mutual consent there's little prospect for getting through the term of the agreement."

"Barring litigation, of course."

"Well, ordinarily I would agree. But if ever there were unusual circumstances, this is it, sir. After all, a nuclear device has exploded in our client's area—the venue, if you will—and there is a clause providing for discussion of termination owing to acts of God and extenuating circumstances and—"

"And yadda-yadda. Et cetera, et cetera."

The icy brain behind the baby-doll face caught her employer's mood. "Ditto, ditto. And so on and so on . . ."

Marshall Wilmont could stand only so much sitcom banter. "If I might interject, it seems that with the Lebanese Army and the U.N. and just about everybody else in the region swarming through that area, a temporary peace is about to break out."

"Concur," Carmichael added. "It's ironic, isn't it? A small nuke goes off, and suddenly everyone wants to get along. Even the Israelis and Iranians are talking, though of course neither side is going to admit it."

Derringer leaned back in his overstuffed chair, hands behind his head. "You know, it could be that Hezbollah will be the big loser, once the damage is fully assessed and the bodies are buried. Nobody with an ounce of objectivity thinks anyone but Hezbollah was behind the nuke, and those who claim otherwise are just going to look damned silly."

Wilmont cocked his head. "So you think that Iran and Syria will try to put a happy face on their role in this?"

"Guarandamntee it, Marsh."

"Well, the Lebanese and the Israelis aren't going to buy it." When Derringer made no reply, Wilmont added, "Are they?"

The president of SSI abruptly brought both hands down on his desk, loudly. "No, they're not going to believe it, but I'd bet my retirement that they're going to pretend that they do."

Wilmont's bleary eyes widened in recognition. "Big-picture considerations. Regional politics and foreign aid; that sort of thing."

"Yadda, yadda," Derringer rejoined. "And ditto ditto."

49

NORTHERN ISRAEL

Omar Mohammed and Bernard Langevin watched the IDF limousine depart Northern Command headquarters. They waited until it turned the corner before either spoke.

"Do you think he'll get his full payment?" Mohammed asked.

"Well, he has so far. His nuke is the real deal. Without the documentation I can't tell the remaining shelf life but it looked good enough to scare me out of my knickers. You know, it was smart to hide the bomb inside the blast zone. The ambient radiation would cover any trace of the weapon, assuming there was any, and not many people would spend much time looking there."

Mohammed pivoted on a heel to return to the headquarters' air-conditioned comfort. His Banana Republic attire was beginning to show unseemly perspiration stains. "Tell me, Bernard. Do you think he really killed his compatriots?"

"I don't know. Not that it really matters. Either he's a murderer or an opportunist. Maybe both. In any case, he prevented another nuclear detonation, and whatever else he's done in his life, that's a plus." Langevin thought for a moment. "Omar, what do you think of the guy? Personally."

"I believe he is who and what he says. Our Israeli friends may have a file on him, but in any case they will know the facts soon enough."

"So why'd he turn? I mean, he spent his whole life fighting. It looked like he had a clear shot at a worthwhile target on this side of the border. Presumably he could have set the timer and scooted for safety if he wasn't into self-immolation. So why does somebody like that suddenly get greedy for money?"

Mohammed cocked his head and stroked his goatee. "Bernie, this is an interesting man. As a case study, that is." The native Iranian pulled a notepad from his jacket. "Esmaili has a world of experience. Revolutionary guards, the Iraq war, special operations, cooperation with Hamas and the Palestinians, and the last two or three Lebanon conflicts." He looked up. "He's in his early forties and he's been at war for almost thirty years. My reading is that he simply got sick and tired of the constant fighting. He seems to think that he has earned a rest."

Langevin was unconvinced. "I'm not so sure, Omar. I mean, that could be true, but to what extent can we really know? After all, he could have simply set the timer and disappeared after the explosion."

Mohammed placed a fraternal hand on Langevin's shoulder. "My friend, I think that he did not want to be used anymore. Twice he told me that the imams and the hierarchy used up a generation of naïve young patriots and religious zealots. But the old men who sent them out to die always remained safely behind. Always." He shrugged. "As for the money—that was probably convenience, not entirely greed."

"You think he could've got more than two million?"

"Almost certainly, based on his knowledge of Hezbollah operations alone. Of course, it required good faith on the part of the Israelis, but at this point in his life, I believe that our Mr. Esmaili decided he had nothing to lose by trusting his enemy." Mohammed arched an eyebrow. "And he's a shrewd businessman: two million is quite a bargain."

Langevin looked around to ensure that no one overheard. "How long do you think he'll last on the outside?"

Mohammad stroked his beard again. "Oh, eventually the facts will be known, by intention or by mistake. But wherever he goes, I would not wager his surviving long enough to spend his money."

"Well, maybe his information will do some good before then."

Omar Mohammed indulged in a wry smile. "I would wager a goodly sum that if Imam Elham remains in Lebanon very long he will receive some unexpected visitors one night."

Bernard Langevin, PhD, smiled in recollection. "As our young friend Breezy would say, 'Hoo-ah the unexpected visitors.' "

50

DULLES AIRPORT

"There they are." Derringer caught sight of Delmore's bald head towering above the crowd.

Most of the SSI staff was on hand to meet the team returning from Lebanon. *Or at least the survivors,* Derringer told himself. He just noticed Jack Peters. "Jack, why'd you come all the way out here?"

Peters shifted his feet. "Well, I feel a kind of obligation, Admiral. Frank and I recruited Pitney and now . . ."

He shrugged beneath his raincoat. "He doesn't really know anybody else from the office."

Derringer watched his talent scout greet Pitney with a warm handshake.

"Robert, welcome back."

The shooter was obviously surprised. "That's good of you, Mr. Peters." He scanned the reception committee. "I didn't really expect a crowd like this."

"Well, we just want you guys to know how much we appreciate what you did. All of you."

Pitney absorbed the meaning without comment.

"How are you? Really."

"Oh, tired but okay." Robert Pitney paused for a moment. "I thought I knew more or less what to expect, but I didn't. Not really. Chris tried to tell me that in his own way." He glanced at Nissen, exchanging handshakes and hugs. "I guess I'm glad that I went, because I learned something."

Peters cocked his head. "Yes?"

"I learned that the price you pay for seeing the show is steeper than you think." He stared at a travel poster, then said, "I guess I'll spend a lot of time wondering if it was worth the price of admission."

Amid the greetings—heartfelt and pro forma—Sandy Carmichael sought out Brezyinski.

"Breezy! Welcome back, guy." She gave the door-kicker a warm hug that took him by surprise. He squeezed her in return.

"Thanks, Colonel Sandy." He sucked in some air. "It's so . . . good . . . to be home."

She patted his arm. "Mark, when you've had time to settle in, come see me. Matt Finch and I will be reshuffling the go-to roster and we'd like to discuss some options with you."

"Well, thanks. A lot. I mean, I really do appreciate it. But I'm not sure what I want to do after . . . what's happened."

"Breezy, you can do just about anything you want. Like J. J. Johnson. He's on our full-time training roster so he doesn't deploy to field operations unless he asks to." She studied Brezyinski's face closely. *He's tired and hurting. This isn't the time to make a decision.* "Why don't you go see him in Idaho?"

"Yeah, I've been thinkin' about that. I mean, I want to see Bosco's family in Washington State. I could see the Double Jay on the way back."

Derringer and Wilmont gathered the ten operators around Chris Nissen. SSI's founder knew it would be a few days before the full team was assembled again. "Gentlemen, welcome back. Welcome back." He shook his head. "You did an extraordinary job." He raised a fist to his mouth and gave an unnecessary cough. "Ah, we're planning a memorial service for Frank . . . ahem . . . and the others. It'll be at Arlington next month. Check with the office and we'll have the details."

Green ventured a question. "Admiral, what about Jacobs and Malten? Last we heard they were still in Beirut."

"No, they came home day before yesterday. The doctors finally released Malten to travel."

Barrkman leaned toward Furr. "Damn, they missed all the fun."

"Yeah, unless Malten calls taking a round through the guts some kind of fun."

Wilmont recognized that Derringer did not want to say much more, and imposed his bulk between the admiral and the operators. "Fellows, we have some vans waiting as soon as your luggage is ready. This way, please."

As the crew proceeded to the baggage carousel, Carmichael eased up to Derringer.

"They look bushed, Admiral. And I don't mean the travel."

"Well, some of them have been through an ordeal. I saw you talking to Brezyinski."

"He's still dealing with Boscombe's death. I think he will be for quite a while." She looked up at her boss. "Maybe for the rest of his life."

Derringer took Carmichael's arm and turned away from the crowd. "Sandy, I don't want to appear an opportunist. I think you know me better than that. But after this mission, SSI's future is assured. It didn't look good a couple of months ago, but handling the backpack nuke is a major coup for us."

The Alabaman furrowed her forehead. "Admiral, how can we publicize that? The Israelis must rate it beyond top secret."

"Well, I talked with General Varlowe today on that very matter. You know how Beltway insiders love to be— inside. The word *will* get around, even if it's not quite the full story. Insiders will hear that we saved Israel from taking a nuke."

"So we're some kind of deniable heroes."

Derringer merely gave her a small grin, slightly cynical around the edges.

After an awkward pause, Carmichael spoke her mind. "Mike, I'm certainly glad the company will survive. I mean, I'm not ready to retire, and I still enjoy the work. But, you know . . ." Her southern accent trailed off.

"Well . . ."

"Tell me. Please," she prompted.

"Well, we turned a corner in Lebanon. It's not going to be the same without Frank and Steve, is it?"

"No, it's not." Her voice was soft amid the background babble.

"You mentioned you're not ready to retire. But I'm not so sure about me."

Sandra Carmichael could think of nothing to say.

51

HORSETHIEF RESERVOIR, IDAHO

"You know, Bosco came here to see me before the African gig."

J. J. Johnson made another cast and landed his fly within eight inches of his aim point. Dissatisfied, he whipped the graphite rod backward, flexed it twice more, and tried again. The Woolly Bugger alit three inches from the floating leaf.

Brezyinski nodded. "Yeah, he told me about that. Said he convinced you to come along."

Johnson laughed aloud. "That turkey! I already decided to go. Just wanted to have some downtime with him so I played him like . . ." He grinned. "A fish on the line."

Breezy regarded the erstwhile Foreign Legionnaire. "I guess you guys became pretty good buds, too."

Johnson shrugged. "Well, you know how it was. Hell, you were everywhere I was: Pakistan, Afghanistan, and Chad. Yeah, the B Man was some kind of operator."

Breezy made his own amateurish effort at casting. Clearly his heart was not in it, even as an accuracy game when the fish weren't biting. At length, Johnson asked, "How'd it go with Bosco's family in Ellensburg?"

"Oh, okay I guess. His old man wasn't around much but I talked to his sister. They wanted to know . . . well, you know."

"What it was like when he checked out."

Breezy nodded, still staring at the lake.

Jeremy Johnson was a worldly young man, not quite

thirty. He allowed his fly to drift for a moment, reading Breezy's mind. "What'd you tell them, Breeze?"

"Ah, the usual stuff."

"Like, it was instantaneous. He never felt a thing."

Breezy shot his colleague a sidelong glare, then relaxed. "Yeah, never felt a thing." He bit his lip in concentration. "Maybe it's even true. He was dead when I saw him."

Before Johnson could respond, Breezy added, "I'm seeing a counselor."

"No, I didn't know. But that's good, Breeze. It helped me, after . . . you know."

Brezyinski gave a knowing nod. *After the ragheads flayed you like a salmon with that strip of belted tire.* He had seen the scars on Johnson's back and legs. *He felt guilty because he talked under torture. Anybody would've talked.*

Breezy felt better about sharing his thoughts. "I tried the VA but they're always overworked. So SSI got me a private shrink. I see her twice a month. It really helps, you know?"

"Sure do." Johnson cast again, picking a different spot. "What've you learned so far?"

"Well, I said that I couldn't understand why I was so shook when Frank was killed but I hardly slowed down for . . . Bosco. I mean, I had a lot of respect for Frank but we weren't close or anything. He usually rode us about our laid-back attitude, you know."

Johnson laughed. "Tell me about it!"

"Anyway, Ms. Cottin—Michelle—says that I empathized with Frank because I was trying to save him and watched him die. I mean, I heard his last breath and I saw the light go out of his eyes. But with Bosco it was almost like, 'Bye, guy.' I just looked at him and then Steve Lee pulled me away. Michelle says that I had a subconscious resentment toward Bosco, because he was such a good bud and checked out without saying good-bye. How weird is that? I mean, it's not like he had a choice!"

"What about Lee? You tried to save him, too."

"Well, that's different, I guess." He paused to gather his thoughts. "Ah, hell, J. J., I dunno. I didn't know him real well, either. I've talked about it with Michelle and I think there's not so much grief there because it was his choice. At the time I thought he was just looking for an easy way out, and I couldn't carry him or anything, so I gave him the needle. But now I know that he was really looking to give *me* an out—saving the radio and whatnot. So no, I don't have as much heartburn about him."

"This Michelle sounds like a cool lady."

"Hoo-yeah."

Johnson turned to regard Breezy. "What's that mean?"

"Well, she's almost a babe."

"Oh, c'mon, Brezyinski! You're not hitting on your shrink, are you?"

Breezy laughed again. "No, of course not! It's just that . . ."

"Just what?"

"Well, sometimes I wonder what she looks like undressed."

Johnson suppressed his own laugh. "Brezyinski, you are one sick puppy."

"Well, of course I am!" He was smiling in the afternoon sun.

"Lemme guess. She's a good ten–fifteen years older, married to a millionaire investment broker with six kids."

"Yeah, that's pretty much in the zone. Her husband's a surgeon. Based on her diploma I think she's eleven or twelve years older. Three kids."

"Pardner, I think Ms. Cottin is doing you a ton of good."

Breezy made another cast, better than before. "So do I, J-Man. So do I."

AFTERWORD

Writing about Lebanon is a challenge. Among other things, there is no consensus on subjects as basic as the number of governates in the country. As one source said, "Not even we Lebanese can agree on that, or anything else!"

Spelling of some place names also is problematical: there are at least four spellings for the city and governate of Nabatiyeh, including contradictions among official Web sites. Finally, we opted for the most common rendering, which narrowly edged out "Nabatieh."

The villages of Amasha and El-Arian are fictional.